ADVANCE PRAISE FOR *PERENNIALS*

"From the lush Mississippi setting and lyrical writing, to the flawed yet engaging characters, Julie Cantrell's *Perennials* is an engrossing reading pleasure. I loved this story of a fractured family and a prodigal daughter, and the healing power and connections that tending gardens brings to their lives. Like an artist, the author uses a delicate brush to carefully illustrate the joys and pains of life's growing seasons, and of learning how to surrender old hurts to find forgiveness. This is a book to read more than once."

—KAREN WHITE, *NEW YORK TIMES* BESTSELLING AUTHOR OF *THE NIGHT THE LIGHTS WENT OUT*

"Family drama, small-town pressures, and life's unexpected turns are all set within the charming parameters of a Southern perennial garden. Add the literary links to Faulkner and Welty, a soul-stirring romance, and Cantrell's lyrical story-telling skills, and you've got a heartwarming tale that is sure to outlast the seasons. You'll love *Perennials*!"

—MARY ALICE MONROE, *NEW YORK TIMES* BESTSELLING AUTHOR OF *BEACH HOUSE FOR RENT*

"Like the perennial plants that give the story its namesake, Julie Cantrell's characters survive drought and flood, sunshine and storm. Readers will see reflections of their own lives as they travel along with Lovey when she returns to the rich Mississippi soil to bloom again. If Julie Cantrell isn't on your reading list, she should be."

—LISA WINGATE, NATIONAL BESTSELLING AUTHOR OF *BEFORE WE WERE YOURS*

"With languid prose and vivid description, Julie Cantrell's novel unfolds as beautifully as one of her protagonist's favorite flowers. Cantrell weaves moving and inspirational stories that make her one of today's most beloved storytellers. Perennials may be her most breathtaking yet."

—KRISTY WOODSON HARVEY, BESTSELLING AUTHOR OF *SLIGHTLY SOUTH OF SIMPLE*

"You can leave home—but does home ever leave you? That's the question at the heart of Julie Cantrell's stunning new novel. With a story that's at once classic and unlike anything you've read before, *Perennials* is as lush and entrancing as the gardens described within its pages."

—Camille Pagán, bestselling author of *Life and Other Near-Death Experiences*

"In *Perennials*, Julie Cantrell has written a love letter to her home state of Mississippi, Deep South summers, and flower blooms that can heal the soul. Through main character Lovey's return trip home, we see what it means to keep 'Family First' no matter what. And her journey home is much more than just miles traveled—it's a glimpse into a life full of heartache and longing, the illuminating light of truth, and the redemptive power of love."

—Lauren K. Denton, author of *The Hideaway*

"I don't think there is anything prettier than the words written by Julie Cantrell. *Perennials* is a beautiful story of redemption, full of rich and colorful characters. Five stars."

—Celeste Fletcher McHale, author of *The Secret to Hummingbird Cake*

"Full of southern charm, this evocative family saga delves into the weight of our relationships and the roles played by fate, redemption, and love. Beautifully written, Julie Cantrell's *Perennials* is a must read, especially for those who believe in the power of second chances."

—Karma Brown, bestselling author of *In This Moment*

"In *Perennials*, Julie Cantrell offers a modern Southern family saga brimming with traditional family values and contemporary problems. Cantrell's well-paced story, beautiful prose, and lush descriptions effortlessly carry you through the estranged, yet enmeshed, lives of sisters Lovey and Bitsy. The novel is deftly woven with bits of Mississippi history, literature, and landscape, adding to this immersive read that goes right to your heart, and makes you remember what's truly important."

—Amy Sue Nathan, author of *Left to Chance*

"*Perennials* is much more than a testament to the South and the healing power of family; it is a love letter that speaks to the deepest longings within us all. Julie Cantrell is a master."

—Billy Coffey, author of *Steal Away Home*

"Oxford, Mississippi—In the span of only a few pages, author Julie Cantrell, in her new novel of the South, took me from a place I'd never been to a place I now feel I need to go. With tenderhearted prose and characters full-to-blooming, *Perennials* is a poignant family drama that reminds us all what it means to return to our roots and come back home."

—James Markert, author of *The Angels' Share*

"With her proven ability to peel back the layers that expose the frailty of the soul, Julie Cantrell has created another evocative tale that tackles tough themes like trust, loyalty, truth, and the familial ties that bind us, whether we want them to or not. A story that will settle in and stay with you, *Perennials* is a masterpiece not to be missed."

—Catherine West, author of *The Things We Knew* and *The Memory of You*

PRAISE FOR *THE FEATHERED BONE*

"Deeply emotional, moving, and full of amazing imagery, Cantrell's latest is a triumph. Although some of the pain on the pages is incredibly difficult to read, this novel is stunning in its ability to convey the different meanings of slavery and being trapped in untenable circumstances. The ending is healing; this is a book to be savored and pondered."

—*RT Book Reviews*, 4½ stars, TOP PICK!

"The author of the Christy Award–winning *Into the Free* and Carol Award winner *When Mountains Move* has written an excruciatingly dark and disturbing novel about the devastating impact of sex trafficking on two families . . . Her portrait of loss and heartbreak will leave readers reeling."

—*Library Journal*, starred review

"Julie is a master storyteller who weaves a compelling story around the issue of human trafficking and the fall-out in the lives of friends and family whose very existence became a daily struggle to hold on and to put one foot in front of the other."

—*Mississippi Christian Living*

"From the beginning, this story gripped me. Julie Cantrell is a wonderful wordsmith, and *The Feathered Bone* offers deep insight."

—Francine Rivers, *New York Times* bestselling author

"A stunning story that takes us through tragedy, heartbreak, and ultimately to both courage and redemption."

—Patti Callahan Henry, *New York Times* bestselling author of *The Idea of Love* and *The Stories We Tell*

"*The Feathered Bone* is not to be missed."

—Michael Morris, author of *A Place Called Wiregrass* and *Man in the Blue Moon*

"*The Feathered Bone* is haunting and hauntingly beautiful, a heart-wrenching story about how one woman, Amanda Salassi, rises from the depths of despair to discover that freedom and miracles do exist. Seeing pure darkness enables her to appreciate the light of love and hope."

—Allen Mendenhall, *Southern Literary Review*

"*The Feathered Bone* is at once heartbreaking and uplifting, tragic and beautiful. And it is also a book that reminds us that even in our darkest hour, there is still hope, still reason to go on, still reason to forgive, to be alive, and to love."

—David Armand, author of *Harlow* and *The Gorge*

"Emotionally gripping, *The Feathered Bone* will break your heart, but Julie Cantrell's masterful skill as a wordsmith will not leave you broken. If you believe beauty can emerge from devastation, this story is for you. If you don't, this story is for you."

—Susan Meissner, author of *Secrets of a Charmed Life*

PERENNIALS

OTHER BOOKS BY JULIE CANTRELL

Into the Free

When Mountains Move

The Feathered Bone

PERENNIALS

JULIE CANTRELL

THOMAS NELSON
Since 1798

Perennials

Published in Nashville, Tennessee, by Thomas Nelson. Thomas Nelson is a registered trademark of HarperCollins Christian Publishing, Inc.

Published in association with the literary agency of WordServe Literary Group, Ltd., www.wordserveliterary.com.

Interior design by Mallory Collins

Thomas Nelson titles may be purchased in bulk for educational, business, fund-raising, or sales promotional use. For information, please e-mail SpecialMarkets@ThomasNelson.com.

Library of Congress Cataloging-in-Publication Data

Names: Cantrell, Julie, 1973- author.
Title: Perennials / Julie Cantrell.
Description: Nashville, Tennessee : Thomas Nelson, [2017]
Identifiers: LCCN 2017023285 | ISBN 9780718037642 (paperback)
Subjects: LCSH: Domestic fiction. | GSAFD: Christian fiction.
Classification: LCC PS3603.A597 P47 2017 | DDC 813/.6--dc23 LC record available at https://lccn.loc.gov/2017023285

17 18 19 20 21 LSC 5 4 3 2 1

For my children,
and for all children,
and for the child in all of us—
May you always know the truth: you are loved.

The trust of the innocent is the liar's most useful tool.

—Stephen King

PROLOGUE

"Falsehood flies, and the Truth comes limping after it."

—JOHNATHAN SWIFT, *THE EXAMINER*, 1710

Summer 1979
Oxford, Mississippi

"Four!" Bitsy cheers, twisting the lid to her firefly jar. I race behind my only sister. She's eleven, which means she's three years bigger than me, and that's enough to make her boss. Fisher says she's not the boss of me, but Bitsy says she is and that's that.

A summer day in Mississippi can last a whole year long, and today is one of those whole-year-long kind of days. Even the leaves are lazy, leaning big as hands from the sweet gum tree with not so much as a breeze to keep 'em company. If it weren't for the trees, we'd have already melted. But they stand heavy and green and full of shade, so I don't mind the heat much, especially now that evening is settling over us.

"I got four too." I hold my Mason jar up high to Bitsy's eyes.

The lightning bugs flash against the glass and Bitsy says, "Good job, Lovey," so I give her my best smile, the kind I wear on Christmas mornings.

"Six." Fisher snaps his lid against the rim. "We win!"

His little brother, Finn, reaches for the jar with a pair of five-year-old hands that look like Fisher's, only smaller. Both boys are covered in bug bites and dirt and everything Mississippi, same as us.

"Lovey? Bitsy?" Mother calls from the porch using our nick-names because no one ever calls us any other way. When I was little, I couldn't say the name Elizabeth. Bitsy was the best I could do. Eva was easy to say, but my folks noticed my "lovable nature" and took to calling me Lovey. At least that's the way Mother tells it. We can't see her from way out here in the pasture, but we can hear when she yells, "Supper!"

The sun is on top of the redbud tree looking like a lollipop by the time our father, Chief, waves from his truck. "Wanna ride?"

Bitsy shakes her head no, so I do the same. Chief drives on up the gravel lane, smiling 'cause he's happy to be home. At least that's what he tells us every night at supper.

"Y'all hungry?" I ask the boys.

Fisher shrugs. "I dunno." He says this like his lips are stitched together, so I take that to mean yes.

"Well, come on then." I wave my arm, which is the same as saying, "Follow me if y'all wanna eat with us," and they do. But first we all stand barefoot, letting the shade-cool grass tickle our toes as we uncap our jars. Even without lids, the fireflies don't leave the glass, so we tap the bottom and cheer, "Fly, fireflies. Fly!" We say it faster and faster until we fall to the grass laughing because our tongues won't roll the words.

When all fourteen fireflies finally fly away, we race each other home for supper. Fisher wins, as always, and I come in second for the first time ever.

"Only 'cause I let you pass me," Bitsy says.

Fisher shakes his head and says Bitsy is a liar.

When we reach the porch, Chief is standing in the driveway talking to some man I don't know. Mother comes outside, says, "Go get washed up."

"Who's that?" Bitsy looks at the man in the big-striped tie. Mother wrings her hands in her apron and doesn't answer, so we all figure it's one of Chief's clients.

Everybody calls our father Chief, even Bitsy and me. Mother says the name stuck from back when he played football at Ole Miss. Now he's a lawyer, which means he helps people obey the law. But sometimes they don't obey the law, and then he helps them do better next time.

This client is probably somebody who didn't obey the law, because he has a mean-man look on his face. He must not know Chief either, because he calls my father Mr. Sutherland. But neither of those things bothers me half as much as his daughter. She's marching over to the porch like she's one of those broody mama chickens who doesn't like us to take her eggs. I don't know her name, so I'm gonna call her Moody Broody because I sometimes like things to rhyme. "Why are y'all so dirty?"

Fisher laughs. Finn laughs. I give her the stink eye. And Bitsy, well, Bitsy looks like somebody just stepped on her toes. Hard. Only her toes are just fine 'cause I can see 'em, and maybe they are a little muddy on account of us playing barefoot all day, but who cares?

"We aren't dirty." Bitsy holds her fists on her hips like she's punching herself into a pinch. If she were a flavor, it would be sour.

"Look at your feet." Moody Broody's got a voice like a chicken too. Loud and squawky-talky. "And your hands. Your clothes. You sure seem dirty to me."

Bitsy's eyes start to look like glass, which usually means she's gonna cry, only this time she bites her lip until her eyes go back to normal again. Then she turns to Fisher, Finn, and me. "Let's go."

But I'm not done yet. If Moody Broody wants to tell us we're dirty, then I want to know why she's dressed like a church lady. "Why are you wearing Sunday clothes? You going to trial for something?"

She huffs, and I almost ask her if she *is* laying an egg, but I don't because, one, it would be rude, and two, she's already strutted back over to Mr. Mean-Man Face. Besides, Bitsy repeats, "Let's go." So we go.

"Got ourselves two extra boys tonight?" Chief leaves his hat at the door.

Mother smiles. "Found these two in the backwoods. Haven't a clue where they came from, but they say their names are . . . What'd you say again, boys? Was it Fisher and Finn?"

Finn's the baby, but even he knows Mother's joking. Their family farm is right across the street, but they eat supper with us most every night, and we all like it that way.

Mother places the hot butter-bread in the middle of the table, and we know what to do from here. We bow our heads, close our eyes, and wait until it's time to say "Amen." Then we pass the potato salad, chicken, and baked beans until everybody fills a plate. Finally, we eat.

"I see y'all met Blaire Dayton," Chief says. "Her family's new to town."

"Always nice to make another friend," Mother adds.

My sister takes a bite of beans so she doesn't have to talk about it.

"Not that kind of friend," Fisher says. "She hasn't been at school as much as a week, and she's already thinkin' she's somethin'."

"That right?" Chief is asking questions about Moody Broody, but I get the feeling he's really asking about her father.

"She called us dirty." Bitsy's face twists like a kudzu vine.

Finn shrugs. "We are dirty." Even his voice is little, but he always comes up with something funny to say.

Everybody laughs but Bitsy. She's too busy staring at Mother's pearls and her pink-polish fingernails. Her face looks hound-dog sad. I get a funny feeling that something just happened, and that Bitsy will never catch fireflies with me again.

"Who wants to help me in the garden?" Mother calls upstairs where I'm still in bed with Bitsy. She got the big bedroom because she's the big sister, but she lets me sleep in here so we can talk until we fall asleep at night and talk again when we wake up come morning. Mother says it's fine as long as we, one, don't argue, and two, get up in time for chores. We don't. And we do.

When I jump out of bed to help Mother, Bitsy pulls the covers over her head. "You'll end up with dirt under your nails. Gross."

Bitsy thinks she's all grown up. I know she's not. I hurry and change into a pair of cutoffs and a halter top. Then I skip away, leaving my sister in bed.

Mother works at the flower shop anytime somebody has a wedding or dies, but nobody is getting married or buried today, so she meets me in the garden—her favorite place, and mine too.

Together, we pull weeds, water the beds, and deadhead the zinnia. I do get dirt under my fingernails, but I'm happy, and Mother is too. So are Fisher and Finn, dragging their fishing poles out to the pond. Bitsy will probably come out acting all nice as soon as she realizes Fisher is here. That's what she usually does anyway. She can be as grumpy as a tomcat, but the second Fisher shows up, she's all of a sudden giggling, leaning onto one hip and turnin' her body all catty-cornered-sideways, as if she needs Fisher to hold her up straight.

When Mother and I finally go in for lunch, I smell my sister before I ever see her. "You're making my throat itch." I rub my neck, wishing she'd go eat outside and take her too-much-perfume with her.

Bitsy's face scrunches. "Well, if I make you itch so bad, then you can sleep in your own room from now on."

Mother must not hear, because all she says is, "You look pretty, Bitsy."

I give up, grab my sandwich, and head for the pond. Fisher and Finn have a can of worms and two bluegill in a bucket, but they sure do smell better than Bitsy.

1982

I'm eleven now, and Bitsy says that makes me way too old to build a tree house. Bitsy says a lot of things, so I keep looking through Mother's gardening shed while my sister stands with her arms crossed like she's nothing but a knot. "Why do you always act like you come from some trashy family? Running around like we can't afford shoes."

"Sticks and stones." That's what Fisher told me to say when she's being mean to me. She's hardly ever nice anymore, so I say it a lot. Now I give her my best you-don't-scare-me look and try to get out of the shed before she makes me mad. Ever since Blaire Dayton moved to Oxford with her fancy dresses and her snotty attitude, Bitsy's turned wicked. She won't do anything without her stuck-up friends, and they all get on my nerves. Fisher's too, but that doesn't stop them from flirting themselves into a frenzy over him, as if he cares one bit.

I walk sideways, trying to scoot past Bitsy with my arms full of scrap wood. The longest board drags low behind, knocking the gas can over with a *thud*. I hurry-drop all my stuff, but the fuel is already in a pool by the time I set the can up straight again.

"You're in for it now." Bitsy shakes her head like she loves to watch me squirm.

"Not unless you tell."

"Smells so bad, they're gonna know whether I tell or not."

"It was an accident!" She makes me so mad I want to spit.

"Never would have happened if you'd stop running around like some backwoods redneck."

"Stop talking!" I yell, dragging my boards all the way to the cedar tree where Finn and Fisher are supposed to meet me. It's been three years since Blaire called us dirty, and Bitsy has been too afraid to break a sweat ever since. Truth is, she probably wants to build a tree house as much as I do, but she's too worried somebody might see her having fun for a change. Well, too bad for her. She can sit and polish her nails all day if she wants. I'm gonna use my brain. And my hands. And my feet. Even if I do get dirty doing it.

I leave Bitsy to her mood and try not to let her ruin my day. I've been on the hunt all week, gathering scrap wood, nails, hammers—pretty much anything we can put to good use. I've already got the piles all sorted, and now I'm standing on the second-high branch, nailing boards to the tree. I'm working up what Bitsy would call a "white-trash sweat" when I smell something much worse than gasoline.

A long, black roll of smoke rises up toward me, so heavy and thick it's hard to see through to the bottom.

I feel my way down, jump hard to the ground, and run as fast as I can through the woods, over the fence, through Mother's gardens. I race around the roses, snagging my T-shirt on thorns before I reach the shed.

"Fire!" I yell, but my voice can't make a sound.

"Get the hose!" Bitsy shouts, coughing. She is already dragging one across the yard, even though she's wearing a brand-new sundress. I hurry to grab another, but the flames are high and I think this is more than a two-hose kind of fire.

"Quick! Move back!" Chief has run all the way from the barn. He shouts as he tugs the hose from Bitsy. "Go call for help."

My sister hurries to the house while Chief and I fight the fire. The heat hurts my eyes, but I keep them wide open because the shed is cracking and popping now. Kind of how it sounds when we snap green beans, only much, much louder. I'm spraying water on the boards, but it doesn't help. The flames are halfway to the roof, and they don't seem to notice the water one bit.

"Back up, Lovey!" Chief has never yelled so loud. He pulls me toward him. "It's likely to come down."

The two of us move closer to the house and keep our eyes on the fire. We spray the grass around us, and I pretend the water is an invisible shield like in the cartoons. I'm still shaking, but all the fire in the world can't touch us as long as we stand together and keep our hands on the nozzles. Next to my father I am safe.

"Lucky the wind died down," Chief says, because that's what Chief does. He finds the good. "And that nobody was in there." He's always counting his blessings, but this time he counts too soon, because all of a sudden Fisher comes runnin' out of the shed—the burning, smoking, hot-as-hades shed!

I rub my eyes, trying to make sense of what I see, but it really is Fisher. He's come right through the door, even though it's nothin' but flames, and he does it just in time, too, because as soon as he hits the grass, the roof starts caving in. The crash is loud and low, kind of how an avalanche might sound, I guess. Like thunder.

As the walls fall, the dark-gray smoke fills with little orange stars. They spin up and down, like fireflies, but these aren't fireflies and the whole sky is a danger. I'm sure not worried about the sparks, though, 'cause all I see is Fisher. He's thirteen and he's carrying Finn in his arms the same way somebody would carry a baby. Only Finn is no baby. He's eight years old, and his hands are on fire. On fire!

Chief hurries to the boys and pounces on the flames, using his own body to smother the fire. Then he jerks the old pair of work gloves from Finn's hands and throws them to the ground. I soak them with my hose until the fire finally dies.

In a daze Fisher feels his own chest and legs, trying to figure if he might have burns like his brother. He lifts his shirt, but he can't find a wound.

Finn's eyes are wide, like he can't blink them, and the fire has singed his eyebrows down to nothing. He's always been small for his age, and now he seems even more like a little boy. He looks at his hands, and when he sees his skin has peeled away, he screams. It's a cry I have never heard from anybody, and one I hope I never hear again.

"You'll be okay." Chief keeps saying this, but his voice is shaky and his head moves back and forth like he's telling his own self no. By the time firefighters show, the shed is nothing but a black-gray pile, which is exactly how I feel watching lines grow deep across my father's face.

Chief carries Finn to the truck, and Fisher squeezes in close beside him, both too scared to talk. "You boys are lucky to be alive," Chief tells them, but I'm guessing they don't feel so lucky.

My father tells me to go inside and call Mrs. Oaklen. When she answers, she is already blurry-talked. That's what Fisher calls it when she's had too much "sauce." I tell her the shed burned and that her boys were in there. "Fisher's fine," I say, hoping she might not think to ask about her other son, but she does, so I tell the truth.

She doesn't ask for more because she's already dropped the phone. All I hear is her crying and yelling as she runs.

While Mrs. Oaklen is leaving her house, Mother drives home to ours. Her station wagon is still rolling when she jumps from the seat and runs toward Chief's truck in a panic. She looks back just as the oak tree blocks it from heading down the hill, but she doesn't stop to worry about her car because she's too busy yelling. "Are the kids okay? Tell me they're okay!"

Bitsy puts one hand across her hip, cocks her scrawny-bony self to the side, and points to the smoldering shed. "Lovey did it!"

"What?" The look on Mother's face is . . . I don't like it.

"She spilled the gasoline. And then she started the fire."

"Oh, Lovey. What have you done?"

What have *I* done? I swallow hard and squeeze my hands tight into fists, trying not to lose my breakfast. Or cry. "It was an accident," I say, too mad to look at Bitsy.

Chief stands long and tall at the door of his truck. The whole sun sits on his shoulders as if even the day is holding its breath like me. Then Bitsy steps toward him, using her best tattletale squeal. "It's all her fault." She points my way. "Lovey did this on purpose! You know how she's always building those campfires."

The last of Mother's lilies crumble with the ash. Right along with what Mother would call my "sense of trust." From the seat Finn and Fisher stare into the haze, their blue eyes a match in both color and fear. They don't say a word but the message is clear. They blame me.

"I spilled the gasoline. But I didn't start the fire." I turn to my sister and yell, "You're a liar!"

"We'll talk about this when I get back home." Chief uses a tone I know better than to challenge. "And, Eva, it's not nice to call names."

He drives away as I mumble to nobody but myself, "It's not nice to tell lies."

ONE

May 2016
Phoenix, Arizona

"At what point do we admit we get paid to lie?" My assistant, Brynn, eyes the empty conference room down the hall, then the clock. The biggest campaign of our career is on the line, and with less than an hour before our big meeting, today's the day we seal the deal. Or lose it.

"I prefer to think of it as a little coat of shine." I pass her a tin of Altoids, hoping the sweet sting of peppermint will ease her nerves.

I wasn't always a liar, but time has worn me down, and I now find truth a watery thing to hold. It's been decades since I spent long, leafy summers clipping crinum lilies from Mother's gardens, playing in the shadow of trees. I've replaced soil with salary, literature with lunch meetings, and all things Southern with a dry Arizona predictability.

Here in this Phoenix high-rise, I now earn big rewards for veiling the truth. Although within the buzzing corporate hive known as Apogee, we prefer the more respectable term—advertising.

Brynn replies, mint pinned like a marble against her cheek.

"Presentation set to view. Leave-behinds stacked at each seat. Rose water chilled." When I offer a grateful grin, she adds, "You taught me well." A brown braid falls from her shoulder, revealing a tattoo beneath the ruffled sleeve. Youth, she's still got it. I don't.

I straighten my skirt, a modest knit I chose from Jansana's latest line, hoping to please my clients. "Now, power stance." I take the position of Wonder Woman, inching my legs hip-distance apart with hands on waist and chin held high. My strawberry-blonde locks, tightly cropped, are fighting gray strands that seem determined to stake their claim.

Lifting her arms into a victory V, Brynn aims for a double dose of superpower. It's a trick we learned from a TED Talks video, our latest obsession. We hold it for the two-minute span, and then she reacts. "It really does work!" She stretches her spine a bit straighter, surging with confidence.

Offering an I-told-you-so wink, I rearrange a vase of Mexican elder, a broad burst of flowers I clipped on the way into the tower this morning, a sign of good luck. In these parts the white clusters can fade from the tree by early spring, but we're far into May already and they're still producing their notable cloud-like blooms, a rebellious showing my mother would appreciate.

I push the vase to the side of my desk and close my planner. It's been color coded to keep me organized, providing a detailed task list for each and every day. When the bright-blue tab snags my sleeve, I can no longer ignore its labeled reminder: *Annual Personal Goals.* I jot myself a quick note: *Reassessment due.*

Then I lead the way to our fourteenth-floor conference room where we will soon welcome Jansana's CEO, president, and chair of their all-female board. Known as The Trio, these women have launched one of the most successful activewear companies in the world, a multibillion-dollar corporation recognized for trendy yoga gear and celebrity endorsers. If we play our cards right, they'll hire us to handle their advertising, a goal I've had for at least five years.

I fiddle with the silver chain around my neck. The dime-size charm weighs against the hollow of my throat. It's the symbol of an hourglass, a graduation gift from my parents. Engraved with the words *Your time is now*, it serves as a daily reminder that the sands are always shifting, that life won't wait for any of us.

"We get this one shot, Brynn. One."

In response, Brynn breaks out in the famous Eminem song "Lose Yourself," singing the catchy "one shot" phrase about making the most of life's opportunities. She nails the rap rhythm with ease while I prepare the presentation, tweaking the angle for optimal lighting. Her youthful performance delivers a pierce of envy to my ribs, but laughter wins and I offer a playful bow of respect. She's earned it.

"Always swore I'd never sell out." Brynn settles into one of the twelve chairs, spinning her pen atop the oval table. "Two years in the Peace Corps and now look at me." She tilts her laptop my way, noting the new spreadsheet as proof we've each become one of the minions.

I give the stats a sideways glance, then turn my attention to the flash of yellow creosote out the window, a fresh burst of bloom to follow yesterday's scant dose of rain. "I wanted to be a horticulturist," I admit. "Florist. Flower farmer. Someone who comes home with dirt on my hands at the end of the day."

I get lost in my childhood fantasy of living happily ever after on a small Southern farm, growing eggplants and bell peppers, selling poppies and peonies. "That was before my sister ran me out of my own life." My stomach clenches. "It's ironic, really. Bitsy was the fact bender, not me."

"Good ol' Bitsy." Brynn gives her best Scarlett O'Hara impression, lifting her eyes to the side with a long, slow blink, as if she's in that posh marriage bed telling Rhett Butler, "I'm thinking about how rich we are."

"Three years older and a whole world wiser. At least that's what she'd tell you."

"Yeah, but she's a *liar*," Brynn jests, exaggerating the trigger word. After years of hearing me talk about my family, she thinks she's got us all figured out.

I start a pot of coffee, allowing the fragrant French roast to carry me home to my mother's kitchen. While the brew bubbles, I arrange cranberry scones and give Brynn another piece of my childhood. "I was eleven when Bitsy blamed me for setting fire to my mother's gardening shed. It was the first time I called her a liar. Chief didn't like that one bit."

I don't say how I longed to be my father's favorite, how it stung when he would choose Bitsy to sit beside him in the truck, letting her shift the gear stick every time he popped the clutch.

"I get it." Brynn rolls her eyes. "My sister's a drama queen too."

"That shed burned down more than thirty years ago, and I can still smell the stench of melted lawn mower tires."

"That would be pretty hard to forget." Brynn tilts her chair, rolls her pen through her bangs.

What I don't say is that Bitsy's fire burned more than Mother's shed. Much more. But the memory of Fisher rushing from the flames, his younger brother, Finn, ablaze in his arms, well, that part of the story has never found voice.

Our curious barn cat watched the entire act unfold, her amber eyes peering between fence posts, her wet black nose poking through to investigate the happenings of the farm. The cat knew the truth. Bitsy knew the truth. I knew the truth. But my parents, well, if they knew the truth, they weren't saying. And that nearly killed me.

"Sounds like you're feeling a little homesick today." Brynn pulls a card from her tote bag, then slides the envelope my way. It reads, *Happy Birthday, Eva!*

"You remembered?" At forty-five I'm way too old to expect anyone to recognize my birthday, but as I tear open the seal, I'm blushing like a schoolgirl. The image depicts an army of firefighters rushing in to extinguish a cake set aflame by countless candles. Inside is the inscription, *Who says old ladies aren't hot?*

"Funny." I drag the syllables, then smile.

She shrugs. "I do hope some sexy firemen show up at your door today." She has countered the comedy by placing a small pack of cosmos seeds inside the card, signing with pristine penmanship: *Thanks for being the kindest soul in the cosmos. Wish big!*

I shake the seeds against their paper shell, a sound much like the flutter of wings. The gift warms my heart. "I do love flowers."

"I know," Brynn boasts, and I pull her in for a hug, grateful she walked into my Arizona office seven years ago in need of an internship. Who knew this scrappy millennial would, in time, become my best friend? "We're also getting tattoos. My treat."

Like many her age, Brynn has inked herself to chart the milestones of her brief thirty years. The one in view is a henna-style elephant commemorating her two-year stint in India. Noting my reluctance, she pleads her case. "Come on, you can get one that only shows up under black light. Your mother will never know."

"Oh, trust me. She'd know." No matter how many years and miles we have between us, I still fear I'll let my mother down.

Today, I am about as far from Oxford, Mississippi, as life could take me. Fifteen hundred and thirty-six miles from the family farm and Bitsy's lies, the smoldering shed, and Chief's disappointed stare. From this high-rise view Arizona offers not a single magnolia. No pink-tinged azaleas or fragrant gardenias. Certainly no carpeted fields of clover. As I prepare my presentation, I am no longer the cross-my-heart-hope-to-die truth teller in pigtails. In fact, I now spend my days doing exactly what Bitsy taught me to do best. To lie. And not just to lie, but to keep everybody coming back for more.

TWO

"Eva, come in." Our new chief creative officer stands near the window looking like Lisa Rinna, coffee in hand. Her mug's inscription makes a stark statement: *Deal with it.*

I grit my teeth and enter. A middle-aged powerhouse, she took the position less than a month ago and has already laid off 20 percent of our team. Known as "The Dragon," she's the last person I want to deal with this morning. Or ever.

"Was on my way to the reception area," I explain. "Meeting The Trio at ten."

"Thought you might like a little pep talk before they arrive." She doesn't offer me a seat, so I stand beneath an abstract painting with bright-orange circles stamped across darker shades of blue. As if chosen to complement the art, her navy business suit fits tapered at the waist, a fashion that feels far too serious for our creative firm where even top executives appreciate a quirky sense of style. Framed certificates, awards, and diplomas claw the wall behind her, but there are no family portraits, no vacation pictures, no handmade drawings sketched by young children. No sign of a life beyond this.

"I like you, Eva. I do, so I'm going to tell you all you need to know to seal this deal."

Knowing she has threatened every employee with layoffs and benefit cuts, I doubt she cares one bit about my success, but I listen respectfully, eyeing the clock.

"You want to stay alive? Follow two rules." She taps her manicured nail on her mug as she lists each point. "Never admit you're wrong. And *never* say you're sorry."

Before I can respond, the hour hand hits ten and I am called to greet The Trio. I politely excuse myself, grateful for the rescue.

Right on time, I lead our top-tier clients to the conference room. "Have a seat," I invite. "Enjoy brunch." They are counting on me to convince the masses that in order to achieve personal peace and harmony, they need to purchase a hip pair of Jansana yoga pants. Plus a mat, straps, blocks, wedges, and eco-friendly water bottles. Doesn't matter one bit if I believe it. I have to make other people believe it. So I've learned to charm my way through it, despite the buzz of my own conscience.

Brynn serves as a hospitable host, doling out pastries while asking how they prefer their coffee. I lead a round of small talk, filling chilled glasses with rose water and topping each with a delicate pink petal the way Mother taught me to do. These women may be movers and shakers in the Arizona business world, but one should never underestimate the power of good old-fashioned Southern etiquette.

Once everyone is served, I prime them with a brief overview of Jansana's advertising history, playing highlights of their company's past commercials while comparing them with top competitors.

"Here's the thing." I spotlight an image of an athletically fit model as she strikes crow pose. Wearing a fashionable pair of Jansana yoga pants, she presses her hands into the mat, her fingers resting just above the famous logo. "We all know nobody really needs this gear. I lead a yoga class every Saturday in Sedona. I teach old ladies in sweatpants and we do just fine."

The chairwoman smirks. A previous head of the Legacy Ball, she's a society heavyweight and the idea of sweatpants seems to humor her, exactly as I hoped.

I display a clip of our Saturday yoga session, Seniors at Sunrise. After nearly three years of intense exercise and the strenuous process to become an instructor, I have worked hard to wear Jansana's Lycra pants without shame. So has Marian, a ninety-year-old widow in even better shape than me.

Unlike the other seniors, Marian's body is lean and defined as she moves through a familiar twelve-pose rotation, shifting her flexible frame from mountain pose to mountain pose with lunges, planks, and folds in between. I use the lingo, reminding The Trio I know yoga and I'm the one to sell it to the world.

The final image shows Marian and me, our hands folded at heart center, our muscles taut beneath our unforgiving pants. "So how do we sell something nobody really needs?" I ask. "First, we acknowledge it's not a need. It's a want. A reward for making our personal well-being a priority. We practice yoga because we want to feel better. We wear Jansana for the same reason."

I display clips of women wearing the company's products. A mother crossing the finish line of a 10K, her toddlers laughing in the jogging stroller as she propels them through the race. A grandmother tackling rapids in a bright-yellow kayak, her granddaughter rowing bravely alongside.

"What do you think when you see these people? Better yet, what do you feel?"

The chairwoman leans in, smiling, and I seize the moment. "Yes, that! We want to stir emotions. See? That's key. We feel inspired. These are the kind of mindful citizens we all want to be."

Two heads are nodding and the third is tilted, intrigued. I keep sharing images of positive people as they practice yoga, meditate, and bike. "We don't sell gym gear. We sell an attitude—products that foster a healthy mind, body, and spirit." As the images rotate, the marketing slogan is tagged beneath each: "Feel good. Do good. Be the good. Jansana."

When the last screen is presented, the CEO lifts her glass of rose water. "Thank you, Eva." The moments drag as she takes a sip. Swallows. Then returns the glass to the slick surface with a slight *clink*. "I like your approach. But is anyone else concerned this may be a little too . . . cliché? Cute grandmas? Kumbaya?"

Silence all around. No smiles. My pulse quickens, but I don't yet offer a defense. In the quiet I count to ten, a trick Mother taught me back in second grade, saying it would help "cool my beans when a hot head started to show itself."

The president thumbs through the leave-behind, examining the media buy, the timeline, the budget.

"It's not the most original tagline. But that's why I'm certain it will relate." I move closer to the CEO, who's still with me. "There is power in the familiar. And in this case, we're aiming to bridge current trends and root values. Combine the old with the new, which is essentially the entire purpose of yoga."

She eyes her partners, holding the poker face I've seen many times.

"Here's the thing." I turn off the projection. "We can twist these figures any way we choose. But if we really want to sell yoga gear—sell anything—we have to tell a story. A story that tugs their hearts so much they'll want to enter the narrative. They'll buy Jansana because they want to *be* Jansana. See?"

With the slightest rise of her lip corner, the CEO finally nods. "I see."

Then the president breaks into a smile. "Strong work, Eva." When she stands, the others follow her lead. "I'm ready to roll with this." She adjusts her suit. Tailored to accentuate her Jansana-esque figure, the Chanel tweed doesn't show a single crease. "Set a production schedule?"

"By Monday," I assure her, escorting the three executives back to the elevator. Their spiked steps combine to form a symphony of ticks and tocks, each thud moving us closer to deadline, closer to payday, and farther from truth.

By the time I make it back to my desk, Brynn is already celebrating. "Nailed it." She gives me a high five. "And on your birthday! Happy hour. Tonight. No excuses."

I throw a glance toward the oversize clock, a contemporary piece that fills the entire wall with its jolting ticks. Then I look north toward Sedona, eager to begin my two-hour route to my weekend home.

Brynn senses doubt. "Come on, just an hour. Tops. I've already invited the others." She looks around the room at our studio peers, all friends to some degree or another. "Here," she adds, pulling out a pad of sticky notes and jotting with big, bold letters: *HAPPY HOUR*. She attaches the pastel paper to my planner with a dramatic swipe. "I've added it to your list. Now you have no choice."

Our laughter is interrupted when Brynn is summoned with a last-name-only screech. "Maxwell!" It's a cringe-worthy howl, evoking flashbacks of fingernails on blackboards. Having never known life before cell phones and computers, it's likely Brynn has never seen an actual chalkboard, but it puts her on edge nonetheless.

As she eyes the cubicles left empty after last week's layoffs, Brynn's spirit plummets. "Time to feed The Dragon."

"No fear," I say, suppressing my own worries of job loss. "We've got Jansana now. She won't touch us."

"Yeah, but all the more reason." Brynn grimaces. We both know our CCO would do anything to save her own neck. Especially since she was transferred with the task of increasing profits. She could play her ace—send us both packing and rake in the Jansana proceeds once we seal the deal. She's got us dangling by strings, a puppet master of the worst kind.

As Brynn heads into The Dragon's den, my father's mantra echoes: *"Always have a plan."* I roll my fingers through the tabs of my planner until I reach the blue one: *Annual Personal Goals.*

Every year on my birthday I reassess my life, examining my progress and drafting a new list for the coming year. But this morning I would do anything to avoid the duty. For the third year in a row, I have failed to complete my personal goals. *"Failure is an F-word,"* Mother always says. *"And we don't say the F-word."* She also says, *"Fat is an F-word,"* but it never stopped Bitsy from hurling hurtful comments my way for decades. This gets me thinking about the other F-words in my life: Finances. Fiancé. Family. Future. I hate F-words.

I return my focus to something I'm good at. I'm already finalizing our test audience when my cell phone rings. Mother. For privacy, I move toward a sleek row of windows where I savor the view of

Camelback Mountain, the highest of Phoenix's seven summits and one that always makes me want to head for the hills. With any luck Jansana will be my golden ticket. I'll snag a hefty bonus, retire to my house in Sedona, and live an authentic life with plenty of time outdoors. No more cubicles. No more advertising. No more lies.

"How in the world am I old enough to have daughters nearing the fifty yard line?" Mother's bubbly tone rolls through the phone, a perfect match to her polished Southern style.

"Nice football analogy, Mother."

"Hotty Toddy!" The one and only Laurel Sutherland cheers the signature chant from our Oxford farm, where Ole Miss athletics infiltrate every part of the culture. "How are you celebrating the big 4–5?"

"Oh goodness, Mother. I'm way too old for all that. Let's talk about your anniversary."

"It's right around the corner," she gushes. "Fifty years! Can you believe it?" At seventy-eight, Mother looks only half her age. Bitsy lucked out and got those good genes: petite frame, Southern grace, the blonde-hair-blue-eyes flawless gift of beauty. I, on the other hand, take after our father, Chief: strong Irish arms, steady feet, and a passion for all things genuine. Who would have guessed I'd be the one creating ad campaigns, spinning ideas until they're spit-shiny enough to sell?

After a long-winded description of the anniversary bash, Mother finally comes up for air. "Sounds incredible," I say, stringing off another list of F-words. "Friends, Farm, Field-to-Fork catering—what's not to love?"

"I keep telling her not to go all out with this thing, but you know Bitsy." Mother buzzes with excitement.

No doubt my sister will host a magazine-worthy bash, arriving with her picture-perfect family in tow. Handsome hubby. Bow-tied son. The ever-dainty Mary Evelyn in sundress and sandals. Nothing means more to me than being their aunt. If only Bitsy would let me be a part of their lives again. For now, I bury the pain and say, "I'd love to help."

"Wish you would," Mother says, as if it's all my fault that I haven't been a part of the planning.

I don't bother defending myself. My sister has always excelled at putting up a good front, friending her way to the title of homecoming queen at Ole Miss, just as our mother had been before her. And then going on to marry the quarterback, just like Mother. My role was to serve as the chubby little sister who fumbled along in Bitsy's shadow, invisible and unseen—the scapegoat nobody ever believed. It's been decades since I left Oxford, and nothing has changed. Bitsy does no wrong. I do no right. And everybody seems to prefer it that way. So I keep my distance and focus on the positive, of which there's always plenty to find in my folks.

While Mother names the party guests, Brynn exits The Dragon's lair and mouths, *"All okay?"*

I cover the mouthpiece and whisper, "Mother." Smiling, Brynn makes a beeline for the break room, then reappears, carrying a tray of cupcakes. One by one, our coworkers join in singing "Happy Birthday" as they head my way.

Mother keeps talking, unaware of the impromptu party taking place in my honor. Only when the voices grow closer does she finally stop midsentence. "Is that . . . Are they singing 'Happy Birthday'?"

"Yep." I am once again surprised it means so much to me. Maybe forty-five is hitting harder than I thought. I blow out the silver candle, trying to decide what I want to wish into my life this year. Sadly, only one idea rises—Reed—and he's the last thing I need.

Shifting my focus to something that makes me happy, I picture my mother surrounded by her plush Southern gardens, the green growth so feral and verdant it swallows all sorrow. At once, I am smiling again, so I wish for flowers, longing for the magic mood their blooms bring me. Flowers, now that's an F-word I like.

After swapping flame for smoke, I treat myself to a dose of icing from the candle's waxy stem. "Sinfully sweet," I announce, thanking my coworkers as they snap up cupcakes and scurry back to their desks.

Like meerkats, they bob in all directions, as if we're occupying an African plain. One looks one way, another scouts behind, while a third sits and a fourth stands. I imagine Marlin Perkins narrating the scene on my favorite childhood television show, *Mutual of Omaha's Wild Kingdom*. As a girl I would stretch across the living room carpet, propping my head in my hands as I learned about tigers and lemurs and all things wild. What would Marlin say about us? The thought pulls me deep into a daydream.

"Members of this group spend most of the day working alone in little boxes. The alpha female maintains rule by dividing the tribe, inciting fear, and ousting those who dare resist. Sensing a possible coup, she is showing force. Tensions are mounting."

"Lovey? You still here?" Mother's voice draws me back. A lifelong daydreamer, I'd honestly forgotten she was on the phone. I offer a sincere apology, but she knows my mind and takes no offense. "Will anyone be joining you for the anniversary party?"

"Not likely." I end with a rise, hoping she'll change topics before she mentions another F-word: Fallow—the worst one of all. It's been her greatest disappointment that I have yet to deliver her a grandchild, and every birthday serves as a reminder that the odds are decreasing by the day. She's asking if I'm bringing a date because ultimately that would mean a chance at marriage, a family, a child. Any proper Southern lady would have already acquired all of these long before her forty-fifth birthday.

There's nothing I want less than to show up solo in a town where everyone will assume I'm either (A) cold, (B) gay, (C) selfish, or (D) mentally ill. They can imagine no other reason a woman my age would not have a man. So there I'll stand, pinched between Mother and Chief—the model couple who still make sweet eyes across the dinner table after fifty years of marriage—and Bitsy and Whitman—the poster family for all things classic about the South.

No wonder I hit the road at eighteen. A misfit knows when it's time to cut her losses and run.

THREE

Surrendering to Brynn's pleas, I join her for happy hour at the downstairs hangout. "Prickly pear margaritas." She orders the trendy Arizona drink, then turns to me. "Two-for-one! We'll get a head start before the others even leave their desks."

"I've really got to hit the road." I let her take both drinks for herself while I prod the barkeep to pour me water instead.

"But it's her birthday!" Brynn offers him the last pink cupcake from the morning office party.

The long-haired gin spinner eyes my bare ring finger and adds a thin curl of lemon to the glass. "Twenty-five? Thirty?"

"You guessed it." I'm kind, but I don't return the flirt.

"You work upstairs?" He lifts his chin and gives me his best smile. It's the sort of pearly-white grin I could use in a commercial. I nod and file it away for any future campaigns that highlight toothpaste or mouthwash or, heck, Viagra.

Brynn is enjoying the exchange, so he shifts to her. "Might want to bring your friends with you more often, Brynn."

I'll tease her later for being on a first-name basis with this cad. When he makes another play, I nudge Brynn toward a table where we can talk in peace.

"Why do you do that?" she asks, a drink in each hand.

"Do what?" I brush crumbs from the chair and plant myself facing the exit.

"You won't give the man a fighting chance."

"Been there. Done that." I survey the room, eavesdropping on various conversations just enough to escape my own.

She blows her bangs from her eyes, revealing a tinge of pink dye in the under layers. "And?"

"And it's not worth it. You just haven't learned yet." I silence the drum of guilt. Maybe I shouldn't press such a jaded view onto a girl who is still naive enough to flirt with a bartender. And yet, part of me feels obliged to warn her of the wicked ways of the world.

Brynn downs a long sip of one margarita. It's the color of iced tea, a brackish tint that reminds me of Sardis Lake back home. Throughout my childhood our family's party barge served as a perch for lazy summers on the water. For the first time in years, I long to go there again, to swim in those warm, calming currents and let the Southern sun sing to my soul. Brynn may not yet understand the games people play, but she has been right about one thing today. I am homesick!

I glance at the bartender, who is already seducing another patron. Seeing my case is proven, Brynn takes aim. "How old are you again?"

"Forty-five." I look her square in the eye, refusing to admit the number is bothering me. What I'd give to go back in time, start again.

She nods toward the corner where an old man watches the door, his eyes glazing over with defeat. "Eva, you know I love you. But listen. It's been, what, three years? Since the Reed Incident?"

"Wow. We're calling it the Reed Incident now? My life, the

screenplay." The mention of his name pulls my gaze deep into her margarita.

"Well then. It's time to pen a happy ending. I have a friend. His name is—"

"Brynn, I know you mean well. But don't get too invested in this script." Before Reed, I'd been on dates with every kind of man imaginable: doctors, farmers, teachers. An engineer. One guy who had made millions by patenting a specific kind of gate latch. Another who had spent two decades traveling the world with nothing but a backpack and camera. But that was before.

"There's a lot more to life than work, Eva."

"You think?" I laugh. She doesn't. "I'm good. Really. I spend my weekends in Sedona. I teach yoga. And I've got wonderful friends like you." I give her my best *cheese*-smile, which reminds me of my sister's kids and how long it's been since I've seen them.

Behind her, our coworkers arrive, cheering as they distribute party hats to strangers around the room. A friend from sales toots a plastic horn and shouts to all within earshot. "Happy birthday, Eva!" Their revelry induces a round of applause from folks who have gathered for a little Friday fun.

"How did you know I wished for flowers?" I smile, accepting a beautiful bouquet and offering hugs in return. "Are these . . . Michaelmas daisies?"

"Asters, yes." Our marketing guru nods proudly toward the others, who obviously relied on her for the gift.

"I thought they bloomed in fall," I say, impressed.

"Special order." She winks, eyeing Brynn's drinks. "And speaking of orders . . ."

As our coworkers make a dash for the bar, I am taken back to Mother's porch where clusters of French hydrangeas overlap the wooden planks, the same purple-blue color as these asters. I pass the flowers to Brynn for inspection. "See? I've got friends."

"Everyone adores you, Eva. No doubt." She looks again at the lonely old man, then at me. "But it's not the same. My sister hasn't dated since her husband split. I'm just saying, I don't want you to end up alone."

"I'm happy, Brynn. Honestly. Very happy." Once again, I spin the truth.

For the next two hours I lace my way through Arizona's maternal curves, restless as a child. Mile by mile, I trade city lights for stars, stretching toward Sedona. As the pregnant moon lures me, my pulse begins to slow. My mind steadies.

It's after nine when I finally steer away from blacktop, tucking my Audi beneath the contemporary yellow awning that welcomes me home. No matter how exhausted I am each weekend, turning into this drive rejuvenates me in a way nothing else does. Friday . . . one of my favorite F-words.

It's been a couple years since I put an offer on this adobe. Once I caught my breath from the Reed Incident, as Brynn has coined it, I needed to escape the habitual haunts we had shared in Phoenix—when he wasn't living his double life, that is. As soon as I saw this place, I made a bid. My heart would have it no other way. The earth-toned construction of the southwestern one-story, the century-old cacti dotting the yard with thorns, the bright-pink bougainvillea that bloom all summer. It was too much to resist, especially nestled against Thunder Mountain, one of the peaks Walt Disney supposedly had in mind when he constructed his trademark roller coaster. I like to think he could never really replicate the "Happiest Place on Earth," but I give him credit for trying.

I drop my keys in the kitchen where I'm greeted by a picture of Bitsy's children. They stand, suntanned and smiling, in front of the namesake amusement park ride. Now at fifteen and twelve, they have each grown more than a foot since that photo was snapped, but despite my pleas, Bitsy no longer sends me pictures. If it weren't for Facebook and Mother, I'd never know if Trip had won his high school soccer game or if Mary Evelyn had landed the lead in the middle school musical. Of all the cruel things Bitsy has done, stripping me of her children is by far the worst.

June 2013
Oxford, Mississippi

"One more twist." I work my fingers through my niece's long curls. It's her tenth birthday, and she's eager for friends to arrive. I wrap the final loop, layering another daisy into her floral crown. "Perfect!"

Instead of smiling, Mary Evelyn holds a pensive stare. "Mama says you can't come to my birthday parties anymore."

"What?" I stiffen. Bitsy has been particularly cold to me since I arrived two days ago, my spirit and my heart both broken by Reed. As usual, she can't feel an ounce of empathy for me and has opted, instead, to pounce while I'm weak.

"Says y'all can't get along."

"Aw, she's just blowing smoke." I wave it off with a sigh. "Nothing will ever keep me away from you." I wrap her in my arms and pull her close, determined not to let Bitsy harden this sweet soul.

I shake the memories away, avoiding the hurt. Little did I know Mary Evelyn was right. It's been nearly three years since Bitsy let me attend the birthday parties. Three years since I was abandoned not only by the man I loved but by my very own sister too.

Moving through my weekend routine, I give a scant dose of water to the succulents and take inventory of my meager food supply. After a steamy shower, I fluff my pillow and fall across the bed. Alone. As an owl hoots from the cottonwood, I count the nights since I've been held close by someone I love.

I grab my planner from the nightstand and remove the sticky note: *Reassessment due.* I can't put it off any longer. I open the tab and review last year's entry.

1. Fat: I will lose the final ten pounds and run a half marathon.
2. Finances: I will land an A-list client, securing early retirement.
3. Fiancé: I will fall in love with a better man and learn to trust again.
4. Family: I will make peace with Bitsy and regain my role as aunt.

Using my highlighter, I code Goal #1 (Fat) in green. Indeed, this goal has been met. I write *Spa day* and promise myself a reward for that shiny half-marathon medal that now hangs in my closet next to my size 6 skirts.

Replacing the green with yellow, I color Goal #2 (Finances) to show it is nearing completion. I'll submit the final details to The Trio this week, and then we'll put ink to the Jansana contract. While the real reward will be retirement, for now I write, *Car wash and detail*, promising myself this small prize in return for hard work.

Next, Goal #3 (Fiancé). I sigh and scratch a big red line, nixing it completely. I no longer believe this one is possible.

Finally, Goal #4 (Family). I eye my phone. Three more texts from Mother.

7:32—Fly home and help us plan the anniversary party?

8:07—It'll be much more fun if we do this together. Right?

9:13—The Lady Banks are almost gone. Let's get you here!

This last one is typical of Mother. Throughout the year she sends a steady flow of photos and garden updates. From winter's camellias to summer's impatiens, the months are tracked by bloom. I scroll back through old messages, feeling more homesick than ever, especially when I read a series from early spring: *Daffodils onstage.* Then, *Take a look at these marvelous Japanese tulip trees.* And her favorite, *Forsythia!*

It's already near eleven in Mississippi, a little too late to call Mother. But Bitsy, well, maybe she'll assume it's an emergency and finally answer. I stare at my phone, trying to find the nerve to put myself in her aim again. Then I go for it. I call, just as I have countless times before. But this time, she answers.

It's been months since I heard my sister's voice on the line, and yet she speaks as if nothing is wrong. She's good at what I call scratch-off-lottery kindness, the sort that gets your hopes up only to reveal nothing but an empty promise beneath that layer of silver shine.

My sincerity softens her, so she tones it down a notch, saying, "I suppose I should be the one calling you. Happy birthday, Lovey."

"Thanks, Bitsy. I dropped a gift in the mail for Mary Evelyn's birthday. How are the kids?"

"They're asleep." She offers nothing more and my walls go up, but I don't dare let her know she has hurt me.

"Okay, well, I've been trying to reach you for a while now. We need to talk about the anniversary party."

"It's all falling into place. No worries."

I can tell she is wearing one of those overstretched too-tight smiles that means everything opposite of kindness. I plant my hand between my knees, fighting the urge to bite my nails. "I'd really like to be involved." I turn to my Notes page, ready for instruction.

She releases a dismissive laugh. "Come on, Lovey. Have you ever thrown a party? Even once?"

Once again she patronizes my efforts, as if I'm still nothing more than an annoying little pest, tagging along to ruin her day. I stay quiet. Hosting elaborate client events has become second nature. How can she not know this about me?

"That's what I thought. I'll take care of everything. All you need to do is show up."

"We really should do this together, Bitsy. It's what they want."

"It's what who wants? You mean Mother?" Her vocal cords tighten, causing her to sound even more like a cartoon character. Then she shifts to a steely tone. "I'll tell her you called. Don't worry."

"Bitsy, stop. This is ridiculous."

"It certainly is!"

"Oh, come on. You host incredible events. It's your thing. I get that. But this is different. We owe it to Mother and Chief. It's not about us. It's about them."

After a long silence, she yields. "Fine. How do you want to contribute?" She snaps each word like a rubber band.

"Well, I don't know. What's the plan?"

"See? You have no idea what's been going on. I've been working on this for half the year. At least. Now you want to swoop in at the last minute and take all the credit."

"You think I want to steal your spotlight? That's what this is about?" I adjust the comforter and climb between the soft, cool sheets.

"You've been doing this my whole life, Lovey. I won't have it." She sounds like a teenager, huffing furiously through the phone. "You love to fly in just long enough to prance around town as if you're too good for Mississippi. Too good for us. Not this time."

"I don't think I'm too good for any of you. I just want to help."

Silence. Then, "Do whatever you want. You always do." She disconnects the call. End of conversation.

FOUR

"I live for you. I live for you too." I am greeted before sunrise by the soothing coo of doves, every note a vow that they'll never have to fly solo through this world. Brynn's words from happy hour come back to haunt me. *"I don't want you to end up alone."*

Pushing anxiety aside, I walk a brisk half mile to the base of Chimney Rock where a dozen like-minded souls are waiting for me to lead Seniors at Sunrise. Boulders and yucca plants stake their claim, but I find room near Marian, the feisty ninety-year-old I featured in the Jansana pitch. We spread our mats and begin stretches.

By the time we've finished our sixth sun salutation, the rays are warming us while songbirds offer notes of prayer. I reach my arms high and draw my palms together to strike Vriksasana, but the calm cannot hold me. The same thought keeps rising. I have all these good pieces of my life—a successful career, a loyal tribe of friends, a healthy body, and an active mind. But everyone seems to think I need a man. What if Brynn is right? What if I'm only a half step away from spending the rest of my life alone?

It's been a long time since my mind raced like this. I refuse to go back to the black spin of insecurities Reed left inside me, so after an hour of yoga, I follow Marian toward a nearby trailhead, hoping to clear my worries. We enter through the Peace Park where she stops at the Amitabha Stupa, a Buddhist shrine that towers thirty-six feet toward the sun. I step aside as she gives the prayer wheel a spin, the vertical cylinder a blur of inscribed verses.

Suddenly, I'm a child of the South again, perched in front of a living room television where contestants spin for prizes. How long has it been since I've watched *The Price Is Right*? I've come so far from my roots, I can hardly remember visiting my grandmother in Jackson, racing to bid the nearest price. This was a thrilling challenge because if Bitsy and I could work the simple math, we could earn a prize: bouncy balls, Silly Putty, jewelry, even books! Grandma would celebrate the win, making us feel as lucky as the contestants on TV.

But here in Arizona, I have no television and no family. No tie to those simple traditions that always meant so much. Maybe that's why I've been feeling lost, unanchored. Alone.

As the prayer wheel slows, Marian makes her three loops around the tower, its tapered top glinting bright. At this hour the park is silent, and a gentle breeze pulses the prayer flags. They dangle from the pitched peak of the stupa, speckling the sky with vibrant color.

I weave my way down the trail where a smaller shrine sits humbly, nearly unnoticed in the underside of the mountain. Known as the White Tara, she is shadowed by a long, thin stretch of Italian cypress and the looming male stupa glowing gold against a cloudless blue. I slow, envisioning all the women who have come here before me. Many have left offerings: cedar beads and oranges, handwritten prayers and stones. Anything to say, "Here I am. See me. Hear my cries."

But I don't want to focus on my fears, so I head back uphill where the sun calls my name. When I round the bend, Marian rejoins me, zipping alongside with a cheerful smile as I try to match her gait. An ideal Jansana model, she's exactly the kind of woman I strive to be. Confident. Resilient. Strong. A widow for more than twenty years, she's one of the most independent people I've ever known. Perfectly content conquering life's challenges on her own. If Marian can do it, why can't I?

We climb for an hour, as wind chimes ring out from the piñon pines, their hollow notes a bell-toned base to birdsong. When we break for water, Marian labels the landscape, pointing in each direction. "Coffee Pot Rock. Chimney Rock. Capitol Butte."

Her water is carried in a dented canteen that makes my shiny Jansana tumbler seem absurd. She takes only two small sips, while I down half, trying to quench my thirst. "You sure you're ninety?"

She laughs and asks my age.

"Forty-five. As of yesterday."

"Your birthday?" Her skin has been weathered by the high-desert sun, but wrinkles don't seem to bother her. When I nod, she points back toward the shrine. "Some say the stupa is a source of blessings. Prayers answered. Wishes granted. Be sure to put in a request."

I'm a skeptic, but I leave her spiritual beliefs unchallenged, telling her about my wish for flowers and the fateful delivery of daisies. She smiles with a wisdom that soothes me, as if nothing could surprise her anymore.

As we tackle Sugarloaf Loop, Marian labels a warbler here, a towhee there. By the time we summit, she has identified an entire trail of birds, shrubs, and wildflowers. Now she steps off the path toward a cluster of cactus blooms. "Hedgehog." She leans in for a closer look. A few of the bright-magenta flowers have already fallen against the rocks, a reminder that in a space such as this, time has a deeper measure.

"You amaze me. You know that?" I scramble to reach the cliff where an early-morning hiker has beaten us to the top. With his shirt and shoes removed, he sits cross-legged, playing his flute to the winds. Like Marian, he seems ageless, and I'm inclined to think these two are on to something by living so far beyond mainstream conformity.

The flutist bows with a quiet, "Namaste," and we return his greeting. "This is a song of forgiveness," he explains. "To help us heal from past hurts and let go of the pain."

He's known for playing from the knoll near Kachina Woman over in Boynton Canyon. A colorful character, he delights tourists by handing out heart-shaped rocks and words of wisdom, but today he's come here, away from the crowds, and we are honored to listen.

As he plays, Marian sits stiff-spined against the rise. She closes her eyes and enters deep meditation. I find my own private perch and do the same. Focusing inward, I count out twelve beats, breathing in for a count of four, holding it for another four, and then exhaling for the final four-count. I think of nothing but the inhales and exhales, the space between. With the sun beating down, I finally begin to enter the deep state of peace I've been struggling to secure all morning.

My brain settles, my heart slows, and each breath echoes with an internal roar. There is no longer any hint of Reed or Bitsy or Mother or Chief. No concern about layoffs or deadlines, financial security or retirement. No thoughts of my single status or the ticking of the clock. I feel Free, my favorite F-word of all.

"This next song is for strength," the flutist says. "This is to help us rise again when life pushes us down. A tune to keep us moving forward."

His notes echo across the mesa, drawing me deep. I focus on the scars that linger from a lifetime of betrayals, the paralyzing fear of daring to trust again, and the even greater worry of what may happen if I don't.

I keep my eyes closed against the sun, and light and shadow begin to bend behind my lids. Red-orange-black, the spin intensifies. Dots become dashes become lines become spirals, until slowly, ever so slowly, an image begins to form.

The shape is not static. It is . . . alive, in motion, and while my mind can't quite reason it, I am being greeted by a woman, a grandmother, it seems. She is smiling, engaging with me as she draws near. Is this what Marian would call a vision?

With each step toward me, the woman becomes more defined. I have never seen her, and yet I feel as if I know her, as if I have always known her. And she knows me.

Many names rise for her, each one voiced in waves of echo: Kachina Woman, Hera, Kuan Yin, Mary. Whoever she is, she is timeless and omnipotent, representing all things feminine and calming and wise. It's clear she has come here today for a reason. She has come here for me.

She walks in silence, with arms outstretched, sprinkling a trail of white feathers at each side. Then she begins to turn, slowly. The feathers spiral out around her, the soft white plumage clipping the wind and drifting down to the ground. As the feathers fall, she beams joyfully, her raven hair falling long against her back, her eyes aglow with a sacred light. She doesn't speak, and yet I hear her words: *Strong. I am strong.*

When my phone buzzes from my backpack, I hurry down from the ledge, keeping quiet so as not to disturb Marian. In contrast, Chief booms loud from Oxford. "Lovey? You okay?"

I can't imagine what his reaction would be if I told him I am at the Sugarloaf summit with a flute player and a ninety-year-old spiritual guide, sunning myself into disorienting visions. He'd be on a plane with the preacher before I hung up the phone. "Of course, why?"

"Your mother's worried sick. Says you haven't responded since last night. She's convinced you're pinned in some canyon."

I sigh, resisting the urge to add *S* back to *Mother* on my contact list. I take a quick peek. Five texts and three missed calls from *Smother.* "I'm hiking is all."

"I figured as much. But while I've got you on the line . . ." He pauses, clicking his tongue as he's always done when he's searching for a way to word his thoughts. "Lovey, your mother and I, we're concerned you and your sister just aren't where you need to be with one another."

"That's nothing new."

"Well, we see the anniversary as a chance to make things right. And that's what I'm asking you to do."

"Why don't you ask Bitsy to make things right? Why is it always my responsibility to fix all the problems in this family?" I don't actually say any of this, but I want to.

"Eva?"

I step back. Chief hasn't called me by my given name in decades. Now he says *Eva* with disappointment, the same way he did when the garden shed smoldered and questions came from every direction—all aimed at me.

In the distance, Steamboat Rock, Cathedral Rock, and The Fin frame the scene as Marian meditates and the flutist plays. "I've tried, Chief. Many times, especially in the last few months. I just called her last night, in fact, hoping to talk about the party."

"Well, try again, Lovey. This is important. To your mother. And to me."

I don't bother pleading my case about Bitsy hanging up on me. Just like I stayed quiet when they blamed me for leaving the gate open all those years ago, setting Chief's sheep loose in the road. So many things I've never explained, like how I wasn't the one who painted *Go Rebs!* on the bridge as a teen. A long line of false accusations, Bitsy's lies that everyone accepted as truths. Instead, I cave, as always. "If it makes you happy, I'll call again. But it's not going to make any difference."

"I can always count on you, Lovey. Now, let me tell you about the surprise I'm planning for your mother." He shares a down-to-earth chuckle that stirs all things sweet in my heart. "What's the one thing she loves most? Other than family."

"Easy. Dolly P." Named after Dolly Parton, Mother's Cavalier King Charles spaniel is a diva in the most Southern of forms.

"She counts as family."

"True." I smile, imagining Dolly P.'s one-bark greeting, her own sweet version of "Hello." "Well, I guess next would be her flowers."

"You got it. I'm building a garden. A memory garden. Every bloom will remind her of something. You and Bitsy being born. A vacation. Our first date. You get the idea. I've been working on this for a while. We've got a lot of good memories. But in order to make this work, we need to take a road trip or two. All of us."

"Listening." I lean against the rock face, its surface warm and rough.

"We need to go as soon as possible. That way I can do the big reveal at the party, like on those HGTV shows your mother watches. I was hoping you might fly down early."

"How early?"

"Tomorrow." He doesn't laugh.

"Tomorrow? The party isn't for, what . . . more than three weeks from now?"

"Not even a month of your time, Lovey. You're long overdue for a visit home anyway."

I look toward the sky and try to muster some courage. For the first time in my life, I tell my father no. "I'm sorry, Chief. I can't."

He clears his throat, as if he's taking extra effort to guard his words.

"Look, I'd love to take a month's vacation with you, but I'm in the middle of a very important campaign right now. Jansana. It's huge."

He doesn't even acknowledge I've said *Jansana*, the world's fourth most profitable athletic brand. "Lovey, we know you've got a lot of responsibilities, and we admire you rightly for it. But people get out of work all the time for emergencies, and, well, this is what I would call a family emergency."

"Oh yeah? How's that?" I say this in jest, but in response, Chief's laugh is forced, a sound much more like a cough.

"Because your mother wants you here. *Needs* you here. That's reason enough."

A long, tense pause spreads between us. Chief speaks first. "Look. I know it's not easy for you to leave work. But your mother . . . she . . . I don't know how to tell you this."

My blood pressure rises to premeditation levels as I imagine the worst. "Is she okay?"

He sighs, clicks his tongue again. "Have I ever asked you for anything?"

I shake my head, even though he can't see me.

"Listen. Fifty years is a lot to celebrate, and, well . . . she's a bit nervous is all. It's an emotional time, and we need you here with us, together. You know what I always say, Lovey. Family First."

"That's why you need me to rush down there? Because Mother is emotional?" I'm not sure if I'm relieved my mother is just feeling overly sensitive, or if I'm angry with Chief for implying something worse. Relieved, I'm definitely relieved.

"Is that a yes?" Chief launches the question as if he's throwing a touchdown pass, expecting the best from his receiver. No wonder he won so many awards back in the day. He won't settle for anything less than a win.

"It's a yes-I'll-ask-my-boss," I mutter, unwilling to let my father down no matter how frustrating the situation.

"Atta girl."

With that we say our good-byes, and I make a quick escape back to the summit. My father's favorite F-words echo with every step: Family First.

FIVE

Early Tuesday morning, Mother has me on the line before I've even left for work. "Lovey? Please don't ever worry me like that again. You head off into those mountains and then you don't even answer your phone? Send proof of life. That's all I ask."

I move the yoga ball to the corner of my Phoenix home studio and roll up my mat. "Sorry."

"Oh, for heaven's sake. Take me off speaker. I can't hear a word you're saying."

Even at forty-five, I do as she says. "*Influential*," that's how Chief describes her.

"Now, tell me you're coming to Mississippi?" She ends every sentence with rising intonation, her way of keeping the conversation going. The porch swing creaks, and I picture Dolly P. curled snug in her lap. If she knows today marks three years since the Reed Incident, she doesn't say. No matter how badly I've needed her emotional support, she avoids the subject with all she's got in her.

Here in Arizona, morning has already broken through, highlighting the overstuffed bookshelves that anchor each wall of my exercise room. "I really need to get ready for work, Mother. I can't possibly ask for leave if I can't even get to the office on time."

"Good point, Lovey. But . . . keep me posted?" She blows me a kiss before disconnecting, and I file this in my brain: *Ideas for an Air Travel Campaign—when long distance just won't do.*

I hurry outside to water my plants before the heat rises. A modest stucco adobe built beyond the urban edge of the city, my Phoenix home is smaller than my Sedona shelter, but this one, too, is fronted by bright bougainvillea. I planted them years ago, and now the blooms turn pink as watermelon, rising up from terracotta pots to frame the door. Their thorns form a fierce defense. Makes me wish I, too, had a shield of sharp barbs.

It wasn't so long ago that Reed and I discovered a pair of elf owls in the front yard saguaro. With rounded heads and white brows, they are nearly as small as sparrows. The pair's puppylike yips would fill the air with a sweet sort of mewing, and their loyal devotion seemed to symbolize our future. Mates for life.

But now it's their defensive strategy that impresses me most. The way they tuck themselves inside the cactus, high above the prowl of predators, perched more than twenty feet aboveground with a wall of thorns separating soil from nest. It's a nearly failproof design, but even they have a backup plan.

1. Surround yourself with a wall of defense.
2. Go limp when attacked.
3. Flee when you have the chance.

The first to arrive at the office, I take a look at my planner. Tuesday, May 17. Three years, and the cut still bleeds. I open my lower desk drawer and uncover a stack of framed photos. After Reed's confession, I pulled these memories from my shelf, shutting the hurt behind lock and key. Today, I take a peek for the first time in ages. The blow is brutal.

One of the images shows us smiling in Oahu, the knee-high pineapple fields sprawling behind us. We'd shared a fresh bite of the tropical fruit, and then he'd kissed me, laughing and saying I tasted like paradise.

The photograph is stacked with others, all snapped during exotic trips to Santorini, Nepal, and Bali. That was before I started storing vacation days and spending too much time at the office. With one look I'm dragged back three years. The weekend I had just turned forty-two, and the night I thought Reed would propose.

May 17, 2013

I've driven almost an hour to meet Reed near the Tortolita Mountains north of Tucson. He's reserved a table for two at Stem, an upscale destination that's earned rave reviews.

With a glance in the mirror, I fix my hair, grateful I have yet to find any gray. I add a smidgen of blush and a quick stroke of mascara, hoping to draw notice to my Irish green eyes. "*Lucky eyes.*" That's what Chief calls them.

It's nearly seven when I reach the patio, and a waiter is already lighting flames for sunset. An insufferable group of businessmen call to him, demanding drinks "before the sun goes down." The waiter nods, moving to the outdoor bar where he serves them shots of tequila followed by cerveza. The men brag about their first-class flight status and early-morning tee times, so I tune out, focusing instead on the arid swell of sagebrush. The mountain peaks are subtle, rising slow above scatterings of wildflowers, most on the tail end of bloom. Saguaros shadow the horizon, like titans, with flashes of red-tipped ocotillos leafing out from recent rains.

Reed is late—again. A pattern that's worsened in recent months. I pace, poolside, where the smooth surface breaks only for the bright-orange torch flares. The flickering flames serve a fair match for the sun as the golden globe dips low behind Dove Mountain.

In response the earth sings out in passionate notes, morphing from a timid silence into an aria of melon, tangerine, and pomegranate. Foraging bats add their faint, rhythmic clicks, and my heart hums in response. I am tuning in to the screech of a barn owl when the smell of Reed moves through me. Calvin Klein. A scent I chose last Christmas, not that he needs any tricks. He kisses my neck before speaking, and this is all it takes. It's been four years since his hospital hired our firm to handle a fund-raising event. Four years, and he still gives me chills.

I spin to face him, resisting the urge to run my fingers beneath his shirt right here and now. With my job in Phoenix and his in San Antonio, the wait between visits has become hard to handle. "Just in time." I smile. "Can you get over this sunset?"

He turns toward the bar. "I need a drink."

I stay by the pool, giving him a chance to wind down from the long commute. By the time he returns, the stars are taking center stage and I'm hoping his nervous jitters may mean he'll pop the question here, beneath the moon. There's nothing I want more than to move to the next phase of our relationship, and it would be the ultimate gift for my birthday weekend. He indulges in a long swig of Buchanan's. On the rocks.

"Hard day?" I rub his shoulders. "You're in knots."

He sighs. "Acoustic neuroma Wednesday. Got the best of me. Larger than what showed on the MRI. Threw every unexpected curve at us. On top of that, the chief of staff called a meeting this morning. Had to squeeze that in before I left for the airport. I'm beat."

"How's the patient?" Guilt surges. Despite all these obligations, he's shown up here for me. I pulse my fingers across his neck, but instead of melting in response, his muscle tenses.

"He was stable when I left." The hand-cut ice cubes clink as he finishes his drink. "Let's eat." He turns and I follow.

We are led to a romantic corner table, another perfect spot for a proposal. As usual Reed doesn't miss a detail. It's what makes him a good surgeon. And a good partner—most of the time. I learned years ago to focus on the positive and let the rest slide.

As we are seated, Reed explains he's already read the menu online. He orders for us both, but I brush it off, assuming he's either exhausted or rushing through the meal so he can take a knee.

For him, a rib eye, rare, and a full glass of Malbec. For me, he chooses pan-seared trout on a bed of pilaf, served with a side of arugula and a dose of chardonnay. Then he turns his attention to his phone. It's not unusual, given the nature of his job, but he's not himself tonight, and I'm struck with a fear that the situation at work may be more dire than he's described.

Admiring the silver vase on our table, I press near the single white bloom. I expect it to transport me home to my mother's garden where the perfumed roses bait me long before I ever reach them. But unlike Mother's, this one has no fragrance, so I slide the vase aside and survey the room instead.

The crass businessmen are now discussing stock market trends at their table. They speak loudly, as if we should all be impressed by their lofty returns. Behind them, a young couple sit close together, oblivious to the obnoxious banter. They are holding hands, whispering, smiling.

"Probably on their honeymoon," I say, hoping Reed catches the hint.

At a table by the window, a young redhead flirts with a much older man. She leans closer and his gaze travels down her dress. Tempted, he reaches for the locket that dangles strategically between hems of soft green fabric. As he plucks the charm from its daring divide, light catches his wedding ring—something the young woman is noticeably without as she cups his hand in hers.

Her high-pitched giggle fills the room, and I try not to judge. But I imagine the man's wife back home caring for children, paying bills, cleaning floors. I look back to Reed, grateful I am not with that kind of man. I may not have the storybook marriage, two kids, and a double garage, but at least I've never been used like that.

I wrap up the final details for The Trio before Brynn makes it into the office. Ten months on this Jansana campaign, and now all we have to do is sign the contract and put the plans into play. My parents are being persistent, but how can I dare risk losing it all now? Especially with recent layoffs and The Dragon's itch to make more cuts?

"Morning." Brynn tumbles into her chair mere feet from my own. She carries a caffè latte in hand, her name sketched in black above the cardboard sleeve. It's misspelled, as it has been every day since the good barista flew the coop.

"Why, hello there, Brine." I exaggerate the mispronunciation while giving Brynn the best smile I can offer. If there's anything I learned from a Mississippi childhood, it's to stash a sorority grin in my pocket, locked and loaded. But Brynn has been my friend for nearly seven years, so even my best Katie Couric impression can't fool her.

"Not good?" She rolls her chair closer, brows pinched, head tilted.

"Oh, you know. Mother guilting me. Bitsy causing trouble. Chief pressuring me to fix it all. The usual." I turn to my computer and don't mention the painful three-year anniversary.

"Look on the bright side. It's Team Building Tuesday!" Brynn mocks The Dragon's attempt to "boost morale." Despite our resistance, we are both wearing burgundy, the closest we could get to wearing red—the *color of the day*. "Welcome back to kindergarten," she snarks.

The Dragon walks by moments later, trailed by her assistant. "Nice to see you sporting the team colors this morning, ladies." Then with pursed lips she hands us a revised list of Office Rules and adds, "Sort of."

She's barely out of earshot when Brynn hunches over my desk. "Go, team!" She tosses the rules into the recycle bin, unread. "Somebody needs to get a life."

I file mine for a later look and scan my calendar, trying to find a way to please my parents and still keep my job. "I've just put the final touches on the Jansana budget. Polished and ready for green light. I'm hoping to submit it to The Trio today, secure sign-off, and move right into production."

"Ahead of schedule, as usual." She sips her latte.

"Let me ask you something, Brynn. How would you feel about me tag teaming from Mississippi?"

She spins toward me, ruffling her brows. "What are you saying, Eva? You want me to take the lead?"

"You're ready for it." I smile, hoping to build her confidence.

"Did someone die or something?" She tilts her chin with genuine concern. I laugh, and Brynn's eyes widen. "Well, what is it? We've got a gazillion things to do for the shoot. I can't babysit these clients on my own."

"Yeah, I know. It's just that my parents are pressuring me to spend the next few weeks back at home. Fiftieth anniversary and all."

"Geesh! Couldn't be worse timing." She waits in anxious expectation, prompting me to give in to reason.

I click my pen and eye The Dragon. Then I sigh. "It's hard to tell my parents no."

"Not your strong point?" Brynn teases, lifting her intonation to form a question the way Mother does. When she adds, "Right?" all I can do is laugh. Even Brynn knows the matriarch's tricks.

The Dragon prowls around the office, then closes her door a little too hard as she answers her phone with a scowl. Clearly, she's in no mood for reasonable discussion. After days of indecision, I finally make up my mind. "Mother's not going to like it, but this *is* Jansana we're talking about."

Brynn shifts into robot voice. "Danger, Will Robinson!"

"Trust me, I know. But if anyone back home really wants to see me, they can come to Arizona. They haven't been here in years."

"Right?" Brynn says again, tickled by how effective Mother's strategy really is.

I am writing a polite e-mail, trying to let my folks down easy, when I receive a video call. "This is new." I show my screen to Brynn, who looks as surprised as I am.

"Your mom's using FaceTime?"

A jolt of nervous adrenaline shoots through me. "Maybe you *are* right about someone dying." I'm only half teasing as I hurry to the conference room, concerned. When I connect the call, it isn't Mother's face that appears. Instead, I'm more than surprised to see a ghost from the past.

"Fisher? Oh, gosh, what's wrong?" My voice rises in both pitch and volume.

"Everything's fine, Lovey." Mother's voice echoes from the background.

Beside her, Chief chuckles and tugs the phone his way. "Sound just like your mother."

Together, my parents stare goofy-eyed into the cell phone. "Isn't this just wonderful?" Mother sings. "The kids keep telling me to get on the Snapchat too."

"What in the world is going on down there? You scared me."

She moves into full view. "All my friends use this FaceTime thing with their grandkids, but you know us. Your father still can't figure out the microwave, and I can't even change the channel with that ridiculous clicker. Way too many buttons. Looks like a cockpit!" My parents have always presented a humble wit. One of the many things I love about them.

"Fisher here was kind enough to give us a hand." Chief moves the screen again. The lens fits all three of them now, but all I see is Fisher's smile.

"I'm here with my crew." Fisher tugs his rugged ball cap: *Oaklen Landscape and Design.*

"Got some drainage issues down by the barn," Chief says. "Fence work too." I assume the real reason he's hired Fisher is to help build the memory garden for Mother's surprise, but why didn't Chief tell me he'd be involved?

"Nice of you to help, Fisher." I am talking too soft, too sweet. Am I flirting?

"It was nothing. Besides, it's a win-win." He leans in from behind my folks. "Now, if the landscape business goes bust, I can add technology coach to my résumé." He smiles, and man, it still gets me. His look hasn't changed much over the years. With a bit of stubble and a small scar across his right cheek, he's still a charmer, a down-home contrast to Reed's highbrow arrogance. Once again, I find myself wondering how life might have been if I had made different choices.

"Good time to talk?" Chief asks, ever the considerate one.

"Sure." The conference room is walled behind glass, so The Dragon paces within view. Normally, I'd keep close watch, but I can't take my eyes off Fisher. He's already stepping away from the phone, a thoughtful attempt to grant us a private conversation, so I speak quickly, trying to stall him. "How've you been, Fisher?" I really can't believe they pulled him in on this call. I wish they had given me a heads-up. I would have checked my look in the mirror. "What's it been . . . five, six years since I bumped into you at The Grove?"

He comes close again, smiling. "Almost seven, I think. We beat LSU 25–23. Can't forget a night like that."

"November 21, 2009." Chief is grinning. There's no better way to get him fired up than to discuss the bitter Ole Miss rivalry. Mother may mark the seasons by bloom time, but Chief divides the year according to baseball, football, and basketball seasons. "Good thing Les Miles can't read a clock," he adds, and the men share a laugh about the infamous blunder that cost the Tigers the game.

With Fisher's stint as pitcher for the Rebs, he's the son-in-law Chief always wanted. If only I hadn't flown like an elf owl right into my thorny shell, accepting the first scholarship I could find to anywhere other than Ole Miss. Little did I know Arizona would still be my home long after I earned that college degree, nor that Fisher and I would go nearly seven years between conversations. I never could have imagined that.

Draped in heirloom pearls, Mother appears ready for a sorority luncheon or a Garden Club tea, but after fifty years with Chief, she holds her own in the football chat, remembering key players by first name . . . Dexter, Shay. It takes generations to work up that kind of polish, along with the Southern social graces she and Bitsy have perfected. When the ice shifts in her glass of sweet tea, she shifts her attention back to me. "So the real reason we asked Fisher to set this up for us is because we have a surprise for you, Lovey. Wanted to see your reaction when we give it to you."

"For your birthday," Chief explains. "Few days late is all." He wears a faded T-shirt, not so different from Fisher's. Both the kind of men who prefer a hard day's work to a round of golf.

"Fisher, you want to tell her the good news?" Mother lays on the charm.

"Happy to." Dark-brown sideburns frame Fisher's ball cap, and the sun has graced his skin with a tempting tan. If anything, he's more handsome now than ever. "Your parents booked you a flight. Looks like you're coming home. Tomorrow."

"Tomorrow?" My chest tightens, but Mother is cheering and Chief looks pleased to have pulled off yet another surprise.

I eye The Dragon. "Guys, that's a kind offer, truly, I thank you, but I can't just hop a plane tomorrow."

"Sure you can. People do it all the time." Mother's tone lifts. She's clearly delighted.

"It'll cost a fortune," I argue.

"We already took care of that," Chief says, as if there's no room for debate. My eye begins to twitch. Their secret weapon has always been guilt.

"You've got plenty of vacation time saved up, right?"

"Yes, Mother, but I can't just—"

"Come on, Lovey." The shift in her voice troubles me. "I need you here. For moral support. There's no telling what your father has up his sleeve."

"She's got that right," Chief teases. Last year, he secured prime seats for Mother's favorite Broadway musical, flying her to New York with backstage passes for *The King and I.* For their fortieth, he held an invitation-only dinner at City Grocery and somehow convinced Dolly Parton to attend—the real deal, wig and all. Mother framed a photo of her with the country icon, keeps it in the kitchen and says she's inspired to see "a woman who is fully alive."

In complete contrast to the singer's jovial spirit, The Dragon gives me a glare from across the work space. I stiffen and pretend to be negotiating a steel-toed business strategy, pushing aside a modern-day *9 to 5* fantasy in which Brynn and I hold The Dragon prisoner until she grows a soul. "All I can promise is I'll do my best."

"That's all we ever ask of you, Lovey." There's a pinch in Chief's pitch as he rounds the syllables, almost as if he's trying not to cry. I've seen my father in tears a few times before. When we buried our dog Huck beneath the elm. Again, when Mother dislocated her knee on the tennis court, buckling in pain as Chief rushed to her aid. I've been told he lost it on my first day of kindergarten and again when I drove away for college. And, of course, when my grandparents passed away. He's not a man who fights emotions, but if he's crying, he's got a reason.

"Chief? You okay?"

He nods but hesitates before saying, "Yep."

My parents have never once sent me a plane ticket. Never insisted I hurry home. "What is it?"

"Eva." My real name again. Second time in days. My spine shoots a warning. Chief and Mother offer each other a knowing gaze. Finally, my father turns back to the screen. "I don't know what more I can say. Just come home. Don't waste another day."

Whether Chief explains it or not, his message is clear: I need to go home. And after this emotional exchange, the choice is easy. It no longer matters that I have the biggest advertising deal of my career on the line or that The Dragon has laid off 20 percent of our workforce with a thirst for more. Even my retirement goals seem insignificant in comparison to my family's needs. If my father wants me home, I cannot let him down. Family First. Simple as that.

In the center office The Dragon lurks beneath the mural of little orange circles. The shapes are stamped like gaping mouths, as if fish are trapped behind the canvas fighting for air. I move toward the painting, trying to breathe. Without looking my way, The Dragon gestures for me to enter.

"Update me on Jansana." She moves three lipstick-stained mugs to the side of her desk, making room for a fourth. Her sidekick places it there to cool before scurrying out of earshot. He doesn't bother to close the door behind him.

"I'm on it, but—"

"Good." She turns toward me now, but I don't fidget or sway. Instead, I plant my feet and hold eye contact, removing all emotion.

"There's a situation. Back home."

"Home?" She's stumped. Unlike our old CCO, The Dragon has not bothered getting to know any of us. She stands cold in her tailored suit, as if she doesn't really care if I answer or not.

"Mississippi."

The pause is long. Then she takes her jab. "I should have known." She sighs before throwing another punch. "Let me guess. Pickup trucks. Shotguns. I bet your family still believes the South will rise again. And you ditched them all for the first ticket out of town."

Insults spray like buckshot, but I ignore her scoffs. There's no point in telling her the truth—that my hometown is a literary mecca filled with poet laureates and Pulitzer winners, a university community more diverse and well-read than any she's probably visited, much less called home. She looks toward the hall as if hoping for an audience.

"I'll be gone a few weeks. I have the time saved."

This snaps her back. "A few weeks? But you have to manage this campaign."

I glance at Brynn, who now looks pale against the sun-washed work spaces. She shakes her head, as if she knows what I'm saying in here.

"Brynn can handle it at this point. Plus I'll work remotely and manage any issues from the road." I start walking before I change my mind. It's quite possible I've slit my own throat. "I'm sorry, but I've really got to get home."

"When?" The Dragon shouts behind me as I head toward my desk.

"Now."

From their cubicles, more than a dozen coworkers watch the exchange. My imagination runs wild again as I picture a room of caged animals, their spirits broken. I grab my leather tote, then stuff it with my planner and laptop as Brynn watches openmouthed like the abstract fish that hang on The Dragon's wall. "Don't worry. I'll be with you every step of the way."

"Not if she fires you!"

"Even then. You got this!" I snag the pack of cosmos seeds she gave me, move the vase of Mexican elder blooms to Brynn's desk, and head for the exit. If I don't leave now, I never will.

SIX

On board the plane, I am relieved to find a seat without neighbors. But the privacy doesn't last long. A woman in the adjacent row leans over, launching a conversation. "Can't remember the last time I saw a flight that wasn't overbooked." She opens a bag of trail mix. "Where you headed?"

I eye the cabin, unsure she's talking to me, but I'm the only one in her range. "Memphis."

"Well, I know you're flying to Memphis, dear. But where to from there? I'm going down to Mississippi. You?"

I slide my window covering up. "Same."

The woman takes a bite of her snack before saying, "Apparently, no one in their right mind flies from Arizona to Dixie." Her laugh is loud, and the other travelers turn our way, the whole half dozen of them. She does have a point, and I'm betting the few who are making this trip certainly wouldn't have put their jobs on the line to do so. Maybe I really am losing it.

If it wasn't for the fiftieth anniversary, I'm not sure I'd ever go home. As much as I miss north Mississippi's tree-covered hills, my stomach tenses at the thought of seeing Bitsy, so I do a mental power stance and give myself a boost of courage. What's the worst that could happen? One, she won't bother to show up at the airport with our folks. Two, she will show up but she'll launch an attack before we even hit the interstate. Either way, I won't let her hurt me. Not anymore.

As the flight attendant gives her emergency spiel, I lean against the window and slide through time again, returning to Sedona, where Marian and I spent this past weekend exploring more than trails.

May 14, 2016

It's nearly noon by the time Marian and I start our descent, following the stone cairns down to a Native American–style medicine wheel. From the sky, it may look like a hoop of rocks with four stony spokes intersecting to form a smaller center ring. A lasting marker representing the two oldest symbols: a circle and a cross.

"I've hiked this trail for years," I confess. "But I've never walked the wheel."

"It can be a good tool," Marian says. "I have one in my yard." She wipes her brow, slowing her step. "My husband helped me build it." She looks to the sun as if he's watching over us. "Alton. He was a good man."

"So they do exist?"

"They do." She smiles sheepishly, her short white hair offering a stark frame around her tanned face as she comes to a stop at the wheel. "Maybe the stars aligned for Alton and me, but I never once regretted my choice to marry that man. He gave me no reason."

I try to think of happily married couples. Chief and Mother.

Maybe one or two more. The rest have divorced, either on paper or in heart. "My parents made marriage look easy. If I could find me a man like my father, I might change my mind about the whole marrying thing."

"You never married?" Marian's pitch rises. In Mississippi, anyone who spent even one morning with me would know my entire history, but here there are boundaries. After almost a year of sharing Seniors at Sunrise, Marian still knows little more about me than the way I look in the downward dog position. Which, now that I think about it, is quite a lot.

"I kind of have a tendency to fall for the wrong men." I try not to sound defeated. "The last one's name was Reed. Wasted some good years on that one."

Marian's gaze deepens, and I adjust with the uneasy feeling she's peering into me. She sees. "How long have you been without him? This Reed guy?"

"Few years, more or less." I don't tell her it will be three years exactly this Tuesday.

"That right?"

I shift uncomfortably.

"Seems to me you're stuck, Eva. Have been for a few years, *more or less*." She smiles, as if she knows I'm still marking the anniversary on my calendar, dreading the day's arrival.

"Nah. I'm long over Reed." A nervous laugh spills through. "I'm just not ready to give it another go is all."

"Ready or not, it's the only way."

I picture my planner, the red line crossed through Goal #3: Fiancé. I shake my head, standing firm on the matter. "Can't set myself up for that. I won't. Never again."

Marian takes my hands in hers, holding my stare with a pensive sincerity. "You can't give him that power, Eva. He's already taken enough."

"Oh, if you only knew!" The sounds slide hard between my teeth.

"Then you have to reclaim your life. Don't let him steal one more day." She pulls a small spray bottle from her day pack and moves into the center circle of stones. "Maybe it's time you give the wheel a try."

I dismiss her suggestion, but she continues in spite of me.

"It's divided into four sections. You see? Helps us process the lessons of our past so we can move forward. Think of it as a rite of passage."

From the center of the wheel, Marian sprays liquid sage. I'm feeling nearly depleted by our noon-day hike, but the scent works its magic, recharging me as she sings in the Lakota language. With her white hair and eyes the blue of a peacock plume, Marian looks no more Native American than I do with my Irish ancestry and my freckled skin, but she is considered a spiritual guide by many and has earned a respected reputation for her sensitive nature.

"As you walk the circle, follow your instincts," she coaches. "Don't question yourself. Just keep moving until you feel the urge to stop."

I make nearly three complete loops before planting my feet a few steps from the place I first entered.

"Good. Now think about this, Eva. Everything is moving in a cycle. We breathe out, the trees breathe in. They breathe out, we breathe in."

She rings her arms around in a giant arc. "Everything—an endless loop. The sun, moon, earth—all round, and they all move in a circular path. Just like us. No beginning. No ending. Just eternal movement, constant change." With her steady cadence and parsed delivery, she sounds much like a minister from a small-town church back home, genuine and sincere as she strives to settle my soul.

"Even the tides move in and out. Inhaling and exhaling, a rhythmic exchange. We are made of that very same water, stardust, light. It's all connected. That's the circle, Eva. The circle of life."

I trace a slow circle in the dirt, my Jansana fitness shoe clinging to dust as I revisit the seasons of my forty-five years. Again and again, my brain spins through the time I spent with Reed, trying to reason through a story that makes no sense. Marian is right about one thing: I am living in a loop that never ends. Every time I think I've moved past it, something triggers me right back in time, and the pain becomes as real as the moment it all happened.

"See where you've stopped? This place in the wheel means you are leaving winter. Entering spring. You're coming back to life, my friend." Marian places her hand on my shoulder and lures my focus toward her. I try to still the quiver of my lip, knowing full well she means a cold and barren season for my soul.

"Just remember, Eva. The harsher the winter, the more vibrant the bloom come spring."

"Lovey! Perfect timing!" Mother rushes to greet me near baggage claim where prerecorded blues songs play through the sound system and aromas from barbecue restaurants taunt the tourists. Insisting I not waste money on a rental car, my parents have driven more than an hour to meet me here in Memphis—the nearest commercial airport to Oxford. A touchstone for fans of Elvis, Beale

Street, and the legendary Sun Studio, this port city is banked on the Mighty Mississippi and opposite of Phoenix in every way.

As she glides near, Mother is all smiles in her high-priced Neilson's ensemble, kitten heels, and Coach clutch. Impressive, as usual, although when she hugs me, my fingers brush bone beneath her blouse. While she's always maintained a petite frame, she's smaller than ever and doesn't seem to weigh more than ninety pounds now, at most.

She eyes my travel wear, a sleeveless Jansana dress and a comfy pair of Tieks, plus a thin cardigan to ward off the chill of the plane. "You look fabulous, Lovey. I've never seen you so fit!" She takes a step back to give me the once-over. It's a scan much more invasive than the airport security check. "Luggage?"

I tap my carry-on, a battered hard-shell that has carried my gear through twelve countries and all fifty states. As far away from Mississippi as I could go.

"That's all you brought?"

I shrug. Mother would never travel without two full bags of beauty products and another set for shoes. She also objects to anyone holding up the line to load a carry-on into the overhead bin. We don't always see eye to eye.

"Okay then. Let's get you home." Escorting me to the door, she calls Chief from her phone. "We're heading out now," she tells him, because as always, they've got a plan.

She leads me outside just as a luxury SUV pulls up to meet us. It's an oversize, freshly waxed beast of a vehicle that reminds me of something a secret agent might drive. I'm surprised to see Chief behind the wheel. Despite a decent run in the NFL, he's a good ol' farm boy at heart, much more suited for his trusty F-150 with too many dents and dings to tally. This high-end gas guzzler doesn't fit.

"Going green, I see." The sarcasm slides past Mother, but my father laughs as he moves around the obscene tank for a hug. He walks stiff-kneed from old football injuries, and my imagination swings to a vulnerable gazelle limping across the savanna. Nothing about Chief has ever suggested weakness, and it pains me to see him this way. As he pulls close, the cedar smell of his aftershave helps to comfort me.

"How's my girl?"

Emotions get the best of me now, and I hold my father longer than I should. It's been three years since I retreated here for safety after the Reed Incident, only to fly back to Arizona licking even deeper wounds. Scars remain.

Never one to cause a scene, Mother prompts us. "We'd better get going."

I give in because, with Mother, there's no other option. "Want me to drive?"

My offer draws a stern glare from Chief, and Mother says, "Oh, don't be silly," insisting I ride shotgun as she climbs into the back with Dolly P.

The dog's pink bow is centered above her doe-eyed gaze, which is all it takes to hook me. When I switch to that high-pitched motherese used only for babies and pups, the spaniel responds with tail wags and affection, convincing me I really do need to get a pet.

"I don't like this whole curbside pickup routine," Chief admits. "I'm not a wait-in-the-car kind of guy. Goes against my upbringing."

"Such a romantic." I smile, offering an exaggerated sigh. I can't take my eyes off my father. His aging skin gathers in folds around his neck and the corner of his mouth tapers into a slant-droop. He's above eighty now, and for the first time I see him as an old man. The quake hits me hard.

"Your hair's nice." Mother reaches from the backseat to feel my short crop. It's already begun to frizz from the humidity, and even though it's not yet June, the walk to Chief's car was all it took in such clammy air. "Although I admit it makes me feel ancient to see my child going gray. I could call JoAnn. Get you into the salon."

And so it begins. The subtle criticisms that suggest I'm letting her down, failing to live up to the Southern belle standard she and Bitsy have perfected. JoAnn has done my mother's hair for decades and would probably love nothing more than to give me flawless blonde hair to match.

"Don't worry. Now everyone will just assume I'm *your* mother." I boost her ego, even though the statement is quite possibly true.

"Shush." She examines her roots in the mirror. When I tell her the chemicals are toxic, she replies by saying, "Oh, honey. What isn't?"

"Still teaching yoga?" Chief changes course.

"Every Saturday. All I can squeeze in for now."

"We're so proud of you. Aren't we, Jim?" She's the only person who calls my father by his given name, and even that is short for James. James and Laurel Sutherland, long considered one of Oxford's most elite couples, although they'd argue otherwise.

"I'm the old lady who teaches seniors at the park. It's not pretty, but I enjoy it."

"Old!" Chief laughs again, a warm roll through my soul. "If you're old, what's that make us?"

"Old*er*." I wink.

"You've really made a name for yourself, Lovey. We see your ads everywhere. The home and garden collection, those are my favorite." Mother sits back, repeating to herself, "So very proud."

"I didn't head that campaign."

"But you're part of the team," she argues. "And those ads are brilliant!"

As Chief drives us south on I-55, trees blur into streaks of green, and after years of dry desert sighs, this colorful palette is a delightful relief. When we cross the state line, Mississippi welcomes us with her delicate spring dance. Bright, bold ribbons of wildflowers partner with hardwoods to shade the mud-slowed waters. The scene soothes my spirit, and I finally work up the nerve to say what I've been thinking. "Bitsy didn't want to come?"

"She's busy with the kids is all." Mother makes an excuse, as usual. Chief glances in the rearview, a cue to Mother, who quickly launches a conversation about the dog instead. In typical Southern fashion, they prefer to stick with something generic, superficial, safe. Three years since I've been home for a visit, and my sister hasn't shown up to greet me. She's being cruel, and they know it. But I let it slide.

It takes a little more than an hour to reach Oxford, and by then I am caught up on all of Dolly P.'s latest canine excursions. I've heard the updates about the men in Coffee Club, and I've received a crash course in the whereabouts of Mother's sorority sisters, an active group who now volunteer for the Garden Club and the food pantry. Mother lost her only sibling, a brother named Levi, decades ago in a car accident, but she has a closer relationship with her sorority sisters than I've ever had with Bitsy. It almost makes me regret my stubborn refusal to enroll at Ole Miss and go through rush with my high school peers. Almost.

As we near Oxford, the traffic spikes on Highway 6. I barely recognize my hometown. The charming college community with locally owned bakeries and elegant boutiques is now cloaked behind a mask of overpriced neighborhoods, an expansive car dealership, and a confusing redesign of the main intersection, plus a slew of fast-food franchises. "What happened to keeping it local?"

"You've stayed away too long, Lovey." Mother looks at Dolly P. when she says this, as if she's fighting tears.

I try to let the guilt wash away, unable to say what I want to say. That I'm sorry. And that I'll never again push my family aside for anything. Not for a job. Not for adventure. And certainly not for a man. I do as I've been trained, though, and keep the conversation neutral.

"Why'd they clear so much land?" I stare in disbelief at the new developments. "Do they have any idea what people in Arizona would give for trees like that?"

No one answers, so I focus on the traffic. While nothing compared to Phoenix congestion, it's a big shift from the Oxford I knew and loved, the small community that inhales one hundred thousand people for Ole Miss football weekends and then exhales them away when the stadium lights go out, leaving us with quiet roads and a ten-minute commute to anywhere in town. "Almost feels like a game day. Where in the world are all these people going?"

"Yeah, boy. Now you know why we bought this baby." Chief pats the steering wheel. "Those students whip around here like a bunch of bats."

"But it's summer," I argue. This has always been the time of year when twenty thousand students take their leave, gifting locals with prime parking and a dinner-hour table without a wait.

"They hardly ever go home anymore. Why would they? Show up with their daddies' credit cards and live like kings," Chief says. "Got hit twice last year. They can ram their Beemers into this little lady all they want, but they'd better be ready for a trip to the body shop." He taps the wheel again, proud.

"Oh, Jim," Mother counters with a softness only she can offer. "We were students once."

"Yeah, but . . . it was different then."

Now she turns to me. "It goes so fast, Lovey. Seems like yesterday this handsome man got down on one knee in your grandma's kitchen. And here we are. Fifty years later. Who knew?"

"I knew." Chief winks in the mirror. Mother blushes and pats his shoulder from behind. He reaches his hand over hers. *Why can't we all be loved like that?*

After three full light cycles, we finally make it past the crowded intersection where billboards announce two new franchises soon to come. A fierce indignation stirs in me. "Seems this town's a half step away from orange shorts and hot wings."

"That's just how time goes, I guess." Chief tries to find the humor.

"Time." Mother sighs and looks out her window. "Our only true enemy."

I fumble with the charm around my neck, the small silver hourglass they gave me for high school graduation. The same one that traveled with me during my exchange year abroad, watched me land my job at Apogee, and heard Reed's confession when life as I knew it all came crashing down. Maybe Marian is right. Maybe time really did stop for me that night at Stem. Perhaps while the rest of the world has been moving forward, I've been stuck in a moment. A very bad, sad moment.

May 17, 2013

Nearly ten minutes have passed without eye contact from this man I adore. I give it another shot. "Reed, I've been thinking. This long-distance thing is getting hard on both of us." I'm hoping he will get the hint, take the leap.

He's put his phone down but still avoids eye contact as he reviews the wine list. "Yeah. I've been thinking the same thing."

Something in his tone . . . isn't right. I wait, eager for him to continue. When he doesn't, I try again. "Maybe it's time I launch my own marketing firm. I could do that in San Antonio. Don't you think?"

He peers at me now, an awkward twist to his lips.

I'm not sure how to read his expression. Is he puzzled? Surprised? Upset? "What?" I shake my head.

His face is strained. "Are you suggesting we move in together?"

"Well, not exactly." An awkward giggle falls from me. "I was hoping we might talk about a wedding. It *has* been four years, after all. I'm ready."

His silence is not the response I was expecting. Flustered, I try to clear the air. "You've obviously had a long week." I reach for his hand, but he doesn't respond.

A stark distance in his eyes suggests he's miles away. It's the look he gets sometimes when he's tired or hungry or stressed. "Eva, you do know I'm already married, don't you?"

I laugh at first, but he doesn't break a smile. My arms begin to tingle, tense, all in response to the truth he has just put to voice. Reed stares hollow-eyed and smug, in control of it all.

The tabletop candle that moments ago glowed with a hint of romance now casts a deep shadow between Reed and me. Here, in the stretch of darkness, I lose my bearings.

"Don't give me that look. This whole thing has been a fantasy from the start. You know that."

My lungs become weights, pulling me under, safe from the burn. I try to take hold, but the world remains above the surface, muffled beyond sense as I sink deep.

As usual Reed hasn't missed a detail—the flickering candle angled just so; the sleek vase with its single white rose, petals yellowing along their crinkled rims; the soft thud of china plates as they are placed before us, brushing the ivory tablecloth like lips to a cheek. My mind goes every direction. The situation feels like an orchestrated scene, as if we are on the silver screen. Indeed, Reed should win an Oscar for his performance. He has never broken character. Not once in four years.

Sensing the tension, the waiter leaves our plates without asking how he can be of more service. Reed lifts his knife and begins to saw his steak. A blood-red rib eye, extra rare.

"Eat." He talks through a mouthful of meat, half-chewed.

Who is this man? Not the person I believed him to be.

The seared trout rests untouched in front of me, my hands too numb to find a fork. "I don't understand," I say. The first words I've managed.

"What's not to understand?" His knife points toward the ceiling.

I stare at the rose, the one I welcomed moments earlier, before the whole world washed away. I'd hoped for the scent of my mother's garden, a breath of home. No heirloom here. This flower too . . . a fake.

Reed exchanges his knife for the goblet, then downs the rest of his Malbec, red like his steak. "You had to have known." His tone is flat. In fact, his mouth lifts into a spiteful smile, the same look Bitsy gave me the day of the fire. He's enjoying this.

I finally find his eyes. They hold nothing but an empty gaze. This is not the man I love. The man who promised to marry me in Mississippi and honeymoon in New Zealand. "How could I have known?"

"Come on, Eva." He smirks again. "I've been on my phone with her right in front of you more times than I can count. That's one of your problems. You don't pay attention."

Her. The thought of his unsuspecting wife brings waves of nausea. "Kids?"

"Of course." He laughs the words. He laughs!

"I trusted you." My voice sounds weak. Small.

"How many times have I told you, Eva? Never trust anyone. You're too naive. Like a child. That's always annoyed me." He takes another bite. Tilts the empty wineglass toward the waiter, who sweeps in for the rescue.

"Excuse me." I remove myself from the seat, a soft gold fabric I had complimented not even an hour ago, when I slid into this prime corner spot expecting Reed to propose. Now I fumble my way toward the restroom as his second glass of wine is being poured behind me.

My mind can't decide what matters, what doesn't. I focus on the wrong things. One man's cuff links shine bright, peeking out from the sleeve of his dark sports coat, but I can't make out his face. From across the restaurant, the redhead's laugh echoes, but a woman in the restroom repeats her greeting twice.

"Are you okay?" Her mouth moves soundlessly as she steps closer, and a strained concern gathers across her forehead. The creases pull much like those of a wedding gown, its fabric yielding and soft, easily manipulated. Like me.

"Ma'am?" the woman whispers.

I offer a thin smile and slide into a stall, closing the door behind me. As I lean against it, my own weight becomes more than I can hold. Above me, the lights are distorted. I press my sweaty palms to the door and try to stand upright. My ears ring and my heart races. Now I know what people mean when they say they are *scared senseless* or *out of their mind*.

"Can I help you?"

I grab some tissue and dab beads of sweat from my hairline. The words won't form. *Help me?*

SEVEN

"Home, sweet home!" Mother cheers as we make our way up the gravel lane. A troop of crape myrtles salute us, their bony limbs contrasting with the giddy azaleas as we turn the curve.

Landscaped without flaw, the grounds are idyllic, as if a fictional character could be living just around the bend. When Chief's loyal black lab, Manning, runs up the lane to meet us, thoughts of Dorothy and Toto spring to mind. "Bitsy and I used to pretend this was the yellow brick road."

Chief pats my knee. "Glad to have you home, Lovey. It's been too long."

Emotions surge as I remember my childhood fascination with *The Wizard of Oz* and Chief's stern warnings about tornadoes. *"They come hungry, and they leave full."* That's what he would say as he held the storm-shelter door, telling us to *"hurry quick"* and *"climb inside."* Mother always kept one hand on my back as I'd lower myself into the safe room, a backyard shelter used by many in these parts. I always hoped we'd emerge after the storm to find a gang of cheerful munchkins from the Lollipop Guild.

Together, the four of us have huddled through many a storm,

listening to hail slam the hatch as the winds grew fierce. We'd pass the time by singing or playing games, and sometimes Mother would read aloud, raising her voice above the downpour as if even the gusts had no power over her. We kept a few books there on hand, including a copy of *The Wizard of Oz*. I can still hear Mother assigning parts, encouraging each of us to impersonate the colorful characters. My favorite was Glinda, the Witch of the South. She was described as being "kind to everyone . . . a beautiful woman, who knows how to keep young in spite of the many years she has lived." I wanted to be the good witch, but Bitsy always got to play that role.

The storms never lasted long. On occasion we'd exit the safe room to find our property stripped of a few trees or shingles, but we were the fortunate ones. Never a casualty to count aside from a few "tornado chickens." Most of the hens we'd find days later, clucking behind a downtown gas station or pecking away in some stranger's yard with hardly any wear aside from a missing feather or two. But a couple were never to be seen again, and that always pinched.

Now, as Chief parks beneath the shagbark hickory tree, my stomach settles. Indeed. It *has* been too long.

"Bitsy plans to meet us in the morning," Chief says, insisting he be the one to carry my luggage from the car. "I figure we'll head out no later than nine."

"You still won't tell us where we're going?"

"No, no," Mother interrupts. "Surprises are much more fun. Now come see the gardens!"

Dolly P. stays on our trail as Mother leads me through the pebbled paths. Dogwood blooms have already fallen, cushioning our steps to the sun-soaked beds where vibrant lilies are in bloom. "I just kept toying with combinations until . . . this!" Mother cups a spectacular melon mix, its edges delicate, crinkled like a pageant dress.

My own hands move effortlessly, pulling a withering stalk from the first round of daylilies and uprooting any stray shoots daring to invade the bed. As a child I learned to deadhead the zinnia, pamper the peonies, and divide the irises nearly as soon as I took my first steps.

"There's no place I'd rather be." I surprise myself by the truth in this. For the first time in years, I don't want to leave.

I follow Mother past hot-pink roses, all in early release. When I lean in for the ancient fragrance, my heart settles to a slow, smooth beat, transporting me back to my high school graduation party, when friends and family gathered right here.

Fisher and I had been madly in love for a couple of years, but I had no idea he was about to pop the question. He was still playing baseball for Ole Miss, and I was barely eighteen—nowhere near ready. My parents had married late in life, and unlike most of my friends, weddings had never been a part of our family conversation. But there Fisher stood, ring in his hands and hope in his heart.

I grew faint, shaky. My entire future flashed before me: wedding, babies, grandchildren, conformity. The whole idea was terrifying, but we *were* in love, after all. I convinced myself that's what really mattered. That people had married this young before. That it wasn't the craziest idea in the world.

Maybe . . . just maybe we can make it.

I let Fisher slide the ring on my finger. And I whispered the word *yes.*

Then, from the fragrant row of gardenias, Bitsy gave me a glance. It was subtle, nothing anyone else seemed to notice, but with one twisted brow and a drawn cheek, she made clear I was making a mistake.

A week later, as I flipped through magazine pages of wedding gowns, Bitsy stood behind me in the kitchen where only I could hear her.

June 1989

"You know what's sad?" Bitsy asks. "It's likely Finn will never marry, what with all those scars."

I dog-ear a page corner, marking a dress I like. "I'm sure he'll find the right person."

"Probably not, Lovey. He's never even had a girlfriend."

I look up. She's staring right at me. "He's still young, Bitsy. Give him time."

"Time's the problem. You and Finn may be on good terms now, but it won't be long before Finn looks at you and Fisher and your happy little family, and he starts to feel bitter. He'll resent you."

"You don't know what you're talking about." Despite my resistance, Bitsy's warning takes hold.

"But I do know. Fisher loves you, but he loves his brother more. You're setting yourself up for a whole lotta hurt down the road. Trust me."

And that was the final blow. It no longer mattered how much I loved Fisher, how much he loved me. Marrying him would mean trapping myself in a space of never-ending guilt and shame, and staying in Oxford would mean a life lived in the wake of my sister's attacks. There was only one way I could ever escape Bitsy's lies and Finn's pain. In a panic, I rebelled. Tears fell as I told Fisher, "I'm sorry." I accepted the scholarship to Arizona State.

By summer's end, I left Mississippi and all I had ever known of love.

"My Lady Banks are nearly gone," Mother says, zapping me into the now as she moves toward the few remaining blooms that wrap the front-porch pergola. The miniature roses are based by billowing hydrangeas and a climbing sprawl of clematis, whose impressive purple flowers haven't yet stolen the show.

I tuck myself beneath the arbor, settling into a rocking chair my grandfather made by hand. Mother takes the swing as Dolly P. jumps into her lap, demanding a head rub.

"I can't believe you're really here," she says, and then her voice grows somber. "Why *has* it been so long, Lovey?"

It's not like Mother to talk about such things, and I sense she has mustered all her strength to do so. She's steeped in the practice of ignoring hard truths, pretending the ugly parts of life don't exist and focusing solely on the pretty pieces. For that reason alone, she's spent nearly eight decades skimming the surface, never facing what swims beneath the shine.

But now it seems she's ready to dive deep, and I'm caught off guard. *Why has it been so long?*

I am no longer with Mother on the porch. Instead, I am lured right back to the Reed Incident, and once again I'm moving through moments as if time doesn't really exist. How can I tell her the hurt I still carry? Not from Reed's betrayal, but from the response I received when I ran home for help.

All my life I'd take a hard knock, never expecting the world to go easy on me, but when Reed betrayed me, it was more than I could handle. I needed my family to stand up for me, help me heal. Instead, Bitsy attacked, Chief stayed silent, and Mother told me never to speak of it again.

June 2013

"A married man. Who does that?" Bitsy glares.

I pass the milk and sugar, hoping to help my family understand. "I never would have gotten myself into that situation, Bitsy. I didn't know." I pour myself a second shot of caffeine, filling a mug made of Mississippi clay.

"That's what they all say." She rolls her eyes. "I mean, seriously. How could you date a man for four years and not know he has a wife? And worse . . . kids? A quick Google search is all it takes."

"Good coffee," Mother interjects, as if we'd better make peace at any cost.

I ignore the warning. "You don't think I searched? I found nothing. Only a website from his practice and a LinkedIn profile."

"I don't believe that for a second. What I do believe is that my sister is a home wrecker."

"That's not fair, Bitsy." My voice elevates, and I try not to shout. "Search for yourself. There's not one family photo, not a single mention of his wife. He's a master manipulator, I'm telling you. A con of the worst sort."

"Girls, must we talk about such things?" Mother butters pancakes with a disappointed look.

"Well, if I should have known about his family, then you should have known too, right?" I throw it back at Bitsy. "Y'all thought he hung the moon."

"Don't expect me to carry your cross." Bitsy stares coldly, crunching every syllable. Ice.

This does it. "You always want to blame the person who gets hurt instead of the one who does the hurting. I guess that means you think I knew when you were hooking up with Harland Henson behind my back?"

I let this long-held secret come tumbling out, one of many wounds Bitsy delivered during childhood. "My first boyfriend stolen by my only sister. How much more Jerry Springer does it get? You'd have taken Fisher too, if he had let you. I know all about how you tried to kiss him while I was getting dressed for prom."

She slams her hand against the table and her coffee spills, a dark stain seeping across the vintage linen tablecloth.

"Enough." Mother moves between us, butter knife in hand.

The three of us pause, frozen in a standoff, waiting for someone to make the next move. As usual I'm the one who gives in. But this time, I don't apologize. Instead, I turn my back and head for the door, then slam it. Hard.

Bitsy follows me out beneath the hickory. Far beyond Mother's earshot, she spits these words: "Nobody believes you, Lovey. You've always been a liar."

"I know the truth."

"Do you?" She shoots me a glare that means to challenge. "So that's why you're about to run away again? Because you're telling the truth, right?"

That's all it took to send me back to Arizona. But I don't tell Mother the real reason I've stayed away so long. Instead, I pet Manning and say, "Time just got away from me, I guess."

"Bet they don't feed you like this in the desert." Chief savors another bite. Thanks to greenhouse transplants, we spent the afternoon harvesting a basket of tender yellow squash and zucchini—the first of the season. Roasted with hand-pressed olive oil, the fresh produce serves as an early supper, dished with homegrown herbs and a piping-hot bowl of fettucine. For dessert, Mother's peach pie, baked from preserves and balanced with a heaping scoop of vanilla ice cream, all drizzled with a warm, dark loop of honey tapped straight from my father's hives.

I fall back against my chair and cover my bulging belly. "What in the world have I been thinking? I'm never leaving y'all again. Never."

"I hope not." Mother gazes at me, and I have rarely felt so loved. Despite the enticing spread, she has barely eaten, and her frail frame seems particularly noticeable now as she declines dessert.

"Just a little slice?" I nudge the pastry her way as Mother brings two photo albums to the table.

"Nothing has much of a taste these days." She shrugs. "Besides, I'm watching my sugar."

I've read about people losing their appetite, even their sense of taste as they age, but it seems odd for her to act as if this is normal. I don't push, but I do worry as she opens the albums and begins reminiscing about the early years. As we flip through the pages, I am met with a carefree little Lovey, a joyful spirit who spent her childhood laughing and exploring these red-dirt ravines.

"Your mother's been organizing all the old photos," Chief says. "Quite a job."

"Don't want you girls to ever forget the good times." She gives me a hopeful smile.

Indeed, she has managed to preserve an entire childhood of delightful moments, pure joy on my face in every shot. And there's another thing about the story these photographs tell. Nearly every image shows me stitched to Bitsy's side. Proof there was a time when nothing could have kept me from her.

"I wish Bitsy would have joined us." Despite all she's done to me, I miss my sister. I miss her children too.

"She's got a pretty full plate." Mother reverts to making excuses again. "A teenager and a middle schooler. That's a lot to manage." Then she lowers her jaw, as if I wouldn't understand. Maybe I don't, but Mother would never acknowledge I, too, have a lot to manage back in Arizona. It's a world as foreign to her as Jupiter, and why I've chosen to live there as an unmarried woman with no children of my own is beyond her.

As the family stories surface and memories take hold, I realize why Bitsy hasn't bothered returning my calls. She's got everything she needs right here in Oxford. I'm the one on the outside looking in.

After the dishes have been cleaned, Chief and I take a long walk, with Manning leading the way. "Just look at all the lightning bugs," I say. "It's the little things, you know?"

This makes my father smile, and the spark is not lost on me. "Won't be long before the rest of the bugs return too."

"First time I came home from college, I couldn't believe the noise. Cicadas. Crickets. Frogs. I had to raise my voice just to talk over all that buzzing and croaking."

He looks toward the pond. "Funny. I hardly even notice anymore."

"I'm telling you, Chief. I've traveled half the globe. There's no place as alive as this."

My appreciation draws a pleased grin and a story from his own youth—a day spent nabbing tree frogs with his cousin Ted. As the sun begins to set, fireflies dance above the wildflowers, spreading wide across the horizon and shining out their sparks of light. It brings me right back to childhood, when Fisher, Finn, Bitsy, and I would spend warm summer evenings filling Mason jars, counting our catch.

Chief shares my delight. "You used to think they were magic. Remember?"

"Those vacations in the Smokies? Best ever!"

His smile grows broader, revealing a slight discoloration between his real teeth and the dental bridge he's worn since a particularly brutal tackle in the NFL. "One of the only places in the world where they all light up at once. You were only about four, I think, that first time. Long before all the tourists starting showing up in droves. Soon as those signals fired, you were hooked."

"Looked like someone had strung a bunch of Christmas lights through the forest. The kind that blink." I can still picture the swell of firefly lights stretching out between the trees. Then they all went dark. Couldn't see a thing. But just when I thought it was done, another wave of light flared, then another. The beetles would shine and then dim as if the trees were breathing in light, inhaling and exhaling, again and again. That same old circle of life Marian talks about.

Chief closes the gate behind us, the metal latch releasing a steely sound. "I've never seen anything else like it."

"You told me we were in Neverland."

He chuckles. "You believed every word."

As we reminisce Chief and I move beneath the redbuds, their bright-pink blooms long gone. The legume pods are already forming, bobbing like miniature sugar snaps in the slight evening breeze. By season's end they'll become dry, rattling as if the tree is a shaman, blessing all who pass.

When we reach the barn, our old tack room calls with its smell of leather saddles and rusted bits. Years of riding lessons have left their mark here, proven by shelves of trophies and award ribbons, saddle blankets, and boots—all turning to dust by the day. Even with a limp, Chief's pace is fast as he makes his way through the indoor riding arena. This is where he taught Bitsy and me to polish our tack and place our weight in the stirrups, insisting, *"If you can work a horse, you can do most anything."*

Summer 1977

"Posture, girls. Are you a princess or a pauper?" Chief stands in the middle of the arena. Bitsy rides her Hanoverian. I have my Paint. "One more round."

"Then can we plant the trees?" I've been itching to get my hands in the dirt ever since Chief came home with a truck full of crape myrtles.

He clicks his tongue. "Show me better posture, and it's a deal."

I do as he says, press my toes and pull my chin proud. I'm six, but Chief says I can already handle my horse like a champ.

"Atta girl!" He claps and smiles big at me.

"Watch this!" Bitsy yells. He turns like she wants him to do, so I finish my circle on my own.

When Bitsy comes back around, Chief helps us remove the saddles, store our tack. We give the horses water and hay. Then we lead them to the pasture and head for the truck. Chief has parked it so we can unload the trees. "Lovey, you're in charge of the white ones. Bitsy, you take the pink." He counts ten big steps between each mark and challenges us to use different languages: *Uno, dos, tres. Un, deux, trois.*

The hose has been running, so the dirt is soft for digging. Perfect for mud pies. "You know what the man at the garden center told me? He said these aren't really trees at all," Chief teases. "They're actually a bunch of old ladies. At night they throw big parties, and sometimes they leave glitter on the ground. Wait and see."

This makes my sister smile, so I dance around and sing, "Glitter! Glitter!" until she tells me I'm being a brat.

By the time we get all twenty in the ground, they stand tall as our horses. To celebrate, Bitsy says we can have a pixie party. I bring leaves and flowers, and she makes a big circle around one of the trees. When we finish decorating, Bitsy stomps her foot and yells, "Summon the sprites!" I wave a branch, speaking "in tongues" to call the fairies.

Bitsy plays the part of queen, so I fill one of the plastic pots with mud. Then I crush acorns as seasoning, and I sprinkle tiny crape myrtle petals on top of the pie. Bitsy says it's pretty, so I let her have it.

"Yum!" She pretends to take a bite. Then Bitsy pops open one of the buds. "This is Grandmother's purse." She presses it until the pale-pink petals peek out between the seams. "This is Grandmother's handkerchief." She pulls the petals, and we find their tiny yellow centers.

I jump in to tell the best part. "And this is Grandmother's gold!"

Bitsy gives me a glare. "Stop stealing all the glory."

I follow my father through the barn, out toward the path where we counted his steps so many years ago. Now the knobby limbs of

the crape myrtles form a seasonal overhang for the walking trail, just as Mother had in mind when she planned the design. Chief reads my thoughts. "Remember when we planted these?" I smile. He does too. "That's the kind of stuff that made you, Lovey. Don't ever lose hold, you hear?"

When he talks this way, I feel a surge of nostalgia, and I wonder if life could be good for me here again. What if I dared return home to stay?

I push aside the thought as Chief shows me the hillside where he'll be installing Mother's surprise garden. It's a serene space, ideal for both shade- and sun-loving plants. He maps out the plan, explaining it may be "a little bigger than expected."

"I think it's perfect." I cup his forearm lightly. "You're on to something with this garden, Chief. Every flower a memory. I can't wait to see it all come together."

His satisfaction is palpable as we walk together past the pond. I was barely three, four at most, when he built this wooden pier and taught us how to bait a hook, always making sure we'd "leave some limp" so the worm would dangle in the current and attract the biggest bass.

Now lean reeds line the bank. Like the Reed I loved, each stands hollow inside a hardened case, casting shadow on all that come close. Nearby, the faded canoe rests onshore, its peeling bow beneath water, the wooden paddles nowhere in sight.

"Remember when you girls sank that canoe? Took Buzz and Juke and me, all three of us, to pull it up outta there. Liked to never got her freed."

Gentle laughter spools between us as I remember Chief's two best friends. The three men could spend a full day in a fishing boat and still hang out for hours after they made it back to the farm. I wonder if I've been too petty all these years. Have I been making a big deal over nothing? So blinded by my own pain that I could no longer see the good right here at home? I take a long look at my father, a man who has shown us nothing less than love from the start. "We had a magical childhood, didn't we? Bitsy and me."

The air spills heavy and long from Chief's lungs, and I have a brief glimpse of how horrible life would be without him. I give him my full attention, noticing the receding hairline, gray and thin, the darkened age spots dotting his forehead, the slight tremor to his hands. He seems to respond in kind, trying to process a daughter who has returned nearly three years older since her last visit home, her own hair graying, her skin lined with wear.

"I've made my fair share of mistakes along the way, Lovey. But I can tell you this. We tried to do everything right for you girls. I swear we did."

Half of me wants to hug my father and assure him I wouldn't change a thing. But the wounded half wants to tell him how badly I needed him to stand up for me. How much his silence has hurt me. Instead, I loop back around to something safe.

"So . . . tell me more about this memory garden."

He refuses to reveal another detail, savoring the surprise and opting instead to put me to work. We carry five-gallon buckets to the strawberry patch, where he says the plush red berries have had a successful spring harvest. Seizing the final drops of daylight, I wrestle the dark-green bunchings that droop from the eye-level arbor, a new method Mother has been tinkering with the last few years. Together, Chief and I pluck the last of the crimson berries from their stems. Even though I'm stuffed from our early supper, the temptation is too much. I pop the treats into my mouth, and Manning does the same, nibbling the ones I offer and returning affections tenfold, his black tail whacking the ground with a loving *thud, thud, thud.*

The size of gumdrops, they release their warm, sweet juices on my tongue. "Taste of my childhood." I savor the tangy-sweet berries, and Chief seems pleased. His strong jaw sets firm against the sunset and his steady frame is balanced tall beside the trellis. "Why can't every man be like you?"

"Ah . . . I'm no saint."

"I never expected to find a saint." My voice softens. "But I'm starting to believe Mother got the last good man."

Around us, the fireflies take it up a notch, a display of dancing stars. "He's out there, Lovey. And he's missing out on a very special lady, I'll tell you that."

Chief puts his arm around my shoulders and we make our way home, buckets in hand, the season's-end strawberries rolling as we stroll. When the sun sinks, it's all I can do not to let my head fall against my father's shoulder and cry out all the hurt. But I never have cried on my father's shoulder, and I doubt I ever will.

EIGHT

Waking up in my childhood bed brings another wave of nostalgia. "No one ever comes in here but you," Mother said last night, defending her choice to let my room stay undisturbed for decades. Equestrian ribbons dot the bulletin board alongside photos of Fisher and me. A few graduation cards are tacked to the border while album covers coat the walls—a timeline of my life.

I circle the room, touching the gritty album sleeves and processing every sting I endured in this space.

Gene Loves Jezebel—the day Bitsy drove off without me and told the drama teacher she had no idea why I hadn't shown up for auditions. Lie.

The Cure—a Halloween party I couldn't attend because Bitsy told Mother she had seen me smoking cigarettes. Lie.

The Smiths—a deep dive into darkness after Bitsy and her mean-girl tribe ganged up on me in the commons area, telling everyone there was only one reason people called me "Lovey." Lie.

Despite the pain at the time, none of those scars compares to what Reed put me through. If only I could go back a few decades and have a talk with that young Eva. I'd sit her down and tell her straight: *"Buck up, Lovey. Don't let Bitsy push you down. She's got no right to run you out of your life, your home. The good stuff is here. Now. And it can be yours."*

But that's the thing about life. There's no going back.

"Morning, sunshine." Mother taps my open door to find me walking down memory lane. She kisses my head, as if I'm still a girl, blanketing me with the classic fragrance of her Chanel No. 5. "Hungry?"

"I'll cook." I run my hands through my cropped hair as a half attempt to start the day. It's only now that I notice the smell of bacon wafting from downstairs.

"Already done." Mother eyes the clock. Red digital numbers proclaim 7:53. "I haven't known you to sleep this late in years."

"Me either. Sorry I wasn't up to help with breakfast."

"Glad you got some rest. Chief's gone to Coffee Club. He'll be home soon for our trip." She nods toward the window. "Bitsy's already outside."

Great. That's all I need, Bitsy accusing me of making Mother cook. No matter what I do, she always finds ammunition for another attack. I step toward the window. Her white Volvo SUV is in the drive, the liftgate open to reveal Trip's soccer balls and Mary Evelyn's dressage gear.

"Why don't you go say hello?" Mother points toward the hammock where my sister's bare feet flash rhythmically between two magnolias. The white blooms are as big as the soccer balls in Bitsy's car. *"Everything was bigger then,"* Mother used to say, claiming magnolias were around when dinosaurs roamed the earth.

From my window I roll the floral curtain between my hands and try to get a better view of my sister.

"I always hoped you'd outgrow the whole sibling-rivalry thing.

Whatever it is that keeps you at each other's throats, I wish you'd both just let it go."

"In all honesty, Mother, an apology would do wonders, but Bitsy has never apologized for anything in her entire life."

She pauses, weighing her words. "People don't always say they're sorry, Lovey. You have to find a way to move on without it."

Mother begins to make my bed, and I hurry to help. "Kind of hard to let something go when it's still happening."

She draws her lips into a tight frown, as if I'm the greatest disappointment of her life. "You think you're the only one who has ever been hurt?" She snaps the pillow to fluff it in its case, clearly convinced her own pain far exceeds my own.

"That's not what I'm saying." I place three pillow shams. She resets them. "Of course I'm not the only one who has ever been hurt. But it's a little different when you're betrayed by someone you love, and even worse when she does it on purpose. You don't know how that feels."

"Well, maybe not. But I do know how it feels to lose my brother."

I don't know what to say. I never knew my uncle Levi. He died before I was born. But Mother always took us to the memorial service during Advent season, and she still adds a plant to her garden each year on his birthday.

She looks at me now from across the bed, her eyes steady and sad. "I'm telling you, Lovey, if something happened to Bitsy today, you'd never forgive yourself. This stuff would seem trivial. You both seem to think you have all the time in the world to figure this out. But time won't wait on you. You have this moment, this day. If that."

I gather all my courage and head out near the magnolias where Bitsy is stretched in the hammock. Her eyes are closed. "Morning."

She doesn't respond. Instead, she keeps right on pretending to be asleep, even though she's giving herself away by tapping her foot: *one, two,* and *three*; *one, two,* and *three.* It's the tempo we'd fall asleep to every night, sharing a bed because neither of us cared to sleep alone.

I refuse to beg, so I leave her alone and head straight for Mother's gardens. When I pass the shed, memories flood through, and I'm jolted back to the Sedona medicine wheel with Marian.

May 14, 2016

"There's a reason the wheel is still used today. The ancestors have a lot to teach us." Marian encourages me to examine the cycles I have already completed and the lessons that haven't yet been learned. "What's your earliest wound, Eva?"

"Wound?"

"Yes, the first time you can remember being deeply hurt."

"You mean, like stitches?" I think of a bike accident, a roller-skating injury. A fall from the diving board.

"More of an emotional wound. Something that hurt your heart."

She probably expects me to reach back to age three, four. But instead I am taken to the garden shed, with Bitsy blaming me for the fire. "That's an easy one. It's a wall that's held tight for decades."

"Maybe it's time to tear it down," Marian hints, suggesting I go back to that moment, become that eleven-year-old Eva again.

For the first time in years, I shed my armor. It's not an easy leap, so Marian continues to guide me as I tell her about Fisher looking up from the ground, roaring a fearful cry for help. Chief rushing in to smother the flames, rolling Finn against the grass until the shock wore off and the scared little eight-year-old started to scream. And later, when Mother called us together, demanding truth. That's when Bitsy made the choice that set us both on a tumultuous trajectory. She didn't stand up for me. She didn't take my side. She chose, instead, to hurt me, and she smiled as she did it.

"How do you feel when your mother believes Bitsy?"

"Hurt," I admit, barely a whisper. "She had no reason to doubt me." I say louder, "None."

"And how do you feel about Bitsy when she betrays you?"

"What kind of person likes to hurt other people? Especially someone who loves them?"

"Does anyone defend you? Comfort you?"

I shake my head.

"Does anyone believe you?"

I whisper, "No."

"What do you want to say to that little girl? The one who spilled the gasoline but who didn't purposely start the fire?"

I can barely talk, but I speak to the child within me, the naive, trusting little girl who believed my loved ones would never harm me. The hopeful, innocent Lovey, who looked up at her parents with full belief that they would stand with her in the world, protect her from the lies and the hate and the hurt. But they did no such thing. Bitsy attacked again and again and again throughout my childhood, and no one ever held her accountable for a thing. No one ever took my side. I speak to that little girl locked deep, and I tell her now, "Don't worry, Lovey. I see you. I believe you."

Mother leans over the squash plants, turning on the drip line to give them a morning drink. Beside her, I pluck the yellow knobs while they are still small and tender for the pan. Adding them to the basket of carrots and beets I've already harvested, I praise Mother's green thumb.

"Started these in the greenhouse." She runs her hands across the prickly leaves of the squash plant. "The black plastic warms the soil. Gave the transplants a boost when the temperatures dipped. Isn't it nice to see them coming in already? Cucumbers and zucchini too." She points accordingly. "My earliest start yet."

I lean over to admire the big yellow squash blooms, a lure that nearly got me in trouble as a child when I brought them to Mother as a bouquet. She never shamed me for it. Instead, she raved about how beautiful they were and helped me add greenery to anchor the centerpiece. How long has it been since I felt this peace? Sun on my face, wind against my skin, dirt on my hands, Mother's soft voice finding its way to me between the garden rows. If only we could stop time. I'd stay right here in this moment forever.

Under the canopy, Bitsy still pretends she's asleep. We're nearly half a century old and yet still children. "Chief called from the diner. Running a little behind schedule."

"He really enjoys that Coffee Club, doesn't he?"

"Ragtag group of early risers." Mother smiles. "His kind of people."

My father's tribe gathers at a family-owned diner where they've been served no-frills bacon and eggs since the fifties. It's the kind of place where everyone knows the names not only of their fellow patrons but of the cooks and the waitstaff too. *"Good enough is good enough."* That's what Chief says about it. I've always thought that would make a marketable slogan for the diner, but they have no need to advertise. They've got a steady troop of loyal customers who keep coming back for more.

"He needs to pay a friend a visit at the hospital before we head out."

I watch Mother for any signs of concern. "Should I be worried? Seems to be limping more on that bad knee."

"He's good, Lovey." She wears her polished grin, as if she's trying too hard to convince me. "You should see our friends. I keep saying the Garden Club should set up a proper reception right there in the hospital lobby. Seems to be where we socialize these days."

I offer a sympathetic smile, so she softens her tone and speaks more sincerely as she kneels over the row of young cucumbers. "I won't go out that way."

"I don't want to think about any of that."

"Hear me, Lovey." She sits straighter now, her knees against the earth, her gloved hands pressed flat across her thighs. "I want to lie down in that hammock and smell the flowers until I take my last breath. And then y'all go find a pretty place right here on the farm. Scatter me in the pasture of wildflowers. Let the clover cover me and the honeysuckle swallow me whole. That's what I want. You understand?"

"Seriously, stop, Mother. You aren't anywhere near that point. You're still young!"

She holds a stoic gaze. "Well, we can't pretend I'll live forever, can we?"

"Sure we can." I smile, but she doesn't. Instead, she looks at me as if it's the last time she'll ever see me, and it makes my bones buzz. "Is there something you aren't telling me?"

She stays quiet and still, then looks off into the fields where the morning glows gold. "Betsy Hughes passed last night. Got the call this morning."

"Oh my goodness, that's terrible. She's only, what, late seventies?"

"Seventy-six. Two years younger than me." She shakes her head. "It's gotten so I dread to answer the phone."

It's hard to think of my parents aging. Someday holding Mother's hand as she takes her last breath, or waking to the call that my father is no longer with us. My eyes water at the thought, and I push it away. Far away. I can't imagine how hard it is for them to watch their friends fade, one by one.

"Buzz Roberts had a heart attack. Your father's age, you know? He's over in the rehab unit now, flirting with those pretty therapists and driving Marge crazy."

"Ugh. He's always been such a scoundrel."

"He has." She laughs. "It's not just us old folks, though. You remember Rebecca Tipton? Graduated with Bitsy?" I nod and pull more weeds. "Cancer's back."

"Again?" I look at Bitsy, trying to imagine her tolerating chemo, hair loss.

"Spread so fast with this relapse. She's spent most of the last few years being sick from the treatments. I'm not sure it's worth it."

I shake my head and move to a bed of carrots. "Hard call."

"The family has her with hospice now. Only a matter of time." Then Mother looks toward the clouds and sighs. "But isn't everything."

NINE

"I promised to make an altarpiece for Sunday services," Mother says. "Don't let me forget?"

"I'll help," I say, eager to work the flowers with her again, a hobby we spent hours sharing throughout my childhood. As the hummingbirds sip nectar, Mother's mention of church leads me to think of Marian and her magnetic energy out in Sedona. They may come from opposite ends of the spiritual spectrum, but both of them press me to leave the past behind. To forgive Reed and Bitsy. To heal and move forward. *Why can't I let things go?*

I keep a gentle rhythm, swaying my chair against the moss-kissed porch. Part of me feels at ease here at home, as if everything can pick right back up where I left off. The other half still feels like the outsider, always looking in on a family living life without me.

The creaks of the planks take me back to simpler times, when my sister was speaking to me. When Fisher and I would spend long summer days exploring these woods as if we were Tarzan and Jane, John Smith and Pocahontas. The roles were clear, and I was never alone.

"Life used to be so easy," I say to Mother, who rocks steadily beside me. Dolly P. rests on her lap, spoiled and loving it. Above us, the Lady Banks wrap the arbor while carpenter bees inspect the last of the fading blooms. Their nearly scentless display reminds me of the tabletop rose from the Reed Incident. I do my best to avoid the trigger, focusing instead on the incessant buzzing of the bees, their flight paths blurring the memory.

Under the magnolias, Bitsy still hasn't left the hammock. "I don't know which is worse," I confess. "Her verbal assaults or this threatening silence."

Mother sighs. "Do either of you even know what you're angry about anymore?"

I don't bring up the Reed Incident or Bitsy's criticisms. Nor do I mention the time she stole my boyfriend, turned my friends against me, or reported me to the teacher for cheating. Love keeps no record of wrongs. *If only it were that easy!*

"I don't know, Mother. It's almost as if this is the norm now. Like we just kept pulling ourselves through the muck, and then one day, we woke up and realized we had lost hold of the rope. Maybe there's no turning back."

"Nonsense. Sisters need each other."

"She doesn't need me, Mother. Look at her. She's never needed me."

"That's where you're wrong, Lovey. She's always needed you. Even if she didn't act like it, you can't just run off to the other side of the country and leave people behind."

I exhale, hoping not to sound too defensive. "I've called her every week, Mother. For years. She rarely answers. Won't return my calls. Won't even let me see the kids. I'm not the one causing this tension. Never have been."

"She pushes people away is all. That's her nature."

"Anyone who won't do as she says." I turn my attention toward the hammock. "Besides, did it ever occur to you that maybe I was the one who needed her?"

I leave it at that, unable to bring up Reed and his traumatic betrayal. I don't mention the number of times I realized his lies went much deeper than I had even begun to imagine. The nights I cried, wishing I had a sister, someone to stand up for me. Someone to help me reclaim my worth. But Bitsy abandoned me when I needed her most, leaving me to wonder if perhaps my sister is not so different from Reed. Both of them, liars.

Thankfully, Dolly P. saves us with a bark as Chief's old Ford comes rumbling up the lane. It's a sound that settles every fear. A sound so comforting, so healing, even Bitsy stands from the hammock and makes her way to the porch.

She wears a preppy floral sundress fitted to her petite figure and anchored by a dainty pair of strappy heels, as if she's just stepped off the pages of a magazine. Stopping by her Volvo, she grabs a straw handbag to coordinate the Southern belle ensemble. Even her soft blonde curls fall perfectly atop her shoulders, with no sign of gray beneath the dye.

"You look beautiful." I offer praise, always a good place to start with Bitsy, who glares at my loose linen tunic as if I've been sleeping under a bridge all week.

She holds her designer bag in the air. "Draper James. I'm addicted." She doesn't mention my weight loss, but she does give me a long once-over. Fat. At least that's one F-word I can scratch off my list.

Chief parks his truck beneath the shagbark hickory before heading for the roomier SUV. "Sure is good to see all three of you in one place this morning."

I give my father a hug and he matches it. Then Mother and I make a final sweep of the house before piling into the oversize vehicle. When I climb into the back beside Bitsy, she stares out the window, trying to avoid the fact that I actually exist. It'd be funny if it weren't so obnoxious. Oblivious to Bitsy's act, Chief announces his hearty, "All systems go," and we hit the road.

As we reach the end of our narrow lane, a pickup truck is pulling in. Without room for both vehicles to pass, the driver is forced to stop and reverse back out to the county road, waiting for us to exit. Chief lowers his window and steers near the truck. Sure enough, Fisher smiles from behind the wheel, *Oaklen Landscape and Design* inked across the door. My skin buzzes, a charge I haven't felt in years.

"We're heading out," Chief explains. "Need anything?"

"No, sir." Fisher treats my father with utmost respect. Beside him, two younger employees fill the bench seat, dressed for a day in the heat. Mother has no idea they're here to work on her memory garden. She thinks they've come to handle an issue with the fence, redirect some water runoff before the big party, but when she asks him about the job, Fisher simply nods and asks, "Did Lovey make it in yet?"

Thank goodness he can't see through the tinted glass because my cheeks feel so warm, I'm probably pink as a stargazer lily. When Chief lowers my window from his front control panel, I have no choice but to offer a greeting. My voice comes out like one of Dolly P.'s chew toys, squeaky and strained.

"Good flight?" Fisher leans his elbow over the window, his tanned arm stretching from a faded blue T-shirt, his bicep bulging beneath the slack cotton sleeve.

"It was." I nod, and five spectators watch for sport. "Thanks for helping my folks."

"Sure thing." That smile again! Matthew McConaughey's got nothing on this man. "It's good to see you, Lovey. You haven't aged a day."

Bitsy snorts, but I tilt my chin with a bashful note of gratitude.

"Let's catch up while you're here?" He looks at Chief, then back at me, as if he's asking my father's permission.

"Sure." I've turned pink again, and this time he sees. He may not be the same boy I loved all those years ago, but at his core, I get the sense he hasn't changed all that much. Kind, respectful, forgiving. How could I have steered so far off course?

Chief slowly accelerates and wishes the crew a good day. As my window lifts, I can't take my eyes off Fisher's smile. "I'm kind of surprised he still lives in Oxford. Figured since his folks lost their farm, he might hightail it."

"Nobody in their right mind ever leaves this town," Bitsy says. "You know that."

"Well, he did go on to State after baseball." Chief reminds us that Fisher studied landscape architecture in Starkville once he got his business degree from Ole Miss.

"Starkville. Doesn't count." She's probably rolling her eyes.

"I left too. Remember? For the pros."

"Sure. But even if people do leave for a while, they always come back." This one's from Mother, who gives me a look as if I've broken all the rules.

I let it slide because Fisher has left a peace in me that even Bitsy and Mother can't combat. With his genuine soul, he was like a big brother when we were kids. Until he became more than a brother, kissing me behind the Ole Miss stadium my sophomore year in high school—a night I'll never forget.

"Hasn't changed a bit," Mother says. "Still cute as ever." Then she beams at me. "He's still single too, you know? Never did settle."

"He's not exactly single, Mother," Bitsy chimes in. "He's dating Blaire Dayton. Nearly a year now. Talk of marriage all around town." Then she looks right at me and turns the sword. "You blew your chance with that one. Trust me."

What Bitsy doesn't understand is that I stopped trusting her long ago. I don't give her the thrill of a reaction, even though the thought of Fisher with a girl like Blaire makes my stomach churn. I can't imagine a worse match. I haven't seen Blaire in years, but all I can think about is her standing near our porch as kids, lifting her nose in the air and asking us all why we're so dirty. She was the alpha of Bitsy's mean-girl tribe, and I can't imagine why in the world Fisher would show her any interest.

"You ask me, he probably could have continued playing baseball," Chief says. "Minors at least. Likely more."

"But Finn wouldn't leave Mississippi, so they went to Starkville together instead." And there it is. With one fell swoop, Mother has shot straight to the heart of this tender topic. She might as well put it to words because we're all thinking about Finn and the fire.

"How is he?" I ask, a ball of steel in my throat.

"Finn? He's good, Lovey." Chief tries to settle any worries. "Studied landscaping with Fisher. They run that company together now. They've made it work."

"He's got three kids," Mother adds. I don't let on to the fact that I already know this. That I've always kept tabs on Fisher and Finn, allowing the what-ifs to rock me to sleep sometimes. "His son's in class with Mary Evelyn. Isn't that right, Bitsy?"

Bitsy continues to stare out the window, offering nothing more than a stark, "Yep." Six years older than Finn, she was late to the game of parenthood, putting Whitman through two years of medical school only to watch him drop out. Then waiting for him to earn his MBA before finally starting fertility treatments. It's yet another parallel she shares with Mother, who waited for Chief's NFL days to end before launching our family—a plan few understood at the time, but one I have always admired.

"What's this song?" Bitsy changes the subject. "Can't for the life of me get it out of my head." She hums, sprinkling the melody with a few scattered lyrics, "kicking around . . . hometown."

"Pink Floyd." I am stunned. Bitsy never would have listened to that kind of music when we were kids. Floyd. Grateful Dead. That was my crowd. And Fisher's. "Basically my personal anthem all through high school." I used to play it on repeat while she stuck to Casey Kasem and his American Top 40.

"Trip's too." Bitsy sighs. "Plays it nonstop."

"Guess he takes after his aunt Lovey." Chief catches my eyes from the rearview. My temperature must jump two degrees at the thought of my nephew having something in common with me.

"I'd love to see him," I say with as much restraint as I can manage. I learned long ago, the more I push, the more Bitsy pushes back. "Mary Evelyn too, of course."

"They'll be out of school soon for summer," Mother says. "Plenty of time for you to catch up."

"Not really." Bitsy crushes my hopes. "They'll both be leaving for camp after finals next week."

"Shipping them off again?" Chief's disappointment is clear. I observe carefully, surprised to see my father challenge Bitsy on any level, especially when it comes to her children.

"It's good for them," she argues. "Makes them more independent and, besides, they love it. Soccer camp has given Trip a real advantage with the scouts, and Mary Evelyn is getting serious about dressage. It's time to kick it up a notch. Especially since we've paid about as much for that new horse as we did for our house."

"Well, I just don't get it. Seems to me they can do all those things right here in Oxford." Chief holds the line.

I stay quiet, but Mother intervenes. "We *would* love to have more time with them, Bitsy. And they haven't seen Lovey in years."

My sister exhales. Then says, firmly, "They're going to camp."

With that, the exchange is silenced, so I search my phone until I find the Pink Floyd playlist. Chief helps me connect to the sound system, and I sing along to the band's classic hit about the rapid passage of time. Before I know it, Bitsy joins in. Together, we croon about being stuck in a small town, getting another day closer to death. This is all it takes to snap me back again, when the four of us would pile into the living room for impromptu Saturday-morning dance parties or late-night games of *Name That Tune*. I can't help smiling, and surprisingly, my sister is too, as if the music is chipping away the wall between us, drawing us all together the way a familiar melody tends to do.

Mother grins contagiously, nodding to the rhythm, and Chief seems to be sitting a few inches taller as we continue from song to song all the way to Batesville. We scroll through our favorite childhood tunes, straining to hit Frankie Valli's high notes for Mother and crooning along with Sinatra for Chief before taking a hard 180 for a Willie Nelson classic that resonates with all of us. Slowly, tensions subside, and mile by mile we begin to behave like a united family again.

When Chief turns south on the interstate, I pry for hints. "Jackson?"

"You'll see." He enjoys the glory of the guess and won't budge.

Now that my sister has lowered her defenses, normal conversation might be an option. I start with my heart. "Catch me up on the kids. How are they?"

Bitsy pulls her phone from her bag and begins to fill in the missing years. Birthday parties, summer camps, first-day-of-school snapshots.

"I should be part of their lives," I half whisper, struggling with the depth of this divide.

"You should," she says, as if it's that simple. As if it's all my fault.

"Did they get the letters I've sent? The presents?"

She nods.

"I've tried, Bitsy. I've really tried."

My sister says nothing. Instead, she stares at the photos and pretends she's done no wrong, as if the entire situation is out of her hands and I'm the only one who can fix it. The old, painful wounds begin to throb within me. *Why doesn't Mother say anything? Why won't Chief defend me?* Once again, no one stands with me. I've been screaming my truth since childhood, but no one hears.

TEN

"You were right, Lovey. Jackson." Mother stares at a row of homes lining the shade-draped street. Much like the historic houses that flank Oxford's square, each dwelling is anchored by hefty porch columns that have surely seen their fair share of social gatherings in a not-so-far-away past. When we turn a corner, Mother points to an abandoned storefront. The original signage can still be seen, faded and hand-scripted across worn brick. "Mr. Fieldman used to own that place. The nicest man. He'd let us choose a mint if we could answer a riddle." After a sigh she adds, "It's true what they say. Gone in a blink."

As Chief steers us through my mother's childhood, I'm sad to see that these once-posh neighborhoods have now become some of the most underserved parts of the city. Bitsy's voice crinkles with concern. "Where on earth are you taking us?"

"The long way around." Chief doesn't seem bothered by the poverty. My sister, on the other hand, wears her thinnest smile while staring at a slew of upturned garbage cans littering the lane from the morning's pickup.

I look beyond, to the treasures that remain. "Brings back memories of Grandpa and Grandma."

Chief smiles and turns down the familiar boulevard where my grandmother always welcomed us with warm cookies and even warmer hugs. Their large antebellum porch was once an active social hub of Jackson, hosting high-society garden parties and Easter egg hunts. Now the yard is overgrown, the house in disrepair.

"Oh, Jim," Mother says with tension in her throat. "My parents put so much into this home."

I focus on the positive. "Needs a little TLC is all."

Bitsy looks at me as if I've lost my mind. With some missing shingles and peeling paint, there's no denying the house is in poor shape, but it's certainly not the worst on the street. I find the neglected yard enchanting, a place where nature still gets to decide what grows and what doesn't.

"Look, Mother. The French hydrangeas." If there's anything to lift Mother's spirits, it's flowers, and they do bring a smile. I lower the window and snap a photo, the bountiful blue blooms just beginning their display. "I used to hide in those bushes."

"You sure did." Mother perks up even more. "If I called you to help with the dishes, you were out the door lickety-split." She is laughing now, and the sound of it soothes me. "I had done the same thing, of course, when I was a girl. Loved those flowers more than any other. Mama would send me out with a box and some snippers. It was my job to gather cuttings for her luncheons, and I was proud to help."

"I'm glad you remember that." Chief pulls into the driveway. "Welcome to the first part of your surprise."

I eye Bitsy, hoping she won't ruin this.

Chief and Mother lead the way across a path of mossy stones and past-bloom clovers before tackling the overgrown porch steps. A chaotic mass of honeysuckle wraps the column, welcoming us with her intense fragrance.

"Your grandpa used to say these flowers smelled like danger." Chief moves a vine to the side so we can pass more easily. "He didn't care for all the stinging insects they drew to the porch."

"True, but none of us ever got stung, even when we'd pick the blooms to make a batch of homemade jelly." Mother leans in to smell the bright-orange trumpet flowers, and from the smile on her face, it's clear she's been transported.

Without waiting for a knock, an elderly woman steps out to greet us. Her wrinkled hands and slow steps suggest she's likely in her nineties, but she seems more sturdy than frail, even with a hunch in her spine. While her body can't compare to Marian's, I get the sense her spirit would hold up in equal measure. Her hair matches the mottled planks of the porch, and I liken her to the overgrown yard—wild and strong and full of purpose.

"You must be the Sutherlands." Our host steadies herself with a wooden cane that bears colorful messages for *Grammy*. With a freshly pressed church dress and orthopedic shoes, she welcomes each of us with a firm handshake. "Right nice to meet y'all. Call me Vaida."

Bitsy fakes a smile, drawing her arms closer to her waist. In contrast, my parents greet Vaida warmly, accepting her kind offer to "come on inside for a pour of strong coffee." She warns we may "catch a chill" because she's "kicked the AC down to make it work a little overtime on account of the heat."

As soon as we cross the weathered threshold, the disheveled exterior is replaced with an impeccably clean space inside. With each step memories begin to flood, and Mother thanks Chief at least four times before we pass the expansive foyer, her eyes drawn wide with wonder.

Vaida encourages us to make ourselves at home, and with her

guidance, we explore her tidy dwelling as a group, moving at a slow pace in order to process the past and to allow for our host's "kinked hip." She speaks with a clear mind, not a hint of dementia. "I'll be one hundred come October, Lord willing."

She shares her family's plans for a big celebration, and Mother and I both sing her praises.

"I keep telling the Big Man upstairs I won't be able to manage much longer, but he keeps on giving me another day, another day. Can't for the life of me figure out what else he needs me to do down here." Dark-brown age spots dance across her cheeks as she laughs. I watch, impressed, hoping I, too, live to be one hundred and that I'll still find humor in things when I do. Reminds me of something Mother used to say: *"Happy is a choice."*

The high ceilings and sparsely furnished rooms allow for easy movement through the two-story abode. As Vaida wrestles the stairs, I keep close behind in case I need to catch her fall, but she stays steady all the way to the top. I imagine my mother as a toddler, my grandmother guarding her every step. Will Mother see a hundred years like Vaida? Will I someday be shadowing, worried she may fall and break a hip?

In each room more memories rise. Grandpa's snoring during a Sunday-afternoon nap, or the lilt of Grandma's voice as she would read us a story. The savory draw of her homemade soup on the stove, or the chill of banana milk shakes and watermelon Popsicles.

"We used to race down this hall," I tell Vaida, running my fingers across the smooth wooden wall. "Seemed a mile long back then. I could do four cartwheels back-to-back."

Bitsy nods but stays quiet.

"Ah, yes. Mine do the same." Pointing to the countless photos on display, Vaida assigns names and stories to each of her loved ones. "Little Macey, she's the baby. Look at all those rolls, will you now?" She squeezes her hand as if she's pinching the infant's thick thighs, laughing as she describes her great-great-grandchild. The love is pure, and it makes me wonder why she lives here alone if she has such a large extended family.

"You keep this big place up all by yourself, Mrs. Vaida?"

"All by my lonesome." This certainly explains why the paint is chipping and why a flurry of weeds have claimed the yard. "Everybody's so busy all the time." She shakes her head. "Back in the day, we'd stick together. We'd make time, you know? Now they're all spread out, this way and that, and ain't nobody showin' up for Sunday supper."

Mother and Chief signal sympathy, and my heart sinks. In contrast, Bitsy grins proudly, insinuating she's the good daughter, the one who makes time for our parents. She hasn't uttered a peep since we pulled into the drive. In fact, she seems so far out of her comfort zone here, she doesn't seem to know who she is. It's a sad truth that makes me feel a little sorry for my sister.

We exchange a few more family stories and head toward the kitchen, where Mother lights up. "Y'all see this?" She moves to the center of the room. "This is where your father proposed to me." She steps onto a rag rug that lines the floor. "Right here."

Chief grins like a schoolboy, shuffling toward her with a nervous step. The original wood planks have since been coated with linoleum, a soft spread beneath his feet. "Feels like yesterday," he says. Then he tries to take a knee on the rug, garnering surprised reactions from all of us. As he lowers, his joints strain, so I reach out my hand to steady him, letting his warm palm press tight against my own.

Once stable, my father cranks up the flattery, replacing my

hand with Mother's as he gazes into her eyes. "You've made me a very happy man, Laurel. Very happy."

My mother blushes, something I've rarely seen from our confident matriarch.

"I couldn't afford much of a ring back in the day, so I'm hoping this might make up for it." Chief reaches into his pocket and pulls a small velvet box to hand. When he opens it to reveal a new ring, Mother gasps. I do too. It's a simple setting, with four round stones lined across the platinum band. Each must weigh at least a carat. "A diamond for each of us," Chief explains. "A reminder that we're better together. Family First."

My stomach tilts with emotion, and even Bitsy rushes to get a closer view of the stones. When she offers a sincere smile, I half think she may be thawing.

"You sure found yourself a right fine man, Mrs. Sutherland. Right fine, indeed."

Mother beams in agreement, and Chief takes it up a notch by popping the question. "Laurel Sutherland, the best thing I ever did was ask you to marry me. And I'd do it all over again. Would you?"

"You know I would." Mother leans low for a kiss right here in the kitchen.

This causes Mrs. Vaida to cheer, and Bitsy and I are a mess. As Chief slides the ring onto Mother's finger, her tears shift to laughter. "I never would have guessed you'd have something like this up your sleeve."

"Aw, shucks." Chief shakes it off. "I've got a lot more comin' your way. Just wait and see." Then Bitsy helps me pull Chief to his feet, and he asks Vaida if he can show Mother what he *really* called about.

"Surely," she says. "Just wish I had a cake ready to celebrate the special occasion."

Of course, we tell her there's no need for anything more than this, and we all make our way back to the porch where I greet a soft gray kitten with a silly, "Hey, meow."

Bitsy rolls her eyes, so I pick up the fluffy feline. I move her paws like a puppet, as if the cat is speaking to my sister in a comical tone. "Meow you doin', Bitsy?"

Mother plays along, in spite of Bitsy's reluctance. "We're purr-fect. Thank mew for asking."

I crack. And Vaida does too. But the battered porch has caused a shift again, and Bitsy reverts back to her stone-cold smile, refusing to take part in such a lowly scene. I resist the urge to tell her she's "*gotta be kitten me.*"

In the meantime Chief has turned his attention to the boisterous row of hydrangeas bordering the porch. I step down the broad front steps to examine the plants from ground level, their summer leaves already back to life, their blooms barely peeking out in search of sun.

"The first time you brought me to meet your parents, your mother served coffee cake right here on the porch."

Mother pulls her hands over her heart and smiles.

"I was a nervous wreck that day, so I clipped a hydrangea for you, trying to impress."

"It worked." She shrugs toward Vaida, and I pet the kitten, grateful for my parents, for my family, for all of this.

"Not at the time, it didn't," Chief counters. "You told me it was bad luck. Remember? Said they'd been planted too near the front door and that you couldn't accept them, not from me."

"Oh my goodness. I did say that, didn't I?" Mother's memory is firing. "That's because people used to say it would make a daughter unmarriable to plant them near the house. I was certain I'd end up an old spinster, no matter how many times Mama insisted she had broken the spell." She touches the limber leaves. "I was worried you were marking me. That we'd be jinxed from the start."

"That's not what I was taught," Vaida interjects. "I always say, if you plant a hydrangea, you're sure to find a love that lasts. Loyalty. That's what they mean to me."

"See there? I knew what I was doing all along." Chief's lips stretch into a broad smile, his most attractive feature despite the dental bridge. Mom offers him a peck on the cheek and he accepts, giving Vaida a wink of appreciation.

"Well, here's the real surprise. We're taking some clippings," Chief says. "Right here from your mother's hydrangeas."

Mother clasps her hands with glee, a much grander reaction than the one she expressed when he gave her the ring.

Chief is loving this. "Thought it might be nice to plant her flowers back at home. If we're lucky, maybe the girls will take care of them long after we're dead and gone."

"Don't talk like that," I say. And I mean it.

Mother's eyes mist again. "Jim, this is the most thoughtful gift anyone has ever given me. Honestly, how in the world did you come up with all this?"

"I'm just good like that." He pulls a small pair of pruning shears from his baggy pocket, then spins it around his finger like a cowboy's pistol.

"A ring? Now clippers? What else you got hidin' in those pockets, dear?"

Chief pulses his eyebrows suggestively, and Mother howls with laughter.

The kitten watches from the porch as we find the perfect stems to trim. Mother prompts us to aim for those without buds, measuring each about four to five inches in length before snapping them a couple of thumb-lengths below the lowest leaf node.

"Run out to the car and grab the pots, will you, Lovey?"

I do as my father asks, finding his secret stash in the back where he's filled a cardboard box with plastic planters. Each one has been stocked with good soil, ready for the transplants, and by the time I return, Mother is eager and waiting. She trims the base leaves, then snips half the leaf from the top of each stem. Her shiny new diamonds draw my eyes as she passes the cuttings my way. I plant each of the rootless stalks into moist soil, enjoying the feel of earth against my skin. Together, we fill ten planters, while Bitsy stands stiff-necked on the porch, keeping us beneath her on the ground below.

Vaida seems pleased, singing praises while we work. "You really have found yourself the last true gentleman, Mrs. Sutherland."

Mother places the final container in the box and turns to me. "Oh, I'm sure there's still one more out there. Lovey just hasn't found him yet."

ELEVEN

One block over, we survey the park where we used to play. Back then, the swings would have been filled with children, each of us avoiding the sizzling heat of the metal slide. Today, however, the swings hang broken from rusty chains, and no one plays.

While the monkey bars stand empty, three teens have congregated near an ancient magnolia, swapping cigarettes and stories beneath the fair-bottomed leaves. Most of the flowers have already burst open, stretching their wings after a spring spent bound by tight cocoons. Now the blossoms are as big as the basketball shifting round and round among the young men. *"What goes around comes around."* That's what Brynn says. But truth be told, I've never wanted revenge for all Reed did to me. And I have no desire to hurt Bitsy. I only want the people I love to stop hurting me.

Just around the corner, Chief offers snow cones. Near the stand, a patch of wild orange calendula and a few heady sprays of yarrow grow in an unruly sprawl. Their bright colors seal the deal, and I surrender. "Why not?"

Chief pulls the car to a stop, remembering my favorite flavor, Wild Cherry Larry. Surprisingly, Bitsy claims her own Gilbert Grape, Mother opts for Spear-a-Mindy, and Chief goes for Lucky

Duck Rainbow—a colorful concoction of blueberry, banana, and strawberry for the young at heart.

Once served, we settle on the wobbly benches, fighting bees for our sugary treats. For the time being, Bitsy and I remain at peace while our parents spoil us with an endless shower of time and attention. The four of us are laughing, eating snow cones, sitting in the shade of an elm on a whole-year-long kind of day. Once again, all seems right with the world.

"It's been, gosh, twenty years since I've had one of these." My confession seems a shock to the rest of my family.

"I bring the kids all the time in Oxford," Bitsy says. "We go the first day they open each summer. Tradition." She shows me more pictures from her cell phone—the children holding their seasonal treats, their lips tinted to match their favorite flavors.

"Sure do miss them." I pull the phone for a closer look. I took such pride in being Aunt Lovey, and I wish more than anything that Bitsy would say they miss me too. Instead, an awkward silence follows, so I concentrate on numbing the pain of my brain freeze, tapping the roof of my mouth with my tongue—a trick I learned as a kid.

"It's good you're in town for Mary Evelyn's birthday party," Mother says.

My breath catches. "Party?"

"Oh, it's just a small thing for a few of her friends." Bitsy waves it off. "Little tea in the garden. Etiquette lessons. No big deal."

"I'd love to go." I take the risk, praying it works.

"Of course you'll go," Chief says.

No one counters, and Mother changes subjects before Bitsy reacts. "You know, Lovey, I never did understand why you split with Fisher. You were so good together."

I glance at my sister. "Bad timing, I suppose."

"I don't think he's ever gotten over you. Still swings by the house. Always says he's looking for work, but we both think otherwise."

"True," Chief says, without emotion.

"Why didn't y'all ever mention that to me?"

Bitsy takes her jab. "Nobody figured you'd care."

"Of course I care."

"You already made your choice, Lovey. No point in trying to change it."

I try to picture Fisher with a girl like Blaire. It doesn't fit. "What's she like now? Blaire?"

"Gorgeous, as always." Bitsy's energy peaks. "Teaches my Barre class. Zumba and Spin too, but I don't always make it to those."

I no longer enjoy the snow cone, imagining my weight creeping back to unwanted digits while Fisher walks the aisle with a perfectly fit Zumba instructor. I poke the ice with my spoon-tipped straw, the sound slicing away the image. "Are they engaged?"

Chief and Mother pay close attention, and I can almost feel them holding their collective breath.

"Any day now," Bitsy says. "Aren't you happy for him? After all these years, he's finally found someone. And not just anyone . . . Blaire!"

Thank goodness my phone rescues me with a ring. "It's work," I explain, relieved to answer the call from Phoenix.

I barely finish saying hello when Brynn interrupts. "Did you get my e-mails?" She sounds panicked.

"No, why? What's wrong?" I turn my back to gain a semblance of privacy.

"Jansana called a meeting. It starts in an hour. I can't run solo with this." Brynn's speaking fast, loud.

"It'll be fine. I promise," I respond with a slow pace, hoping to calm her. "They probably just have a few questions."

"But what if they're pulling out?"

"This late in the game? Not a chance."

"You don't know that. Anything can happen."

I step away from the table and talk her down from the ledge. "Now, listen, Brynn. You know this campaign as well as I do."

"No, Eva. I don't. I've always been your sidekick. First your intern. Then your assistant. Now your teammate. Even your best friend. But I've always followed your lead. And maybe I like it that way. I don't want to be responsible if this falls through."

"It won't fall through, Brynn. But if it makes you feel better, I'll join the meeting."

"Yes! Please, yes!" Her relief is palpable.

Chief and Mother eye me curiously, if not with concern.

"I'm on a road trip with my family right now, but I'll find a way to call in. No problem." She thanks me repeatedly. "But, Brynn, all you need to do is be yourself. You know this stuff. I've sent you all the data they could possibly want. You helped me create the concept start to finish. And you excel at making people feel comfortable. I have full confidence you could do this without me."

"I haven't told The Dragon." Brynn sounds a little less anxious now, but her pitch is still strained. "Think I need to clue her in? Send her an invite?"

"Why bother her with a bunch of what-ifs? She'll shred your confidence, and that's the last thing you need right now. It's better to steer clear until you have more to tell her. That's what I would do."

"So . . . you're sure. You'll handle the meeting?"

"Of course. And, Brynn? One more thing." She waits for it. "Power stance." Finally, laughter and a long exhale.

As we disconnect, I'm hit with a blast of questions from Mother and Chief. I give them only enough information to quiet them, hoping not to make them feel guilty about taking me away from work. Bitsy seems unimpressed, even when I describe the big campaign.

"You sound like Whitman," she says, slow and monotone. "Work, work, work."

I don't react. Instead, I reply by asking about her husband, Whitman Strayer II, a med-school dropout turned venture capitalist who now helps Oxford's elite decide what to do with all their money.

"He's fine." She adds nothing more.

"Still traveling a lot? Last I heard he was partnering with investors in Atlanta? Birmingham? Dallas? Looking for start-ups."

"Yep. As I said, he's fine." She gives me a glance that warns me to back off, so I turn my attention back to the landscape, eager to drink in every gift Mississippi offers.

Behind the picnic table, a batch of invasive kudzu has crept in from a steep ravine. With no natural balance to keep it in check, the Asian species now abuses its power, growing thick, leafy webs across everything in reach. Even the trees with the deepest roots have fallen victim to this vicious vine.

As Bitsy's words echo, I wonder what lesson the kudzu wants to teach me. Have I, too, done better in foreign soil, opting to grow far from the challenging conditions of home? Have I been able to thrive out there in Arizona, living without any real competition? Or am I nothing more than a wayward transplant, an aimless seed taking more than my fair share?

With our tongues tainted from the colorful dyes, Bitsy and I climb into the backseat like two young kids. Within minutes Chief pulls up to our next surprise destination. Mother becomes radiant as he parks in front of a pristine Tudor revival, the historical home of Pulitzer Prize–winning author Eudora Welty. The house rests across from Belhaven University, a picturesque Presbyterian enclave that anchors the community Welty and her parents once called home. This stretch of Jackson is undergoing regentrification, an effect that transports us to a simpler era, to a quiet street where children played freely beneath arching bowers of hardwoods, where all that stood between sunrise and sunset was a leisurely lunch and a book or two.

"Jim, you are something else!" Mother cheers. Bitsy and I clamber behind them, making our way to the well-kept museum. It's a next-door home purchased to display the author's accomplishments, an honorable collection the down-to-earth garden lover would likely find a tad pretentious.

As we enter I am immediately drawn to an arresting sketch of a younger Welty. The ink profile has been perched on a shelf in the foyer gift shop, allowing the writer to greet guests with her confident stare. It's as if she wants to make clear she is a bold and daring soul, a woman of her own means who will give her name away to no one.

While Mother, Chief, and Bitsy move ahead, I can't take my eyes off this portrait. I can hear Eudora's voice, steely and Southern, breaking the words with her infamous cadence, a flutter of hurried syllables parsed with a few that drag. *"Eva, listen. Liars only have as much power as you give them. Claim your own truth."*

When I give the front-desk employee a strange glance, she smiles in return while organizing a stack of bookmarks. "Questions?"

Indeed, I have many. *Do you hear voices? Has anyone ever received a message from Miss Welty?* But I don't dare admit these ridiculous notions. Instead, I regain my composure and discuss the price of the sketch, Welty's works, and the hardcover garden books that would make a nice addition to Mother's coffee table.

"That's what won her the Pulitzer." The young clerk pulls *The Optimist's Daughter* from the shelf. "Start with that one."

We exchange a few back-and-forths about Mississippi authors, listing a long line of Southern scribes whose works have stood the test of time. "Welty truly is my favorite," she insists. "I've always admired Eudora and her mother. They were very progressive, independent."

I confess I know little about Eudora's mother, so the kind employee tells me about Chestina's challenging childhood. Turns out, the elder Welty was just fifteen when hired as a West Virginia schoolteacher. To reach the classroom, she had to travel long distances on horseback each day to the crossing point of the Ohio River. Then back and forth she'd boat, commuting to the mountain schoolhouse.

While this may have been too much for another girl of her age, Chestina had already proven her grit. When her father had taken ill, she had accompanied him on an icy winter trek all the way to Baltimore, only to have him die of a ruptured appendix. She then had to manage alone, transporting his deceased body back home on the train. After such hardship, Chestina became a determined spirit, and despite the responsibilities of being the eldest child and the only female in the family, she made the bold decision to leave her family's rural home and build a life of her own.

I take another look at the daring sketch of the young Eudora. "No wonder she faced life with such a courageous heart."

"Yep. Her mother's daughter."

As another visitor enters the gift shop, I take my leave. Passing a display of Eudora's many honors, I think deeply about the woman whose claim to fame is not the wealth or accomplishment of some husband or child. In fact, the younger Welty left this world having never become a wife or a mother at all. And yet, here we are, surrounded by people who admire her for the mark she left on our hearts. It's her words we remember, and the truth she delivered in them.

Mother, Chief, and Bitsy have already followed a docent to the back, and I find them in a small, quiet room filled with gardening books. Mother shares some of her favorite Welty quotes, all from heart: "'Welcome!' I said—the most dangerous word in the world." And "Beware of a man with manners."

"Better a man with manners than a man without." Bitsy smiles. Leave it to my sister to try to put Eudora in her place.

"I don't know. I think she may have been on to something." I fumble my fingers along the spines.

The docent straightens a tilted hardcover, apologizing because the house is "all kinds of slanted." A retired public school librarian, she's a well-spoken guide with a teacher's heart. She and Mother dive deep in conversation about an exhibit panel on the wall. It's an image of Welty's many titles, arranged chronologically to show her extensive contribution to American literature.

"Eudora offered such an authentic voice," the docent continues. "Way ahead of her time. She graduated high school at sixteen and was the only girl to have an outdoor graduation tea, right there in the yard." She points to the Welty family residence next door.

"Like the birthday tea we have planned for Mary Evelyn." Mother smiles at Bitsy. Then she looks my way. "I can't wait to show you the charms we ordered."

My heart leaps, but I don't dare say a word. Can't risk giving Bitsy any reason to resist.

"Eudora's party was different from the formal events her classmates hosted, but like her mother, she loved the garden. They worked together, creating their own designs."

Mother drapes her arm across my shoulder, drawing me close.

"Eudora enjoyed planting the bulbs: spider lilies, jonquils, daylilies. And she was particularly fond of the Camellia Room."

"Again, just like Lovey." Mother beams my way.

I blush, clenching the book to my chest, happy she remembers. "I do like camellias. Bloom just when winter sets in."

The docent seems pleased. "If you have time, the film starts in five."

Chief follows her into the hallway where I'm certain he's working on his garden plans. Mother plays along, pretending not to notice his antics. With arms now crossed, Bitsy steps back toward the window.

"You know, Eudora didn't always live in Mississippi," Mother says to me. "She was a lot like you, Lovey. Graduated high school and couldn't wait to run off and see the world."

"Really? I always pictured her as a homebody."

"Nope. She only moved back to care for her parents. By that time, she'd already made plenty of connections, and she was able to keep writing from here." Mother points to the image of her extensive collection. "Thing is, though, she may never have achieved any of this if she hadn't had the guts to go find herself first."

TWELVE

After the documentary, we thank the docent and depart the welcome center, heading toward the official Welty home next door. It's nearing time for the conference call with Jansana, so I leave Bitsy, Mother, and Chief to enjoy the rest of the tour without me. Then I switch gears to the Phoenix tower where Apogee seems a whole world away.

In the shadow of Welty's towering pines, I search for a quiet spot to work. Across the street I find a bench on the Belhaven campus and call in early for the meeting. "Any updates?" I ask Brynn, reassuring her that I'll lead the conversation.

"All I know is they have a few questions, whatever that means."

"Let's assume the best," I say, trying to calm her nerves. A squirrel scrambles at my feet, clearly accustomed to student snacks. I have nothing to offer, but he keeps me entertained as he scurries between my bench and another, where a college girl shares cheese puffs with him. She's one of only a few summer stragglers in sight.

Within minutes The Trio joins in from Arizona. I don't pretend I'm in the Phoenix conference room. Instead, I get real, confessing my family road trip and giving them all an image to laugh about—a squirrel holding a cheese puff in his tiny pink hands, nibbling away as his cheeks inflate by the second. I hope it shows them I'm well-rounded, able to juggle a million balls while maintaining a calm-cool-collected sense of humor. Instead, they fail to laugh, and the silence is louder than the raucous crows cawing in the oak limbs above me.

"Well, I hope you're enjoying your vacation." The president speaks with a sharp tone, giving me no pardon. It's not like her to be so crude, and I fear Brynn may be right to worry. "While you're off playing with squirrels, we're working hard on this campaign. And there's been a bit of a ruffle in the timeline, Eva. We've got an unexpected chance to make headway in Prague, and we cannot miss this opportunity. We need to push the project up four months. At least."

"New deadline?" I ask, worried a four-month jump will put us in a real crunch.

"Mid-July."

I work through the production schedule in my head, trying not to panic. "All four videos by July 15?" No wonder she's stressed.

"At the very latest. Tell me it can be done."

I imagine Brynn pacing the conference room. There are so many people involved in shooting commercials, and coordinating the various teams gets tricky. We're bound to lose some actors, at the very least, and that doesn't include securing locations. But I don't dare say this. Instead, I talk through a smile. "I'm certain we can find a solution."

"Excellent. I knew you'd come through. We can't lose Prague, Eva. This is key, you understand?"

My throat tightens, but I somehow manage to channel a bit of confidence, forcing a smile as I say, "Absolutely."

When the conference ends, Brynn rattles off a list of concerns. I listen patiently and then waste not a second more. "Well, we've got some calls to make. Want to divide and conquer?"

She agrees, and I break down a task list for each of us, taking notes on my phone with Brynn on speaker.

"No need to panic quite yet," I tell her. "We have almost two months to get everything in place. We can do this."

"From start to finish, Eva? Those locations required permits. Travel. It's not doable." Her voice is tense, and she sounds quite like the squirrel who is now chirping at my feet, the ponytailed cheese-puff supplier long gone.

"We can do it, and we will." I try to convince the both of us, but my little fur-friend objects, shaking his fluffy tail now to match his nervous chitter. It's a warning, reminding me of all the reasons this new deadline won't possibly work.

After a few anxious calls to production, casting, and graphics, I dash back to meet my family. When I find them in the backyard garden of Eudora's home, Mother puts one arm around my waist, the other around Bitsy. "I'm so happy to have both my girls with me." Surrounded by phlox and lilies, snapdragons and cornflowers, Mother is absolutely glowing.

"I'm happy too." I try hard to push all thoughts of work to a far-back corner, at least for now. Mother's passion is contagious, boosting my energy as I bend to brush the bearded irises, their upright standards drooping to meet the falls and beard.

"You do realize . . . some of these stem from roots Eudora tended with her own hands." Mother leads us through the garden, tapping plants with a tenderness reserved for babies and the elderly, as if she's escorting them into or out of this world.

Bitsy seems almost as moved as I am, even admitting she'd like to come back with the kids. When I touch the camellia leaves, shiny and smooth, Mother smiles. "That's the Lady Clare. Named a character after this plant in *Delta Wedding*. See? She really did speak my language."

"Which is why I brought you here," Chief says. "Remember when you would read aloud to me? Imitate each character?"

Mother laughs, naming her favorite Welty story, "Why I Live at the P.O." With a dramatic Southern drawl and a double dose of sass, she emulates the narrator: "But here I am, and here I'll stay. I want the world to know I'm happy."

"Yes!" Chief's surprise is falling into place, and I give him a wink of approval. "You remember what she took with her when she moved to the post office?"

"Let me think." Mother enjoys this challenge. "A fan. Maybe a pillow? Gosh, I can't remember. The radio. She definitely took the radio."

"Something else." Chief bobs his head toward the garden, dropping a hint.

"Ferns!" Mother cheers. "She took the fern. And she tried to take the four-o'clocks too, but her mother wouldn't let her."

"Yep. She was plucky, like you, Laurel." The three of us laugh, knowing full well Mother is indeed what one might call *plucky*.

"Why'd she move to the post office?" I try to remember the story.

"Because she got tired of her sister lying all the time," Mother says. "So she packs up her things and makes herself a home right there in the P.O. Some people kept on believing her sister, but she didn't care anymore. She said, 'As I tell everybody, I draw my own conclusions.'"

"And that's why I love your mother," Chief says to Bitsy and me. "Because she draws her own conclusions."

"Boy, do I!"

We share another round of laughs before Bitsy leans to read the placard beside the roses. I watch her now and see slivers of the girl I adored as a child, the big sister who peered into my jar of fireflies and said, *"Good job, Lovey!"*

"You know what else Eudora used to say?" Mother looks at me, then Bitsy, stressing her point. "Life doesn't stand still."

It has been hours since breakfast and the snow cones have done little to hold us over, so when Chief insists we stop for lunch at one of Jackson's most posh eateries, no one objects. As we enter the restaurant, we are relieved to find the space cool from the air conditioner.

"Order me a glass of pinot," Bitsy says. Then she and Mother head for the powder room, each complaining about the humidity.

As we take our seats, Chief sneaks me a list of flowers he's secured from the Welty docent. "Text this to Fisher for me, will you? I wrote his number on there for you." He's clearly enjoying this game.

I try not to let on to the fact that I am indeed eager to text Fisher. Instead, I tuck the list into my purse. "Sure. After lunch."

During the meal I consume every last bite of my shrimp and grits, relishing the uniquely Southern combinations: tart lemon juice, savory scallions, crisp bacon, and a dash of paprika all mixed in with freshly grated Parmesan and creamy white cheddar. It's been tossed with sautéed wild mushrooms and minced garlic, cayenne pepper, and Gulf shrimp, all atop a bowl of steaming Mississippi Delta stone-cut grits. My belly sings a psalm of thanks with every flavor-punched drop, and that doesn't even count the homemade biscuits baked big as fists and the silver-dollar pickles fried deep with salt. Drown it all together with a swig of syrup-sweet tea, and the name of this country song would be "Welcome Home."

Bitsy seems to savor her pinot much more than her serving of gumbo, accepting not one but two more pours despite the lunch hour. Chief, on the other hand, devours the smoked pork tenderloin bedded atop smashed potatoes and thick, dark puddles of gravy. Mother, once again, barely touches her meal, a summer bowl from in-season farmer's market finds. "How's your salad?" I ask, worried she may not be enjoying her dinner. "You want my biscuit?"

"No, no, thank you. I'm still full from breakfast is all." She smiles and pats her stomach even though she only sipped coffee this morning, avoiding her food while I consumed an herbed frittata made from farm-fresh eggs plus a crisp slice of bacon. With her petite frame Mother has never been a hearty eater, but now she's withering away in front of us and no one else seems to notice.

"Are you sure you're feeling okay?" My forehead gathers in a pinch, something Botox prevents for both Mother and Bitsy.

"Of course, Lovey. Just too excited to eat, right?" She turns to Chief, who provides the confirmation she desires. Bitsy remains oblivious and returns the conversation to center around herself. The rest of us oblige, giving her the praise she craves.

Regarding her son's soccer coach: "Maybe he'll let Trip captain the next game."

Her daughter's recent dance lessons: "Of course Mary Evelyn deserves the lead!"

Her husband's latest investments: "He's always had a head for money. You've both done so well for yourselves."

And the conversation goes on like this all the way through dessert, when Mother takes only one scant bite of the crème brûlée, insisting Chief finish it off for her even though it's one of her favorite treats. No one mentions this odd behavior, so once again, I feel like the outsider, as if they all know something they aren't telling me. I want so badly to come right out and ask what's going on, but Mother would not appreciate being backed into a corner, that's for sure.

By the time we leave the high-class eatery, Chief nudges me again to send that text. I climb into the SUV and do as I'm told.

Hi Fisher. Lovey here.

About to send you the Welty flower list per Chief.

Please stay tuned.

I hit Send and add the lengthy list of flowers for Mother's garden.

Gardenia, mimosa, honeysuckle, philadelphus, vitex,
spirea, yaupon, camellia, four-o'clocks, ferns.

I'm giddy to see Fisher's reply: Thanks. What time will you be home?

Me: Heading back now.

Then him: Perfect. Can't wait to catch up.

He can't wait to catch up? I cover my smile with my hand, but Bitsy glares as if she's on to me.

"Who are you texting?" She says this more as a threat than a question. Then she leans over, reads my screen. "Is that Fisher?"

I have not come home to cower to Bitsy's bullying again. This time I draw a line. "Your brazen disrespect of my personal boundaries continues with age, I see."

"We're having such a good day, girls. Let's not do this." Mother shifts to discuss the heat and the need for rain. Safe terrain once again.

We do our best to keep the conversation neutral, but as I'm without a husband or kids of my own, no one seems to know what to talk to me about. They don't know enough about Arizona or advertising to make a conversation of that, and yoga is equally as foreign. So we spend the two-hour drive home talking about Bitsy and her kids.

With every detail I feel closer to my niece and nephew while trying not to resent the years away from them. In the end, I choose to focus on the good, grateful for this time we have together and hopeful Bitsy will let me see them soon.

THIRTEEN

"Going to check on Fisher's crew. Join me?" Chief doesn't say this to Bitsy or Mother. He speaks directly to me, and I accept the offer as a gift, following my father along the eastern boundary of our land. Together, we take the long way to the barn, exploring the riparian buffer where rows of red maples and sycamores crowd the river's edge, their limbs fighting for light. Beneath these arbors the waters have always run dark and brown, but now they are spotted with oily rings, iridescent where the sheen meets sun. What once was a sacred childhood sanctuary is now clogged with agricultural runoff from farms upstream. I picture the clean mountain springs back in Arizona, where rock-bed creeks run clear and cold. *What would Marian think of this?*

"Shame, isn't it?" Fisher joins us riverside where we spent long, lazy days watching our fishing lines loop the currents. "They won't stop pumping poison."

"Crop duster wiped out my bees again this year," Chief says.

"What?" I'm shocked. "We ate your honey with the pie."

Chief shakes his head and explains it came from the farmer's market. "Second year in a row I got nothin'. Crop dust across the street. Wipes out our bees."

I am indignant. "You should be able to protect your own property."

"Doesn't work like that," Chief says. "Can't keep the bees in. Can't keep the chemicals out."

Fisher, too, seems bothered, shuffling his feet and looking across the street toward his childhood home. "Don't worry. I'm gonna buy back my family land. We'll make this whole stretch organic back here, give the bees room to roam."

Chief releases an appreciative chuckle. "If only I can hold out that long."

"It won't be long," Fisher says. "Haven't told anyone yet, but . . . we're working out a deal right now. Hope to close by year's end. Granted, it'll take some time to clear out all the toxins, but we gotta start somewhere."

Chief and I both step back in surprise, and Fisher keeps his gaze toward the land his grandparents farmed, then his parents. It's a few thousand acres of rich bottomland, parceled off when his folks divorced.

"I've been trying to buy that place for years," my father says. "Never made it to market."

Everyone in town knows the story. The divorce got messy, very messy. The entire property ended up with greedy attorneys in lieu of payment. They've been leasing it to a farmer for decades, harvesting cotton, soybeans, corn, and sweet potatoes while they wait for the last of the pine stands to mature.

"The house still empty?" I ask.

"Ridiculous, isn't it?" Fisher removes his ball cap with a frustrated tug. "Their hunting buddies stay there sometimes. Otherwise, sits unused. That home survived the Civil War but barely made it through that crazy divorce."

My father is quiet for a minute. Then he puts his hand on Fisher's shoulder. "I'd like to see you get your land back, son. Maybe I can pitch in, help you seal the deal."

Fisher fumbles with his ball cap and nods with humble appreciation. "Thanks, Mr. Sutherland. I think I've got it covered." From the shift in his eyes, it clearly wasn't lost on him that Chief just called him son. Fisher's own father flew the coop long before the divorce became final, bailing on nearly every adult responsibility in his life, including Fisher and Finn. Some say it was the fire that sent him away for good, that he couldn't handle his son's burns or the painful recovery.

I don't know if that's true or not, but he's the kind of man Chief has always described as "*rich in harvest; poor in spirit,*" or one who "*can't find his way through the eye of a needle.*" It's no secret Fisher looks up to my father as a mentor, and Chief feels equally fond of him.

"So how about you show us this garden." Chief turns toward the hill where Fisher's truck and landscape trailer block any view of the secret that rests on the other side. Mother would only discover it if she hiked to the top and over, or if she came around back from the barn, neither of which she is likely to do before the party. Her regular flower gardens are down near the house, and the produce patches are scattered in sunny, raised beds between those blooms.

The three of us climb up the hill where the higher, dryer hickories merge with white ash and winged elms. Then down toward the back path where Fisher's crew is hard at work. The walk is nothing Mother can't handle. It offers a gentle trail that weaves its way around and up to the shallow summit, making the majestic spires of Arizona seem a world away.

"You can see here, the back side of the hill is a gradual slope,"

Fisher explains. "Opens up to the field where we have full sun. We'll use permaculture techniques to distribute water evenly across the landscape. Slow the flow with contours, letting it spread and sink as needed. This'll give you less erosion and more natural irrigation."

"Excellent." Chief is clearly impressed, and I am too. Behind the equipment trailer, Fisher's crew is digging beds and filling them with compost-rich soil, a fertile base for the many flowers they've already delivered.

"I followed your advice. Tried to represent the seasons of your life together." Fisher speaks sincerely, as if the romantic notion isn't lost on him. "We'll wind the beds up from the sunny pasture, through the shady portions. Mix trees, shrubs, and flowers to create textured layers."

He goes into an in-depth explanation of permaculture forest gardens, describing the levels top to bottom with labels such as canopy, subcanopy, woody shrubs, herbaceous plants, ground cover, and the like. His words are music to my veins, the dialect of my soul. He, too, lights up as he points out the vines that weave through it all, and when he shows us the root layer, his hands scoop fresh soil as if it were gold.

"We'll form a walking path all the way up from the barn. It'll end by winding around a labyrinth." He stops at a freshly leveled ring atop the hill. "Here."

"Labyrinth?" I'm surprised by this.

Fisher scratches his chin. "Something simple. I'm thinking a coil of stones with some pebbles mixed in, maybe some hardy grasses. Was hoping it could represent the cycles of life, like the garden itself. Too corny?"

"Absolutely not," Chief says. "Laurel will love this!"

"She will," I echo.

Fisher exhales. “So we’ll include mostly perennials, scattering some annuals in for a little extra color. Make sure something will be blooming year-round. What do you think?”

“Perfect!” Chief offers enthusiastic approval. “Lovey? Why don’t you run get some of those hydrangeas from the car. Your mother won’t notice a couple missing. We’ll leave the rest for her to plant down below.”

“You still like to garden?” Fisher asks.

“Of course.” I give him my best smile, nothing like the ones I’ve come to rely on back at Apogee.

He gives his chin a quick dip. “I’ll find you some tools.”

I hurry back to the house where Mother and Bitsy are poring over the menu for the anniversary party. In the background a television plays quietly, airing one of the home and garden commercials Apogee recently released. Mother looks my way, trying to bring me into the conversation. “What’s your opinion, Lovey? Will the charcuterie board and marinated vegetables be enough, or should we add fruit too?”

“Fruit,” Bitsy answers before I can say a word.

“What else will you have?” I move to examine the options.

“I’m thinking small plates served tableside,” Bitsy says smugly, offended I’m being included. “Duck sliders, shrimp ceviche, and crawfish tails with grit cakes. You know, tapas style.”

“Some of this is out of season, but I do have my favorites.” Mother is alight.

“Sounds incredible.”

Bitsy shoots another phony smile, which makes me think she’s the one who needs to spend a little time digging in the garden with Fisher. He's good medicine, and the dirt is too. She continues without asking for input. "Caprese salad with tomatoes and basil fresh from our farm."

"We'll serve our peaches," Mother explains, ecstatic that her favorite chef in town has agreed to whip these into delicate pastries. "Blueberries too, plus black bean cakes and smashed sweet potatoes. I'm drooling just thinking about it."

"Man, I feel sorry for the people who aren't invited," I tease.

"I'd invite the whole town if I could. The more the merrier, I always say."

"We can swing a bit more." I look toward Bitsy for backup. The two of us are footing the bill for the party, our anniversary gift to Mother and Chief. Thanks to Whitman's investments, Bitsy has very deep pockets and could easily pay for an expanded guest list, but she doesn't offer, doesn't even acknowledge the chance, so I don't press and Mother handles it with her usual tact, making a comment about how there really isn't room for more anyway. I do my best to change the subject. "What do you plan to give Chief? For a gift?"

"Nothing big. Besides, at our age, the only thing we really need is more time." Mother's voice becomes solemn now, and she looks down to talk to Dolly P. "Sure do wish I could give him that."

I offer her a quick sideways hug and explain that Chief needs my help in the barn. Then I slip upstairs to change. When I come down in shorts and a T-shirt, Bitsy stares. Clearly, my toned physique has drawn shock.

"You're looking so fit and trim, Lovey." Mother offers praise. "Yoga must be your calling."

"Oh, I don't know. But it's the only kind of exercise that's ever really hooked me."

"I wouldn't call it exercise." Bitsy stabs again. "You sit. You breathe. You stretch. How hard can it be?"

Mother points toward the back of the house where a sunroom full of gym equipment has perched mostly untouched for years. "Maybe I should give yoga a try. If it weren't for my yard work, I'd probably weigh a ton by now."

"Speaking of weight . . ." My glance finds Mother's collarbones as Bitsy continues to side-eye me, smiling only when Mother looks her way, always putting on a good act when someone else is watching. "You've lost a lot."

"Oh, you know. Old age. It happens."

Once again, she dodges the issue. When they turn their attention back to the menu, I make my escape, grabbing a few of the potted hydrangeas and heading for the memory garden. I pass Chief along the way, and he thanks me for keeping this surprise under wraps.

"Of course." I take pride in the fact that he trusts me. "And speaking of secrets, please don't tell Bitsy I'm working with Fisher."

He laughs and agrees it would be in everyone's best interest to stay mum.

FOURTEEN

At the top of the hill, Fisher is on his hands and knees eyeing the ground. "What d'ya think, Lovey? Look level to you?"

I step back and walk the ring that will form the labyrinth. After viewing it from every angle, I nod. "Wouldn't shift an inch."

"Now that's what I like to hear." He stands, dusting the knees of his faded jeans. They look as if they've seen a decade's worth of wear, a down-to-earth appearance that suggests he still harbors a humble heart. The kind of man who is all things opposite of Reed, and all things good for my wounded spirit. As he makes his own loop around the labyrinth, small clouds of dust jet beneath his booted steps, reminding me of a bedtime story Mother used to tell us when we were young. It was about a man known as a cloudmaker.

Bitsy and I would climb into bed with Mother snuggled between us, our heads tilted against her chest. Her breath always smelled sweet like warm apple cider, her shoulders soft from lavender lotion. She would prop against the pillow, holding the book between Bitsy and me so we could both see the pictures while she read aloud.

Spring 1977

"Cloudmaker had a special power." Mother reads with her quiet voice, which is her way of telling us it's time to settle down. "But the townspeople didn't much care for this strange man who walked around stirring up clouds all the time."

"They're mean to him." I point to the picture. Some boys are throwing eggs at the cloudmaker, laughing like it's funny.

"You're right, Lovey. They called him names and told him to bring his silly clouds somewhere else. So one day, he got tired of everybody being mean to him, and he got up and he walked away. Nobody even bothered to tell him good-bye."

"Show us the party." Bitsy turns the page before Mother gets the chance.

"The people were so happy the cloudmaker was gone, they threw a party to celebrate," Mother reads. "The sun was shining, the sky was blue, and the people cheered. But they didn't realize what they had done."

"Because the sky *stayed* blue!" I already know the ending.

"Right again, Lovey," Mother says. "Next day, no clouds at all. And the next and the next. Soon, the flowers started to die. Then the vegetables stopped growing. Then the fruit trees too. The people tried and tried to give the plants enough water, but no one could replace the rain."

"They need the cloudmaker," Bitsy says, and I say it too.

"They sure do." Mother leans close to Bitsy, then to me. "That's when the people finally realized they had made a very big mistake!"

"Big!" we shout.

She turns to the happy-ever-after part and reads with a quieter voice, so we won't get all wired up again. "They all set out to search for the cloudmaker, but they couldn't find him anywhere. He wasn't at the beach. He wasn't at the park. He wasn't in the woods."

"He's on the mountain." Bitsy says this.

Mother keeps reading anyway. "But then someone saw something they hadn't seen for a very, very long time."

"Clouds!" I say, and Bitsy points to the picture.

"Right again, girls. There, at the top of the highest mountain, were some clouds. And guess who was sitting up there under those clouds?"

"Cloudmaker." I yawn as I answer.

"Yep. He was sitting up there making tiny little clouds just for himself. So the people climbed and climbed, all the way to the top, and when they finally reached him, they said they were . . ."

"Sorry." Bitsy and I fill in the blank.

"They were sorry for being so mean, and they begged him to come back to the village so he could make it rain again."

Then Mother switches to talk deep like the cloudmaker man. "'Well, have you learned your lesson yet?'"

I turn the page to show the answer.

Mother smiles, like she always does when we get to this part. "The cloudmaker surely could have said no. He could have left the villagers to live without rain forever. He could have been mean to them, like they had been to him. But instead, he chose to be nice. He said, 'Now you understand. Every person is here for a reason. Even me.'

"'Especially you,' the people cheered, finally seeing the cloudmaker's worth."

My eyes start to droopy-close while Mother reads the last two pages. "When all the people got back to town, they threw another party. This time the cloudmaker was the guest of honor. Everyone brought him presents and ate cake, but the best part was that they all became friends. The cloudmaker was so happy, he danced. And when he danced, his boots made clouds. The clouds made rain, the rain made flowers, and the farmers grew food. No one was mean to the cloudmaker ever again."

"The end!" I say, opening my eyes big and giving Mother a hug. She squeezes me tight and kisses me before turning to do the same for my sister.

"Now say your prayers." Mother climbs out of bed. She stands in the doorway for a long time, watching us count our blessings before she turns off the light. She is wearing her thick, comfy robe with little pink roses on it, and her hair is pinned back because she has already washed her face. Mother says our smile is our superpower, and she's got a big one. "I love you, girls. Bunches and bunches."

"Love you more," we both say at the very same time. So, of course, Bitsy calls jinx and says I owe her a Coke.

As these tiny clouds rise beneath Fisher's boots, they put a whole new spin to the old folktale. I haven't felt this kind of attraction since, well, since Reed. Maybe Brynn is right. I am forty-five now, and time *is* ticking. It could be crazy to fathom the fantasy, but I find myself wondering . . . would Fisher dare to go there again after all this time? And if so, would I?

I offer him the French hydrangea cuttings I've brought from the car. "Where should we plant these?"

He takes the plastic pots and moves them to a tilled plot of soil that's sure to receive a dose of sun each day. "I'm thinking we'll plant a few limelights here too. Maybe some lacecaps and oakleaf. Create a hydrangea room with a few varieties." He shares the same hill-country drawl as others from these parts, with a tinge of university speak that is only surface level, at best. One beer or a heated discussion, and he would be right back to full-on twang. Everything about him feels like home.

Behind us Fisher's crew is busy unloading a large supply of perennials from the trailer. I lend a hand, carrying black pots stamped #1P or #3P depending on size. The larger ones I leave for the landscapers, who are far more muscular than I will ever be. Fisher does his share too while supervising the whole operation, calling out names as he gives directions: dahlia, gladiolus, gardenia, just to name a few.

"Mock orange," I say, adding two more pots to the stash, excited these sweet-smelling blossoms will bring a thrill each spring. "One of Mother's favorites."

"Always a bestseller," Fisher agrees. "People love it, especially Faulkner fans."

"What's Faulkner got to do with it?"

"Supposedly, he got the name wrong. Called it a syringa in one of his stories."

"Syringa? Like the lilac?" Mother has taught me my fair share of gardening lore, and I am realizing how much I miss the lingo. In Arizona no one talks of life in terms of when the flowers bloom.

Fisher shakes his head. "Who knows what he was thinking."

"Ooh, you know I love a mystery!" It's decided. I have officially become a flirt, and I imagine William Faulkner would approve of the developing drama. Give him something to write about, at least.

A Nobel Prize–winning Oxford boy, Faulkner became infamous not only for his way with words but also for his ability to capture the day-to-day lives of his people, my people. An observer of human behaviors, he examined the conditions of the heart, collecting stories with his trusty typewriter and a bottle of bourbon. If he called the mock orange a syringa, he certainly may have been drinking too much, as some claim, but perhaps he simply made an honest mistake, identifying the shrub in the way his neighbors did.

We tend to forget, after all, that he was just a man. A man who spoke the language that swam around him. I assume he did his best to preserve that language on the page so that someday, when he was dead and gone, the rest of us could sink our toes in the same cool waters and savor the dip back in time. As much as locals may have misunderstood him, he gave them the gift of immortality, and for that, I do believe, they should thank him.

I toy with the scaly bark, enjoying the fragrant white blooms. "My friend Marian says we shouldn't limit something by its name anyway."

"Smart friend." Fisher moves closer, shadows my hands, touches the leaves.

"She is." I smile at the thought of my feisty yoga partner back in Sedona. And suddenly I'm spinning through time again, making my way back to the cliffs of Chimney Rock, where Marian climbed with me in the morning sun, labeling plants and birds and mesas while the flutist played.

May 14, 2016

"It changes the way we move through the world, when we assign a name for things." Marian walks at least ten steps before elaborating. "Did you know the name for that hedgehog cactus? Before I told you?"

I shake my head. No telling how many times I've walked past

the familiar desert plant without ever really thinking about what kind of cactus it was.

"What changed then? Once you knew the name?"

"Gives meaning to it, I guess. Lets me file it so I can pull the information later and use it."

"Yes, but is that a positive or a negative?" Having spent most of her life in Sedona, Marian speaks in terms of energies as if they are a natural part of everyone's vocabulary.

"Positive, I suppose."

"In many cases, yes." She doesn't sound convinced. "But in other situations, perhaps by assigning a label to something, we define our expectations of it. It can no longer be as it chooses to be."

I twist my lips, curious.

"When someone looks at me, they're likely to draw a name to mind, even if they don't know the name Marian. They tag me with a description: *old, widow, woman*. If I accepted those labels, I'd probably be in a nursing home somewhere, my brain turning to jelly with my bones."

"I can't imagine."

"That's because I decided a long time ago not to fall into a box." She pulls herself up a particularly steep part of the incline, knocking a few loose rocks down the slide as she climbs. "It doesn't matter what people call me. Fact of the matter is, I'm all that encompasses this human journey, and change is constant. That can't possibly be summed up in one little word."

I adjust my hourglass charm across my neck. What would Marian think of Fisher? I imagine she'd tell me to let the universe have its way. That what's meant to be can be, if I don't let fear get the best of me.

FIFTEEN

Fisher removes his heat-soaked ball cap and wipes his brow with his shirt, revealing a toned set of abs that would hold their own against a guy half his age. "Geesh, Fisher," I tease. "What's your secret?" A sheen of sweat catches light between each muscular ridge.

"What's yours?" He scans my body quickly, with restraint, before respectfully lifting his eyes back to mine.

"Staying single!"

"Well then, I'd say single looks good on you, Lovey." He chuckles in a friendly sort of way, and I blush yet again, turning to focus on the job at hand. Side by side we work, and it feels like old times. It wasn't all that long ago when we spent our days running wild through the mayapples and buckeyes. We constructed forts in the trees, cutting thick bamboo stalks and painting *Keep Out* warnings with the fuchsia stain of pokeberries. Our bodies work in sync now, like they did back then, and few words are needed between us.

As a team we drop well-soaked roots after each dig. Then I smooth the soil back into place with bare hands, opting to feel the cool earth against my skin as we move on to cuttings and first-years, saplings and pass-alongs. We sweat and electricity builds between us, surging and shifting, increasing its charge. Each time his arm meets mine, my spine reacts with an energetic thrum.

And now, as his finger clips my wrist beneath a mangled mass of roots, I don't look him in the eye. Instead, I'm lost in all those childhood lessons of Eden. No wonder the story begins in a garden. No wonder God called it good.

When Fisher finally suggests we take a break, I agree. We step to his truck where he plucks two icy water bottles from the cooler and passes one to me, the tip of his hand touching my own. Everything about him makes me feel safe. And for the first time in years, I begin to have hope again, as if love may be more than a fairy tale after all.

With the trailer removed we sit on the tailgate, shoulder to shoulder, barely an inch of air between us. My feet swing from the steel overhang, reminding me of bonfire parties and Saturdays at Sardis Lake. Heat rises between our hips, and it has nothing to do with the sun.

"Tell me everything," I prompt. "Catch me up."

"Could take a while." He looks toward the west where the sun is dipping lower by the second. Behind us his crew begins packing their things to call it a day. "How 'bout we go for a walk? Watch the sun set over the fields?"

When he leaps from the tailgate and offers me his hand, Eudora Welty's voice comes through the haze of seduction: *"Beware of a man with manners."* I ignore her warning.

As we walk, Manning follows us out to the fields that once

belonged to Fisher's family, the very ones he hopes to buy back from the lawyers before year's end. Divided by crop, the rich bottomland has been planted for seasonal rotations. Corn is already nearing eye level while the cotton shoots are just finding their way above our shins.

Fisher follows my gaze toward the rows. "I've convinced the lawyers to let me tackle some of their irrigation issues. The farmer was happy for the help. You probably can't see it, but I took a laser to the furrows. Slope at a ten-degree grade now. Allows for more natural flow." He points to a line of poly pipe, rolled out to distribute water from the river pump. Like a long white tube sock, it snakes the cornfield, shooting small arcs from each well-planned blowhole. "They were on pivot for years. Finally convinced 'em to switch last spring. When I get it back in my name, I'm gonna work the land even more. Use the same permaculture techniques I'm using for the memory garden. But this is as far as I could push 'em for now. Change comes slow, you know."

"You're passionate about this." I peel back a stalk of corn to investigate the silks, still tucked inside. Their new strands glow bronze against the setting sun, triggering another flashback to days when Fisher and I played chase through the crops.

"It's all I've ever wanted," Fisher says. "To farm my family land."

I bite my lip but finally give in, asking the question that needs to be asked. "What about Finn? Is he on board?"

"One hundred percent. Couldn't do it without him."

Manning darts between the cornstalks, splashing through the watery furrows until he's completely out of sight. Black birds scatter above his path. It's the only way I know he's already passed the turnrow, leaving us far behind to take a dip in the creek.

"And that's how you make a dog's day," I jest. "He's probably a muddy mess by now."

"Finn's lab does the same thing. Can't keep him clean."

My hands tense into fists. "How is he?"

"Finn? Old and married like the rest of our friends. We're the only ones who held out, seems like." He shifts his gaze, far and away.

"I mean, how's he *doing*, Fisher?"

His pause is heavy. "Honestly, he's good now, Lovey. If it weren't for the scars, no one would ever guess he'd survived such a thing."

I exhale. The burden has been with me since childhood, hard and heavy on my heart. Bullies can be found in any town, and Finn found more than his share here when we were young.

"He met Alice down at State. Three kids now. Happy family. He's handled it much better than I have. I guarantee."

"Me too," I say, unable to express how sorry I am for spilling that gasoline, how much I wish we could turn back time and prevent the whole thing from ever happening. We both share the heft of it.

As the sun sinks lower, we walk the outer loop. Here, the pines stretch tall in rigid rows, like dominoes waiting to be set in motion. "Fisher, there's something I need to say."

He slows his pace, so I continue.

"I spilled the gasoline that day, so the whole thing *is* my fault, but I assure you, I did not set that fire. You had promised to help me build a tree house, remember?"

He picks up speed again, and I stay with him as he talks. "We had come ready to work, Finn and me. Had gone to the shed for tools. I saw the gas had spilled, but it didn't worry me none."

"I was already up in the tree, nailing boards up the trunk. I could smell the fire long before I saw it."

"The tires." He scrunches his nose as if he can still smell it too. "From the mower. That thing went off like a bomb."

"I came running, yelling for Chief." The memories rise now, fast as flames and suffocating like the smoke itself. "By the time I reached the shed, Bitsy was already dragging the hose. We did our best, I swear we did. But . . . we . . . we didn't know."

He threads his hand around the bend of my elbow. Pulls me to him with a gentle press. "It's okay, Lovey."

We stop walking now, both of us. "All I remember is you yelling for help, and Finn. Scared speechless. I couldn't understand what was happening." My voice cracks as my mind fills with images I have long suppressed: Finn's gloves on fire, his hair singed from the heat, his face red beneath the soot, his hands . . . melting.

"We were all too young," Fisher explains. "People always ask me, why didn't we just come out? Run for safety when the fire started? But you have to put yourself in our shoes."

He has no idea how badly I wish I could do just that. Have the fire burn me instead of Finn.

"We were in the storage closet, behind all your mother's flowerpots, back where Chief stashed old tools he never used anymore. We were both down on the floor, digging through metal toolboxes, plus the radio was on and we were singing and laughing. It was hot in there, too hot, but by the time we realized there was a fire, the door was already full of flames. I think we were both too scared to run through it. I mean, I don't know how to explain it, Lovey. I just couldn't think."

"You were thirteen, Fisher. Even adults go into shock like that."

"But Finn was eight. I should have helped him. Kept him safe. Instead, we just hid in the corner, yelling for help. Never dawned on me that no one would come."

"We didn't hear you, Fisher. We were all yelling too, and the water was running, plus the fire was pretty loud—paint cans exploding, wood popping. We were so focused on keeping the flames away from the house . . . We had no idea . . . 'til you came running out."

He nods. "Yep. I kept shouting at Finn, telling him to run. To get out. But he couldn't move. He was crying. Tell you the truth, Lovey, I've never been so scared. Sparks up against our skin . . . couldn't breathe. There was no time left. I jerked him up by the shirt, but he pulled away. That's when he fell."

"His hands?"

He nods. "He was wearing some of Chief's old gloves. They hit the fuel line when he touched the ground. All it took."

I shudder, the image too much to hold.

"He wouldn't listen. So I picked him up. And I ran. Made it out. Somehow. Whole shed came crashing down." He shakes his head. "Lucky."

"I'll never forget that feeling, Fisher. When I saw you. When I saw Finn . . . his skin . . . Fisher, it was . . ."

"I know." He trembles.

"Bitsy pointed the finger at me. Convinced everyone I had done it on purpose. Made no sense. I swear to you, Fisher. I never would have done anything like that. I was in the tree the whole time."

"I know that too."

"You do?" I'm without breath. All these years I've carried this blame, and he removes it just like that. Why have we never had this conversation? Why have I been so sure he blamed me?

"Of course I do, Lovey. Finn knows it too."

"He does?" It's as if he's given me the whole world with these words.

"Everyone does." He adjusts his cap and speaks as if this is common knowledge, having no idea the shift he has set in motion deep within me.

"Everyone knows I didn't do it?" I speak slowly, needing to hear this again.

"Of course." He holds my gaze with a steady patience as I struggle to put two and two together. "I always figured Bitsy did it, tell you the truth."

"Bitsy?"

"Bitsy." He says this matter-of-factly, as if there's no reason to doubt his claim.

"Oh, I don't know about that. I'm sure it was just an accident. Some electrical glitch or something. It wouldn't have taken much to light that gasoline, especially on such a hot day. Besides, even Bitsy wouldn't be that cruel."

"Are we talking about the same Bitsy? Lovey, think about it. How many times has she tried to get you in trouble?"

"Yeah, but petty stuff. Sibling rivalry. Nothing like this."

He holds my stare for a long time, as if he's debating whether to say more. "You want me to be honest?"

"Always." I don't blink.

"I think she couldn't stand all the time you and your mother spent working together in that garden."

"What are you saying?"

"I'm saying . . . y'all had that bond, the flowers, something Bitsy lacked. So she burned that shed to the ground, trying to destroy what the two of you shared."

My words take a while to surface, and when they do, they are soft, sad. "I . . . I never thought of it that way."

"She's been jealous her whole life, Lovey. You're bound to know that much."

"Jealous of me? Oh, come on. That's ridiculous. She's the golden girl. Homecoming queen. You name it."

"She may wear the crown, but she's never had half the heart you have. That's why she tries to break yours."

Fisher's assessment pulls me to a still, quiet space, and I focus on the sun, now a thin, plum slip across the horizon. "You think . . . you really think she set that fire on purpose?"

He nods.

"She wanted to ruin Mother's gardening equipment? And blame me?"

"I do." He speaks as if he's surprised I haven't known this all along. "Remember when she broke the only purple crayon in the set? Your favorite?"

I nod this time.

"And cut all the hair off that doll you won in the first-grade raffle?"

He's right again.

"She nailed your 10,000 Maniacs record to a tree and told us all to use it as target practice. Insisted you didn't want it anymore. I should have known better. I'm sorry for that, by the way."

I can't help smiling at this apology, even if it arrives a few decades after the matter. In tune to my emotions, Fisher pulls me in for a compassionate hug, his arms wrapping around me like wings. My head rests against his chest, and I surrender to the comfort of being held by this man, a man I still love. A man who says he believes me.

SIXTEEN

"Up and at 'em!" Chief roars his optimistic cheer from the foyer. I'm already opening my eyes as the sparrows bring me to life from beneath the sweet gum tree, their simple tune accompanied by migrating songbirds of every vibrant hue. Scarlet tanagers, prothonotary warblers, and my personal favorite, the indigo buntings who have returned with their striking blue feathers and silvery bills. The trees are alive, and they sing to tell us so.

Downstairs, Mother starts her piano playing. I leap to my feet as she tackles a Bogus Ben Covington tune, a satirical jam about Adam and Eve. Years ago, these lyrics made us laugh as we sang along and danced in the living room. This Saturday morning, to the backdrop of these jubilant melodies, I work through a condensed yoga routine in my bedroom. After a few inverted poses and a four-minute plank, I'm good to go.

By the time I end my shower and make it to the kitchen, Mother has moved from the piano to the table, where she peers over her reading glasses, working a crossword puzzle. "Fisher's crew just pulled up, in case you want to say hello." One eyebrow lifts, letting me know nothing gets past her.

"Bitsy says he's nearly engaged, Mother."

She adds ink to the white-spaced word cubes. “There’s no reason to fight it, dear. Whatever it is you and Fisher have together, it’s got a life of its own.” She says this with exaggeration, enjoying the tease. “Time to let love bloom.”

“Wow, you’re coming up with some winning lines there, Mother. What kind of crossword puzzle is that? Soap Opera Catchphrases? Bored Housewives?”

She laughs. “Say what you want. I’ve been around long enough to know a good thing when I see it. You and Fisher . . . well, that’s a good thing.”

I shuffle my feet, half hoping she’s right. “What about Blaire?”

“What about her? She runs around behind his back, from what I hear. And I guess you already know she left Ron Howington at the altar a few years back.”

“Are you kidding?” Heaven knows Fisher suffered enough when I returned his engagement ring. The last thing he needs is another rejection.

Mother shakes her head. “You know I’m not one to gossip. Blaire may be a good person for all I know, but for Fisher, she’s a heartbreak waiting to happen. And I care about Fisher. We all do. I don’t want to see him end up with someone who doesn’t appreciate him. Just like I don’t want you to end up with someone like Reed ever again.”

The mention of Reed snaps my spirit. Every fiber severs, sending pieces of me far and away.

July 2013

“Eva. This is Meghan. Reed’s wife.” She announces her name before I can crawl to a safe space. It’s been almost two months since Reed confessed his double life to me. Somehow I found the strength to drive away from the Tortolita Mountains that night, and I've spent the last fifty-two days striving to regain some sense of dignity. I certainly never expected this call. Especially in the middle of a workday, trapped by the confines of Apogee.

"I have questions, Eva. You owe me that, at least."

"Of course." I bite my lip. "Give me a minute?"

Mere feet from the phone, Brynn is watching another TED Talk. Across the cubicle, coworkers shield themselves behind earbuds and computer screens. I muster all the courage I can find and move to a conference room.

"I've been married to Reed for nearly twenty years. My family is everything to me, you understand?" She weeps, and I can't bear to hear the pain she carries. "I found a text on his phone today. Several, in fact. He's met you in Arizona? Told you he loves you?"

It's clear she expects answers, but I stay silent. I'm angry. Not with this poor woman, whose hurt must be far worse than my own, but with Reed, for deceiving not one trusting partner but two. As her story unfolds, it becomes clear that Reed is still playing us both. Four full years in a relationship with me, and his wife is only finding out today? He's too good a con for this to be a coincidence. I want to warn her. Tell her he preys on trusting people like us. That this is some sick part of his game. Instead, I listen, wishing I could erase the past, save her from this suffering.

"Is any of this true? Please, Eva. I need to know."

There's no right way to do this, so I follow my heart and start by offering an apology. "I'm so very, very sorry, Meghan. I know you have no reason to believe me, but I never knew he was married. I would never choose to be with a married man. Never."

She catches her breath. I've been there, shattered by the one person you trust most in the world. The one you love and the one you believe loves you in return.

"He says nothing happened between you." I can hear the hope in her, wanting, needing me to say her children are safe, that her family is not about to be destroyed.

"Reed says a lot of things."

The rest comes in pieces, as she demands the whole story. I struggle through the truth, not sure she believes a word I say. How we haven't talked for a couple of months. That when I found out he was married, I ended it immediately. "Part of me wanted to reach out to you. But I didn't want to cause any more hurt. I figured, well . . . I guess I hoped your marriage might survive all this."

"I still don't understand. How exactly do you know my husband?" Meghan struggles to process the details, asking me to explain it all again, as if the words will suddenly fall into place and make sense of this. No logic could ever validate Reed's choices. I know. I've tried.

"He's not well, Meghan."

"You don't know him."

"You're right. I only thought I knew him."

She doesn't respond, so I try to break through. "Truth is, Reed is a con. I was nothing but a pawn."

"Keep talking," she says, as if things are beginning to come clear.

"I loved him, Meghan, like you. Trusted him completely. I never imagined he had a family. Never once crossed my mind."

The syllables slash across the phone, but I know how it feels to want the truth, so I answer every question and give her the shameful details, explain that yes, Reed said he loved me, and yes, he supposedly planned to marry me, and yes, he promised we would live happily ever after in our dream home by a lake. I confess to the international vacations and romantic getaways. I describe the way he broke the news of his marriage the very night I expected him to propose.

She sobs, and I fight my own tears, tears I have no right to cry. And when her grief takes the shape of anger, I absorb that too, as I should. She's right to say I owe this to her, and so I do my best to deliver, focusing only on her pain, trying hard to ignore my own.

As my coworkers call it a night outside the conference room, Reed's voice comes through the phone. He is arriving home from work, edgy and tense. I hear him yell for Meghan, slam a door. "Dinner isn't ready?" His voice comes closer, and I shiver as he demands to know who's on the phone.

"It's Eva," she says without emotion. Such strength.

"Eva who?" His volume lifts. "What are you doing, Meghan?"

My bones begin to shake in response. I've never heard anyone treat someone this way, but she seems to accept it without much shock. Despite the games Reed played with my life, I never saw his temper. Never once. This is yet another mask he wears, and I get the sense he's set this whole thing up just to watch us squirm.

He yells louder. "I told you. She's a friend. Nothing more." The names he calls her are brutal. She is in real danger now.

"You hear this?" she questions me, confronting his lie with a sideways move. "He claims you're just a friend."

The pain in this is unbearable. Not just accepting that Reed doesn't love me anymore, but facing the reality that he never did.

Something crashes in the background, and the verbal assault escalates. I have never met Meghan, but to hear her treated this way, to understand the level of cruelty Reed delivers . . . "Meghan? You need to get out of there."

The phone disconnects. I'm left with nothing but dead air.

I dial her number. It goes immediately to voice mail. I try again. Nothing. I call Reed. No answer.

I am pacing again, unsure of how to help this woman. I call the San Antonio police. My hands shake as I report my concerns. They seem unconcerned, so I press for a safety visit, insist I remain anonymous. Only when they agree to visit the home do I finally hang up the phone, fully aware that if anything happens to Meghan, it's my fault.

SEVENTEEN

"Go easy on that door," Bitsy teases Trip, who comes bounding into the kitchen with a big hug for Mother. And for me! Standing at least six feet high, he's a half foot taller than I am now.

"Trip, my goodness. You're a man!" I can't get over it. "Since when does fifteen look like this?"

When I ask how he keeps the girls away, he laughs with teenage smugness. "I don't." Then he opens the fridge, helping himself to leftover peach pie.

Mary Evelyn comes trailing in behind Bitsy, and Trip offers a slice to each of us. It's not yet breakfast, so we all decline. At twelve years old, my niece stays back and takes in the scene before allowing me to hug her. An introverted personality trait I can relate to, but still, it hurts my heart.

"I hope this means you're going with us today." I pour Trip a glass of milk.

"Yep," he says between bites.

Chief stretches the suspense, refusing to tell us where we're headed. Bitsy drops a box of muffins on the table from the local bakery, and the rest of us circle. I dole out the plates Mother has been using for fifty years, and she steps in beside me, passing napkins and glasses before saying, "Every man for himself." We indulge.

"Trip has practice at five." Bitsy eyes her phone, scans her calendar. "And Mary Evelyn has a lunch party at noon. Ballet at three. Riding lessons at six."

"So we'd better get a move on then." Chief jiggles his keys in his pocket to encourage a quick bite. We all talk over one another as we devour the muffins, and everyone eats but Mother, who sips coffee in silence while watching the chaos around her. Within fifteen minutes Trip snatches the last of the banana-nut muffins, smiling as he taunts his sister with the final bite.

"Head 'em up, move 'em out." Chief sings the classic *Rawhide* verse, reminding me of lazy rainy afternoons spent watching Westerns with my father.

The kids and I wrap up the jingle with an enthusiastic, "*Rawhide*!" Then the six of us pile into the family tank and Chief drives us just a few miles up the road to Rowan Oak, home of the late William Faulkner.

The historic estate can barely be seen from the residential street, where Chief parks roadside. Together we stroll the long gravel path through the property, letting the neighborhood noise fade into the trees. As we near the iconic row of eastern red cedars, I remember how Chief would scare the dickens out of us with tales of Judith Sheegog, a spirit who supposedly haunts these grounds. I question my niece about the famous folktale, pointing out the massive magnolia where Judith's grave reportedly rests.

She sighs. "I'm kinda too old for that, Aunt Lovey."

The sound of those two words, *Aunt Lovey*! Never has there been anything sweeter. It's all I can do not to sweep her up into my arms, but I figure if she's too old for ghost stories, then she's way too old for public affection. I try my best not to blow this, giving both kids time to let me back into their lives.

Mary Evelyn must feel bad about her response because she draws close to me now. "You are coming to my birthday tea, aren't you?"

I smile and wrap my arm through hers, our elbows holding the hinge. "Wouldn't miss it for the world. Still can't believe you're going to be a teenager!"

Bitsy stays quiet, walking ahead as if she doesn't hear, so I steer to the safe side. "Either of you know why this house is called Rowan Oak?"

Trip answers, confident in his knack for spouting random facts, a habit that's earned him the moniker Trivia Trip. "Named after a tree." He speaks in an overconfident voice and rubs his chin, acting the part of a learned scholar.

"Two trees actually," Mother says. "The live oak and the rowan tree. Ironically, neither are on this property."

"Faulkner probably did that on purpose, don't you think?" I can picture him now, all smug as he imagined future tourists flocking in search of the rowan oak. Not only would they fail to find the mythical tree, they'd also come up short in search of both the rowan and the live oak.

"He did seem to have a peculiar sense of humor," Mother admits with a smile. "The rowan is actually a symbol of protection."

"From evil spirits." Trip teases Mary Evelyn with a spooky voice. He looks back toward the circle garden where the magnolia roots have long been at war with the brick paths.

"More like tax men and nosy reporters," Mother says. "I think Faulkner was searching for his own little corner of the world, a safe and peaceful place to call home."

"Might have helped if he had put down the bottle," Bitsy snips, ever the critic of other people's lives. No one mentions the fact that she's been nursing many a wineglass in the days since I've been home. Typical of her to project her own sins onto someone else.

Chief grunts in response but keeps us moving between the cedars. They loom over us like giant sentinels, holding their position in two linear rows, insisting we embrace Faulkner's Mississippi—a place that was at once both magical and maddening. Some say the cedars were planted to cleanse the air after the yellow fever epidemic, a legend that adds to the mysterious dance of light and shadow taking place beneath the aromatic boughs.

Despite the morning hour several quilts dot the lawn where students have gathered around the black locust. With guitars and ukuleles this carefree group strums, while a middle-aged couple whispers against the courtyard wall, ivy weaving its way between them like a jealous lover.

I text notes on my phone, jotting the names of plants as we walk. Were we to venture inside the Greek Revival home, we could see Faulkner's outline for *A Fable*. This novel won both the Pulitzer and the National Book Award, but I've long been more impressed by the fact that the plot points were written by Faulkner's own hand across the walls of the study, including a secret section he tucked behind the door to prove we never know what tomorrow might bring. But today, we skip the house with its stately white columns and head past the scuppernong arbor.

"Well, shoot," Chief says, disappointment clear as he reaches a tangled mass of wisteria. "I thought they'd still be in bloom."

The wisteria vines have nearly devoured an iron pole that struggles to support their weight. Having already finished their first spring cycle, their purple petals cloak the grass now, holding dew beneath the morning light.

Bitsy and Trip shade their eyes from the sun, and I move closer to examine the thick web of vines. Trip takes a seat even though the iron bench seems too small and ancient for his sturdy frame. Off-balance and faded, the bench arcs to connect with others just like it, looping the pole to form the center of the English knot garden whose geometric privet hedge circles us all.

Mother lets her hand fall softly across the shoulders of Mary Evelyn, who already stands nearly as tall, while Chief grasps one of the woodsy stems for closer inspection. "Y'all know how kudzu and English ivy tend to take over? Won't stop growing 'til nearly everything else is dead?"

"Yes, sir," Trip says politely, and all I can think is how happy I am to be here, to share this time with my niece and nephew.

"Well, wisteria is nearly as bad." Chief tugs the vines. They interweave beyond the pole, reaching high into tree branches to overhang the garden. "Been known to take the roof off a house, swallow a car, even pull down a barn or two."

Mary Evelyn's eyes grow wide. They are green like mine and anchored by a full-flowing swath of strawberry-blonde waves, same color as my own before the gray started setting in—a nod to our Scots-Irish ancestry. She looks more like me than she does her mother, and also like me, she adores Chief. He pulls a few spent blooms from the ground and dew shakes loose, sprinkling my shirt and drawing a laugh from Mary Evelyn, who leans in to inspect. "You can probably imagine how pretty these are when they're still purple and new."

When she nods, Chief adds, "Well, don't be fooled, young lady. I'm gonna tell you something I don't talk about much."

No stranger to their grandfather's spur-of-the-moment sermons, both kids tune in, knowing there's a lesson to be learned. The rest of us do too.

"A long time ago, there was a woman who looked about as pretty to me as these flowers when they bloom."

"You'd better be talking about Mother," Bitsy teases.

"Actually, no." Chief shakes his head with regret. "Someone else. I came home and, well, Laurel was waiting at the door. Word had already gotten back to her."

"Can't get away with much in a small town," Bitsy says to her children, a tone of warning.

"True," Mother agrees, unnerved, as if nothing Chief could say would make her love him less.

"That's a good thing too." He speaks to the kids, emphasizing his point. "Because your grandmother here made it clear that I'd better toe the line. And you know what? She was right."

"Always is." I smile, impressed as ever by Mother's graceful composure.

"Absolutely," Chief says. "Truth is, I had put my own family at risk. So that afternoon, Laurel took me to the woods and showed me some wisteria, just like this here. It had covered an entire tractor and half a hay barn on the neighbor's property. Plus a tree or two." Chief turns to Mother. "You remember what you said?"

"I do." She gives him *the look*. Same one she gave me when she thought I had smoked a cigarette or cheated on an exam. "I told you, some things need to be kept at a distance, or else they destroy every good thing within their reach."

"Yep. That's what she said." Chief nods meekly before he turns back toward the kids. "And to this day, we still don't let wisteria grow on our property, no matter how pretty it is."

I move my hands to my pockets, feeling a surge of guilt for touching the risqué plant. Trip grins in response, as if he knows what I'm thinking.

"So here's the thing," Chief preaches on. "Y'all know how Laurel and I tend to think life is like a garden. It's important to plant ourselves near the right people."

Trip plays along, speaking in his professor voice again. "Beware the vines!"

"You got it." Chief nods. "In a healthy family, there's a balance. Every life can flourish. But if there's no equal balance, everybody suffers. Few survive."

Mother smiles Chief's way, with a fondness reserved for soul mates of the truest kind. "You need to know two things in life, just like when you weed a garden: When to say yes. And when to say no."

Bitsy shifts uncomfortably, as if she can't imagine any other outcome for our family. I, too, feel sickened at the thought of my parents ever suffering any form of infidelity, even the threat of it. But looking at them here, together, I realize no marriage is safe from such dangers. The important part of the story is that Chief easily could have tended the wrong plant, devoured our mother's spirit, destroyed the rest of us who shared space beside him. But he didn't. And that one choice has made all the difference, not only in our lives, but in the lives of every generation that will follow.

With his hand now entwined in Mother's, Chief leads us through the grounds of Rowan Oak. He continues to point out various plants, adding sweet stories one by one, and I take notes to share with Fisher.

Near the gazebo, Bitsy eyes the large camellia and tells the kids about their earliest hide-and-seek games. "Mary Evelyn chased a rabbit from the boxwood once." She offers a heartfelt smile. "You thought that was where the Easter Bunny lived. Remember?"

Trip gives his sister grief for this, but his teasing stops when Mother suggests we take a few family photos by the barn. She points toward the structure's green roof, a contrast to the rough-hewn logs and chalky chinking. We each take turns behind the camera, capturing various group photos before moving north of the tenant house where the catalpa tree rises wide and sturdy like a wizened groundskeeper. I fiddle with the English ivy that has crept its way from roots to branches, just as Chief warned. The effect provides a textured backdrop, ideal for a few more snapshots. When a considerate tourist offers to take a photo of our entire family, Mother beams, overjoyed, as we all gather close together for a few takes.

Once the tourist has returned the camera, I nudge the others toward Bailey's Woods where ancient oaks and hickories mark the trail. The trunks are so thick, Trip and I can barely link our arms around them. "I challenge you to find the oldest."

Trip accepts, wrapping trunk after trunk, trying to gauge the girth of sweet gums, beeches, and oaks of all sorts—red, white, and post. By the third or fourth tree, Bitsy shouts a warning: "Don't come complaining to me when you get poison ivy!"

He keeps at the hunt while Mary Evelyn balances her way across a fallen hickory. Having collected a few pods from a crape myrtle, I seize this opportunity to share our childhood poem about grandmother's purse, teaching my niece to pop open the seams in search of treasure. While she may be too old for ghost stories, she smiles when she finds the floral handkerchief and gold within, proof nobody outgrows such simple wonders.

The six of us share memories until the trail's end at the university museum. Then we follow the peaceful wooded path back toward Faulkner's house, weaving past yet another honeysuckle patch. The strong fragrance prompts my eyes to water, but I snap two white flowers, stealing them from the oversize bumblebees who surround the near-twenty-foot vine with a constant hum.

"White flowers are my favorite," Mary Evelyn says. I want to add a Chief-like homily, tell her I need her in my life as much as the flowers need the bees, somehow convince her she needs me too. But I don't dare push the boundaries for fear Bitsy will slam me out again.

"You know how to drink the honey?" I pass her one of the blooms.

When Mary Evelyn shakes her head, I mourn for her—so out of touch with nature, unfamiliar with even this basic childhood milestone. I lift my own flower, chest-high, and model the technique from my youth. "See this little green part? Where the flower was connected to the stem?"

Mother overhears and joins in, elated for the chance to teach the proper vocabulary. "That's right." She leans over us. "Now give that bud a little pinch, just above the calyx." She guides her granddaughter with gentle hands. "Go ahead and break through the petal. Just don't squeeze too hard or you'll ruin the inside parts, and that's where you find the sweet stuff."

Trip plucks his own flower from the vine. "Now pull, softly," I say, showing both of them how it's done. "Just until this tiny white string comes out."

They mirror my moves.

"That's called the style," Mother says patiently. "It's the female part. So what you want to do is pull that style until you see the little green stigma at the end. And when the stigma hits the edge, all the nectar squeezes into a little drop of sugar. You see?"

"Now drink!" I say, as if making a toast for one of our make-believe fairy parties. The innocence of our childhood!

"Tastes good." Mary Evelyn pulls another one from the vine. Trip nods confidently as if he's known this secret all along.

Mother steps ahead, trying to catch Chief and Bitsy again, but the kids and I stay back, sipping nature's candy, sharing a secret the rest of the world forgets: How to stop and take notice. How to care.

When the kids and I finally leave the trail, we spot Chief, Mother, and Bitsy already walking toward the car. We hurry to catch our crew, and I'm struck with a sudden rush of what-ifs.

What if I had made different choices from the start? What if I had stuck around to watch another year of seasons spin here in Oxford, staying to see the daffodils bloom or to wander beneath the privet tunnel hand in hand with Fisher? What if we had kept right on kissing until the naked ladies emerged near the Osage orange? What if I had lingered long enough to see cape jasmine arrive, her voluptuous white bundles an aromatic call for summer love? Or even longer, when the spider lilies burst open in the fall and the yellow autumn light fell low among mossy roots? What if I had stayed through winter, forming snow angels with my lover beneath the icy cedar boughs? What if I had not let fear defeat me after Fisher knelt before me in my mother's backyard garden, ring in his hand and happy-ever-after in his heart?

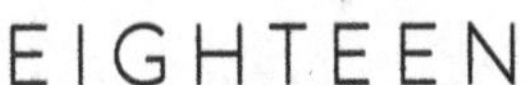

EIGHTEEN

Mockingbirds wake me with angry squawks as they chase a blue jay from the hickory leaves. While the birds battle for terrain, a squirrel skitters across Mother's trellis. It's a path he's taken countless times since my arrival nine days ago. He's heading toward one of the feeders Mother keeps stocked with seed. As I stretch beneath the covers, an eastern bluebird joins the scene, his bright wings a stark contrast to the rust-toned breast feathers. As fledglings chirp from his birdhouse nest, the sun gives birth to a new day.

I rise, stretch, and take a look at my phone: Call. ASAP. It's way too early for Brynn to be texting. Something is definitely wrong.

She answers with a warning cry, much like the alarms of the jays. "Eva? Listen. The Dragon got wind of the new production schedule. She's wanting to know when you'll be back in the office. Has she called?"

I glance at my phone log. "No."

"She's not happy, Eva. I don't know how much longer I can stall her. I'm dreading going in today. What am I supposed to say?"

"Don't worry. I'll give her a ring. Smooth the waters."

"I can't tell you how much she scares me." Her voice tenses.

"Don't let her shake you, Brynn. I'll handle it. Promise. Even with the new deadline, everything seems to be moving on schedule from my side. Any kinks for you?" Outside, the sun continues to rise, shifting shadows and reminding me how quickly time is moving.

"Much better than expected," she admits. "Everyone seems to understand. No complaints, other than that graphics intern."

"Intern? They put an intern on this account?" This does upset me, and my voice suggests as much. "I'll give them a call too."

"Well, I don't know if he's *officially* an intern, but he sure does act like one. Annoying. Overconfident. And slow." She pronounces *slow* as if it's a two-syllable word.

"Hmmm . . . wasn't so long ago I hired an intern much like the one you describe." I say this with a smile, and I'm certain she can hear the kindness.

"Ouch! But thanks for making me laugh."

"Best I ever hired. You know that."

"Yeah? Well, if you want us to keep working together, you've got to make that call, Eva. First thing." With that, she relaxes, shifting to boast about her latest boyfriend, a dentist who has made it past the three-date cutoff, a rarity for Brynn, who is known to sideswipe an online prospect faster than I can learn his name.

"Standards," she always says, quick to nix any potential suitor who poses with a shirtless selfie, a gun, or a fishing rod on the online dating sites she frequents. *"Because . . . cheesy."*

That's my Brynn. Her requirements include a professional-level degree, a six-figure salary at minimum, and no ex-wife or kids. "Plus teeth," she always adds. "Teeth are a must." But when it comes time for a second date, she's got even tougher criteria. Her motto is "Never settle." Certainly a rule I admire and one that will take her far in life. But somehow this dentist has made the cut, and she's flat-out giddy about date number four.

She's giving me the scoop when Fisher's landscaping truck finds its way down our gravel lane. I seize the first polite opportunity to end Brynn's call. Then I dress and stroll downstairs where Mother greets me with coffee. "Helping with the grounds crew again today?"

"Actually, I thought we might work your gardens. Together. It's been a while."

"It has indeed." Her glow suggests she's charmed. "But maybe you should make sure Fisher doesn't need a hand. Your father's concerned about getting that drainage worked out before the party. Worries we won't have enough parking without it."

Good ol' Chief is playing this one like a champ.

After moving to the kitchen, I add a little cream to my coffee before Mother joins me at the table, offering a tray of fruit and some quinoa toast with avocado. "The kids were so glad to be done with finals yesterday. Did you talk to Mary Evelyn? Seems a little nervous about her birthday tea this afternoon."

"Hope it's not on account of me. You can't imagine how much I've missed them." I eye the fruit on Mother's plate, barely touched. "Sure you're feeling okay?"

She nods and opens the paper, reading aloud about a local who is making it big on Broadway. "Isn't it exciting?" She's clearly avoiding the topic, even as her bones protrude from both wrists, angling out like pins. I know when to back off.

The story of the local actor makes me think of Bitsy's engagement in the Big Apple, a romantic summer proposal in Central Park that caught us all off guard. "I'm surprised I haven't seen Whitman yet. Think he'll be at the tea party?"

"No telling. He travels a lot these days." Mother keeps scanning the news. "Bitsy stays so busy with the kids. I guess they kind of do their own thing."

"When's the last time you saw him?" I sip my coffee.

"Oh, you know. He's here and there."

I try my toast, then take another approach, hoping to learn more. "Bitsy doesn't seem very happy, does she?"

Mother looks up from the paper and holds a pause before answering. "No, Lovey. She doesn't."

"Did something happen? With Whitman?"

She removes her glasses, holds them in hand. "I'm hoping they're just going through a rough patch. Everybody has those."

"Not you and Chief."

"Oh, sure we do. You can't spend fifty years together and not hit a dry spell every now and then. Any gardener can tell you that. Trick is knowing how to adapt." She sips her coffee. "Gotta keep growing. Whatever life brings."

"Easier said than done, Mother." I put it in garden terms to lighten things back to Mother's comfort zone. "Seems to me, Bitsy is withering."

She takes my hand now and stares the way she did when she told me my grandmother had passed away. "Why do you think I insisted you come home, Lovey? I keep trying to tell you. Your sister needs you. No matter how much she pretends otherwise."

Fisher's voice reaches me before I crest the hill. The familiar sound brings comfort, but what I'm not prepared to find is Finn at his brother's side, planting a camellia. Despite the early hour, both men have already worked up a sweat, straining until the hefty root-ball finds proper footing.

"One down, four to go," Fisher says, turning my way. "Ready to get dirty?"

He's definitely kicking this up a notch with this R-rated version of our childhood joke. I let it slide.

"Turning out to be a tough project," I say, impressed by the scale of the garden. Wrapping the entire hill, the top labyrinth is partly ringed now by a substantial four-level wall of stone, something I'd expect to see on the Ole Miss campus or a historic homestead, but nothing I could have imagined here at my family's farm. The large gray boulders are no easy weight to haul, so a five-man crew has been brought in to manage the task with a Bobcat. "Skid-steer? Seriously? Had no idea it would be this intense."

"Yeah, well . . . you know Chief." Fisher stands. "Go big or go home."

Finn stands too and heads my way, pale-white scars still etched across his cheeks. "Long time no see, old friend." He removes his glove and his hand reaches mine.

I try not to react to the tight texture of his palm, the long-healed layers stretched thin. The damage draws pain within me, but I smile. "It's so good to see you, Finn. Fisher still making you do all the work?"

"Don't you know it." He elbows his brother, and they share a good-hearted jab at each other's expense.

"Well then . . . I'm here to help." This earns me two grateful grins from the men who once knew me best in this world. Better even than Chief and far better than Reed. Reed never saw me swim in the creek, climb a tree, or catch a bream. Reed never helped carve my initials in the fence post or search high and low when my dog Huck went missing. Reed, I now realize, never knew me at all.

As the three of us construct the garden, Finn's scars keep drawing my eye. It's been so long since I've seen those stark-white marks where pigment was scorched away. When Finn catches my gaze, I turn. "It's all right, Lovey. I'd stare too."

He's caught me off guard, and I stammer, "I'm sorry, Finn. It's just . . . it's been a long time is all." My eyes must convey what my mouth fails to say because Finn moves closer, this time with his arms stretched wide.

"Aww . . . come here, girl." He wraps me into a hug that is as comforting as a homemade quilt. "You know I love you like a sister." I surrender, not daring to resist affection of this nature. "But you're right about one thing. It *has* been a long time." He pulls away now, and I catch Fisher watching us.

"Too long," Fisher says.

"I'm really sorry, Finn. I shouldn't have stared."

He opens his palms, laughing. "You know what Chief always says: 'Never trust a guy without scars on his hands. Any man worth his salt has banged himself up a time or two.'" We all find humor in this, as Finn erases all tension.

"Tell you what," Finn continues. "Why don't we go out to eat tonight? You've never met Alice, and she's been wanting to try that new restaurant on the square. Would earn me back in good graces after missing her cousin's baby shower last weekend."

"Doghouse?" I arch my brows.

"Big-time." He laughs, proof the fire has done nothing to break his spirit. "Seriously. You gotta help me, Lovey. Silent treatment for a whole week. I can't take another day of it."

When Fisher shines his irresistible McConaughey grin, I'm sunk. "What kind of friend would I be if I didn't help?"

Finn gives his brother a you-can-thank-me-later grin, every wingman's championship gesture, and I realize my parents aren't the only ones working behind the scenes to draw Fisher and me together again.

"Still need to pick up petit fours and sandwich squares." Mother nudges me to the car while reading her list of errands. She's moving a mile a minute, checking her watch. "Party starts in two hours."

"We're doing good," I say, trying to ease her stress. "Already made the place cards, finished the centerpiece, and wrapped the charms." I load the last box of gifts into Mother's Infiniti. Then I close the liftgate and we're on our way.

After a quick stop at the bakery, we head for Bitsy's house. Just north of town, it's a custom two-story she and Whitman built a decade ago. The home stands exactly as I remember, and despite requiring extensive upkeep to maintain its grandeur, the property is meticulous. While she hasn't touched a flower bed since the day Blaire called us dirty, Bitsy has long been admired for the pristine landscaping, with many of the blooms transplanted straight from Mother's gardens and Fisher's crew in charge of the show.

Perched high above the lawn, the broad porch displays full glory too. The architectural pride of every true Southern home, it boasts massive hanging ferns with potted annuals anchoring the door. I park in the side slot, and Mary Evelyn comes to help us unload.

"Happy-happy birthday!" I sing, giving my niece a big hug.

She thanks us both and admits she's a little nervous about the tea. "Just hope they don't think it's too lame. The whole charm school thing? Etiquette lessons? I thought it would be kind of fun, but now . . . I mean, what if they hate it?"

"It'll be great," Mother says. "They'll be happy to be with you. No matter what."

Bitsy meets us at the front door and takes the bakery items to the kitchen. We follow her through the house, then out to the poolside garden where she's already set a table for the six teenage girls to dine.

"Pretty," she says as I position the shallow centerpiece of althea.

"White flowers are Mary Evelyn's favorite." I give my niece a wink and hope she feels special.

"You have the name cards?"

I pull an envelope from the bag, and Bitsy assigns each guest to a seat. She looks up and seems sincere when she says, "Thanks for doing the calligraphy."

"Happy to help." I smile.

Bitsy has already set the table with antique china, crystal goblets, and polished silver, so Mother finds another task, organizing gifts on a smaller table nearer the pool.

Mary Evelyn paces between the two. "What if no one comes?"

"Oooh . . . then we can have all the petit fours to ourselves!" I tease.

She's still laughing when she spins around and yells, "Dad!"

"How's the birthday girl?" Whitman heads our way from the back door. Tall and muscular, with peppered hair, he looks like a typical desk jockey who hits the local gym each afternoon for weights. Add that to his golf course tan, and he and Bitsy still seem able to hold their own in a town of young frat boys and sorority girls. Ageless, both of them.

When he places a gift in the pile, his cologne fires a trigger. Calvin Klein. The same fragrance Reed wore. It's all I can do not to bolt when he leans to give me a hug. "Good to see you, Lovey." Then a kiss for Bitsy. "Where's the kids' table?" he teases, full of charm.

Mary Evelyn swats him playfully and pulls him in close for a picture. "Are you staying for the party?"

"Of course. Which one is my seat?" He moves around the table, pretending to "oust one of the guests" to make room for the "father of the queen."

Mary Evelyn is laughing, chasing along, and Bitsy captures it all on her phone until Whitman claps. "Okay. Put me to work."

"Kitchen?" Bitsy asks. And they head off to manage the food and drinks.

Mother and Mary Evelyn examine the gifts while I walk the grounds, eager to see Fisher's landscape design. I stroll past sweet peas, snapdragons, and larkspur, all in bloom. Beyond the corner, rounded rows of phlox form colorful borders, and a group of lush peonies are full of buds, nearly opened. I'm making my way back to the porch when conversation leaks through an open bedroom window.

"Where have you been, Whitman? It's been weeks."

"Ridiculous how you always wanna keep tabs on everything I do."

"You can't keep doing this. I didn't even know if you were dead or alive."

"You're nuts, you know that, Bitsy? Completely nuts."

His volume lifts, and I step behind a sycamore trunk, out of view. I've never been one to eavesdrop, and the guilt is hard to swallow, but I stay anyway, longing to be a part of my sister's life.

"Can't you see what this is doing to your kids? Do you even care?"

"Don't you dare use the kids to threaten me." His voice booms louder, angry.

"I'm not threatening you. I'm begging you to stop this. Whatever it is, we can work it out."

Silence.

"The kids need a family. A good family. That's what we signed up for."

"You think I signed up for this?" he shouts.

"What's so wrong with *this*? Look at those kids. Who could ask for more?" Then after another long pause she adds, "Whitman, please. Don't do this. Not today."

Chief pulls into the driveway, and I step casually from behind the tree to meet him, hoping I haven't been busted. Together we enter through the front door, and I call out Bitsy's name, hoping to give fair warning.

We find her in the kitchen, where she's putting sandwich squares on a three-tier stand. "Grab the scones?"

I do as requested, then fill another tray with fresh grapes and berries. Whitman comes in, shakes Chief's hand, smiles as if all is normal. The men exchange jokes as Bitsy works nervously in the corner, avoiding eye contact with Whitman and keeping focused on the tasks at hand.

It's all I can do not to put him in his place. But Bitsy looks to be barely holding on, and right now all that matters is we make it through the party for Mary Evelyn. When Trip comes barreling down the stairs, the three men move outside to shoot hoops. Bitsy's shoulders drop in relief.

As guests arrive the party flows smoothly. Mother and I give Bitsy the support she needs, and the quiet, calm event suits Mary Evelyn's personality well. Together, we work through an entire lesson on etiquette, modeling social protocol and emphasizing the importance of respect—both for yourself and for others.

"The napkin should be placed on one's lap from the start." Mother teaches the girls the proper way to use the cloth linens, adding that it's always a nice touch for the host to offer black napkins to guests wearing dark colors to avoid getting lint on their clothes.

Then Bitsy holds her cup of tea as an example. "One would never squeeze the lemon. The juice might squirt on clothing, the tablecloth, napkins, or another person. Yikes!"

"And let's not put the lemon on the lip of the cup," I add. "Go ahead and drop the wedge into your glass. No splash. A dainty drop."

"The spoon should never clink against the glass," Mother says with a smile. "Silent stir."

And it goes on like this throughout the afternoon. The girls are on their best behavior while also at ease laughing, talking, enjoying the fancy affair. When situations arise, we use the opportunity as a chance to teach: "If one needs to leave the table, we simply say, 'Excuse me.' Then place the napkin in the chair until one returns." Bitsy handles it like a pro, and I honestly don't know how she's managing to stay so composed after the conversation I overheard. If I hadn't witnessed it myself, I'd think nothing was wrong at all.

As the tea continues, even I enjoy the etiquette refresher, having forgotten a few of these social rules myself. Finally, when it's time to open gifts, Bitsy teaches one last lesson: "Once finished, place the napkin on the table to signal the server."

With this, she announces they have each passed Charm School 101, and she gifts each of the guests with a quaint silver charm, praising them for lasting the entire meal without their cell phones.

Eager to open her gifts, Mary Evelyn asks me to fetch the boys. I find them on the front porch, where Whitman is the center of attention, swapping stories about his latest business trip to New Orleans. He imitates a street corner salesman in a degrading way, as if he'd last a day in that life.

"Time for presents," I say, smiling at Trip. "Mary Evelyn thought y'all might want to watch."

The men move with me back toward the poolside, where my niece graciously unwraps each present. When she reaches the one from her dad, he steps in for a closer look. She opens the box and pulls out a tight red dress, strapless and short, and I imagine he may have bought it from that same New Orleans street vendor he was impersonating moments ago. Mary Evelyn holds it up, blushing, and Chief shoots Mother a look.

"She's thirteen, not thirty," Bitsy says with a bitter bite.

"You can't keep her under your control forever, Bitsy." Then he turns to his daughter. "The world's a big place, Mary Evelyn. You'll see."

"All right." I step in, take the dress. Put it back in the box. "One last present." I hand her my gift and give Whitman a look that says, *Back off.*

Mary Evelyn pulls an old notebook from the bag and shows her friends, confused. It's covered in doodles, tattered and torn.

"Oh my goodness," Bitsy says. "Where'd you find that?"

"I've always had it. Figured it was time to share the love."

Bitsy laughs and Mary Evelyn asks, "What is it?"

"Your mother and I kept this going for years," I explain. "We'd take turns. Write a letter. Hide it somewhere in the house. Wait for the other to find it and write back."

"Fun!" my niece says. "Trip? You wanna do that?"

"No." He pops a sandwich square in his mouth, unimpressed.

"Please?"

He shakes his head. No chance of changing his mind.

Mary Evelyn flips through the notebook, reading some of the letters aloud, much to the entertainment of Chief and Mother. "You're so lucky," she says to Bitsy. "I always wanted a sister."

NINETEEN

In her dressing room Mother hands me her favorite shade of lipstick. "Might want to add a dash of color."

"It's not a date," I insist, even though I'm wearing a little black dress that falls a tad low at the top and holds its hemline above the knees.

"Sure it isn't." She moves a stray strand of my hair into place. "That's why Blaire isn't going with y'all, right?"

"I'm sure she's teaching a class or something."

Mother gives a little wiggle of her chin, letting me know there is no point in arguing.

"Great. That's all I need. The whole town gossiping about Fisher and me. Especially if they're all rooting for him to pop the question to their favorite Zumba instructor. Might as well sew a big scarlet letter to my dress right now."

"No one in their right mind wants those two to marry." Mother hands me her Chanel No. 5, but I decline. "Not even Fisher, I imagine."

This is what finally breaks me into a smile. Mother leans behind me, standing now to see into the mirror. "You look beautiful, Lovey."

She drops a kiss on my shoulder, and I respond with a humble pat on her hand just as the doorbell rings.

Dolly P. barks once, and Chief opens the door to welcome my nondate into the living room. From upstairs I hear them chatting about the weather, Ole Miss baseball, and the ongoing debate about the university mascot. Their conversation flows easily, with a natural shift and cadence known only to those most comfortable with one another.

"Best not make him wait," Mother says. "Your father'll have him signed up for Coffee Club before you know it."

I laugh and make my way downstairs, determined not to look too eager. Dolly P. pounces after each of my steps, sliding down the wooden stairs with the adorably clumsy bounds only a furball can manage. The men overhear and round the corner, both watching me descend. "This feels a bit too much like prom night."

"Hold up. I forgot your corsage in the truck." Fisher plays right along, helping to quell my anxiety. Then he circles back around. "See? Always have been too corny for my own good."

"True." I make my way toward him while Mother and Chief suggest a few alternative dining options, just in case this new restaurant hasn't officially opened. Then they tell us to have fun and to give Finn and Alice their best.

A nervous energy bounces between us as Fisher leads me to the truck. He opens my door and then fumbles to move some landscape plans from the passenger seat. "Good thing I don't want to impress you or anything."

"Oh, please. You impressed me the minute you agreed to create Mother's garden. That's no small feat."

As his Chevy roars to life, I realize it's the first time I've seen him in anything other than jeans since I arrived. He's quite handsome in his dark-blue chinos and fitted gray button-down. He smells good too, and while I can't put a name to the cologne, it's having its desired effect. I force my attention outside the window, hoping to steady my bones.

The county's free-roaming dogs chase our tires as we make our way down the ridgeline. Evening deer dart from the danger, disappearing into underbrush. Pulses of black-eyed Susans flash from the roadside ditches, where crimson clover recently fired off blooms. Come fall, these wildflowers will be replaced with yellow tickseed and blue-toned mistflower, a constant wave of color to soothe my soul. Reed may have stolen years from me, but he didn't take this. He can never have this.

With Fisher behind the wheel, we navigate the subtle rise and fall of Mississippi's hill country. These gentle rolls will build from this point eastward until they reach the Great Smoky Mountains, where Chief used to bring us camping at least once a year. We were barely old enough to tie our shoes when he first taught us to navigate the misty trails and steal sun-ripened blueberries before the bears devoured them.

Those peaks seemed endless, especially compared to our local high point, Thacker Mountain. It caps at just above six hundred feet and offers no bears nor blueberries nor mystical cloud-covered trails, but now that I'm home, I appreciate this landscape like never before, almost enough to forget the Sedona mesas and high-desert views.

As we near the downtown square, memories surface and the remains of my life are exposed with each passing landmark. There, on the corner, that's where I fell on my bike and ended up with seven stitches across my forehead, pebbles in my knee. That swimming pool is where I spent my summer days in the lifeguard chair.

"Earned myself a whopping three dollars an hour to guard those waters."

"You always did love to swim." Fisher turns my way for so long, he hits the shoulder of the road before correcting the wheel. I don't admit I was ashamed to wear a swimsuit in public, and that I'll never get over Bitsy and Blaire calling me fat in front of the other kids.

We make that corner now, passing the library, a looming redbrick structure complete with classic white columns and a two-tiered porch. "Learned everything I ever needed to know in that building right there," I confess. "How to share. How to return something in as good a shape as when you borrowed it. And how to appreciate a good story."

Fisher laughs, driving slowly uphill alongside St. Peter's Cemetery, where tombstones document the familiar families who have called this community home for generations. "We've got a little extra time. What d'ya say we give it a visit?"

He takes a right toward William Faulkner's grave, parking street side for quick access to the famous tombstone. Its location has been marked by a sign, staked catty-corner from a Methodist church.

Together, we walk to the grave where a few half-empty bourbon bottles have been scattered across the cement slab. *Four Roses.* I read the label with a sigh, an ode to good times past.

"Don't tell me you're too old for the Faulkner Challenge?" He shakes one of the bottles, daring me to take a swig of the lingering liquor. I wave my hands in the air as if the entire idea is absurd, but truth is, I'd do anything to go back to those romantic date nights, kissing Fisher beneath the moon, hiding in the shadows of headstones and trees.

As I move closer, I accidentally kick one of the bottles. It spins atop a smattering of coins before clanking against an adjacent jug. One visitor has even placed a Happy Meal toy on the headstone, right next to a rain-stained hardcover of *As I Lay Dying.* "Someone's got a sense of humor." I point to the book.

Fisher smiles, then stares at the high-dollar townhomes across the street. In the same block lies a set of bungalows where tenants endure the summer with no air-conditioning. Between the two extremes rests the one small church and a home on the historic register. On nearly any given day we could sit right here at the feet of Faulkner's tomb and see the rich, the poor, and everybody in between, all while listening to the clock tower chime, or the high school marching band practice, or the Ole Miss stadiums ring with cheers. Not to mention the aromatic notes wafting in from any number of eateries, some claiming the coveted James Beard Award, others serving barbecue, gumbo, or chicken-on-a-stick from a gas station counter.

I rub my hands across the headstone and Fisher looks my way. "I hated studying Faulkner," he admits. "All those long rants and heavy dialect. I don't think anybody actually reads that stuff."

"I kind of liked it, actually. You remember *Soldiers' Pay*?"

"A little."

"Remember what he said about love?"

He shrugs.

"Said the saddest thing about love isn't just that it doesn't last forever, but that even the heartbreak is soon forgotten."

Fisher hesitates, then leans closer. "Goes to show Faulkner didn't know a darn thing."

We each circle the grave, a bit nervously, until I take a seat on the rough concrete ledge. Faulkner's marker is one of the more modest stones, with vertical columns to frame the family name. From where I sit my feet nearly brush the edge of a second grave, this one belonging to the writer's wife.

"I wonder what poor Estelle thinks of all the bourbon and coins. Drunk frat boys lurching over her resting place." Towering above the grave, one of the oaks is covered by a thick mat of English ivy, and I'm betting that's exactly how Faulkner's wife felt most days, swallowed whole.

Fisher sits quietly beside me, and I can no longer avoid the questions that have been racing in my head for days. "Bitsy tells me you're dating Blaire."

With a sigh he leans back, putting distance between us. "Yeah. That's true."

"Does she still think we're white trash?" I tease, but I can't hide my disappointment. Blaire and Fisher? Not a match.

"She's not like that anymore. Now that she's out of her dad's control."

"Still a con?" I worry Fisher is falling into a trap. Like I did with Reed.

"Money talks, Lovey. Always has."

Money. Power. Control. I've learned the hard way. The most dangerous monsters aren't always the strangers in a back alley. They can be the ones we welcome through the front door.

"How long have y'all been dating?"

"'Bout a year now. On and off. Maybe longer. We've circled back around a time or two."

I pluck a penny from the marker and fumble it in my fingers, an easy distraction. "Bitsy says you may be getting engaged."

"It's come up." He fiddles with the grass, avoiding eye contact.

"Is that what you want? To marry Blaire?"

He, too, pulls a penny from the stash, gives it a flip. "Heads, yes. Tails, no." He tries to laugh it off. Neither of us bothers to look at how it lands.

"I'm serious, Fisher." I turn toward him now. "Are you happy?"

He doesn't answer. And that is answer enough.

"It may be out of line for me to ask you this, but . . ."

He makes eye contact now, pressing me to finish. I steady my nerves and aim for the root of the matter. "I heard she was running around on you."

Fisher stands and kicks the edge of the grave with his Timberland boots. "She's done a few things, I guess. Who hasn't?" He shrugs, kicks again. "Everybody cheats, seems like."

"Do you?"

"No." He says this with conviction. "'Course not. Never."

"Then not everybody cheats." I watch him closely, waiting for more.

The silence sustains us, until Fisher makes another attempt to explain. "Who knows, Lovey? Maybe marriage isn't what we thought it would be. I mean, look at Bitsy and Whitman. They seem to handle it."

"What do you mean, they *handle it*?" I try to read between the lines, and when he doesn't answer, I ask again.

His eyes narrow. "You don't know?"

"Know what?" I rise now to match his stance. "Is Whitman cheating on my sister?"

"Oh, man." He turns toward his truck, clearly upset he's said the wrong thing. I rush behind, demanding details, but he changes his tone, insisting he may have gotten it wrong.

"Maybe so, but I need to hear it anyway." I lean against the truck to stop him from opening the door. "Fisher, please. This is my sister we're talking about."

He shifts his weight, as if unsure.

"Think how you'd feel if it were Finn."

This gets him, and after a pause, he spills. "I don't know how to say it, Lovey. Yes. Whitman cheats. All the time. Brags about having a girl in every town. Doesn't even try to hide it."

My stomach sinks with a sudden sickness. I have a strong urge to rush right to Bitsy and sweep her off to Arizona. Fly her far away from small-town gossip and good ol' boys who never grow up.

"Are you really surprised? Whitman's always been a cheat. Far back as I can remember. It's who he is."

I'm flooded with memories of their wedding, when I caught him with one of Bitsy's bridesmaids. He was leaning in close, brushing curls from her shoulder and giving her his best come-and-get-it grin. I let him know I was on to him, and he smirked as if he didn't care. When I told Bitsy, she was in the bride's room, adjusting her veil before walking the aisle. She told me to mind my own business. Then she drew closer, with heat. *"You really can't stand for me to be happy, can you?"*

"Does Bitsy know?" My heart is pounding and I bend low, pressing my palms against the truck for support.

"How could she not?"

"Because, Fisher. The wife is always the last to know." I scowl at him, angry at every man who ever lived. *Why so many liars?* "I have to tell her."

He touches my arm and I retract. "Be careful, Lovey. She's not like you."

"That doesn't mean she wants a cheat for a husband."

Fisher holds his eyes on mine, and it's clear he doesn't see things so black and white.

"Why would anybody want that?" I'm indignant.

"Maybe she likes her life the way it is, Lovey. There are women who go along with it. Everybody gets what they want. It evens out."

"Or maybe she loves him! This isn't a game, Fisher. It's my sister's life we're talking about. And her children's."

He lets the dust settle before giving in and leaning his hand against mine.

I pull away. "You think Bitsy is happy, Fisher? Really? Look at her."

"I don't know. I'm not Bitsy. But if I were her, I wouldn't have married someone like Whitman in the first place. Don't you think she knew what she was signing up for?"

"So I guess that means you know what you're signing up for? Marrying a player like Blaire?" I let the rest go unsaid.

Fisher stays silent too, but his jaw tenses as we climb back into our seats.

I stare at the A-frame roof across the street, its stained glass windows blue and orange, a cross centered high above the door. Bitsy's wedding took place within walking distance from here in the church where we were baptized. It was an elaborate Southern affair, earning her the cover of *Mississippi* magazine. With fourteen bridesmaids and twice as many showers, the events filled an entire year: engagement teas and girls' getaways, Delta hunting trips for the guys, and equally elaborate bachelor and bachelorette parties. There was also a honey-do shower, a sip-and-see when the bridesmaids' dresses came in, even a racy boudoir shindig hosted by a few of Bitsy's more promiscuous sorority sisters.

Most considered it the wedding of the year, if not the decade, and people still compliment Mother on the flowers, the harpist, the double-decker rental that carried guests to the private reception. More than four hundred friends witnessed Bitsy and Whitman stand at the altar and vow to love one another, to preserve the holy state of matrimony, to remain loyal partners for life.

Did the words mean anything? To either of them? I don't know, but I can only assume Bitsy went into it with as much trust and love as I felt for Fisher and then for Reed. So as I stare at the stained glass windows, all I can think about is saving my sister from a liar, a cheat, and a broken heart.

TWENTY

Fisher puts the truck in gear and drives a couple of blocks to the downtown square where he parks without speaking. Then, after a longer-than-comfortable silence, he exits the truck. He is feeding loose change into the meter when I join him.

"Fisher." I touch his arm with gentle pressure. "I was way out of line. I'm sorry. You and Blaire . . . That's none of my business."

He gives me pardon, extending his elbow until I accept the offer, a kind gesture I never would have received from Reed—a man who liked to walk five, sometimes ten steps ahead of me. I weave my hand through, and we stroll arm in arm beneath the awnings, Fisher's strong bicep taut against my palm, warmth seeping through his sleeve.

"I shouldn't be shocked to learn about Whitman. Should know by now not to trust anybody."

"That's not a very Lovey thing to say."

"Yeah, well, if you'd been burned like I have, you'd understand." I keep my eyes on the storefront displays, disappearing into the brightly colored dresses, pottery made from river clay, and racks of Ole Miss merchandise.

"Maybe you'll tell me that story someday," Fisher says, not prying too much here in public, a kindness I appreciate. When I pause at Square Books, he gives me time to examine the titles. "You know what my mom says?"

I lean my head, wait for more.

"She says it's a really bad way to live when you don't trust anybody. Says it's even worse when you don't trust yourself."

I am still mulling over these words when we enter the restaurant. Finn and Alice are already seated at a table for four. They stand, each of them greeting me with hugs and kindness. The room is small and narrow, so other patrons turn to observe the commotion. A few nod hellos, but none are recognizable to me.

"Finn has been talking about you for years," Alice says warmly. "It's so nice to finally meet you."

She's an attractive woman, with girl-next-door dimples and kind brown eyes. I picture her at home tackling projects the rest of us pin on our Pinterest boards but never get around to attempting. She's the sort of person I'd want to be, if life had gone as planned.

We start with neutral topics: her children, her job teaching kindergarten. But we quickly steer into deeper waters, analyzing the gap between Oxford's haves and have-nots, discussing the current political tensions, the Confederate flag, church.

When the waiter serves our appetizers, the conversation comes to a pause for the first time. "Gosh, we've only been here twenty minutes, and we've already broken every rule of polite conversation," I tease. "Money, politics, and religion."

"Welcome home, Lovey," Finn says. "You never should have left your tribe."

"I second that." Fisher holds up his wine for a toast, and four glasses clink together, serving as our mealtime prayer. With this, we pass the string beans. They've been marinated in a vinaigrette, tossed alongside squash, eggplant, and cherry tomatoes. We pair this with a slice of garlic bread, served hot and toasty from the grill, and I top mine with a dollop of white anchovy bruschetta. The menu claims it has been combined with house chili, mint butter, and radish greens, which delivers a flavor-packed punch. I swoon. "No matter what I say, do not let me get on that plane."

"Y'all heard the lady." Fisher grants me another smile. The more we chat, the more I feel at home, and I realize how much I miss this easy banter. We fill in each other's sentences with a roundabout open flow, maintaining a casual but frantic pace. We are all laughing, talking over one another, enjoying shared portions of panzanella, when Bitsy enters the restaurant, her girl gang in tow. I smile, but she's no longer the vulnerable sister from the poolside tea party. Now she's retreated back behind her shell, hardened and closed.

The sleek, slim row of tables has provided an elegant, if not romantic setting thus far, but now it feels suffocating and small. My first instinct is to rush Bitsy into the restroom and tell her what I've learned about her cheating husband, but Fisher gives me a stark look of warning, so I bite my tongue. For now.

"Lovey? What a surprise." Bitsy eyes our foursome with suspicion but stays on her best behavior. She waves politely to friends two tables down, then greets another walking by. She seems to know everyone here, but she doesn't bother introducing me. Instead, she encourages her party to grab the back table where she'll catch up with them soon.

"How's Blaire?" she asks Fisher, then turns to put me in my place.

It almost works, until Fisher takes a shot right back. "She's great, Bitsy. How's Whitman?"

My sister plays the queen bee, answering cheerfully in true

socialite form, but her eye twitches twice. No matter how much she harms me, I don't like to think of her being hurt. All I want to do is rescue her from the fire.

"He's out of town. For work," Bitsy aims again. I show no reaction as jabs bounce like ping-pong balls across our table. Thankfully, Fisher knows my sister well enough to do the same, but this only makes her swing harder. Finally, she leans in and whispers, with a volume loud enough for all four of us to hear, "You may not know Lovey as well as you think you do, Fisher. Don't say I didn't warn you." Then she stands with a snap and moves to join her friends in the back.

"Some things never change." Finn looks to Alice, as if he'll explain later.

"Sticks and stones," Fisher adds, grabbing a second scoop of string beans. "She's just trying to stir up trouble."

I sigh, certain that's exactly what she'll do. "Blaire knows we came to dinner together. Right?"

Finn takes a bite of his entrée. Alice sips her wine. Fisher looks down at his plate. No one answers.

"She doesn't know?" This certainly flies beyond every healthy boundary I have worked so hard to maintain.

"She will now," Finn says, trying to lighten the mood.

I finish my wine in one long sip. "Maybe it's best I head home."

"Nah, Lovey. Don't let Bitsy ruin this." Fisher reaches for my hand. "We're having fun."

"It *has* been fun, so let's leave it at that." I smile but stand firm. "I'll call Uber. You should call Blaire."

Despite Fisher's protest, I pull cash from my wallet and leave my share on the table. "I insist. Otherwise people might call this a date." I give Fisher a polite but steady stare. "It's not a date."

I suffer all night, one bad dream after another. Finally, I give up and grab my laptop, hoping to get all my worries off my mind. It's not until I dive into e-mail that I remember I was supposed to call The Dragon. Between the garden and Mary Evelyn's birthday tea and the unfortunate nondate, I completely forgot about work, something I'm finding easier to do the longer I stay in Mississippi. I write myself a note and add it to my planner: *Call Dragon.* First thing in the morning, I *will* make that call.

In the meantime I draft some e-mails, confirm the script has been finalized, and send approval to the casting agent, who has done an outstanding job finding actors for the shoot. Women of all ages and ethnicities—one is pregnant and another has lost both breasts to cancer. Authenticity is what I love, showcasing the female spirit of resiliency. *Perfect!* I include in my comments. *Diverse. Modern. Effective. Strong work.*

I've marked twelve tasks off my list by the time I close my computer, a productive hour. Hopefully now I'll get some rest. I listen to my white noise app, I recite old poems, I count backward from a thousand, I sing Emmylou Harris songs. Still, sleep does not come, and I regret having slacked on my yoga routine. Clearly, it's catching up with me.

Instead of worrying over Whitman's crude behaviors and Bitsy's harsh words in the restaurant, I keep busy by sorting through an old box of photos. The snapshots offer flashbacks from simpler times. Sleepovers, living room campouts, Christmas morning mayhem, Tooth Fairy visits. There's one of Bitsy and me playing in Mother's flower garden when even the roses were young. We had threaded clover through each other's hair, wore vines of ivy around our wrists.

In every picture I'm laughing and playing and looking to Bitsy as if she were the center of my universe. In fact, she was. When I reach another first-day-of-school photo, I've had more than I can handle. How I long to find that sweet, innocent Lovey again. The one who trusted everyone, who felt loved by them too. The tender spirit incapable of hurting a fly, always swooping in to save spiders and lizards when Bitsy tried to squash them. The spunky Lovey who was content building camps and catching fish.

Where is that girl with such an open heart? And how can I bring her back to life?

While I flip through the pages, I'm realizing this album is different from the one we viewed together at the kitchen table. Here, as the years are documented, so are Bitsy's jealous side glances, noted in frame after frame when the camera's focus is on me. Is it possible my sister has always worn a mask, like Reed? Even from the start, was she happy and personable to others while secretly trying to destroy me when no one was watching?

I fumble through the images, studying her eyes, her smiles, her posture, following the timeline of our lives. Here, a nervous three-year-old Bitsy holds me in her small hands, her grin broad and proud and happy. Love exists in this smile and in the tender way she cradles me against her lap, the pink blanket tucked carefully around my newborn form. And later, at my first birthday party, when Bitsy stands beside me, teaching me how to blow out the candles and make a wish. She's sincere and helpful in her pose, no jealousy reflected at all. Again, at Christmas. I'm three; Bitsy, six. We are giddily opening a present wrapped for the two of us. We aren't fighting over the shiny strings. We don't care who gets more of the paper. We're completely absorbed in shared delight. What happened to us?

I keep moving through the years, until I stumble across one shot that changes everything. Chief took this photo. I remember the moment, a few days after Blaire Dayton moved to Oxford and called us dirty. I'm eight; Bitsy, eleven. We are in the garden with Mother, surrounded by a jungle of vibrant dahlias. I used to pretend the cupped blooms were beds for fairies and that the miniature sprites camped there, watching over us as we played. I'm taken back now, as if time is just one long drink and I can steal a swallow whenever I want.

Summer 1979

Mother reads to us from my favorite book: *Pippi Longstocking*. She pretends she's different characters and that we are all in Villa Villekulla, but we never really leave this garden.

Pippi is funny. And brave. She lives with a polka-dot horse and a monkey. Which means Pippi makes up all her own rules and doesn't let anybody tell her what to do.

I move closer to Mother as she reads about Pippi going to the circus. Bitsy sits behind her, listening even though she says this is a little-kid story. Mother promises we'll read *Anne of Green Gables* next, and this is the only reason Bitsy pays any attention. I know because she tells us so.

"'He's the strongest man in the world,'" Mother reads. "'Man, yes,' said Pippi, 'but I am the strongest girl in the world, remember that.'"

Then Mother turns to me, puts her hand on my cheek, and

says, "You're just like Pippi, aren't you, Lovey? Strongest girl in the world."

I smile big as the dahlias. It doesn't matter anymore if I ever get to go to Villa Villekulla, because now there's no other place in the world I want to be. I'll stay forever right here in my garden. With my family. At my home. Where Mother says I am the *strongest girl in the world.*

This is when Chief snaps the picture. Just when I'm glowing in my mother's bright light, absorbing all her attention and affection. But what of my sister? Still sitting in Mother's shadow, Bitsy is no longer the smiling, supportive sibling. Instead, her arms are crossed tight across her waist. Her lips are low, and she glares at me with a look that holds only hate. Could this be it? The tipping point? The moment when Bitsy first felt pushed to the side while I relished Mother's full adoration in the garden?

I leave this image and continue sorting. Sure enough, this is the place where the side stares begin. The envious slant eyes, a sign of bitter competition. Fisher was right. It all came down to Mother's affection. Bitsy wanted it all.

Is this why she blamed me for the fire? Could she really have struck the match, as Fisher suspects? Torched the gardening equipment so Mother and I could no longer enjoy working the flowers together? Could a little sibling rivalry really go this far? And if so, how has she held on to that lie all these years?

The vibrating buzz of my cell phone wakes me. Arizona. Oh no! I sit up in bed and quickly answer, pushing the stash of photos to the side. "Brynn? I'm so sorry. I'm about to call her right now."

"Too late." Brynn speaks in a tone I've never heard. "She's pulling you from Jansana."

"What?"

"I tried to tell you, Eva. She's been a ticking time bomb. As soon as I got here this morning, she stormed over and started in on me: 'This is too big a campaign to lose, Maxwell. If Eva can't commit to seeing this through, then I'll have to take it the rest of the way.'"

"This makes no sense. There's no one else with this relationship." I am pacing the floor. "What did you tell her?"

"I explained how you've been working from the road and that we have it under control. Showed her the production schedule, assured her everything is on track. She doesn't care, Eva. This is what we were afraid of."

Outside, dark clouds block the morning sun. "You did everything right, Brynn. I'm sorry I got you into this."

"I can't lose Jansana, Eva. My whole career is on the line."

"Don't worry. I'm calling now." I disconnect and make the call I should have made yesterday. If only I hadn't let small-town drama drag me away from my real life.

"Eva." The Dragon answers only after I make it through her assistant's derisive inquisition. "How's vacation?"

"I'm not on vacation. I'm keeping up with everything. I assure you, Jansana is good to go. There's absolutely no need to worry."

"But I *am* worried, Eva. You must know how much is riding on this campaign."

"I do know, absolutely, which is why Brynn and I have made this project our top priority for more than ten months." I stand at the end of my dresser where framed childhood photos observe the scene. What would that innocent little Lovey think of me now? Going head-to-head with a dragon.

"Top priority? If that were the case, you'd be here working on it in person. This is unprofessional. And unacceptable."

"Did something happen? A complaint or concern? Anything?"

"No, but that's what I'm trying to prevent. You understand."

"Honestly, no, I don't understand. Jansana is my primary focus. I assure you I am not going to drop a ball."

"I've got a lot on my plate. The last thing I want to do is take on a client my team should be able to handle. But let's shoot straight here, woman to woman. You and I both know you can't manage this properly from . . . Where did you say you were again?"

"Mississippi."

She sighs. "You've got twenty-four hours. If I don't see you in this office tomorrow, Jansana is mine. And I don't have to tell you what is happening to people who aren't pulling their weight around here."

The phone disconnects before I can respond, and I feel as if I've been talking to Bitsy. The only difference is, with The Dragon, the stakes are much higher than a wounded ego or a soiled reputation. This woman controls my career, my financial security, my retirement plan . . . my future. I no longer have the option to stay here at the farm. I need to leave Oxford, return to Phoenix, and manage this account the way I've been hired to do.

TWENTY-ONE

From the kitchen I spy my parents on the front-porch swing. Manning sleeps at Chief's feet, his heavy body spread wide against the wooden slats, his breathing lazy and loud. Mother's head is resting on my father's shoulder. With a slow, soothing rhythm, they sway in peaceful silence, hand in hand, watching the sun rise over the pasture as Dolly P. curls in Mother's lap. The lambs are chasing each other around the pond while the ewes circle the trough of fresh hay. All is idyllic here in this world my parents have built for one another. For Bitsy and for me. How can I tell them I'm leaving for Arizona?

A knot in my gut, I make my way onto the porch. Mother has been so happy with us here together. Chief has appreciated the help with the memory garden. And I, too, have experienced my own healing from this unexpected homecoming. A huge part of me doesn't want to return to Phoenix at all, doesn't want to run away again. But I am no longer a child. I have to go back to my real life, finish the job I started, and move into the next phase of my journey. It's called growing up.

My parents both greet me, doling out their full attention. "We were just thinking we'd like to learn yoga," Chief says.

"Seniors at Sunrise," Mother adds with a wink. "Mississippi Edition."

"Seriously?"

When they nod, I'm elated, letting go of every other worry for the time being. I grab some blankets and spread them across the grass, eager to share this part of my life, grateful they're game.

"Go easy on me now." Chief seems intimidated, surprising from a man who held a record-setting passing streak at Ole Miss, excelled in the NFL, and still maintains this farm independently.

Mother stands beside him. "We've never done this, you know."

I ease their fears, starting by teaching them a bit about breath control. In the background a gun enthusiast is shooting off what sounds loud enough to be a cannon, and yet my parents never flinch. The explosions would terrify my Sedona friends, but in these parts, it's par for the course. Thankfully, the birdsong helps to counter it.

"We'll learn some basic positions," I explain, beginning with an easy cross-legged pose for Mother while Chief opts to leave his legs outstretched. I model a basic inhale as we roll our shoulders up and back, expanding the chest to open the lungs. Then we exhale, letting our shoulders sink down, pressing forward again to release the breath.

We stretch the neck, shaking the head slowly with exaggerated yes nods and then a few shakes of no. I help Chief lift his chest to find better alignment, praising Mother for her excellent posture.

As they straighten their sternums, I cue them to pull their belly in to meet the spine, holding their palms together at the chest before pressing them overhead, then down and around, inhaling and exhaling with each full extension and rotation.

We continue through a beginner's session, twisting the

torso, stretching the spine, strengthening the core until they feel comfortable with the basics: tabletop, cat pose, cow pose. Then I challenge them by diving into puppy and downward dog. Chief struggles with these, as well as the forward fold, so he is relieved when we move up to mountain pose, where we focus on rooting down to the earth and rising up to the sun. When we strike volcano, lifting our arms to an upward V above our heads, I'm reminded of Brynn and our power stance back at Apogee, but I push those thoughts aside and try to stay right here in this beautiful moment with my parents.

"Remember to breathe." I exaggerate my inhale and exhale as we rotate through warrior I and warrior II. Chief insists he can handle both, despite his tricky knee, but I keep the hold brief, just in case. Finally, we wind down with a relaxing child's pose, where we focus on a few final moments of meditation.

Regardless of gunshots and nearby farm equipment, my parents stay focused. It's bound to be one of the most peaceful moments we've ever shared. That's the paradox, isn't it? I can stay here and actually live the life I am trying to sell to the world. Or I can go back to Arizona, sit in my cubicle, stare at a computer screen, and produce a campaign that encourages *other* people to live the very lifestyle I'm experiencing right here and now without a single Jansana product in sight.

I teach my parents another bit of lingo as I end the session with a bow of honor. "Namaste. The light in me sees the light in you."

"Namaste." Mother nods toward each of us reverently. "I like that. I don't know why I've never tried this, Lovey. I could definitely start my mornings like this. You should move home, teach all our friends. They'd love it."

"You think?"

"Found muscles I never knew I had." Chief holds his chin high and proud.

The three of us rest now beneath the trees, the morning breeze cool against our skin, the hollow thrums of yellow-bellied sapsuckers and redheaded woodpeckers echoing out between trees. "You really should consider the idea, Lovey. You could live here at the house, take over the farm. Build that flower business you always talked about when you were younger."

"The flower farm?" I recall my childhood dream. "You remember that?"

"Sure I do," Mother says. "You had a whole notebook with plans and price lists. Just like your father with all his goals. Truth be told, I always hoped you'd grow up and do it." She smiles, then laughs a little. "Kind of selfish on my part, I guess. But I thought it'd be fun."

"You never told me that." *How might my life be now if she had?*

Before we can discuss this idea any further, Bitsy arrives, staring with puzzlement as she drives up the lane. It's clear she's trying to figure out why we're sitting on blankets in the middle of the yard like schoolkids.

"What on earth?" she yells from beneath the shagbark hickory, already agitated as she exits the vehicle and darts our way.

"There goes our moment of Zen." I laugh, but it's true. As soon as Bitsy arrives, the energy shifts. I now understand what Marian says about positive and negative forces, how every living being emits a charge and how our own state of mind can be altered by those we allow close to us. *"Surround yourself with positivity."* That's what Marian teaches. Another of her mantras is, *"Find positive people and think positive thoughts. Then you will do positive things."* I imagine Marian would say Bitsy is a squall of negativity and that I would be wise to keep my distance, kin or not.

As I watch Bitsy race toward us, anger brewing within her, my instinct is to flee the storm, find shelter. Especially after her rude behavior last night at the restaurant. But instead, I consider what Pippi might do. I choose to stay. I stand and offer my sister a hug, hoping we can start anew today. She rejects the offer, of course, but I won't let her negative vibe sink me.

"You just missed our first yoga class." Mother helps me gather the blankets.

"Yoga?" Bitsy's eyes dart anxiously despite the frail smile she holds in place. "I thought you didn't believe in all that stuff, Mother. You've said it before. How you don't understand why Lovey got sucked into all this New Age nonsense."

I laugh. Surprisingly, Mother does the same.

"It's not like we're out here doing devil worship, Bitsy. You can calm down. Can't be all that different from your Barre class, I'm sure."

Finally! Mother stands up to Bitsy. I help Chief to his feet, and he hands me his blanket. Then he puts his arm around my sister and says, "What d'ya say we grab some breakfast?"

We all agree, making our way to the kitchen while a familiar whitetail returns to the strawberry trellis, nibbling her own morning feast. Manning doesn't even bother barking. According to Mother this deer has been a daily visitor for two years running and has become the lab's loyal friend—a good reminder that there is more to life than Jansana or Apogee or The Dragon's dreadful demands. And yet I have responsibilities I can no longer ignore. I have to tell my parents about work. No more dancing around it.

"I've really enjoyed being home with y'all." I crack eight eggs into a bowl while Mother mixes flour and milk for a batch of biscuits. I don't know how to tell them I've booked a flight for this afternoon.

"I do wish you'd move back to the farm, Lovey." My mother leans near and kisses my shoulder, both her hands covered in sticky dough.

"Me too," Chief says, pouring water for a fresh pot of coffee.

Bitsy sets the table and stays silent.

"Well, actually, that's something I need to talk to y'all about. I spoke with my boss this morning. Seems I need to fly back sooner than expected."

"How much sooner?" Mother's blue eyes are fixed on me, causing my stomach to churn.

"Today."

Chief hits the brew button and turns my way. "What are you saying, Eva?"

Ugh. He's using my real name again.

"You can't just up and leave," Mother argues.

I sprinkle some cheese and pepper into the eggs, saving the salt for after they've been scrambled. "It's this Jansana campaign I told you about. I've got a new boss, and she's threatening to pull the account from me if I'm not back in the office by tomorrow. That's bad enough as it is, but she'd likely pull it from my partner too. Even if I chose to suffer the consequences, I can't let Brynn pay the price."

Mother shakes her head in protest. "You're telling us you're flying back to Arizona? Today?" Her voice is tight. So much for the yoga-inspired calm and all that positive energy.

"Listen, Mother. I want to be here. More than you know. But I can't win. Either way I'm letting someone down. If I stay, I could lose my job. And without this deal, I may never have the financial freedom to retire."

My argument doesn't seem to sink in. She lifts her hands in the air, upset, and I'm at my end. "Honestly, Mother. Don't you think you're being a bit unreasonable?"

She stares as if I'm speaking a different language, making no sense. It's yet another moment when she seems completely incapable of seeing things from my perspective. "You know what?" I set the whisk down. "You and Bitsy have no clue what it's like for me. You've never had to make it a single day on your own."

Their glares burn through me, and Chief jumps to their defense, giving me a gruff, "Hey, now," but I don't back down.

"Not to mention you've all got the flexibility to travel anytime you want. When's the last time any of you came to visit me in Arizona?"

No one says a word. They all know it's been years, and they know there's no excuse for it either.

"To be frank, I don't think it's fair. I don't ask a thing from any of you, but you act as if I'm doing something wrong because I'm not living solely to serve y'all. I tried to tell you it wasn't a good time for me to visit. I dropped everything to fly here without any notice, but now I've got to go back to Arizona whether you like it or not. I'm sorry, but I've got a job to do. You're more than welcome to fly back with me."

This leaves my entire family speechless. Bitsy stares at me with what could almost be described as a smile, knowing I have once again become the source of disappointment and she can now return to being the favored child.

Chief gives Mother a concerned look. "Sit down," he says, with a voice so authoritative no one dares question him. When I hesitate, he says it again, even louder. I leave the eggs half whisked in the bowl, and Mother moves to wash her hands, the sticky ball of dough unfinished on the bread board. She carries the hand towel with her as we gather around the table, the sound of chairs sliding across the wool rug loud as thunder. Chief has taken charge, and we do as commanded, despite the buzz in my ear telling me to run.

"Lovey, I know you think we're being too demanding." His tone is serious, too serious. "But there's something you don't understand."

Mother locks her hand in Chief's now, her eyes on him too. They glaze as he lowers his voice. "Last month your mother was diagnosed with late-stage esophageal cancer."

My neck tenses, and my voice fails me.

Mother forces a smile, her pale eyes suddenly tired and sad.

"Did you know this?" I question Bitsy. She shakes her head but reveals zero emotions. None.

"We wanted to wait and tell you both after the party," Chief explains.

Mother takes over. "I knew things would change once we told you. I wanted to enjoy a happy stretch of time with my girls while I was still healthy enough to do so."

"Still healthy?" I ask. "What do you mean?"

She sits straighter, her head held high now with a resiliency that both inspires and dismays me. "I'm saying I refuse to give this disease a single day more than I have to."

I shoot questions like arrows, fast and straight. "What's the prognosis? How long have you known? Is this why you haven't been eating?"

"It's not good," Chief says, a crack in his voice. "Stage four. It's already metastasized."

My fists clench with worry, and my jaw barely bends at the hinge. "You can beat it. Right? What's the plan?"

She shakes her head. "I've decided not to fight it." Mother stays calm, her mind already made up.

"Not fight it?" I turn to Bitsy for backup, but she is stone-faced. Stares at the floor.

"I've watched too many friends go down that road," Mother says. "They end up in so much pain, withering away with tubes and treatments. It's not how I want to leave this world."

"Well, that's not an option," I argue, a bold defiance. "You have to fight it. Look at all the people who *are* able to get well. You could go into remission, gain years of time. You have to try."

Mother smiles and rubs my hand. "It's okay, Lovey. I understand. But please put yourself in my position. The doctors say there is less than a 10 percent chance I could beat this, and even then, it's unlikely I'd stay healthy for more than a year. Two at most. I'd rather spend the last few months doing all the things I love with the people I love. Not wasting it in doctors' offices and hospital rooms. It's not my nature."

"But the cancer will make you sick too, Mother. There's no avoiding that."

"True, but I don't want to fight the tides. And I surely don't want to lose my hair. Nothing good ever comes from that." She laughs, giving us her best Dolly Parton accent as she references her vanity.

"I can't believe you're making a joke of this." I look at Chief. "It's not funny."

He nods.

"We need to get a second opinion." I continue my charge. "And a third. I know a natural medicine expert out in Sedona. She's supposedly healed a lot of people, people who had been told there were no other options. I'll call her. We can go today."

"We've already done all that," Chief says. "It is what it is."

Mother looks at me with sad eyes. "This must be very hard for you girls. I'm sorry. I remember when my mother died. There's no easy way to handle it."

I wipe my eyes, determined not to cry. Not to accept this. Chief takes one of my hands in his. Mother takes the other. Bitsy stays distant, but Mother pulls her hand in too, joining the four of us together.

"We don't have a lot of time left," Mother says. "So I am begging you, please don't waste another second. I can't leave my family fractured. I won't."

It's all I can do not to sob, but I give Mother the smile she craves, a weak but honest longing to please her. Bitsy keeps her gaze on the table. I'm not sure she's heard a word.

"Promise?" Mother challenges us both, tugging our hands and demanding a response.

We nod, each of us in our own time, and Mother sighs in relief. "Family First."

There is a hum between us, a buzz of hope, and I want to believe that if we stick together, just like this, we can heal Mother. We can heal us all.

TWENTY-TWO

If I want to save my career, I should be packing my bags and heading to the Memphis airport before lunch. Instead, I'm walking out to the memory garden in search of Fisher. When his ball cap appears above a leafy althea, my entire body steadies. He smiles when he sees me climbing to the hillside garden where he works.

"Morning," I say, my voice still tight with fear from the news of Mother's diagnosis.

"Didn't know if you'd be talking to me today." Fisher speaks from the ground where he transplants a butterfly bush from a friend's backyard, a "pass-along," in Mother's terms. Then he injects an awful British accent: "One must first reach down if he wants to rise up." He covers the base with soil, then mulch, before finally standing to greet me. "I didn't make that up," he confesses. "Just like to sound smart is all." Then his eyes open wider with concern. "What's wrong, Lovey?"

Three workers are within earshot, and I need to keep this conversation private. "Can we talk?" I look toward his truck, and he gets the hint.

Without resisting I let him take us for a drive. He heads back toward the pine flats while I sit quietly in the passenger seat, eyeing parcels that have been stripped bare by a recent tornado. Fisher doesn't rush me. Instead, he keeps the radio off and winds us along the rural back roads while I sort my thoughts. Blacktop gives way to gravel, from which a myriad of red-dirt routes branch out. They're built for powerful pickup trucks and off-road four-wheelers, but the only visible tracks I spot are from the deer, coyote, and dogs who follow the moonlit paths at night.

The road curves beside old slave cemeteries and generational family lands where stories of moonshine outlaws and Union troops still move through the pines. Every acre carries a secret, every homestead hides a shame. Fisher drives and I stare out the window. Despite her scars, I drink Mississippi in like a long, cold sip of something sweet and familiar. I ran away from this place as fast as my feet could take me, and now all I want in the world is to call her home again. To go back and gather all those lost years, spend them here with my mother.

Fisher's steady patience brings me a sense of peace. Reminds me of a phrase Mother used to say: *"Only those who love you most can hear you when you're quiet."*

"Mother has cancer." I say this plainly, half-numb from the shock of it all. "Chief told us this morning. Says it's too far along to fight. She's refusing treatment."

"You mean no chemo? Radiation?"

I shake my head. "Nothing. Plans to make the best of the time she has left."

"How much time?"

"Not much, it seems." I stare out at the fields where Fisher, Finn, and I used to ride three-wheelers before they were deemed illegal. I still wear an oval scar on my leg from the scorching muffler. "That's why they wanted me home. I knew something wasn't right."

Fisher listens with an empathy reserved for the most genuine of hearts, his deep-blue eyes solemn and sincere. "It's good you're home, Lovey. She needs you here."

"I'm not ready for this. I can't . . . I can't lose her."

As much as I want to release the hurt, I don't dare cry. That would make it all too real. "I also have this situation with work." I clench my teeth, steel my voice. "I need to fly back today or I could lose my job. Lose everything, really. Not that any of that matters anymore."

We pass a few tree stands and corn plots before Fisher parks the truck in the drive of a private hunting lease. Bright-orange *No Trespassing* signs dot the oaks and a pipe gate shields the ATV trail. He lowers the windows, cuts the engine, turns my way. It's not our property, but we sit here anyway, surrounded by towering trees and the never-ending songs of nature.

All of a sudden I'm drenched with a deep and intense rush of fear. *My mother is leaving me. I will be alone in this great, big, terrifying world.* My breath becomes fast and heavy, my heart races. "I can't do this. I can't."

Fisher puts his hand on my knee, pressing his palm soft against my jeans. "I'm with you," he says, holding steady until I finally settle. When he offers a long, true gaze of compassion, my heart cracks open, and an ancient love comes spilling through. "I'm sorry I said no, Fisher. I'm sorry I left, all those years ago. Why did I run? Why'd I leave everyone who loves me?"

He leans near, sliding across the bench seat. "You broke my heart, you know?"

I don't respond, but I do know.

"I mean, I understood. You had some sorting out to do." His words are measured, careful, and kind. "But I couldn't chase you,

Lovey. No matter how much I wanted to. I had Finn here, and Mama. I couldn't leave."

"You considered it?"

"Are you kidding?" He draws back and I lift my head.

Our eyes stay focused on each other, and I almost think he'll kiss me. So I turn away. "What happened to me, Fisher? How do I find my way back?"

"Maybe that's what you're doing." He moves to hold my hand, and I feel a healing begin within me, all the way down to my deepest wound. He shifts to his British accent again, quoting gardening lore as a nod to Mother's quirky habit: "Maybe you're finally realizing where your roots should be planted."

My breathing slows, and it's a relief to feel the light break through. "That's what we say in yoga. Root down to rise up."

"I know you've got a whole big life out there in Arizona. But there's a whole big life right here for you too. All you have to do is say you want it."

As we drive back to the farm, I stay on my side of the seat, asking Fisher to fill me in on his relationship with Blaire. "It's not what you think," he explains. "It's not what anybody thinks."

"Say more, please." A long pause fills the air, and I sense he is hiding something. "What is it? Full Monty here, Fisher."

"You really want to know the truth?"

"Nothing less." I hold eye contact.

"Okay." He sighs. "I honestly never pictured my life without you, Lovey. When you left, it . . . it broke me. Really broke me."

"You don't look broken to me."

He sighs again, shrugs. "I've found a way to get by. But . . . you know."

When I wait for more, he continues. "I go to work. I go home. Rise, rinse, and repeat. Finn's got this great wife, kids. And I'm just the fun uncle who never settled down."

"The last thing I ever wanted to do was hurt you, Fisher."

"I know." His voice is heavy, and I wish so badly I could go back, make different choices.

"It had nothing to do with you. You understand? I was suffocating in Bitsy's shadow. And the whole issue with the fire. Felt like there wasn't any room for me here."

"I get that now, I do. But . . ."

"But what?"

"It's been a long road is all. When my dad left . . . It took a lot for me to give marriage a shot."

I nod, and my heart hurts from such knowing.

"You were the one thing I believed in, Lovey. And then you bailed too."

He doesn't have to remind me how much he suffered when his father left. I walked it with him, watching both brothers wrecked by their father's rejection, the crippling damage of feeling unloved, unwanted by the man they loved most. The futile struggle of trying to keep their mother happy once her heart had been destroyed. The childhood trauma that made them tougher than they should have been—old souls.

"We were so young, Fisher. I figured you'd move on, be happier without me. I couldn't see."

"Well, I could see it all, but you wouldn't listen."

"Never would listen to anyone. Too stubborn for my own good."

He laughs. "True."

I fidget with the armrest, then the glove box, anything to avoid the facts. "You really haven't loved anyone else?"

He stays quiet.

I lean against the window, looking his way. "Blaire?"

He turns toward the woods. "She's just somebody to hold, Lovey. And I'm the same for her." He stutters through the next attempt. "We . . . I guess we got tired of doing life solo, and we don't mind each other's company. But it's not a thing, not really. It's just . . . I don't know what to call it."

"I'd like to hear Blaire's version of the story."

He looks me straight in the eye. "She'll tell you the same."

"Then why is she talking marriage?"

"I don't know. I think . . . I guess she's giving up on finding the life she wanted. She's not a bad person. She's just lonely is all. We both are."

These words spin around us, between us. How do I tell him I've been lonely too? Outside, the wind picks up and the taller trees bow to the breeze. "So is that the plan? Marry Blaire?" My throat tightens through this sentence, and a fog of defeat weighs heavy on my bones.

"No." He hesitates. "I mean, she wants to, I guess."

"*She* wants? What about you?"

"No."

He can tell I'm not buying this. "I'm not lying."

Another awkward pause.

"Look, I'd do anything for Blaire. But . . . life just put us together is all. And, well, maybe now life is telling us it's got a better idea."

"Yes, I understand." I can barely say a word between The Dragon's accusations from the other end of the phone. She's trying to upset me, put me into an emotional spin so she can say I'm unable to handle the Jansana campaign. But I'm no longer the naive girl I was before the Reed Incident. I see right through the players of the world now, and their moves are all the same. I stay calm and deliver the facts. "My mother has been diagnosed with late-stage cancer, and I will not leave her." I put her own tactics to work for me here, ending with an authoritative, "You understand."

"That *is* unfortunate," she says, not an empathetic note to be heard.

I move around the house, listening to The Dragon roar. With phone in hand, I straighten Mother's sheet music and cap the pen she's left unopened near her crossword puzzle. Anything to take my mind away from the devastating prognosis as I try my best to focus on work.

"I do believe it would be wrong to remove me from the campaign, but you're the boss."

"I'm glad you understand these decisions weigh heavy on me, Eva. They do."

"Of course." I tread cautiously. "My concern is that Brynn and I have developed strong relationships with The Trio. They trust us. Changing that dynamic at this stage could jeopardize the deal."

"But you aren't here to maintain that relationship. That's the problem, you see?"

As I've learned from a life with Bitsy, I don't react.

"I have to look out for the firm as a whole. Jansana is our top client. We can't take any risks. So in light of the current situation, I have no choice but to step in."

"And I have no choice but to accept your decision, but as you've said, with the layoffs and restructuring, Apogee is unstable. Our clients sense this, and they've been paying close attention. I imagine The Trio would appreciate some consistency, to settle any uncertainties they may be having about the partnership."

"What are you saying, Eva? Spit it out."

"If I'm off the project, then Brynn should take the lead. The Trio would feel less rattled if they keep at least one of us on the campaign."

She hesitates, then adjusts to maintain power. "Of course I'll leave Brynn on the team, but I'll take the helm. She's far too young to handle this."

Pressure builds against my ribs, and I am careful to slow my next inhale. "So that's it then? Brynn and I spend almost a year on this campaign. We bring in the biggest client of the year. We scramble to push a rushed production through at the last minute. And then you step in and take over at the end. Just like that?"

"Don't get emotional, Eva. It's beneath you. Go take care of your mother."

I find Mother in the garden, deadheading roses while Dolly P. and Manning rest at her feet. Like the dogs, I too long to be near her, so we work close together, capturing fragrant petals in a bowl for potpourri.

"We need to show Mary Evelyn how to do this," I say. "Thank goodness Bitsy nixed their plans for camp. So glad they'll be here all summer." Then I tell her what she's longing to hear. "I canceled my flight."

Mother looks at me, holds her breath.

"I'm staying." I smile.

She exhales, grabbing me with renewed strength as she pulls me into a long, tight hug. "You don't know what this means to me, Lovey. You don't know."

I may not know how my mother feels as she clings to me in the rose garden, fully aware that her own final breath is coming due. But I do know one thing. I know, without a doubt, I have made the right decision by leaving The Dragon to her lair and keeping my feet planted close to home. If there's one thing I have done right in my life, it is this.

I open the mailbox and am surprised to find a letter from Arizona. Marian's handwriting is slanted, indicative of left-handers who were forced to adapt to the right-handed tools of that generation. One thought of Marian, and I'm back in Sedona, soaking up the desert sun.

May 15, 2016

"Morning!" Marian parks her bike and joins me in the herb garden. Without hesitation she kneels to help me work. "I'm on the search for a rental home. Know of anything? Something near the trails."

"You're moving?"

"No. I'm opening a studio." She begins to pull weeds. "A simple place for yoga. The arts. I'll need a partner. You interested?"

I look up from planting basil, assuming she's joking.

"There's only one kink," she says, steady as ever. "I don't want to charge for the classes."

"No fees?"

"None at all." She looks up to make it clear there's no changing her mind.

I pat fresh soil around the base of the basil and grab a second batch from the pots. "How would you afford the property if you don't charge your clients?"

She shrugs as if it's a minor detail. It isn't.

"Maybe there are grants available, private donors. What's the hook we could use to get funding? Sell me on this."

"The hook is that I don't believe our modern approach is working." Marian turns her attention to the thyme. "We go about everything in the most unnatural way. Childbirth, food, medicine, even death. Nothing makes sense anymore."

I nod. "You've got a point."

"We need to get back to the natural order of things, when elders would guide us through the healing."

"Elders? You mean the elderly?"

"A bit more complex than that. Not all elderly are equipped to be elders. Some have never managed to mature, despite their age."

"So you want to partner qualified senior mentors with younger people who are in need of direction?"

"Exactly." She smiles. "A way to pass on wisdom learned from life. Think about it. Rehab, therapy, prison. We convince people they are broken, unworthy. We cut them off and tell them they have to find a way to fix themselves before they can come back and be a functional part of society. But that's when they need community support the most."

"So what's the answer? Therapy?"

"I'm not sure that works either. If all we do is talk about our pain, we keep reliving the same moment, often becoming more traumatized with each repetition. We have to do more than just talk about *what* we are feeling. We have to examine *why* those emotions keep rising."

"And you think elders are the answer?" My brows are pinched.

"In most cases we just need someone to believe us. To care. I see so many broken people today. Lost souls everywhere."

When Marian asks if I know anyone who fits this description, I don't mention Reed. Instead, I describe my struggle to maintain peace with Bitsy. "I'm not saying she's a lost soul. I'm just not sure how to reach her."

"Big sisters think they know everything, don't they? I had one too. Never could do right in her eyes." Marian looks toward the layer of white-gray clouds in the distance. They are growing darker, signaling a rare midmorning storm. "But you know what? I'd give anything to have another day with her. Even just one more day."

Marian's advice comes back to me now as I read her letter. It's a brief note, with thoughtful updates about our yoga class, my Sedona garden, the unusual weather. Apparently, she's still on the search for studio property, and she tells me to hurry home so I can help her turn her ideas into an actual retreat center.

I'm brainstorming funding options for Marian's studio when Bitsy meets me in the yard. "The kids are ready to go. We've been looking for you everywhere."

"Just checking the mail is all." I hand her a magazine as penance, and she opens the new edition of *Garden & Gun*. "Bitsy, don't you think Mother should get another opinion?"

"It's her choice." She keeps her gaze on the page. I might as well be talking to the pecan tree beside us.

"She should at least give treatment a try, don't you think?"

"You just can't stand not to have control of the situation." She moves toward the house. I follow.

"You have to stop attacking me at every turn."

"Attacking you? Please." She rolls her eyes, sneers. "You've always loved to play the victim."

"What is it, Bitsy? Why are you so angry?"

"Me? Seriously? You're the one who is angry," she snaps. "Listen to yourself."

"I can't even talk to you," I say, frustrated. "Everybody else gets nice, happy Bitsy. I get this."

She stares at me with heavy lids. "Poor you." Hate. Pure hate.

"Don't you think you're being impossible? One minute you act like I'm a villain, and the next you accuse me of playing a victim. Truth is, I'm neither. I'm just trying to help our family reunite before it's too late. And I can't do this on my own." I block the front door, holding the knob. "You may not love me, Bitsy, but I know you love Mother. Let's call a truce while she's still with us. Then you can do whatever you choose." I extend my hand, hoping to find common ground. "Deal?"

She holds tight to the magazine. "Fine. But don't think for a second this means I've forgiven you."

"Forgiven me? For what?"

She rolls her eyes and opens the door, once again leaving all the blame on me.

"Can't believe it's already June," Mother says, blotting her lipstick as Chief drives. It's been five days since I learned of Mother's cancer, and I still can't process this new reality. When I try to care for her, she resists. When I question the diagnosis, she changes the subject. When I give her names of specialists or links to research studies, she shrugs it off as if there's no hope for recovery. She's made it clear she will not spend one ounce of energy discussing her health. So we skirt the subject as if it's a big, deep ravine between us.

Since the original road trip was delayed, Chief now drives us forty miles east of Oxford to the place where William Faulkner was born. "Twenty years since I've been to this town and hardly anything has changed." I look out the window as we enter New Albany.

"Well, they converted the railroad into a bike trail." Chief slows his speed as we reach the downtown streets. "Forty-four miles each way. Quite a ride."

"Ninety miles?"

"Almost."

"That's nearly the distance from Phoenix to Sedona." I've driven that route each weekend for years now, but the red rock buttes are already fading in my mind. Mississippi and Arizona couldn't be more opposite, and there's no longer any doubt which one feels more like home.

We've already passed the hospital, its multilevel architecture a counterweight to the Walmart distribution complex that keeps many employed in these parts. But now that we're downtown, I'm surprised to see that cars still park in the middle lane of the road and men still pay a slim penny for a straight-blade shave. The iconic red, white, and blue poles let visitors know where to find such service, and from the looks of it, dough burgers are still a lunchtime favorite, skillet fried and sold on the cheap at a colorful cash counter. With flour mixed into the meat, the pancake-thin patties are savored for their crunchy exterior, a recipe born to stretch a poor man's dollar and one that lands the diner on Best Burger lists still today.

This picturesque community is reminiscent of *Leave It to Beaver*, and I indulge the fantasy. Today, I'll walk these quiet streets with my family, settling into the slow, simple rhythms of small-town life. If Bitsy dares to bite, I won't let her see me bleed. She can go right ahead and gnaw on my bones until her teeth fall out, but I'll never run away again.

Chief leads us over the tracks to the Union County Heritage Museum. It's a one-story brick building, with classic columns and a pair of ferns that welcome us through the wide white door. We receive warm greetings from a young woman who holds a toddler in her lap. She explains she's "just watching the desk until the director returns." When the phone rings, her child tries to take the phone, then the pen. Frazzled by the sudden chaos, the mother's eyes widen.

A nurturer by nature, Mary Evelyn wiggles her fingers and entertains the tot, drawing an appreciative smile from the mom who is struggling to jot a message.

The rest of us step into the next room to explore the collections. "Talented curator," I say, impressed with the permanent exhibit.

Trip, our history buff, heads straight for the Chickasaw display, admiring the primitive weaponry carved from stone and wood.

"I heard they may be sponsoring an atlatl contest." Mother points to the ancient spear-throwing tool with her grandson, whose curiosity is piqued.

Chief, too, leans in for a closer look. "Reminds me of that plastic thing that helps me throw Manning's tennis balls." He pulls his arm back as if slinging the tool through the air for an intense game of fetch.

"You should enter," I tell Trip. "You've got Chief's genes. Natural athlete."

Trip shrugs off the compliment, much more interested in the facts he's just read on the display. "Sold six million acres to the government?"

"Treaty of Pontotoc, 1832." Chief taps the placard, filling in the blanks. "There's a sellout in every group. All the government had to do was find the weakest link."

Trip reads the rest. "Says most ended up in Oklahoma."

Bitsy moves ahead to the textile exhibition where she examines a boll of cotton, but Trip asks at least ten more questions. "Was that when they had to walk the Trail of Tears? What if they didn't want to leave? Will they ever get their land back again?"

Chief accepts each with excitement, happy to share some local history with his grandson. The conversation circles through the story of our native tribes, the resettlement of the Chickasaw, and the wars that were fought as French and English explorers claimed new territories.

Near the center of the room, Mary Evelyn now fidgets with a light-up timeline of Union County. "Says here the Indians taught the settlers how to barbecue."

"Hmmm . . . barbecue." Bitsy shows signs of life. "Anybody hungry?"

"It's barely eleven." Mother laughs, indicating she will likely eat little again today.

I keep quiet, capturing every subtle gesture and sound Mother offers, determined not to forget a thing. After discussing a collection of primitive tools, some dating back ten thousand years, we move to a room filled with exotic animals that have been harvested from all corners of the world.

"First time I've ever seen a wild dog." I head toward the bizarre African beast and consider the roles we all play in the world—some predator, others prey.

"What *is* that thing?" Mary Evelyn follows.

"Half hyena, half wild boar?" Trip inspects the animal's strong jaws, large ears.

We're discussing taxidermy when the museum director joins us, her feet forming soft steps along the wooden hallway. With a smile ever as friendly as the young volunteer's, she explains she "had to run a box of fossils up to the school."

"We came to see the garden," Mother says. "Our daughter's down from Arizona. Can you believe she's never visited the museum?"

I shuffle with shame, offering excuses.

The director tilts her head in a way that suggests she understands. Then she gives a gentle smile. "Glad you're here."

With a graceful gait she leads us outside to the Faulkner Literary Garden. We enter through an arbor of wisteria, the branches swollen with dense interweaving, awaiting their second bloom. "We pulled this from Miss Lucy Hawthorne's place, over near Ole Miss," she explains. "Supposedly, Faulkner would stand under this exact wisteria, visiting on the porch before hunting quail on their property."

She points to the placard: *Wistaria*. "That's how Faulkner spelled it." She humbly credits the New Albany Garden Club for such detailed research and exceptional garden design. A few of their volunteers are here this morning, adding fresh mulch to the beds and clipping stalks from the irises that have already begun to fall.

One of the women chimes in, a clump of weeds in hand. "I like knowing whose yard they came from. Don't y'all?"

The others agree, noting which blooms they contributed and giving us a story with each.

"That's like your garden, Grammy. All those pass-alongs."

Mother lights up as Mary Evelyn shows such interest, and I'm charmed she still uses the affectionate term *Grammy* instead of *Grandmother* or the like.

Another volunteer works the roses. Beside her, a plaque references "Retreat" from *The Unvanquished*, mentioning "Mrs. Compson's rose cuttings wrapped in a new piece of paper in her hand."

She notices me reading the quote. "Can't you just smell the roses in that scene? Here." She holds a handful of petals out for us before she drops them into a small basket. "I add them to my bathwater."

The director smiles, then points out the pokeberry, noting it may need to be tied soon. "Isn't it interesting that Faulkner's fictional Yoknapatawpha County was centered around a town he named Jefferson? He was born right here on Jefferson Street," she says. "Forty miles from the university, just like the county seat he created for his novels."

"When we were younger, Mother would treat us to dessert if we could spell Yoknapatawpha and Mississippi." I lift my brows at the kids, a challenge.

Mary Evelyn accepts, singing the familiar childhood spell-song: *"M-I . . . Crooked-Letter-Crooked-Letter-I . . . Crooked Letter-Crooked Letter-I . . . Humpback-Humpback-I."*

"I would've failed y'all completely if I couldn't even teach you that much." Mother laughs, and the whole world lights around her.

With full-moon stepping stones drawing us through the blooms, I stop to read each inscription. Much in the way Eudora's garden has been preserved back in Jackson, this one, too, is designed to link literature to nature, inspiring us to take better notice of both. The director's enthusiasm stirs me as she notes the many plants and the novels that prompted their inclusion here.

- Lemon verbena, which Faulkner described as having an odor you could "smell alone above the smell of horses."
- Honeysuckle, which he said was the "saddest odor of all."
- Lantana, which many believe he described as a "fierce lush myriad-colored paradox."

My favorite is the Carolina jessamine, her twisted vines lining the fence like tangles. From around the bend another group of visitors arrives, and the director takes leave to greet them. As I catch up with Chief, I read a quote from *Absalom, Absalom!* It's a reference to some of the plants that have already lost their blooms: ". . . and you said North Mississippi is a little harder country than Louisiana, with dogwood and violets and the early scentless flowers, but the earth and the nights still a little cold and the hard, tight sticky buds . . . on Judas trees and beech and maple . . . you find that you have been wanting that pretty hard for some time . . ."

In his story Faulkner may have been suggesting a lustful want for the maiden Judith Sutpen, but I take it another direction. As hard as Mississippi can be, I realize now I have indeed *been wanting that pretty hard for some time.*

If only I had known to avoid the wisteria. Instead, I said no when I should have said yes; said yes when I should have said no—and that mistake has nearly choked the life from me.

With a perfect pedicure and even better posture, Bitsy walks alongside the garden's wooden fence. The pickets reach only to her hips, a modest height that would allow for neighborly conversations, and I picture my sister sharing whispers with friends as the flowers capture every secret. She's faced brutal betrayals too, and yet she's still standing. Still mothering. Still holding her own. With such confident ease, perhaps Bitsy has now become the *"strongest girl in the world."*

Chief waves his hand, calling the kids to join us around the spindly redbud. "I've got a story," he says, causing Mary Evelyn to roll her eyes. "Yeah, yeah, but this is a good one."

"That's what you always say." She laughs, and Chief pretends his feelings are hurt. Then he gives a wink to his grandchildren, and they bend toward him as if he's magnetic, the same impact he had on me as a kid. Still does.

I press my hand against the trunk, allowing the bark to form a grooved impression across my palm just as my father makes his own sweet impression on our hearts.

"Some people call this the Judas tree." He lowers one of the branches.

"Like Judas Iscariot?"

Bitsy shines a proud smile at Mary Evelyn, and Trip tries to one-up her. "A traitor in every group."

"That's right, Trip." Chief seems pleased his lessons are taking root. "It wasn't an enemy who told the guards where to find Jesus. It was Judas, a man he loved and trusted."

"Yep." Bitsy says this with an intensity that suggests she knows about Whitman's affairs. I try to read her, but she shifts quickly as if I'm intruding.

My stomach clenches as Chief offers another of life's lessons: "Be careful who we trust. *And* be trustworthy in return."

"I do believe you missed your calling, Brother Sutherland." I turn my attention to a robin, try to avoid the triggers that are firing.

"Amen and hallelujah!" Trip draws me back with a high five. If Welty and Mother share the language of flowers, Trip and I must share the language of sarcasm, a bond even time and Bitsy haven't managed to break.

"Some say Judas was the worst kind of villain, but maybe it was part of the plan. You can't have the good without the bad. You see?"

Now Chief has hit a nerve. "No, I don't see." Bitsy shoots me a look of warning, but I continue. "Judas chose to torture an innocent man. A man who had done nothing but offer pure, unconditional love to people who refused to receive it."

Mother's eyes soften.

"Maybe you're right, Lovey." Chief speaks sincerely. "But Judas was human, like the rest of us."

"Oh, please. Judas knew exactly what he was doing, and he did it anyway. You think he should just wave his hands in the air and say, 'Oops! I'm only human'?"

I'm making a fool of myself in front of the kids, but Chief's story has angered me. Not one thing happened to Reed, despite all the pain he caused. No one has ever held Bitsy accountable for her lies and cruelty. Executives like The Dragon go for the jugular every day, justifying their greedy choices by saying, "It's just business." No matter how much harm these predators cause, those of us left in their wake are expected to let it go, get over it, accept they are "only human."

"You know what, Chief?" I continue. "You're right. We're all imperfect people faced with impossible choices every day. I get that. Every one of us is a messy combination of all that has happened in our lives, all the hurts and heartaches, mishaps and mistakes. But there's one big difference. Some of us choose to love in spite of it all. And some of us don't."

"You're absolutely right," Chief says. "Isn't that the point of the story?"

Mother puts her arm across my back, and Chief takes charge again, looking toward the kids to make his lesson clear. "Despite what we think of Judas, if it weren't for him, we may never have heard the story . . . the story of forgiveness. And love."

I move back into the sun. "Now you're trying to tell me Judas was the hero?"

He shrugs. "I'm just saying it's all connected. Every part has a purpose. The good, the bad, and the ugly."

TWENTY-FOUR

On the way out of the garden, Mother leans against Chief with a nurturing nudge, and I can't take my eyes off her. I try to capture the way the sun highlights her blonde tones, giving her a golden glow. I want to hold this image forever, lock down her every grace, like how her left cheek carries a row of freckles and her lips draw higher to the right when she smiles. I never want to forget the sound of her voice, gentle but steady, or the way she walks, a positive force if I ever saw one. A bit like Bitsy but with less sass, more class. Less bitter. More sweet.

How many more moments will we have? Will the years carry the sound of her laughter with them, erasing this woman who gave me entry into life? How does anyone go on without a mother? How will I?

She leans low over a patch of larkspur, says she used the fernlike greenery in her bridal bouquet.

"I ever tell you kids our wedding disaster story?" Chief steals Mary Evelyn's attention with his humor, so she scoots closer with an eager grin. "By the time it finally dawned on me that Cousin Ted wasn't gonna show up to give me a ride to the church, it was too late.

Operator tried calling everybody we knew, but they were all at the sanctuary . . . waiting on me."

Mother is laughing, soothing every cell within me. "Nearly all of Oxford was there. It was small in those days. Only person missing was the groom!"

"How'd you end up getting there?" Mary Evelyn asks, as if she, too, realizes our moments together are limited and that we can't waste a second more.

"Walked. In my suit! By the time a farmer stopped and offered me a ride, I was all hot and bothered."

"I think his name was Harold," Mother says. "I insisted he sit up front with the family. Remember?"

"You didn't know him?" Trip seems stunned.

"Oh, I'd never do a thing like that now," Chief insists.

"Never." Bitsy gives her kids a look of warning.

"So you see, the moral of the story is . . . you can't trust Cousin Ted." Mother lowers her voice to imitate the slack best man: "'No, Laurel. Haven't seen nor heard from Chief all day.'"

"He thought it'd be funny to act like I was MIA."

"Wasn't funny at all!" Mother wails. "I thought I'd been jilted. My poor daddy was storming through the pews." She imitates her father now. "'I'm gonna wring 'im by the neck!'"

"Chief?" Trip laughs, imagining his grandfather being attacked by the father of the bride.

"Wanted to kill him," Mother says. "Probably would've too, if he really had bailed on me. Daddy never would have stood for that."

Chief agrees. "Put his fist to my face and warned me that better be the last time I ever disrespect his daughter. But that wasn't the worst of it. I jumped out of that farmer's truck straight into a swarm of church ladies. And let me tell you, nothin' stings more than a bunch of angry church ladies."

Even Bitsy is laughing now.

"Oh well, I forgave you the minute I saw you." Mother steals a quick kiss.

Then Chief taps Trip's ball cap and says, "I guess the point is, if Ted hadn't made your mother fear I'd left her, she may never have appreciated the fact that I actually showed up to marry her."

"Oh, I'm not so sure about that," Mother argues. "Most of us know how to find the good. We don't need a dose of bad to make us notice it's there."

"True." Chief looks at Bitsy. "But some of us do."

After the museum visit, we place our order at the counter of Tallahatchie Gourmet, a popular blue-plate café. The small eatery is packed with bankers, lawyers, farmers, and doctors, a catchall for New Albany locals who all take time to speak to one another before finding a seat anywhere they choose. It's the way Oxford used to be, before the growth got out of control and the newcomers outnumbered us all.

The down-home vibe has us feeling sentimental, which keeps Mother talking about her wedding day. She fiddles with her new ring, the diamonds so big they'd draw the attention of a thief in any other town, as she takes us back to the day she said her vows.

"My grandmother put fresh snips of rosemary in my shoes, to bless our marriage. And then she gave me this strand of pearls, passed down for three generations before she clasped them around my neck." She strokes the heirloom necklace, explaining it was her "something old."

As a child I would fidget with it while I was in her arms, letting the soft, round pearls spin beneath my fingers. I imagine the necklace will go to Bitsy and then Mary Evelyn, which is only fair. But for today, it's still draped around Mother's neck, where I hope I'll always picture it best.

"I remember your grandma pinning the zipper on my gown. It had been fickle on her own wedding day, inching down right in the middle of the ceremony." Mother says this with stars in her eyes, as if she's been transported right back to the bridal room, feeling the dress press against her skin. "I could hear the rich, deep moans of the organ as I dressed. And then my father . . . He slipped me a handwritten note just before I was swept away by my aunts. They each added a homegrown flower to my bouquet, tied it all together with a long satin ribbon—my something blue. I also remember a *very* nervous groom." She teases Chief, then turns our way.

"I couldn't believe you were really going through with it, Laurel. But then you came down that aisle, and you looked at me as if I was your everything."

"You were." Mother places her palm against his cheek. "You are."

I stack pink packets of sugar substitute. Will anyone ever vow to love me like that? Does anything real even exist anymore? Or is all we've got now just a world of artificial sweetness?

"Remember our vows?" Chief asks. "The preacher talked about the story of Adam and Eve, how we are told that God pulled the rib from Adam's side because it shows that woman and man were made to be equal partners."

"He said Eve wasn't formed from Adam's feet to be below him

or from his head to be above him, but from his rib, to walk beside him." Mother says this while smiling. "I liked that."

"Yep." Chief nods. "And that the rib came from near his heart, so she would be loved by him, and from beneath his arms, so she would be protected by him. It was the first time I'd ever heard it told that way. Made sense. Still does."

I look at Bitsy. She turns away.

"Remember how the preacher went on about what our vows really mean? Said men have been given certain strengths to protect our families. Never to control them or harm them." He shifts to me now, then Bitsy. "It would have been easy to hurt you girls, your mother. But I can't understand why a man would ever do such a thing. And I don't have a lick of respect for one who does. Power without love? That's what you call abuse."

Silence spreads between us as I keep my eyes on the table, ashamed. How did I end up with Reed, especially after Chief and Mother gave us such a healthy model?

"You know what I remember most of all?" Chief smiles. "That first kiss."

Mother laughs as he leans in to plant another peck. "Can you believe it's been fifty years?" She turns to the kids. "One minute you think you've got your whole lives ahead, and the next thing you know, it's all behind you." She shakes her head, sighs. "Time never bothered asking my opinion."

I tinker with my hourglass charm, wishing I could capture every grain of sand before it all slides away. Wishing I could hold our mother here and never let her go. Wishing I could go back to the start and make everything right again, keep us all together, happy, safe. Unharmed.

We're barely home from New Albany when Mother declares she needs a nap. Bitsy leaves, explaining the kids have plans, and Chief heads to chair a finance meeting at church because Mother won't let him change his normal activities no matter how much he begs, always insisting, "Life must go on!"

I use the time to check in with Brynn. "Eva?" she answers with a whisper. "One sec." I hear the shuffle of papers, the slam of a drawer. Finally, a door closes. "Thank goodness you called. She's blowing it."

"What do you mean, blowing it?" I find a seat beside Dolly P. on the living room sofa, and Brynn gives me an earful.

"Jansana's president and The Dragon. They're about to draw blood."

I sigh. "Mother always said you can't have two alphas in the same pack."

"My money's on Jansana." As Brynn laughs, my imagination takes charge again. I'm sneaking through the African plains where two topi antelopes compete for a mate. Marlin Perkins narrates the battle scene, explaining this species' unusual practice of female-on-female combat. Animals, all of us.

"Is there something specific that's got them worried?"

"Film crew wasn't able to secure all the locations. We're down to the wire now. Nowhere to shoot."

"That's why I always have a plan B. Did they see the alternative locations we scouted? I made a list."

"No."

"Well, here's your chance to shine, Brynn. Present the options. Tell them there's always a solution."

"Don't you get it? The Dragon doesn't listen to a word I say."

"She will this time."

"I'm not telling them," Brynn says. "And you shouldn't either. I'd rather watch the fireworks."

"Oh, come on. Do you realize how much money is on the line?"

"Karma, baby."

"Maybe so, but I can't sit and watch a year's worth of work fall apart. I'll make some calls." Dolly P. nuzzles against me, reminding me how glad I am to be home. "Anything else?"

"No, but seriously, Eva. I'm just not sure it's going to work even with your backup plan. We don't even know if we can lock down those locations now. There's only so much we can do. Besides, you're off the project. No contact, remember? If you interfere, you could cost us both our jobs."

"Think about it, Brynn. If this campaign fails, there's no way The Dragon would ever take the fall. Besides, I want these ads to hit the air. We've earned that at least."

We end the call with Brynn promising to present the list of alternative locations and keep me posted on the progress. Then I head to my room. I haven't had much time to myself since I arrived, and I agreed to help Chief polish his toast for the anniversary party. With his notes in hand, I get to work, shortening sentences and reorganizing his thoughtful words about Mother. I'm almost done when Fisher's truck drives within view. One look and I'm back at the Sedona medicine wheel, trying to heal my wounds.

May 14, 2016

I'm speaking as if we are in a private therapy room and not on an open mountain trail. Somehow Marian has lowered my defenses, guiding me with patient prompts, helping me process a lifetime of pain.

"Now, let's leave that younger Eva in the past. Imagine yourself five years from now. A future Eva, a more mature and healthy version. Tell me, what do you see?"

"This part is easy." I smile with relief. "Retired. Living here in Sedona. Teaching yoga. Not wasting another day in the office."

"And who will be with you here, in five years? When you retire?"

I draw a blank.

"So . . ." She holds the pause long. "You plan to live here alone?"

"Why not?" I stiffen. "You do."

"I'm ninety, Eva." She speaks with kindness, no critical tone at all.

"Yeah, but you were, what, seventy when Alton died?"

"That doesn't mean I've spent the last twenty years alone. I know what it's like to choose the wrong man too." When I lift my brows, she stands firm, making it clear we're here for my story, not her own. "I'm content now, but being alone is not for everyone. We're not solitary animals, Eva. It can wear on a soul."

There's so much I want to say to comfort her, but she speaks first. "Tell me this. What did Reed do that keeps you living in fear?"

My throat tightens. When Marian presses for an answer, I fight the swell of tears, blinking before my cheeks feel the sting. Fear. The worst F-word of all.

"It's okay," she says. "This is what we're here for."

But no matter how patient Marian is with me, no matter how much I want to purge myself of Reed once and for all, I cannot bring myself to tell her what happened. Instead, I keep it locked inside.

Marian touches my shoulder again. "You've done a lot of hard work today, Eva. The wheel is here when you're ready. And so am I."

I sense I've disappointed her, which is the last thing I'd ever want to do. I can't give her what she really wants to hear, so I find something else to confess. "You know, Marian, something strange happened this morning. At the ridge."

She nods, as if she's not surprised.

"I think I may have had a vision." I feel ridiculous. *A vision? What does that even mean?* But with Marian's persistent prods, I spare no detail. I describe the grandmother, her white feathers. The final message, *I am strong*. "What do you think?"

"I think . . . you are growing." Marian puts her arm around me fully now. "Be open, Eva. The answers will come."

I find a stash of stationery and write my friend.

Dearest Marian,

Thanks for understanding my extended stay in Mississippi. No doubt, the Seniors at Sunrise are in far better hands with you.

The fiftieth anniversary party is less than two weeks away. Mother and I have been planning our floral arrangements. This seems to have turned Bitsy a deeper shade of green, but I'm glad to have the extra time with my mother.

On a side note, I've reconnected with an old friend. His name is Fisher, and I'm trying to remain "open." It's terrifying, but as you say, "Fear is the foe."

As for the retreat center, I'm honored to play any role you'll allow, and I'll do all in my power to help you accomplish your goals. Sedona had better realize what a treasure they have in you. I sure do.

Much love,

Eva

As I sign my name, I realize no one in Arizona calls me Lovey. And no one in Mississippi calls me Eva. The split hits full force. What if Reed wasn't the only one living a double life? What if I've been living a lie all along too? Have I been separated from my true self, pretending to be someone I'm not?

All these years I have worked so hard to do the right thing. Build a successful career, make good friends, buy not one but two investment homes. Live a frugal life, never asking for help from anyone. Day by day I have worked hard, with goals and to-do lists and a very specific plan, just as Chief taught me to do. But where has it gotten me? Halfway across the country in a life that's not my own. Maybe I truly have become an invasive species growing wild in foreign soil. There is only one word for such a thing. I'm a weed.

"It sure does get lonely when the sun goes down." Fisher approaches the hammock where I am lying beneath the stars. I don't get up. I'm too entranced by the sliver of the moon. Like a switchblade, its slim, sharp tip seems capable of delivering a fatal wound, and yet it lures me with a light that's not its own. The shine is a mirage, a mere reflection of the sun's generous gift, but there sits the moon, resting high in its noble position, stealing the light of another so it can offer the world what it thinks we want to see.

Fisher draws closer, so I make room and pat the hammock, inviting him onto the fabric sling. We lie opposite one another, our feet on the grass, our eyes toward the black velvet sky. It's a platonic, safe position, and yet my body reacts.

"This is nice." He lets his arm rest against mine. "Whatever this is."

"Whatever this is," I echo, hoping for answers. Above us, a canvas of constellations—each one a story reaching out across space and time. "You worked late today."

"Trying to get that garden wrapped up in time for the party. Think your mother has caught on?"

"Don't worry. She won't blow it for herself."

He gives the hammock a nudge, and we sway, slowly, as he presses his foot, straightens his knee, bends again, repeats. "We've still got a lot of catching up to do."

"Yeah, I'll let you go first." I watch that moon, thinking of danger.

He laughs, then whispers, "On second thought, maybe some things are better left unsaid."

His long, lean body stays close to mine, and the warmth is soothing, despite the humid summer air. Fireflies light around us, and the coyotes have begun to howl in the distant dark, a pitch-perfect pairing with the sounds of the owls. Makes me think of my elf owls back in Phoenix, and the wall of thorns around my heart.

"We could've had a good life together, Lovey."

My spirit sinks with regret. "I was scared, Fisher. Weren't you?"

"Sure, I had fears. Plenty of 'em. But never a doubt."

This brings a jolt. "Fisher, listen." I turn from the stars in the sky, trading them for the ones in his eyes. "I'm not the kind of girl who gets in the middle of another relationship. If you're dating Blaire, you're dating Blaire. Period."

"It's not that simple, Lovey."

I turn back to the moon, wishing away every sharp and dangerous thing that has ever threatened my vulnerable heart.

TWENTY-FIVE

"Happy anniversary!" Bitsy and I greet our parents with breakfast in bed—a tray of homemade waffles, poached eggs, and coffee. I give my sister credit. "Bitsy made the eggs."

"And the coffee!" She nearly yells this, and Mother startles. Then smiles.

Bitsy and I have spent the morning taking wide circles around each other's territory, like cats, maintaining the truce while under Mother's roof. Chief now pulls the serving tray into position, and Mother accepts the coffee, her favorite verse inscribed across the mug: *Perhaps this is the moment for which you have been created.*

From the foot of their bed, I press against the antique mahogany frame. Is my sister's heart responding like mine? Is she, too, swelling with gratitude that our parents share such a special bond, while at the same time grieving the fact that we were not so lucky in love? Is she thankful we have this moment together as a family, while also sad our mother's time is narrowing?

Chief slices into his buttermilk waffle, pairing it with a few mixed berries and declaring it delicious. Mother nibbles her poached egg and repeats his praise, although she coughs when she tries to swallow, reminding us all that time is not our friend.

I give them each a hug and make my way upstairs where I brush my teeth and throw on a comfortable outfit, eager to finish the floral arrangements for the party. But before heading for the barn, I accept a call from Brynn.

"She took me off the account. I'm blocked from everything." Brynn sniffles between clipped phrases.

"What in the world?" I sit on the edge of the bed. Then stand again. "She said she would leave you on it. We discussed this."

"Well, that's not what she did. I took your advice. Presented the alternate location list. But I copied The Trio on the e-mail. Figured it would help because we're so short on time. That's what set her off."

"Of course. If you'd gone straight to her, she would have presented the list to Jansana and taken credit. All would be well. She wants you to be her flying monkey."

Brynn exhales, still crying. "Said she'd handle everything moving forward. Said I'm lucky to still have a job."

It takes a lot to make me angry, but I will fight for those I love, and Brynn is like a sister to me. "Just as we feared. Now that we've got all the work done . . ."

"Yep. She'll end up with all the money too." Brynn's tone suggests I'm not the only one who is fuming. "We should talk to The Trio. Be up front."

I give it some thought. "I think it's time to take this to the next level."

"Samson? No way. He'll say we cause too much drama, turn around and give the account to a man. I'd go straight to the top. Call Mims."

Brynn doesn't realize how fiercely Apogee clings to the chain of command. "Would be a risk," I say, trying to find a better solution.

"And counting on Samson wouldn't be?"

Outside, turtles are coming out to sun near the pond, squirrels are launching their morning hunt for nuts, and birds are flying free. What I would give to escape these ridiculous problems we make for ourselves. Corporate politics, such silly games. "It's time to make a plan. Can you still access the shared work folder?"

"I've got it open now. I've already made fresh backups of everything."

"Perfect. We need to act fast. They'll slay us if they sense weakness." The more confident I sound, the steadier Brynn becomes, so I outline our strategy. "You'll have to visit the alternate locations. Work with the film crew. Do whatever it takes to secure the shoots."

"No way, Eva. If she finds out, I'm gone for good."

I let this stir for a minute. "Okay. Then we'll have to plead our case. Make a timeline. Document everything. Prove we've earned our keep. And one more thing . . . Delete the shared folder."

"Delete?"

I clear my throat, trying to convince myself this is a good idea. "If she wants the information, she can come to me. I'm done letting the bad guys win."

Brynn continues shuffling papers, stapling, clicking keys. Her voice is muffled from holding the phone in place with her shoulder. "She doesn't play by the rules, you know. This'll never work."

"Just remember, we've got one thing she hasn't got."

"Morals?"

"That too." I laugh. "But I was going to say we have each other."

It's already ten by the time I haul the wagon back to the barn, toting floral wire, foam, and tape along with me. I've already clipped

black-eyed Susans, Queen Anne's lace, and butterfly bush from Mother's gardens, dropping the longer stems into buckets of water that now slosh as I navigate the gravel path. A stash of Sweet William should make a nice contrast against the hefty boxwood clippings, and with hydrangea and ivy looped in, we should be set.

Mother has promised not to peek, so she's back at the house making centerpieces with friends from the Garden Club. They all stay a safe distance from the barn where I am now enjoying both the work and the peace.

First, I weave a simple wreath of boxwood for each barn door. Then I manipulate wire around nails, adding cuttings to create a leafy perimeter for the oversize entrance. I let the greenery hang loose, a casual swag that evokes romance and innocence, a style Mother will appreciate.

I stand back and take it in, excited to see the pieces coming together. Next, I add a layer of Queen Anne's lace, its white clusters representative of the bridal veil worn by Mother and Bitsy, never by me. I can hear Mother's voice, teaching me that the flower is considered a weed by many, but she added it to her wildflower garden intentionally. She claims it has *"a rebel heart, its snowflake appearance proof it was never meant to be a summer bloom at all."* With its dark-purple center, this renegade flower represents all things feminine: delicate lace, the symbolic purity of snow, the red stain of suffering, and the long, deep taproot that keeps her growing against all odds.

I'm attaching the final touches when the event planner arrives. Bitsy has been in charge of every detail, but she's hired this expert to make sure the party goes as planned tonight. With a classy twist of auburn hair and a practical let's-get-things-done attitude, the middle-aged woman is already on the ball, directing a delivery driver to back in near the barn. Then she instructs her crew to set out ten round tables at their designated marks, each with six seats to accommodate our guests. Two chef's tables are constructed in the corner; a family table near the front. As she sets the final prop in place, she turns my way. "Have you seen Bitsy?"

"She and Chief are running errands with the kids," I explain, grateful my father swooped in for the rescue.

"You've got the place looking good." The planner walks past the doors with impressive efficiency. "Mason jars for the vases?"

"Mother's friends are on it as we speak. Did you get the fireflies?"

"I did," she whispers, as if even the crew can't be let in on the surprise. "It's going to be magical. Promise."

For the rest of the morning, the team works to make this the most beautiful space imaginable. After draping each table in classic white linen, we secure an overlapping layer of burlap with a rugged twist of twine and ivy, a detail I've carried through to the sliding door panels as well. We set the champagne station with sparkling glass flutes and add place cards to every seat, each name hand-printed with delicate loops of black-inked calligraphy, a skill Mother taught me in middle school and one that has proven an asset more times than I can count.

A tasteful mix of vintage china and silverware is arranged at every setting, stirring memories of Sunday suppers and backyard potlucks. The chandelier is the capstone of the entire display, a handmade combination of Mason jars with holes in the lids. By the time the party starts, a company that specializes in such things will have filled each jar with a healthy stash of fireflies. If all goes as planned, the lightning bugs should begin to flash just before sunset.

"And here's the best part." The planner demonstrates how every jar in the chandelier is easily removed from its attaching hook.

"We'll be able to distribute one to each guest. Then we'll release the fireflies into the pasture. Just as you suggested."

"Wow! I was just brainstorming. I had no idea we could really make it happen. My folks are going to love this!"

"Hope so." She seems as excited as I am.

But as my fantasy becomes reality, I get a sinking feeling that I've just put hundreds of fireflies in harm's way. "It won't hurt the bugs, will it?"

"The company has a fantastic reputation. They breed them specifically for this purpose, and then they set them free."

My expression must reveal my concern because she smiles and adds, "Let's face it . . . Kids have been doing this for generations. It's all good."

By midafternoon I've added long purple trusses of butterfly bush and dotted the remaining spaces with bright-yellow black-eyed Susans.

"Goldsturm. Good choice." Fisher approaches from behind and offers me a glass of iced tea from the kitchen. I gratefully accept. "Sweet William too?" He smiles, and gosh, he is some kind of charming.

"It's kind of a sentimental thing. Mother used to tell us stories about black-eyed Susan and her one true love."

I recite a verse from the familiar childhood poem. "'Though battle call me from thy arms'"—and just like magic, Fisher chimes in, finishing the lyric with me in tandem—"'let not my pretty Susan mourn.'"

I'm speechless.

He shrugs. "What? You think men don't know poetry?"

"Um, yeah."

Laughter now. And then his confession. "All right, I admit, I had to recite it for a college class. Did a project on literature and landscaping. I wasn't too into it at the time, but apparently, it seems to have served a purpose."

Again we speak in sync: "Go figure."

"We're turning into one of those old couples who finish each other's sentences," I say.

He moves closer. I step back, regretting the word *couple* and quickly reverting to neutral turf. "Mother used to sing the poem to us when they would bloom each year. Supposedly, William returned from war to dry Susan's tears. They've bloomed together ever since, with 'a love that never ends.'" I say this with exaggerated drama, waving a handful of blooms in the air while imitating Mother's fairy-tale flair. "I hope she likes it."

Handing me a cluster of Sweet William, he nods. "That's what's so special about you, Lovey. You're always thinking of everyone else. Caring more about others—"

"Except the one time it mattered most." I lower my voice in apology.

"We were too young anyway. Can you imagine? If you had gotten married at eighteen?" He laughs. "What was I thinking?"

How can he defend me, after all the pain I've caused?

"I loved you, Fisher. Always." Now I've said too much.

He leans against the rough barn wood, giving me a blue-eyed look as long and deep as the sea. I turn away, trying to maintain a healthy boundary. "I just wasn't ready."

He pockets his hands, drawing my eyes back to him. "Are you ready now?"

Every part of my heart wants to shout, "Yes! I'm ready!" But with Blaire still in the picture, I can't allow myself this fantasy. All I can think about is the sound of Reed's wife calling me at work and the rage of Reed cursing in the background, demanding she hang up the phone. The last thing I want to do is sidetrack another couple. I can't and I won't. So I turn toward the hill and change the subject, my own little version of flight. "How's the garden? Ready for the big reveal?"

Fisher sighs but follows my lead, looking toward the area where temporary construction panels have been arranged to conceal Mother's grand surprise.

"He's such a romantic, my father."

"Yeah, he told me if I had even a lick of sense, I'd realize romance is the secret to a happy life."

I laugh. "That's Chief for you."

Off to the side, Fisher stomps clumps of dirt from his work boots. "Well, they've made it fifty years, so I figure he might be on to something."

"Yeah, I think Mother found herself the last real cowboy." It's an ode to the ideal American man, strong and masculine yet tender and true.

"Nah." Fisher adjusts his ball cap. "You just gotta know one when you see one."

TWENTY-SIX

By half past five, we're all dressed and ready for photos. My father's casual suit serves as a perfect match for Mother's linen dress. Mary Evelyn and Trip are tolerating the adult affair like champs. And no one outshines Bitsy. With her tightly tailored seersucker, she will surely turn heads.

"Stunning," I say, snapping photos while I stand back in my summer-gray Eileen Fisher—one of my favorites. The kids are all smiles, but Bitsy checks the clock, growing more anxious with each ticking second. She's already downed two glasses of wine, and the party doesn't start until six. Mother gives me a worried look as Bitsy pours herself a third dose of pinot.

"I'll never forgive him. Not for this." She stares out the window, but there is still no sign of her husband. I have neither seen nor heard from Whitman since Mary Evelyn's birthday party, and Bitsy's excuses have worn thin. This seems to be the final straw, and I don't blame her. Apparently, she can take a lot behind closed doors, but if there's one thing Bitsy won't tolerate, it's being humiliated in public like this.

"Don't worry. If anyone questions, we'll just tell them the

truth." I glance at the kids and hope this little white lie can serve as salve for their hurting hearts. "His flight has been delayed, and he's sorry he wasn't able to make it. We owe no one more than that."

Bitsy looks at me now with grateful relief, but the moment is brief and her eyes go cold again. She takes another sip of wine and glances out the window. "Guests are arriving."

"Ooh, we'd better hurry!" Mother cheers, as giddy as I've ever seen her.

Chief directs us all to the golf cart, a multiuse vehicle that has proven handy on the farm's rugged paths. With Bitsy's children dangling from the rear and Mother in the front beside Chief, my sister and I have no choice but to sit next to one another. Our father drives us all to the barn where guests are already parking their pickup trucks and old sedans, high-priced SUVs and luxury sports cars. The parking area alone is a representative mix of the socio-economic layers that form our town, a complicated community if ever there was one.

Chief steers around the vehicles, going off the path a bit and causing the cart to rock across the uneven gravel. The tilt draws my arm against Bitsy's, and my spirit reacts. No matter how far two siblings stray from each other, there is a bond that never breaks. I feel it now, and I sense that Bitsy does too. She resists, though, stiffening and scooting farther to the edge.

As we turn the corner, Mother becomes a ball of light. "Lovey, you have truly outdone yourself." She points out the florals at the entrance of the barn. "And, Bitsy, this setting! I never could have imagined anything so nice. This is what you were born to do, girls. How could anything be more perfect?"

I try to catch Bitsy's eye with a smile, but she heads straight for the wine bar, anxious for another sip.

Chief helps Mother from the cart and she immediately begins to greet guests. She is kind to reintroduce them to me, reviving all the hometown connections I've let fray through the years. One by one, they welcome me home, insisting this is where I belong.

There's the optimistic public librarian who came early to lend a hand, and the hilarious Wilson twins who already have everyone in stitches. The local tennis pro whose energy is contagious, and the kindhearted preacher who baptized Bitsy and me. Mother's sorority sisters, a few of Chief's football buddies, some old law partners from my father's days at the firm. The men from Coffee Club, ladies from Book Club, and loyal friends who have shared fifty years of the couples Sunday school class with my folks—even the widows and widowers remain part of the group, sticking together. My spirit is warmed by these generous servings of compassion, a community of souls who still claim me as their own.

While I'm grateful my parents have such loyal friends in their lives, I'm also ashamed these guests have spent more time with Mother and Chief than I have. Even more upsetting is they aren't yet aware of my mother's diagnosis. We're all supposed to put up a solid front, as if everything is normal. But it's not.

I'm handling the waves of emotions fairly well until Fisher and Finn arrive. While I'm pleased to see Alice, it's the first time I've seen Blaire in decades. No matter how much I try to think of her as a mature adult, all I see is the snob who stole my sister and never let go. On some level, I've always blamed her for Bitsy's change of heart, even if that's not a fair place to aim.

When Fisher reintroduces us, Blaire offers a polite hug. "I still feel like I know you, Lovey. How creepy is that?"

"Quite," Bitsy says, joining us with another glass of wine and a veneer smile. She can't even keep the peace for one night. One night! I swear I have half a mind to take her out behind the barn and tell her if she messes with me again, I'll let our guests know the truth about Whitman. Give her a dose of her own medicine for a change.

Instead, I manage an awkward grin. "Nice to see you, Blaire. It's been a long time." My stomach twists in knots. One thing's for sure. Blaire's Zumba figure explains why Fisher would consider marrying a woman he doesn't love. I could do yoga for the rest of my life and I'd still never look that good in a dress.

Thankfully, Mother steps in to save me, redirecting my attention to a friend from the florist shop, proving once again I need my mother more than I sometimes like to admit. I smile, share small talk about the flower business, and hope no one notices the sweat beading across my hairline. It's all I can do to avoid Blaire and Fisher, so I'm more than relieved when Chief clinks his fork to his glass and offers an official welcome, inviting us to follow him out for his big surprise "before night falls."

Guests gather around the viewing area, and Chief explains his plan. "Y'all know those shows on TV where they come in and do some kind of landscape project?" He winks. "Well, it's time for *the big reveal.*"

"Five, four, three . . ." Trip leads the crowd in a countdown, and the energy surges around Mother. She shuts her eyes tight while Fisher and Finn shift the wooden screens out of view. As their beautiful garden is exposed, the guests ooh and aah. I, too, am in awe. The winding path is wide enough for the golf cart, rising up the slow slope with just enough angle to give depth to the design. Along the way, specific flowers have been layered to form a sensual timeline of our family's most important memories, tracking a lifetime of lessons and love.

When Chief gives Mother the go-ahead, her eyes pop open and her hands fly to her mouth, bringing joy to everyone, cheers all around.

"You're probably thinking the last thing you need is another garden," Chief says, "but this one's a little different." Then he speaks to the crowd. "I'm betting all of you have received Laurel's 'Just Because' arrangements, maybe her centerpieces, corsages, or whatnot."

Juke shouts out, "Can't believe you know those big words, Chief!" Everyone laughs, recognizing the special friendship these men have long shared.

"If there's one thing I've learned by helping Laurel garden, it's that every seed is a story. I sure as heck can't tell one purple flower from the next, but Laurel, well, not only can she tell you its name, she can tell you when she planted it, where it came from, and how long it should bloom before the petals fade. Half her plants have been passed along for generations, many from friends—including some of you."

Mother kisses Chief on the cheek. She's what Marian would call a "bundle of positivity."

"With Lovey back in town, we've spent the last few weeks making road trips, traveling back in time a bit."

"Preach, Brother Sutherland. Preach!" Trip teases, drawing another round of laughs from the crowd. Chief gives him a playful wag of the finger, but we all know he's not in any real trouble.

"I hope you'll continue to tend this farm long after we are gone," he says to Trip. And to me. "I also hope these flowers will continue to tell our story because, when you think about it, if the story lives on, so do we."

He points out the redbud, my grandmother's hydrangea, and

the empty arch that represents the missing wisteria. He shows off a camellia room, much like Welty's. Then jasmine, gardenia, and the mock orange. The plants are numerous, the stories are too, and all lead us up to the top-level labyrinth with its symbolic spiral of stones.

At the crest of the hill, we reach the semicircular perimeter wall. A half arc, the sizable barrier has four levels, two of which are suitable for sitting. Many of the guests find a place to perch, sipping wine and enjoying the evening. I join them, settling against a section that has been shaded from the sun. Its cool stones offer comfort after a long day's work. Those who have avoided the climb can still see and hear my father clearly from barn level, so no one is left out as he explains this last section of his gift.

"I'm not nearly as good with words as Laurel is, so y'all forgive an old man for getting my daughter Lovey here to help me with this speech. She's put a little shine to it, as she likes to say, and I just hope I don't redneck it up too much. Aren't we all glad she's home again?"

More nods with kind eyes, which in turn brings warmth to my cheeks. Bitsy tilts her glass, smiling as if she's got a pouch of venom in her mouth. I don't let her sink me.

Chief gives credit to Fisher and Finn, thanking them for their work. Between the brothers, Blaire smiles. My throat tightens in response, but Chief soon brings me back to what really matters.

"Now, I'm gonna get serious for a minute here. I've got something to say to my grandchildren."

Bitsy pulls Mary Evelyn close, a gentle moment of nurturing that is not lost on me. The absence of Whitman is clear to everyone, and I, too, find it hard to forgive him. Trip fidgets off to the side, trying to play it cool, but his bottom lip is pulled sideways, between teeth, and I imagine his father's no-show is weighing heavy on his heart. When he looks my way, I cross my eyes with a silly scrunch of my face, trying to ease his hurt. It works.

"What do we see when we look at this garden?" Chief pauses, then answers his own question. "Flowers? Stems? Some leaves? That's the part we notice. But what's going on under the surface?" He keeps his focus on the kids. "We don't always see the miracles taking place around us, within us. But that doesn't mean they aren't happening."

Trip kicks at a barren plot of soil near my feet, and sure enough, the tip of a crocus bulb emerges from the soil. He quickly tucks it back beneath mulch. Lesson learned.

"There will come a time when you'll feel invisible, unseen," Chief continues. "A season when you're buried in pain, or fear. Or loss."

"But seasons change," Mother says. "And when we *are* in those dark, scary places, we always have a choice."

"Grow!" Mary Evelyn swings her arms up high and wide, with uncharacteristic drama, as if she, too, is beginning to bloom beyond her shy nature.

"Yes indeed." Mother smiles proudly. "No matter how bad life gets, we must always, always, always continue to grow, preparing ourselves for our next big bloom."

I reach for an elegant gardenia, the sturdy leaves a base for her milk-white gloves. In sight of this debutante's fragrant blooms, a batch of bold-toned zinnia have begun to rise, a rowdy crew of rule-breakers that stand in contrast to the highbrow gardenia.

Mother points them out and continues. "All these flowers you see tonight . . . Wasn't so long ago, they were locked in tiny seed-pods. They could have stayed right there, hidden away in that dark, cold shell. It was a familiar place. Safe enough. But they knew they were born for more. And so they took a chance. And they broke free, determined to find the light."

"Y'all see why I built her a garden?" Chief boasts. "*Now* let me tell you why we invited you here to see it." He clears his throat, then softens his tone. "Laurel and I, we built this farm together, board by board. Reared our two girls here. Welcomed many a friend through the years."

One guest's cheer is followed by his cohort's hearty, "Hotty Toddy!"

Chief lifts his glass but then grows somber. I pull my hands to my lap, clenching my fists as he looks at Mother. This is all becoming much too real. "What you don't know is that Laurel has been diagnosed with esophageal cancer."

This brings a different reaction entirely. Some friends gasp, others reveal looks of distress.

"The prognosis is . . . not good," Chief continues. All eyes fix on Mother, many narrowing with concern. "After a whole heckuvalotta prayer, Laurel has decided against treatment. Instead, she's chosen to live each remaining day to its fullest. A brave, strong forward march."

Mother offers quiet affection to those around her, assuring them she's at peace with all of this. The rest of us are not.

"So we invited you here tonight, to this memory garden, not only to celebrate our fiftieth anniversary, but to celebrate Laurel's life."

Chief turns to Bitsy and me now. "I can't imagine this world without your mother. If I had my say, I'd go first so I could hold the door for her, and I've been asking the Big Man for that favor."

Mother leans close, and he supports her fragile frame. "But I'm not the coach. Never have been. All I can do is find comfort in the lessons Laurel has taught me and accept there is no reason to fear the changing seasons."

"Amen." The actual minister nods sincerely. Others do the same.

"So, with that, I offer another toast." Chief lifts his glass and we follow. "To the devotion, compassion, and kindness Laurel offers all of us—a perennial kind of love."

TWENTY-SEVEN

Once the guests have explored the garden and shared many a memory, some humorous, some sad, we make our way into the barn for dinner. The entire display is breathtaking. No client event at Apogee could top this backyard soiree, and part of me thinks I really could begin again here. Move home, launch a flower farm, open a yoga studio, maybe even host events right here on the property.

As the evening progresses, I do my best to avoid Blaire, but at one point my eyes meet hers and she smiles my way. I return the kindness as guilt scrapes against my teeth. "*Stay open,*" that's what Marian said. So I finally expose my heart again, and look what it gets me!

I've tried to uphold safe boundaries, but I never should have entered such dangerous ground. It's a ridiculous childhood fantasy, believing in second chances and happy-ever-afters and some perfect soul mate who could be "The One." It's high time I move beyond those childish notions of flower farms and the boy next door. I've got a new plan now. I'm going to get through this evening with as much grace as I can muster, focusing all my attention on

Mother. And when it comes to Fisher, I'll mimic the elf owls: Hide. Play dead. Fly away.

As the meal winds down, compliments circle the room, with many praising the produce we've harvested from the farm. The blueberries were a particular success, whipped into sugary popovers and served as an alternative to the peach-pie squares. The servers continue to dole out champagne, with Bitsy eagerly accepting an ample pour. I'm seated between her and Trip when Mother stands from the family table to offer a toast of her own. Her hands are shaking as she unfolds a sheet of stationery, but she manages to keep her voice steady as she speaks.

"It's impossible to top Chief's surprises, so I won't dare try. But I've made a little list of Fifty Things I Love about this man. If you'd be so kind . . ."

The entire barn silences, and Mother begins to read one caring thought after another, all in honor of our loyal patriarch. She looks frequently at my father as she reads, the bond between them strong and visible, even after all these years.

"I love you because you have made me laugh every day for more than half a century. I love you because you let me be me, and you have from the start. I love you for saying 'please' and 'thank you,' and for kissing me good morning and good night. I love you for treating each day together as if it were a gift, not a curse, and for teaching me all there is to know about football, baseball, and, yes . . . even golf."

"Hey now." Chief grins. "Y'all know I drive a mean cart." Laughter echoes. Despite his athletic talents, Chief is notoriously the last man picked for golf events. Still, it never stops him from hitting the course with friends. He's learned to take pride in his high handicap and a club head cover monogrammed with the word *Duffer*—a good-hearted gag gift from Buzz and Juke.

Mother's eyes mist over with tears as she continues her offering. "I love you for building me up and for never tearing me down. For seeing my flaws and forgiving them all. For finding the good in me, especially when I struggle to see it in myself. And for showing our girls how a woman should be treated, with dignity and kindness and equal respect."

I lift my glass. "I second that!" Bitsy keeps her gaze on Chief, ignoring me.

"I love you for knowing when to take a stand and when to take a knee. And for always holding the door for me."

"Always," Chief says.

As she reads through the list, I intentionally avoid Fisher. Instead, I stay focused on my parents and try not to think about the love I've lost.

"I love you for nudging me to pursue my own dreams and for giving me space to grow children, flowers . . . and myself. I love you for all that you are and for all that you have helped me to be."

Then she folds the paper and speaks straight from the heart. "I'm grateful you chose me, Jim. Not just fifty years ago, but again and again, every day of our lives."

Mother leans to give my father the kindest, sweetest kiss I've ever seen, and I'm a ball of tears by the time she pulls away. I'm not the only one. Seems every table is filled with sniffles and tissue grabs, even from these seniors who have surely seen it all by now.

"We'd better offer a double dose of that champagne!" Chief jokes. Cheers replace tears, and one waiter plays along, pouring the next glass to the brim. It's a gesture that earns praise and will likely score him a generous post-party tip. Then Chief raises his glass and says simply, "To friends and family. Life doesn't get any better than this."

"Friends and family." We salute, clinking our flutes. I drink in honor of F-words: Friends, Family, Flowers, Farm, and Faith . . . all the ones that mean the most.

With the party coming to a close, the planner instructs us to choose a Mason jar of fireflies. Then Trip leads everyone out to the edge of the pasture where Chief gives the kids the honor of the countdown. On their mark the lids come off. Many of us have to give the jars a gentle shake, nudging our little friends out into the great, big world just as we did as children, but after a brief transition, the lightning bugs fly free. The effect is magical, and guests exchange youthful smiles as wonder reignites in them.

Mary Evelyn breaks free too, running through the field, laughing as the bugs flash around her. While Trip would probably enjoy it just as much as she is, he stays back and laughs with the adults, taking photos with his phone.

I move his way. "Maybe next summer I can take y'all to see the fireflies in the Smokies. It's a lot like this, but . . . multiply it by thousands."

Trip videos, capturing the magical display on his phone while sharing live footage with friends on Instagram.

"Mind if I see?"

He tilts the phone my way, and his peers are chiming in with comments, all in real time: "Magic!" "I want!" "Bring me!" It's much like I described in my Jansana pitch. These viewers are so inspired by Trip's post, they want to be a part of this experience, this narrative, this *story*.

I look around at our guests. Men and women of various ages, a broad range of ethnic and religious backgrounds. Some wealthy, most not so much. Some more fit than others. It's a mishmash of people doing the best they can each day. But how many have ever bought a Jansana product? Who is selling yoga gear to the average Jane?

"Trip, let me ask you something . . . If someone recorded a fishing video, showing a person catching a big bass, let's say . . . would you notice the rod and reel?"

"Probably."

"If they shared a soccer tournament, an incredible goal shot, would you notice the cleats?"

"Yep."

"So if I shared a video of yoga, you think people might be tempted to buy some Jansana gear?"

"Sure."

"You're a genius!" I wrap him in an enthusiastic hug, sweet as tea.

"We did it." I join Bitsy near the barn.

She half obliges, propping one elbow on my shoulder. "I'm so relieved."

Maybe it's on account of the fireflies, or Mother's toast, or the many memories pointed out in the garden tonight, but this simple gesture renews hope for peace between us.

As the guests scatter to their cars, Bitsy and I load presents into the cart. The crew breaks down tables, folds chairs, and gathers linens for the cleaners. While they work, Bitsy treats herself to a few more glasses of champagne before the carafes are capped, insisting she needs to hold on to the last opened bottle "just in case."

It's obvious she's still upset about Whitman's no-show, but she's been drinking a lot in the weeks I've been home, and the pattern is troubling me, especially now as her steps become cumbersome, her behaviors unguarded, her voice too loud. Seeming oblivious to their mother's indulgences, Trip helps collect the silverware while Mary Evelyn sends every guest home with a Mason jar of perennials. Around us, Mother continues to float on air.

With the work mostly finished, I step aside and make a quick call to Arizona, eager to share my social media idea with Brynn. Once again, she answers with a cry of defeat.

"It's okay, Brynn. I've got a new plan." She listens. "Raw phone footage filmed and shared by the average American."

"I don't follow."

"We'll do a call for submissions," I explain. "Reward people for posting their Jansana stories on social media."

"Like Snapchat? What are you talking about?"

"Snapchat. Instagram. Facebook. Maybe others. We ask our end users to show us how they're enjoying our products." I watch the guests leave, imagining them trying their first yoga class dressed in Jansana gear, stretching across our fields. "But not only us. Show the world."

"I love it!"

"Good. I do too." I relax into a smile. "All this time we've been trying to set up photo shoots at prime locations. Schedule film crews and find the ideal models. It's all an act, Brynn. When it comes down to it, we're trying to sell a more authentic life, but there's nothing authentic about our campaign. If we want to celebrate real people, let's show exactly that."

"Would trim the budget *and* solve the location problem."

"Exactly. We'll still put together a proper ad," I explain. "But we'll compile clips from cell phone footage instead of scheduling a shoot. Easy-peasy."

"What about Prague? And Tokyo? London?"

"This will transfer beautifully to foreign markets. Think about it. Our international audience will see authentic glimpses of normal day-to-day American life. Unfiltered. Unpolished. Nothing but truth. They'll be captivated by footage they rarely see. And then we'll extend the callout to international viewers, celebrate their way of life as well."

"Hashtag Awesome!"

"Let's hope Jansana agrees." I lean against the barn, taking a little weight off.

"We have to convince The Dragon first. Want me to set up a call?"

"Nope. We'll take this directly to The Trio. If they approve, we'll have just enough time to get submissions and meet the deadline. No need to involve The Dragon. She's done enough damage already."

"The campaign isn't even ours anymore. This could backfire. Big-time."

"What do we have to lose, Brynn? I'm not going down without a fight."

I move to a quieter area, back by the path of crape myrtles, and phone the president of Jansana. I leave a voice mail on her private cell, explaining my late-hour call and the time-sensitive nature of the plan. "And one more thing," I say before I end the message. "Let's keep this between us."

It's a gamble. There's no guarantee she won't report this to The Dragon, as Brynn fears. But I'm betting she wants to save her campaign regardless of the impact it has on Apogee, and her only chance of doing that is to take her chances with Brynn and me.

I exhale and return to the barn where Fisher, Blaire, Finn, and Alice have come back to offer help. The last thing I want to do is end this evening by trapping myself between Fisher and Blaire, so I immediately find an out, adding floral supplies to the pile of gifts in the golf cart. I've just turned the ignition when Fisher hops into the passenger seat. "Need a hand?"

"Not sure that's a good idea." My tone makes it clear, but he settles anyway. I can't help but give him a glance. His dark hair has been trimmed tight above his ears, honoring his rigid jawline, strong neck. He looks like one of the firefighters from the birthday card Brynn gave me, but I refuse to be charmed. Never again.

"It was nice to see Blaire," I say, drawing a firm line.

"Yeah, we should talk about—"

"I really don't need to know anything else, Fisher. If you're happy, I'm happy. We'll leave it at that."

He doesn't reply, and I drive as fast as I can make this little engine go, not bothering to avoid bumps along the path, intentionally giving him a rough ride. He keeps looking ahead and gives no reaction to my rude behavior.

"Not many make it fifty years anymore."

"No, they don't." I say this with a bit of a bite.

We reach the house quickly, and Fisher helps unload. We stash the floral supplies in Mother's gardening shed, the one that was built after the fire. Not a single board remains from the original building, and yet all I smell is ruin.

We leave the door ajar and organize the gear back into its appropriate spots: scissors, clippers, buckets, wire. It's not a big job, certainly something I could manage solo, but he works at my side, handing off materials as if I need his assistance. No matter how hard I fight it, each time his hand touches mine, my pulse steadies. He calms me in a way nothing else can. "Fisher, you need to go back to the barn. Find Blaire. This isn't right."

He stops now, holding a Mason jar against his chest until I look his way. "Just hear me, Lovey." He keeps a kind focus, a hope.

I sigh, set another container on the shelf.

"You need to understand." He tightens his grip around the glass and takes a deep breath. "Some part of me has been waiting all this time. Hoping you'd come home again. Believing that maybe . . . maybe, you might still love me as much as I've always loved you."

I speak before I can censor myself. "Of course I love you, Fisher."

His eyes soften with relief, and he moves closer now, too close. I step back, pinning myself against the shelves, but Fisher presses nearer, leaning in tight enough to kiss me. Energy pulses between us, but I fight the longing. I turn away.

"Why is it we never seem to find the right time?" As he speaks, his lips are near enough to shape the wind across my cheek. There's nothing threatening about it, and yet . . . danger. One spark, and we could both go up in flames.

Before I can answer, Blaire speaks from the open doorway. "Fisher?"

This cannot be happening!

Behind her, Bitsy speaks—her words thick and slurred. "Tried to warn you, Fisher. She only wants what isn't hers."

"Stay out of it," Fisher demands. But she moves toward him, finger in his face as Blaire observes in silence.

"You think you know my sister?"

Fisher stays calm, even though Bitsy pokes his chest not once, but twice.

"She's a home wrecker. Ask her!"

Then she turns my direction, stammering through a slew of vicious accusations. "She uses people. She uses people, and she leaves them. It's what she does. She already left you once, didn't she? Ran off thinking she was so much better than you, than all of us. You really think she's changed?"

"Stop this, Bitsy," Blaire pleads, but my sister continues her charge. "Oh, sure. Everybody *loves* Lovey. But trust me, you can't believe a word she says. She lies. Lies so much she doesn't even know when she's lying anymore."

"You're drunk." I reach for her hand.

She jerks away, hitting Blaire by mistake. This proves too much, and Blaire hurries off into the night. Fisher runs after her, leaving Bitsy and me together in the shed.

Now she stumbles, falling against the door frame and snagging her dress. "See? All you do is destroy things. Destroy people."

"Are you sure you aren't talking about Whitman?"

This is what finally does it. She comes at me, full force, calling me everything from crazy to selfish, pathetic to sick.

"Is that what you really believe about me?"

She laughs. Laughs! As if I'm truly the most disturbed human being she's ever known. "I'm the only one who sees through you. I know who you are."

Nothing she says makes sense, and despite my determination to stay strong, I revert to lifelong patterns, defending myself, arguing, trying to convince the both of us that I'm not the horrible person she says I am.

"Can't you see? You want all the attention, all the time. Couldn't let us have a happy night. Have to cause chaos wherever you go." Her voice echoes. Jars rattle.

I step toward the door, trying to catch my breath.

She follows. "You really think we want you here? *Need* you here? Truth is, Lovey, we're all much better off when you stay away."

No matter how hard I fight the hurt, her words bring a sting. Tears rise. I blink them away.

"Oh, here we go with the tears. Poor, pitiful Lovey." She speaks with exaggerated drama. Mean and cruel. "Go ahead. Cry! You always were good at putting on a show."

Behind Bitsy, Fisher's truck pulls from the lane, his taillights blurred by distance and heat. The others have left with him, and my ears begin to ring, just as they did during the Reed Incident. My hands are shaking. My stomach, in knots.

"Why are you saying these things, Bitsy? What have I ever done but love you?"

She stares, cold. "You're not who you pretend to be, Lovey. You're a mess, and now everybody will finally, *finally* see the truth."

"I'm not your enemy, Bitsy." I make one last attempt to reach my real sister, hoping she still exists. If only she could see that I'm here for her, have been all along.

But she glares and ends with two words only. "Just go!"

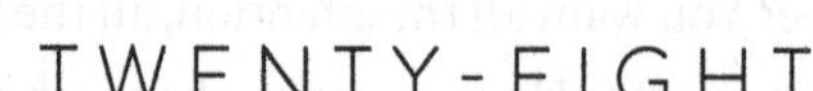

TWENTY-EIGHT

I fumble through the keys on the kitchen rack, a hand-painted frame that decorates nearly every home in Oxford. We were just two of the many kids who made this vacation Bible school craft under my mother's patient direction. My hand clenches now as I grab the key to Chief's old truck and head for the driveway. Far from the glow of Tiki torches, the surrounding forest has shifted to an inky black. The air, too, seems thick and soaked with tar, heavy and hard against my lungs.

The engine growls and I peel away, gravel spitting behind. I don't know where I'm going. Driving fast as Bitsy's demand echoes: "*Just go!*"

I'm four, maybe five miles from the farm before I realize what I'm doing. For years I've been a kettle, simmering. But mile by mile, the pain becomes more than I can contain. With my knuckles white against the wheel, I turn to emptier back roads, and there, away from eyes and ears and judgment, I finally scream away the ache.

I mourn the loss of my sister's love and the years I wasted with Reed. I roar for the pain my choices brought to Finn and to Fisher, and for the fact that my mother now dances with death. I howl for the husband and children I do not have, and for all the mistakes I've made. I wail for that happy, innocent, trusting little girl who once roamed barefoot through these woods, triggering steel-jawed traps in hopes of protecting naive animals, never knowing the one in the gravest danger was me. I cry and I shout and I drive. Drive until the gas gauge goes low and the back roads have me caught in their murky maze.

The old truck can barely produce enough light for me to see, and these red-dirt paths no longer seem safe. Occasionally, another truck zooms past, one with its engine revving, one's horn an obnoxious Rebel battle cry. I make a few desperate attempts to follow, but they lose me in their wake, this old engine no match for modern speeds.

What if Bitsy's accusations are legit? Am I really responsible for destroying Reed's marriage? Have I now come in between Fisher and Blaire too? Is it possible I even carved a wedge between Bitsy and Whitman when I reported his behavior with the bridesmaid on their wedding day? Was I jealous, as she claimed? And worse, did I somehow cause my sister to doubt her own husband? Destroying trust in her marriage from the start?

Maybe I really am as horrible as she wants me to believe. A selfish mess of a soul who only wants what I can't have.

Darkness threatens from all sides, but I press on, trying to reach a road I recognize. My GPS has no signal, and there's not a map to be found in the glove compartment. The sky is starless as I am tossed back and forth through time, trying to line up the plot points of my life.

Age Eight: Happy, confident, trusting, free.
Sixteen: In love with Fisher, hopeful we will have a future together, longing to escape Bitsy's toxic rivalry.

Eighteen: Letting Mississippi go and leaving Bitsy's shadow, even if that means losing Fisher. I see no other way.

Twenty-five: Finishing a year of travel and landing my first real job at Apogee. Hopeful and confident, even though I still miss Fisher and home.

Thirty: Dating but advancing my career. Successful, focused.

Thirty-eight: In love with Reed, content with my job and travel. Planning a happy-ever-after with a man I love. All the pieces finally coming together.

Forty-two: Wake up! Reed is a fraud. My life is not what I believed it to be. Everything shatters as if I'm Jim Carrey's character on *The Truman Show*. My reality was a sham, orchestrated by the one I trusted most.

Forty-five: My age is getting to me. My mother is dying of cancer. My sister hates me. Fisher is with Blaire. My career is tanking. Everything I have ever loved and lived for is being taken from me. And I'm lost, on a dark Mississippi back road, running out of gas.

Right this second: If I add up all the problems, there's only one clear common denominator—me.

The miles grow longer by the minute. I'm beginning to lose hope of finding my way when another pair of headlights peaks atop a far-off ridge.

Back here, anything could happen. Flagging down a stranger could end badly. But with the gas needle leaning a hard left, I am willing to take my chances, betting I could outrun most of the dangerous men in these parts if it came to that.

I flash my lights, slow my speed, and wave my arm, hoping for help, but despite all attempts to draw notice, the driver zooms right past me.

I try my GPS again. Still no signal, which means calling my parents is not an option either. What would I say anyway? "Chief? I'm lost. Can you and Mother come find me?" How pathetic. Maybe Bitsy is right. Maybe I really should pack my bags and "*Just go.*"

I fight the urge to pull over and cry myself to sleep, surrender to self-pity and take the easy way out. Instead, I keep driving, determined to find my way through this mess. But just as I start to regain my senses, the tire catches. In a painful jolt my head slams against the steering wheel.

Suddenly, the truck is sliding sideways. I jerk the wheel and hit the brakes, hard. Too hard. The truck goes into a blurred spin, rotating until the front tire slips deep over the drop of the roadside ditch. At a drastic tilt, I sit, stunned, trying to find the resolve to survey the damage.

With one back wheel whirling midair, there is no longer any chance of escape. From the trench, the truck's aged bulbs shine yellow, drawing a slew of bugs to the hazy beams. I crawl from the seat, cutting my way through the swarm to inspect not one, but two flat tires.

No flash of a porch light. No rebellious rednecks firing guns. No gang of teens drinking beer. With a cloud-cloaked sky, not even the moon offers help tonight. In every direction I find only the long, dark mane of madness eager to claim me as her own.

I check my phone again, walking as far as the headlights will let me. I try to get a call through to Chief, but the service won't connect. I find a spare tire, but only one. So even if I could manage to change one of the flats, I'd still be in a jam. And that would do nothing about getting me out of this ditch.

With no real options I make myself comfortable across the seat, but the fates aren't done with me yet. I've lowered the window to cope with the heat, but now thunder roars and the skies spill. Rain lands hard as hail, leaving tinny echoes on the roof, thuds and thumps across the hood. I hurry to roll up the window but the pane sticks, and I end up half-drenched by the time the glass is sealed.

Here at the bottom of a steep hill, the ditch swells quickly. Within minutes water laps the door, leaking onto Chief's old floorboard as lightning flashes white against the never-ending bullets of rain. I can't imagine the surge will rise enough to matter, but it's an inconvenient annoyance at the very least.

I resort to my old childhood strategy of singing away the storm, turning to the familiar tunes Mother would hum when we were young. Church hymns and nursery rhymes, country standards and folk songs. But after thirty minutes, I've grown tired of my own voice. Dark thoughts creep in. So I do what Chief would do, and I make myself a plan.

1. If I'm lucky, another truck will pass, and I'll try again to flag some help.
2. If not, I'll wait for morning, and then I'll walk until I secure a cell signal.
3. Then I will make the call of shame, admitting to Chief and Mother that I am, in fact, still a child and that I do, in fact, still need them to show me the way.

Within an hour the storm slacks, and my stress levels shrink a bit, even if I am covered in mosquito bites and chilled from the rain. I've just begun to doze off when my phone rings. It's Chief, a miracle of no small size.

"Lovey? You okay?"

"Um . . . yes and no."

"Where are you?"

"Honestly, I have no clue." I fill him in on my absurd situation, saying only enough about Bitsy to let him know we had a spat. I put him on speaker and try the GPS, but the positioning system simply won't work.

"Stay on the phone. We'll figure this out."

Despite his own exhaustion, my eighty-two-year-old father gets into his SUV and heads out into the night to find his long-lost daughter. "So much for a romantic anniversary." I try to make him laugh, but his concern is unshakable, and he is far too tired for jokes.

Again and again the call is dropped, and even when we do maintain a connection, it is weak, our syllables disappearing in the space between us. I'm a mess on this side of the phone as he navigates these rain-soaked hills in the dead of night. Only outlaws and middle-aged flight risks like me would dare roam these roads at this hour. *Why do I continue to make things harder than they need to be? Hurting the ones I love?*

It's a good thirty minutes before Chief's headlights round the bend. I am nothing but nerves by the time I finally see my father safe. And here.

I climb through the passenger door and rush toward his SUV, mud sloshing my calves, apologies spilling from my lips.

"Get in," he says, handing me a towel to dry myself.

I don't make any excuses. I don't blame Bitsy for my choices. I simply climb into the passenger seat with my head hung in shame.

He takes a few minutes to examine the truck, its back wheel airborne above the narrow lane, the front fender dented beneath ditch water. “You’re lucky you weren’t hurt, Lovey. This isn’t safe.”

I nod, the sharp edge of guilt lumping my throat as I rub the towel through my hair. “I’m sorry, Chief. I’m so sorry.”

“What were you thinking?” His fear begins to subside, and his eyes hold a deep reserve of compassion. After a long pause, he must realize I have no answers. “We’d better call for a tow.”

A ten-minute conversation with the wrecker service leaves Chief frustrated. “Could be a while. Students keep ’em busy at this hour.”

“Even in summer?”

“Seems so.”

I lean my head against the window as a heavy night steam wraps us. Damp from rain, I shiver, so Chief turns on the heater to warm me, a gesture I find nurturing and kind, especially when the leather seats begin to offer comfort.

“What were you doing way out here? This time of night?”

As much as I want to pour out my troubles, I’ve already caused him more than enough worry tonight. I stay quiet.

“I’m listening, Lovey.” He says this with a sincerity that strikes me. As he watches me in the amber glow of the dashboard lights, it’s almost as if he’s come here tonight for this very reason, to hear me.

With guarded hesitation, I begin. A small regret here. A half-hearted confession there. But when his voice softens and he shows genuine concern, I let the words flow freely. Before I know it, I’m telling him everything. My whole life’s worth of woes. The unbearable sadness I feel about Mother’s diagnosis. The grief that has already begun to swirl and the fear I have of losing her. The anxieties that are mounting about work, especially having no spouse to share the financial load if Jansana falls through.

I admit to the confusion I'm facing with Fisher, not knowing whether to give this relationship a chance or to get out of his way once and for all. I even tell him everything about Reed, all of it, including my own naive choices that put me in the palms of a predator.

And finally, I admit the absolute destruction Bitsy has brought to my life. I spare no detail. Rewinding all the way back through her lies and my truths and how the two have become muddled in time.

I talk for an hour, at least, right here on this nowhere back road waiting for the wrecker to show. I share every last secret, sin, and shame. And without interruption my father listens. He really listens. He doesn't argue or advise. He doesn't get defensive or tell me I'm wrong. He doesn't make excuses or suggest I got what I deserved for making bad choices along the way. He doesn't tell me I'm being petty or that I should just get over it or that I have no right to be hurt. He simply lets me know he cares.

By the time I've emptied myself completely, I feel thirty pounds lighter. I've finally poured out every last drop of pain that has been brewing within me all these years.

Chief sits stunned in the driver's seat, speechless. "I don't know what to say, Lovey." He has hugged me and said he loves me at least five times during this confession, but now he takes my hand in his. My breath holds tight, as if the whole world is a fragile web and even one exhale could send us tilting again. I don't dare move. "All those things Bitsy has said about you. I know they aren't true. And you need to know that too."

This is when I begin to weep, and it isn't forty-five-year-old

Lovey who finally cries on my father's shoulder. It's the little girl who first felt the fire of betrayal. She leans into her father's broad frame, and she slowly begins to heal.

"You believe I didn't start that fire? That it's not my fault Finn got hurt?"

"I guess I never really knew what happened. Didn't think it mattered either way. Now I see it did matter. It mattered a lot."

I nod and stay quiet.

"You mattered, Lovey. I made you believe you didn't, and I'm sorry for that." He clasps his hands as if trying to put all these broken pieces together again. I expect him to make excuses, argue his case. Instead, he says, "All this time, I thought I was a pretty good dad."

"You were. You are. A wonderful dad. Chief, I'm not blaming you."

"No. I should have protected you from Reed. I should have stood up for you when Bitsy took aim. I'm sorry."

I sit straighter now, twisting the towel, remembering how my grandfather was eager to wring Chief's neck at the very idea of him jilting my mother. "You didn't know about Reed."

"But I should have." He adjusts the thermostat. "I should have followed my gut. Never cared for him much."

My eyes lift in surprise.

"He always stuck to calling you Eva. Everybody calls you Lovey. Didn't sit right with me."

I give him a smile now, albeit a weak one.

"You know what a predator goes after first? An animal separated from her pack. They find the vulnerable ones, the ones who are alone in the world. Fact is, I wasn't there when you needed me, and there's no excuse good enough, Lovey. I'm sorry."

"We all have things we'd change, but you're the best father I've ever seen. Look at the way you love our mother. You gave us everything by giving us that."

"What good did it do if I threw you to the wolves? I wasn't there to protect you, and that was the most important part of my job, as your father. To keep you safe."

"But, Chief—"

"No. Let me finish. Because you're right about Bitsy too. We *have* always given her more slack. That's true, and it's not okay. It was never okay. But I guess, well, I guess I always knew you were the strong one."

"Bah!" If only he could know how weak I feel right now.

"It's true. Your sister could never handle things the way you do. She needed more from us, but we loved you both the same. You know that."

My hands fidget nervously. "I know you love me."

"More than you can imagine."

There is a long silence between us before I finally speak again, my voice soft and pained. "I'm not blaming you."

"Oh, I know you're not placing any blame. But I never thought about all this until now. And, well . . . I guess I should have paid more attention, sorted truth from the lies. Wish I had kept the bad guys from getting to you, so to speak."

I tug at my dress. "I'm making too big a deal of it is all."

"But it *is* a big deal. Now that I know what that man did to you, it's all I can do not to take a bullet to his brains." He grits his teeth. "Makes me sick."

I'm ashamed, wishing I hadn't said so much.

"Hold your head up, Lovey. It's not your fault." He waits until I look his way. "You need to know I believe you. And I believe *in* you. Always have."

All my wounds tie tight together in my throat.

"I can see now . . . maybe by letting Bitsy get away with it all those years . . . maybe I was teaching you it was okay to be treated that way."

"I don't—"

"Hear me out, Lovey. I made it your responsibility to keep the peace. At any cost."

"I try."

"I know you try. You always have. But I made you think you had to try harder. No wonder you ended up with a man like Reed. I taught you love was one-sided. That's my fault. I can see it now."

Chief rubs his hand through his hair. "It's not okay to be treated that way. Not by Reed. Not by Bitsy. Not by anyone." Then his own eyes become glassy and his voice begins to crack. "Thank goodness you fought your way out of that mess."

He fidgets with the driver's panel, and I don't know what to say. After another long silence, Chief adds more. "As for Bitsy . . . something's gotta give."

"I don't think anything can help at this point. No matter how hard I try, she always comes back swinging."

"Well, remember what I said. Judas has a story too."

I roll my eyes.

"Think about it. Regardless of all Judas had done, Jesus forgave him."

"I *have* forgiven Bitsy. Don't you see? She won't stop."

"Listen," he says with a serious resistance. "It didn't matter that Jesus forgave Judas. You know why? Because Judas never forgave himself."

I wince.

"What I'm trying to say is . . . Judas's own shame took him

down. What if he had learned to love again? Can you imagine the good that could have come from his life if he had chosen a different path?"

"But that's not the way the story goes, Chief. If anything, it teaches us some people never learn."

"Look, Bitsy has done some horrible things. But she's my child too, and I won't give up on either of you. All things can be used for good. Even this."

I shake my head, still unsure.

"That's what the story is about. The choice we have when bad things happen."

I stay quiet, wishing he would stop all the preaching.

"Jesus experienced the worst. Betrayed by someone he trusted, destroyed by the people he loved. Public shame, humiliation. He was falsely accused, said to be someone he wasn't. He tried to tell people the truth, but few stood up for him, few believed. They stood and watched, even cheered as he endured tremendous torture, a brutal crucifixion. But despite all of it, he chose to love."

My father keeps his eyes on me, a soft but serious stare as he continues. "It always circles round to the garden, doesn't it? If we allow the ruin to be used for good . . . well then, life comes back. And I believe love can too."

TWENTY-NINE

After an exhaustingly emotional night, Chief, Mother, and I gather in the kitchen for breakfast. "Morning," I say, yawning over coffee as my parents share a kiss.

Chief drops a bagel into the toaster and looks my way. "Get enough sleep?"

"Yeah." I yawn again. "You?"

"Just enough." He gives me a long look, then grabs some cream cheese from the fridge. "What d'ya say we all go out for dinner tonight? Just the three of us."

I nod, not even attempting to hide my smile. A night out with my parents, sans Bitsy. No stress. No hurtful accusations or stares. Too good to be true. "Y'all want to join me for some sunrise yoga?" I grab an apple.

"I'm about to take the ol' tractor for a spin. Gotta clean the coops too. Might even skip church."

I look to Mother, hoping she'll say yes.

"Need to write a few thank-you notes while I have the energy." She pulls a box of stationery to the kitchen table, along with a roll of stamps. A Mason jar of perennials rests in the center, a reminder that the seasons are changing, that Mother, too, will soon fade.

I take a seat. "I'm happy to help."

"Oh, that'd be great, Lovey. But why don't you go ahead with your workout, and I'll have things organized by the time you make it back." When I hesitate, she adds, "I'd like a little quiet time this morning anyway."

I try not to worry, but even her smile is tired. When I press, she insists there's nothing to be done here, so I finish our breakfast and join Chief outside. With the sun on the rise, a perky poplar tree holds the flame.

My father matches my steps, side by side along the path. He smells like trees. "Thanks for coming to get me last night."

Chief doesn't respond.

"I'll pay for the truck to be fixed. I know how much it means to you."

"Money's the least of my worries, Lovey." He slows his gait, glancing back toward the house. His fear reveals itself in furrows across his brow.

I follow his sad gaze, wishing I could ease his worry. "Why won't she try? People beat cancer every day."

Again, he doesn't answer.

"What if we make an appointment anyway? Insist on it?"

"You know she'd never go for that. Besides, the doctors really don't have any answers. There's no good plan."

"Then what? We're supposed to just sit here and watch her waste away?" A surge of anger clenches my neck. I kick a small pine sapling, letting it snap back into place with force.

Chief takes note, stopping now to rest his hand across my tense shoulder. "She's got two bad choices, Lovey. Neither would be easy. The least we can do is respect her decision and help her get through it."

I press a low, dry hickory branch until it splits from the force of the bend.

"We're lucky we've had her with us as long as we have," Chief says. "Lot of people never know how it feels to be loved like that."

This breaks me. How many years have I wasted? I've spent half my life chasing love that wasn't real, when everything I needed has been here all along.

The hourglass hangs from my neck, and I fidget with it now. "I'm not ready, Chief. I want more time with her. With you. I just want more."

Chief shakes his head. "Your mother has a favorite quote about time. From *The Sound and the Fury*, I think."

"Faulkner?"

He nods. "She had it framed. Did you see it? On her dresser?"

My heart sinks with regret. Yet another piece of my mother I have overlooked.

"Says something about how clocks slay time," he explains, as if by framing the quote she can hold tight to the moment she is in, rebel against the shifting sands and stop the forward movement.

I hide my hands in my pockets, hoping they'll stop shaking. "Faulkner really had a way of putting things into words, didn't he?"

Chief holds his green eyes on mine, those same Irish eyes he's always called *lucky*. Then my father draws me near. It's a tight hug, a sincere embrace that says, in all ways, we're going to be okay. He drops a gentle kiss on the crown of my head. "I love you. You know that?"

Tears fall as I say, "I know." And suddenly, the feral child inside joins the weary woman within. Together, their voices become one, and just like that . . . I am no longer divided by wounds. I am whole, and I am free. I am me.

Just as I shift my footing, Chief's weight becomes heavy against my frame. I step back, and he falls, his hand grasping at his chest. His face is flushed, his neck pinched with tension. His throat, too tight for words.

"Chief!" I grab my father above the waist and struggle to pull him toward the shade, to safety. "Chief!" I yell again. He stumbles, reaching to catch himself against the rusting panel of his tractor. He can no longer hold his own weight.

"Help!" I yell toward the house, toward the road, in every direction. "Help!" But only the animals hear me. The odor of gasoline leaks from the aged fuel tank, triggering that childhood panic.

"Breathe!" I shout, this time hovering over my father's body. He has sunk all the way to the ground, unconscious. I yell again. Touch my father's arms, chest. I shake him, easily at first, but then harder and harder, determined to draw a twitch, a gasp. Anything!

Behind me, a sheep bleats near the pond. The sound snaps me back as I fumble for my phone, dial 911. I confirm he has no pulse. Not breathing.

One . . . two . . . three . . . I pound my father's chest and press my lips to his. But no matter how hard I cling to this life, I have no power. No control. I move dazed but determined, until my voice stops counting, insisting, "No, no, no . . ."

With the 911 operator still on the line, the first responders arrive. Time has no meaning to me now. I don't know if it's been two minutes or twenty since Chief clutched his heart and fell to the ground. My mother, seeing their arrival, rushes from the house to join the paramedics. Together, they move as a pack toward the barn.

"Here!" I yell, waving my arms. "Over here!"

Mother falls to her knees beside my father, the whites of her eyes wide with alarm. "Oh, Lovey."

And we know, we both know. Chief is gone.

THIRTY

Mother sits between Bitsy and me in the memory garden, Chief's ashes in an urn beside our feet. The children are in the distance, still in church clothes despite the evening hour. They are inspecting his tractor, as if they, too, find the truth hard to swallow. It's been a full week now since their grandfather fell against the rust, his entire body contracting with pain. Still, it does not seem possible that he is gone.

"My sweet, sweet girls." Mother gives our hands a gentle pulse.

I stare at the ashes, not ready to let go. "We don't have to rush this."

"It's time," she counters, reminding me the clock keeps moving no matter how much we wish it would stop. "Your father would have loved the memorial service. All those stories from our friends. Juke had everyone laughing. And Buzz saying the prayer? Wasn't that something?"

I give her the affirmation she's after, but my heart is heavy and my smile is too. Nothing in life has prepared me for this. How could it have? "I'm sorry," I say for the millionth time.

"Lovey, you are going to have to make peace with this." She rubs my hand softly.

"I keep thinking it through. He was breathing heavy during our walk. Something was off. I should have known—"

"It's no one's fault, Lovey," Mother interrupts. "He just went ahead to hold the door for me is all." She puts her arm around me, tenderly kisses my cheek. "Life has a way of giving us exactly what we need, even when we don't understand it."

Bitsy rolls her eyes, shakes her head. Resists.

"Chief would have told you the same thing," Mother insists. "He had done what he was sent here to do. I'm at peace with that, and I want y'all to be too."

Bitsy has been particularly quiet in the days since Chief's heart attack, even giving me a look of kindness now as Mother continues to quiet our fears.

"Here's the way I think of it." Mother puts her arm around Bitsy now too. "When I'm starting a plant from seed, I let it sprout in the greenhouse first, right?"

We both nod on cue.

"Then I let it go through what gardeners call a *hardening.* I put it out for just a few hours at first. Slowly increase its exposure to the wind and rain, the cold and sun. You understand why I do this?"

We understand, but she continues anyway.

"If I put it straight out into the world, it'd get knocked back, too damaged to reach its full potential, might not even survive. So I have to care for it. Teach it. Give it time to adapt. Only then is it ready to thrive on its own as a healthy, happy plant. You see where I'm going with this?"

A caterpillar crawls across my foot, reminding me there is purpose in the process, even when I can't always see what's ahead.

"You're both in a hardening season right now. That's all this is.

It's scary, I know, and you may feel unsure, unrooted. But there's a steady gardener in control, preparing the soil, strengthening your roots, giving you all you'll need so you can bloom when the time comes. There is mercy in this madness, girls. We're never as alone as it seems."

With my elbows over my knees, I watch the caterpillar maintain her march. I try to picture my life without Chief. Without Mother. Without moments like this.

"I'll be leaving you soon too, you know."

No! my heart screams. *NO!*

"Maybe this is a step in that direction, preparing you to stand on your own, no matter what life brings."

"I'm not ready," I argue. Bitsy nods, in sync with me again after all these years.

"We can't fight the seasons, girls." She eyes Bitsy, then me. "But you both have some work to do. Your time is now."

"What is it you think we need to do?" Bitsy asks, a tad defensively.

I lean closer into my mother, offering support and taking some as well.

"You've both been giving too much of yourselves to the wrong people, the wrong goals," Mother says. "It hasn't made either of you happy, has it?"

Silence. Then I give in. "I only wanted what you and Chief had. I thought Reed was 'The One.'"

"Just remember, you can't give anybody so much of yourself that if he runs off with it, there's nothing left of you. Protect your spirit, girls. It's the only one you've got."

Bitsy looks at me. Then at Mother.

"When it all comes down to it, it's the only real job we've been given," Mother continues. "Get this one spirit through to the end.

And still be willing to love and be loved in spite of all the hurts we endure along the way."

"Easy for you to say." Bitsy sighs. "You married Chief."

It's the first time she's opened conversation about her marriage, and Mother and I both respond with concern, compassion. But our kindness turns Bitsy cold, her typical defense.

"You really want my advice, honey?"

"Sure," Bitsy says with a halfhearted sigh.

"Okay, then. Your grandmother used to say we should never chase a love that leaves us." Then she stands, eyes us both. She lifts Chief's ashes now, ready to send them to the wind. "Sometimes the best thing to do is let go. Even if it's the one thing we love most in the world."

Just before sunset, Mother and I join Bitsy, Trip, and Mary Evelyn in the pasture. The lambs sing out as we scatter Chief's ashes. At our feet Manning whimpers among the black-eyed Susans as if he, too, is letting go. Fireflies ignite, a sensitive reminder of Chief.

That night on the dark, wet back roads, when my life came crashing to a halt, Chief showed up. He listened. He cared. And he gave me the healing I had been seeking since childhood. After I'd spent years stuck in the pain, my father took one look down into that Mason jar, recognized the light in me, and gave me the gentle nudge I needed, reminding me I was born to shine and to fly free. That one pivotal moment was all it took to shake me loose.

"Remember those trips to the Smokies?"

Mother smiles, and I sense she has been sharing the very same thought. That we were witnessing nothing short of miracles right there among those cloud-soaked forests. That the miracles are here with us again, tonight. That Chief is too.

"Well, I was just thinking how much more powerful it is when we're all lighting up together, at the same time. Not scattered out across the darkness."

"Family First," Bitsy says, then sighs. "Something I can't seem to get right, no matter how hard I try."

I suddenly realize this familiar mantra has kept Bitsy trapped in a dangerous place far too long, sacrificing her own safety and sanity in order to preserve what remains of her marriage.

Mother wipes one slow tear and counters the old adage. "I think what Chief really meant was Love First. If we love one another in a healthy way, the family will naturally thrive. But it's up to every member of the team to pull their weight and play their part. Otherwise, it doesn't matter how hard you try, Bitsy. If Whitman isn't equally invested, a balanced partner, it simply won't work. Wisteria, kudzu, English ivy—they'll swallow you whole if you let them. That's not family. That's not love."

When we return to the house, Fisher and Blaire are waiting for us on the front porch. I fight my urge to turn for the barn, choosing instead to greet them with the best friendship I can offer. "We brought supper," Blaire says, giving Bitsy a hug and me a smile.

Mother responds with appreciation and leads us all inside where we are treated to a spread of baked chicken, green beans, macaroni and cheese, and crowder peas. "All made from scratch by Supper-to-Go." Blaire laughs, confessing she's never cooked more than a frozen dinner in her gourmet kitchen.

"Very kind," I tell her, unable to say the rest of what I need to say. That I'm happy Fisher found someone. That I'm sorry I caused any kind of rift between them. That I will always love him, but I had my chance. I'll let him go.

Instead, Blaire is the one who brings up the topic while the two of us set the dining room table. "Lovey, I know this whole thing with Fisher and me has kind of been freaking you out."

Her tone is much like a teenager's, and I want to latch onto her youthful energy, the inner pulse of light she hasn't yet lost in this life. Makes me think again of Glinda the Good Witch, "a beautiful woman, who knows how to keep young in spite of the many years she has lived."

"Fisher told me all about it," she continues. "How y'all have . . . reconnected, I guess you'd call it."

My stomach tightens. Is this it? The phone call from Meghan? The confrontation with the sleazy *other woman*—me? I come up with a frail excuse. "It's not what you think."

"Oh, honey. It's perfectly all right if it is." She smiles, looking into the kitchen where Fisher is uncovering an aluminum casserole dish. "Here's the thing. I care about Fisher, I honestly do, but we both know he's not the one for me. He's wild about you, Lovey. Always has been, and . . . I just want him to be happy. That's all."

"What are you saying?" The fork feels heavy in my hand now, as if every hope is hanging right here in my palm, and this one piece of silver gets to make fate's call. Which way will it fall?

"I'm saying y'all have my blessing. I've never really been the marrying kind anyway. Mama just won't get off my back about it." She laughs, as if my return to Oxford has set her free. "All I ask is that you take good care of him. He's the real deal if ever there was one."

After supper, Mother puts her napkin on the table and her head in her hands. "I'm flat-out beat." No one mentions the fact that she has hardly eaten a bite, yet again, nor that she coughs with every sip of tea. Instead, we suggest she get some rest, and she thanks us for taking care of the kitchen.

As Bitsy leads her kids to the car, Blaire pipes up. "Mind dropping me off on your way home?"

Bitsy's brows furrow. "You aren't riding with Fisher?"

Blaire looks at Fisher, then at me. "Why stand in the way of a good thing? My only condition in all of this is that I don't lose my friend. In fact, I'd like to gain one." She gives me a hug and promises to check back in with us soon.

Without so much as a blink, Bitsy closes her door, starts the car, and leaves Fisher and me alone beneath the great big universe of stars. It's as if she no longer has the energy to hurt me. Perhaps she's finally given up the fight.

At our feet Manning rolls onto his back, requesting a belly rub, and I oblige. "He won't leave my side. Keeps looking for Chief, whimpering."

"Can't blame him." Fisher moves closer, and my worries slow.

"I know I'm supposed to say all the cliché things, like 'At least it was quick,' or 'He went ahead to be there for Mother.' But honestly, I just miss him, Fisher. And I'd do anything to have had more time with him."

When Fisher offers Manning a pat, the lab whimpers, too grief-stricken to wag his tail. "I can't give you more time with him, Lovey. But I do have one thing." He leads me to his truck where he lifts a thick, blue landscaping tarp. I am met with a concrete impression of the Virgin Mary, stretching end to end across the bed.

"Listen to this." Fisher plays a voice-mail message from his cell phone. My throat tightens at the sound of Chief's voice, and Manning barks in response.

"Fisher? Chief here. Hey, I was thinking. There's one more thing I want to add to the garden. I know it's too late for the party, but let me know if we can slip it in next week."

Every bone in me is lightened. Even gone from us, my father has found a way to break through, to remind me I'm not alone, that I've never been alone, and that I will never be without his love.

Through the receiver, he speaks from the great beyond:

"Here's the story. Long time ago, Laurel's brother was killed in a car accident. Levi, you've heard us talk about him. Well, Laurel and I had just gotten married, and I didn't know how to help her through it. I was driving her over to Jackson for the funeral, and we stopped for gas. One of those full-serve places where they'd wash your windshield. I miss those. Anyway, the station was run by a widow lady who lived next door. She had a yard full of flowers, and she told Laurel she could go take a look.

"By the time I grabbed a couple Cokes and paid the bill, Laurel was out of sight. I found her on a bench in the garden. There was a statue of Mary there. The widow woman came up behind us, noticed Laurel was crying. She said, 'Go on and spill your troubles, dear. God hears.'

"I went on back to the station and started checking the air in my tires, tinkering with the oil, you know, just trying to give Laurel some space. When she finally got back into the truck, she told me she wanted to build a prayer garden someday. A place where people could go to find comfort. I guess that's what started her interest in flowers in the first place.

"So, I was thinking, maybe you could help me add one of those Mary statues. Just a little something extra for Laurel. Let me know what you think. And then let's get your farm back, son. You deserve it."

I ask Fisher to play it again. And again. Not able to get enough of my father's voice, his thoughtful request. "Mother needs to hear this."

"What do you say we set up the statue first? Then we can surprise her in the morning."

I wrap my arms around him, and he holds me in a gentle hug. With my hip cupped close against his thigh, his comfort reaches deep within. I haven't felt this kind of respite in decades, not since I left his arms for Arizona. But now I know. This is where I belong.

When I finally pull away, a peace spreads between us. Together, we work to transfer the heavy icon to the top of the hill. Beside the labyrinth, we find room beneath the white oak, a bare, flat space where Mary can watch over the entire farm with her gentle grace.

"Mother's gonna love this." I brush dirt from my hands and help Fisher secure the footing. Mary's arms are outstretched, palms up and open, as if she is ready to receive our sorrows, our prayers, our pain.

"I've got a couple finishing touches I want to add in the morning. Think you can stall her until about ten?"

"Won't be easy. She's been spending most of her time out here." I step back to admire the addition.

Fisher leans in close, kisses my cheek. Despite Blaire's blessing, I still need final confirmation, clarity. A clear conscience. "Blaire?" I ask, a life's worth of hope in the word.

"You," he answers. One sweet and simple syllable. All I'll ever need.

When Fisher's lips reach for mine, I surrender. All that has been spinning within me for years now steadies, stills. I finally understand what Marian has tried to teach me. How we sometimes find the right person when it's not the right time. Or how we sometimes settle for the wrong person because we feel pressured by time. But every now and then, if we're open to it, a few of us get lucky and the stars align. With Fisher pressed against me, I finally get it. Right now, in this perfect moment, we are one with the stars, with the universe, with all that ever was and is to come.

THIRTY-ONE

I've asked Bitsy to keep Mother occupied this morning, allowing Fisher the chance to finish the prayer garden. In the meantime, I can no longer avoid my responsibilities back in Arizona. It's been a week since I've corresponded with anyone from work, so I head to the kitchen and scan the slew of e-mails and texts that have poured in since Chief left us. When I reply to an old message from Brynn, my phone rings immediately in response, signaling a video call from Phoenix.

"Eva? How are you?" Brynn's brows crease with worry. "I'm sorry about your dad." She's cut her hair, a style that makes her look a little older, more professional.

"Love your new do," I tell her. "And the flowers you sent were beautiful." I extend my thanks to the many coworkers who contributed.

She launches a caring discussion, asking about Chief's sudden heart attack, the funeral, even the garden, everything that's happened since our last conversation when I suggested we use an authentic social-media campaign to sell Jansana to the average Jane. "So when are you coming home?"

I sit at the kitchen bar, looking out toward the oak where Mother would push us in the tire swing. We'd pretend to fly higher than the elephants, the treetops, the sun. "Tell you the truth, I actually kind of feel like I *am* home. I'm beginning to think . . . maybe Mississippi is the place for me now."

Wide-eyed, Brynn replies from Arizona. "Serious?"

I smile. Shrug.

"But what about the Jansana offer?"

This stumps me. "What offer?"

"Didn't you read the e-mail?"

I scan my in-box while Brynn fills me in. "Basically, when The Trio got word about your father, the president gave me a call. Wanting details about the memorial service. So I took a risk, Eva. Told her everything."

"My work is done." I shine a proud smile.

Brynn laughs. "You definitely taught me to stand my ground. But can you imagine if I had to fight this bully of a boss on my own? That's a game I'd never win."

"I'm on your side, Brynn. Always will be."

"She couldn't believe what The Dragon had done to us. I didn't even have to suggest it. She went straight to Mims, put us both back on the account."

"Are you kidding?"

"Not kidding. The social-media campaign? Brilliant, Eva. And they all know it was your idea. Plus, get this . . . The Dragon is gone!"

"Gone? As in—?"

"As in, don't know, don't care. She's no longer our problem." Brynn sounds ten times more confident than when I left Arizona. "The point is, karma got her. Plus, Mims mentioned you as the top candidate. Says you're long overdue the promotion."

"No way."

"Yes way. But there's more . . . The Trio has an offer too. Full-time, permanent positions. Just you and me. They don't trust Apogee anymore, but they're happy with our work. Very happy."

I take a sip of tea as Brynn beams from Arizona.

"They even said they'd consider a consulting contract, in case you need more flexibility for a while. Doesn't sound like they'll take no for an answer, Eva. This is big."

"Are you saying—?"

"I'm saying The Trio wants us to leave Apogee and work exclusively for Jansana." She breaks into our slogan with exaggerated pep: *"Feel good. Do good. Be the good. Jansana."*

"That's a life-changing opportunity for you, Brynn. You should take it."

"I will!" she sings. "But you're coming with me, right?"

I give this some serious thought. I could probably negotiate a posh consulting contract, retire, launch the retreat center with Marian in Sedona, and travel back to Phoenix only when Jansana needed me in-house. It's an ideal opportunity, something I would have celebrated just last month, crossing off my annual goals and giving myself a big reward. But now, everything has changed.

"Eva? You *are* coming with me to Jansana. Aren't you?"

My voice drops with sincerity as Dolly P. comes barreling into the kitchen, wanting treats. "I don't know how much time I have left with my mother, Brynn."

"But what about . . . after . . . ?" She won't say after Mother dies, but that's what she's thinking.

"Honestly, I don't know. I guess we'll have to wait and see."

"I can't do this without you, Eva. Please?"

I smile, a genuine show of respect. "You absolutely can do it without me. You've just proven it."

"Well, even if I can . . . I don't want to."

When Mother, Bitsy, and I reach the top of the hill, Fisher is already waiting for us at the memory garden, Finn by his side. The statue of Mary stands reverently between them, taller than both brothers by at least a head.

"Oh my goodness," Mother gasps. "How did you know?"

Fisher plays the recorded message, holding it close to Mother's ear. At the sound of Chief's voice, she clasps her hands over her heart and starts to cry. Bitsy and I both wrap our arms around her frail, thin frame, and she takes a seat on the stone wall between us. She listens attentively as her hands shake with emotion.

"I can't believe this," Mother whispers. "Of course he leaves me with one final surprise." She stands again, smiling weakly, and gives Fisher and Finn each a hug. "You boys meant so much to him. The sons he never had." Both men look away, fighting tears of their own.

Fisher clears his throat and adjusts his ball cap. "Did a little research on this concept of a Mary Garden." He eyes the flowers he planted this morning while Bitsy kept Mother occupied. "Hope you don't mind, I added a few to go along with the story."

"Marigolds." Mother leans low to examine the blooms. "Fabulous!"

Fisher identifies the others too: iris, begonia, bleeding heart. Then he points to the lush green ferns that drape the white oak branch above us. "I thought it'd be nice to place her here, beneath the resurrection ferns."

"Very thoughtful," Mother says, looking at me as if I'd better recognize a good man when I see one. Then she speaks in a more serious tone. "You know, when my brother, Levi, died, he was just starting to find his way in the world. Dating a nice girl, had landed his dream job at a radio station down on the coast. He was happy. Then a drunk driver swerved too far on a rainy road." She snaps her fingers. "Just like that."

"Horrible," Finn says.

Mother nods, moving back to sit between Bitsy and me. "I was just starting out too. Newly married. Life was good. And then I got that call." She shakes her head. "He was gone."

I rub my mother's back softly as she speaks. The bones of her spine protrude beneath her summer blouse; her ribs, prominent beneath her skin. A pressing reminder that our time is short.

"When Jim and I found that prayer garden, we were out in the middle of nowhere. Seemed almost like it had been put there just for me. I wasn't ready to get to the house, to see my parents grieving. And there she was." Mother points to Mary. "A statue exactly like this one. She was waiting there in the garden. As if she knew."

"Maybe she did," I whisper.

Mother nods again. "It was the first time I had stopped to think since the phone call." She pauses. "I've never told anyone this."

She eyes Fisher and Finn, unsure, before continuing. "It makes no sense, I know, but sitting in that garden, crying, I heard Mary speak to me. Just one word. 'Surrender.'"

We all listen patiently, without questioning. Without doubt.

"To be honest, it made me angry. How dare she tell me to

surrender? But then Mary spoke again, clearly. And this time she said, 'Let go, Laurel. Everything will be okay.'"

"I hate it when people say that," Bitsy argues, standing to move around the garden. "Because it's not okay. That's the lie, Mother. Levi died too soon, and it's not okay. Chief has gone just when you need him most, and it's not okay. My husband has destroyed our family, and it's not okay. None of these things are okay, and they never will be."

"You're right, Bitsy. I don't mean to say it's all okay. But in that moment, I stopped trying to make sense of such things. I stopped fighting the loss, demanding explanations. When I did that, when I surrendered, I felt the anger and fear leave me. Just like that."

Bitsy looks at the Mary statue, then at me. When she turns back to Mother, she begins to cry. "Well, I'm not like you, Mother. I *am* scared. And I'm angry too. And I'm certainly not okay."

"We are all scared and angry sometimes, Bitsy. We're allowed that."

"But you want me to accept something I can't. It doesn't work that way."

"When I say I surrendered, I don't mean to say everything was fine in an instant. Some days it still gets the best of me. But Levi's story, my story, your story—they're all connected, you see? Always have been. Always will be."

Even with the men here, Bitsy cries a little harder now, her breaths rushed and shallow. With each exhale she is taking off the masks and crowns that have kept her caged for decades. I sense she is finally breaking free.

Mother taps the seat, encouraging Bitsy to sit again. "I read the other day that they now believe there are trillions of galaxies in the universe. Trillions! Maybe even more. Did you know that?"

Bitsy stays quiet. I lift my eyes to the trees where two squirrels bark from the canopy. So many forms of life around us. What a minor part we play.

"Think about how infinite this creation really is," Mother continues, as if reading my mind. "Sometimes I like to take a step back, use the wider lens. Helps me realize how small my problems are in the grand scheme of things."

"Doesn't make me hurt any less." Bitsy leans against the stone, wipes her tears.

Fisher moves to sit beside me, a comfort I accept with gratitude.

"You have no idea what Whitman has done to our family," Bitsy says. "I don't deserve that. The kids surely don't."

Mother pulls Bitsy into a hug. "Of course you don't deserve it, honey, whatever it is." Then she pulls back to make sure she's listening. "No one deserves to be hurt. No one. Lovey didn't deserve a monster like Reed. Fisher and Finn didn't deserve their father leaving. Look at Finn. He surely didn't deserve to be burned in that fire. No one deserves it, Bitsy, but we all suffer. That's the only guarantee we have in life. Pain."

"You haven't suffered like I have. You don't know."

"You're right. I don't know. But when I hurt, I try to accept the pain as a lesson. Let it teach me."

I listen, learn.

"Think of it this way." Mother leans to pull one of her bright-pink zinnia to hand. "When a flower blooms, its seeds will scatter. Right? Well, let's say some of those seeds land in a parking lot. Others land in a fertile field. Is that fair? No. Some will have real disadvantages, greater challenges."

"But they all can grow," Finn says. "As long as they find a healthy place to root."

"Bingo!" Mother points Finn's way, giving him the win. "Some may have to settle for a crack in the pavement. But once a seed takes root, it can find its way to the light. Become all it was born to be."

Mother hands me the bloom, a bright-pink mound of petals, each the size of dragonfly wings.

Bitsy looks at us with frustration, as if we still don't understand. "Don't you see? Even if the flower manages to bloom, some people will stomp it to bits just because they can."

"She's right about that." I pass the zinnia to my sister.

"But others will go out of their way to water it," Fisher counters. Finn nods.

"Ultimately, that's their choice, not ours," Mother says. "All we can control is what we do with the one little life we're given. Remember what Chief liked to say. Everything in life can be explained by a garden." She counts on her fingers, the way I used to do as a child.

"One, we find a foundation much bigger than ourselves. Two, we establish roots, digging deep into healthy soil. Three, we grow and stretch, always moving toward the light. Four, we fulfill our purpose, blooming and offering love to the world."

She pulls her pinky up for five, spreading her palm wide for emphasis. "And then we can only hope some of that love will catch hold somewhere, and that it will be passed along from one generation to the next."

"Despite all the storms and stomps along the way," I say.

"Exactly." Mother pulses her hand atop my knee and nods toward the statue. "That's what Mary taught me. Our body's death is not the tragedy, girls. It's when we waste our time in life feeling dead on the inside. That's the real reason to grieve."

Fisher and Finn exchange a glance that suggests they learned this lesson years ago.

"That's why I designed the wall like I did." Fisher touches the stones. "Four levels. You see? Birth, life, death—"

"Rebirth." I finish his sentence, and Fisher smiles. "Goes right along with what Chief said about perennials." I speak to Bitsy now. "If we allow the ruin to be used for good . . . well then, life comes back. And love can too."

Mother wipes a tear and moves to the feet of Mary. Then she turns back our way. "So that's it, you see? The only story that matters. We are here to love. And to be loved."

THIRTY-TWO

I head into town to refill Mother's pain meds. Steering off course, I drive around the back streets that surround the square. Childhood memories surface, and I begin listing the presidential names in order, as Chief would challenge us to do as kids. When I drive past Rowan Oak, my father's many sermons rise again, drawing a sting, but then a smile.

From there I head north of town, and within a few miles, I'm passing Bitsy's house. Despite the dissolution of her marriage, everything still appears perfect from the outside. The only thing that looks askew is that her home, while pristine in appearance, is vacant. No light shines from the kitchen. No loved ones gather together on the swing. Not even a dog rests on the welcome mat. This home stands lifeless, starved of the family it was designed to shelter.

I think of my sister now and realize she's become much like this home. An empty shell of the girl I so adored. Where is the Bitsy who dared to host parties for the fairies? The one who laughed with me under the covers, turning pages while Mother read aloud? The Bitsy who helped me make a wish on my first birthday or set out milk and cookies for Santa every Christmas Eve? The sister I have loved my entire life. Is she still inside that shell somewhere, waiting to bloom? And if so, how do I help set her free?

I sit behind my wheel, the engine running. How much pain has Bitsy absorbed beyond that beautiful front door? How many nights has she sat up alone, wondering where her husband has gone? How many cruel words has he thrown at my sister's heart? How many lies? How many sins?

How many times has she needed me when I wasn't here, while all the time I thought I was the only one hurting? If only I had known to zoom out, see the suffering all around me, take in the world with a wider lens.

From the wooded surroundings, a cat prowls onto Bitsy's lawn. Its ear has been clipped to show he's one of many feral strays who has been neutered and released in these parts. I hear Marlin Perkins again, describing the scene:

"On the prowl for prey, the tomcat pounces. A squirrel races up the front yard birch tree, shouting frantic warnings to her friends. But the tom is in close pursuit, his tabby stripes a black-gray blur. Just in time, the squirrel leaps to the roof, leaving the cat at limb's end without a kill."

Watching the chase, I wonder again if we're each born of a certain nature. Some of us predators, others prey. Or do we all enter this world as innocents, with an innate ability to love? Does something happen along the way to men like Whitman and Reed, or were they bad seeds from the start?

With the squirrel out of sight, the cat slouches back onto the porch where he curls into a comma on the swing. Even without the kill, he wins. Like the tomcat, Bitsy chased me from my nest, far from the reach of my familiar trees. I ran from Oxford, from my parents, from Fisher. From all I had ever known of home.

But now, as the cat takes a nap, the squirrel returns to her nest. She's quickly back to gathering nuts, content as ever, undeterred.

As Mother says, Bitsy's journey is her own. I cannot change her nor heal her. But maybe there is still room for me here too. The squirrel survives not by becoming a predator, nor by cowering in fear, nor by abandoning her home forever. But by being in tune enough to know what she's up against, by following her instinct and staying ten steps ahead of the monsters near her nest.

I leave Bitsy's house and drive to St. Peter's Cemetery where I park on the narrow lane. With the late-August sun beating down, I make my way to Faulkner's grave and take a seat beneath the oaks. I've been here only a matter of minutes when my sister drives up, parks.

"Hey," she says, heading my way in a pair of flats, not her usual heels. "I thought that was Mother's car."

She has softened since Chief's death two months ago, approaching slowly now, as if she's asking forgiveness with every step. My hopes are high, but my guard is too.

"Who's with Mother?"

"Fisher's sitting with her for a while."

"Nice of him." She toys with the coins, stacking pennies across the cement border.

"She's getting weaker by the day, Bitsy. Nothing but liquids now. Can barely swallow. The pain is . . . It's hard to watch."

"We don't have much time left with her, do we?"

I shake my head. "It's been a hard couple months." I spin an empty bottle, absorbing the hollow echo it sends against the stone.

"Hard few years." It's a shared sorrow.

A pause pulls long between us, but then she sighs and opens. "Whitman left me, Lovey. For good this time." Her eyes are sad and red as truth claws its way to the surface. Despite all the lies she's told me over the years, this is the real Bitsy speaking. Unguarded and honest. The sister I have been fighting for, resurfaced. "I came home from Chief's memorial service, and he was gone."

"He moved out during the funeral?"

She nods, and I am sickened by his cowardice.

"You should have told us."

"Figured y'all had enough to worry about. But that's why I haven't been able to help you more with Mother. It's all I can do to keep the kids afloat. I try to be strong, but . . . sometimes I can't. I hate myself for that. And they'll hate me for it too, I'm sure."

I offer my sister what Chief offered me on that dark, rainy back road. I listen. I care. She tells me of Whitman's countless affairs with young college students, his reckless investments that have nearly bankrupted them, the twisted psychological abuse and dangerous temper, even his deep dive into drugs. She tells me of things he has done to her, things no man should do to anyone, much less to the mother of his children. And she tells me how long she's stayed loyal and loving, hoping to keep a unified home for her two innocent children.

"I should have listened to you. The day we got married. You tried to warn me, didn't you?"

"I'm sorry I wasn't here for you. You and I, we . . . I didn't know what you were in."

"Yeah, well . . . I didn't even know." She laughs a little. "It's a slippery slope."

I nod. I know how the lines get blurry. How you bend a little here, a little there, and before you know it, no boundaries are left at all.

"The sad thing is, I watched him lie to so many people, Lovey. Little lies. Big lies. Lies I didn't even know were lies. I watched him use people, cheat people. But somehow I convinced myself it was what men do, you know? That he understood the world better than I did or something. I don't know."

My eyes soften. How similar our paths have been.

"But I never imagined he was lying to me too. How stupid is that? For some reason, I believed he loved me. That while he might hurt other people, he would never hurt me. Not our family. Our children!"

She breathes deep. Then starts again. "Turns out, he had been hurting us most of all. I was the last to know. Such a fool."

"Trusting someone, supporting someone . . . That's not foolish, Bitsy. That's love." I pull her close, and she lets all her weight fall against me. She rests her head in my lap.

"I'm a wreck, aren't I?"

"Hush." I try to settle her. "You're beautiful, Bitsy. But you forget that's not all you are. You're also smart. Confident and strong. And you're a very good mother too. You don't need Whitman. Just wait 'til word gets out that you're single again. You'll give Blaire a run for her money, that's for sure."

"Right." She fights tears.

"Who is this woman?" I try to make her smile. "Seriously, when has Bitsy Sutherland ever quit anything?"

"I lost that Bitsy a long time ago." She releases a heavy sigh, the kind that makes me think she's been holding her breath for hours, if not for years. "He hurt me so much, Lovey. Ruined my life, my children's lives. I made the worst choice, the worst! And now look at me." She gazes down at herself with disgust. "Pathetic."

"Bitsy, nothing about you is pathetic. Whitman's choices, that's what's pathetic." I fiddle with the grass at the edge of the grave. It's been worn thin from tourists, but a ladybug crawls to the top of one green blade, minimized even further by the stash of acorns remaining from last fall. Her entire world could fit in the palm of my hand.

"You know what it's like to walk around this town with everyone's whispers and stares? They corner me in Kroger, for heaven's sake. You wouldn't believe the ridiculous rumors. People believe anything."

"Who cares what people think. Whitman can't fool them for long."

"He sure fooled me. Took me decades to see the truth. I stayed and forgave and put up with so much, Lovey, always fighting for the good in him."

"Why?" I ask sincerely.

"Because I love him." She says this in the present tense, which makes my stomach turn. "And I trusted him. One hundred percent. I believed in him. And I believed in marriage. And I believed our children deserved a two-parent home and a full-time father in their lives. Family First, right? But now I know better, don't I? Whitman doesn't want me. He just stayed because he didn't want anyone else to have me. Truth is, he doesn't love me. And he never did."

"I know that feeling." I say this to show we're more alike than she thinks, but Bitsy snaps back.

"No. It's not the same." Then, even louder, "You have no idea how it feels to be me. I was his *wife*, Lovey! And I have children with this man! You were on the other side of it. You always are." She pulls away. In the background the clock tower chimes from the square.

I look to the sky, thinking of Mother and Chief and how *life doesn't stand still*. I'm tired of all the anger and hate.

After a few steely minutes, Bitsy finally loosens. "I'm sorry, Lovey, but you don't understand. You can't."

"Bitsy? Can I ask you a question?"

She keeps her focus on me, listening.

"Why have you been so angry with me all these years?"

"Because, Lovey, don't you see? In a way, you've always been the other woman. You're the one everybody wants."

Her criticisms send me back to Chief's supportive words. *"It's not okay to be treated that way. Not by Reed. Not by Bitsy."* But then I hear another piece of his advice. *"Judas has a story too."* For the first time, I try to see things from my sister's point of view. And just like that, everything pivots.

"You've always done your own thing, Lovey. You never tried to wear the right clothes or say the right words. You, Mother, Eudora Welty . . . you 'formed your own opinions,' right?"

I smile. "Sure, but—"

"Let me finish, please. I need to get it out while I can." She gathers her thoughts. Then says, "You were the real-life Pippi, the 'strongest girl in the world.' I wasn't like you."

"We each have our strengths."

"No, I was chained, Lovey. Always worried about what people would think."

"Not always. I think it goes back to Blaire. When she moved here. Said we were dirty, remember?"

She doesn't respond, so I continue.

"We came in from catching fireflies? Her father was at the house talking to Chief?" I try to trigger her recall. "And there was Blaire, this beautiful new girl, all dressed up and looking down on us like we were trash."

Finally, she nods. "You didn't care what she said to us. But I couldn't stand the idea of her thinking she was better than me, higher class. I've worked so hard to prove I'm just as good as anybody else. Never imagined my life would turn out this way."

"But you *are* as good. Why in the world would you ever think you weren't?"

I finally begin to understand my sister's suffocating insecurity, living in fear that the in-crowd may turn on her, kick her out of the herd. I see now that she's spent her entire life trying to be perfect for everyone else while failing to be true to herself, and in doing so, she has watched me with a fierce and furious envy, a jealousy that grew into hate.

When I joined Mother in the gardens as a girl, Bitsy was too afraid to get dirty. And when I ran barefoot, building camps with Fisher and Finn, she was stuck on the porch swing, painting her nails, yearning for attention from the boys. And when I served as lifeguard, earning money of my own each summer, she stayed flat as a pancake, working on her tan, too afraid to get in the water for fear of messing up her hair.

In her mind, I *have* always been the "other woman," the one not following the rules, the one taking what she wanted, even if that was the simple act of independence.

"You know what's ironic? I always wanted to be more like you, Bitsy. You were the golden girl, the homecoming queen. You ran this town. Still do, it seems."

"Ha! You don't understand anything about this place anymore. You got out!"

"You could have left too."

"You think I don't know that? That's the worst part, don't you see? All these years, I did all I could to put Whitman through school. To build the perfect house. Be the perfect wife, the perfect mom. But every choice I've made has been wrong. And now I'm frozen. Scared to death to make one more bad decision because it'll do me in, I swear."

"You've made a million good decisions too, Bitsy. You followed your heart and married the man you loved. No fault in that."

"Oh, I'm barely hanging on, Lovey. You don't know. I wake up every day trying to pretend my life isn't falling apart. Pretend, pretend, pretend. Heck, I even pretend I'm still blonde, for goodness' sake!" She tugs at her graying roots. "Nothing *real* left at all."

In front of us, Faulkner's headstone stands solid and still, watching our stories play out. The simple inscription reads:

BELOVE'D
GO WITH GOD

I stir the words around my mouth, the infamous punctuation mark a typo etched by a careless inscriber. I picture Faulkner's wife, Estelle, weighing the epitaph options with her daughter, Jill, at their kitchen table. They likely spent careful time before settling on *Beloved, go with God*.

It's a beautiful verse, a heartfelt honor selected not for Faulkner the writer, but for the father and husband who was being laid to rest. Perhaps they even wrote *Belovèd*, to emphasize it as a three-syllable rather than two-syllable word. But then the inscriber fudged their plan. Another lesson that nothing is ever perfect, no matter how much we try to make it so.

I lower my voice and point to the marker. "Isn't it something? After all those long, complicated stories, Faulkner leaves us with this."

She eyes the grave.

"Maybe it's time to end all this anger, Bitsy. Just. Be. Loved."

THIRTY-THREE

November 2016

The air has become thin and crisp, and the entire town carries an autumn tint, a sign that life is on the swing again. The courthouse is gilded by the season's amber light. The steeples and stadiums too. But from Mother's bedroom window, I see only trees. Trees that first took root decades, even centuries before my parents purchased this land. Trees whose seeds were planted by people with names I will never know. People who understood the importance of leaving something good behind, looking not just to the next generation, but to the next and the next, believing entire worlds exist in a single seed, and that every choice leads us one way or another, toward the dark or toward the light.

Outside, in the wind, my favorite oak stands steady and strong despite her falling leaves. She accepts this shedding gracefully, with her head held high, as if she understands that in her giving, others receive.

I try to learn the lessons of the trees. I try.

Mother has been asleep all morning. Her breathing has

become strained, with rattles in her lungs, and we keep her meds heavy to lessen the pain. She has taken nothing but ice chips the last few days, refusing a feeding tube or any lifesaving measures. Bitsy and I have supported her choices, despite how badly we long to keep her here, and the hospice nurses have offered guidance as we grieve.

Mother stirs now, and I move to straighten her covers, adjust her pillow, comfort her. It is gut-wrenching work to watch anyone suffer, especially someone you love. No matter how long I sit with her, pray with her, hold her, I am absolutely helpless in quelling my mother's pain.

Between the constant visits from friends and family, Mother and I have made the most of our time together, laughing, singing, telling jokes. I read Welty and Faulkner to her, even sprinkling in a little Pippi and the story of the cloudmaker. It has been a special journey for us both, with nothing but time. And in the hours, she has shared with me her own life's story. After all these years of seeing her as a perfect matriarch, always poised and polished, as near to flawless as anyone I have ever known, I finally understand her not only as wife and mother, but as a survivor in her own right.

I know her now to be a classically trained dancer, having taken ballet through the age of twenty, and to have spoken fluent French and Spanish in her early years. Until recent weeks, she was still able to play piano and win at canasta.

This woman, Laurel Neely Sutherland, was fierce and bold and brave, more so than I ever imagined. After learning more about her love of Broadway and travel and (who would have guessed it) beer (!), I can now respect her affection for Dolly Parton, realizing she has long admired the country music legend not only for her impressive stage talents but also for her spunk, for standing her ground in a way men don't find intimidating.

"I think she figured it out long ago," Mother explained. "Men take one look, and they underestimate her. That's smart, if you ask me."

This woman, my mother, has perfected her own polished charm. But like Dolly, she is no empty shell. She has spent her life reading and thinking and questioning and seeking. So when she wakes now and pats the bed weakly, I don't hesitate to accept her invitation. I settle beside her, wanting only to ease her pain. It's a heavy role, shuttling a soul into the next world, and I feel there's no right way to manage this.

"It's happening, Lovey. I need to make sure you're ready." Her words are breathy, drawing pain with each pulse of her throat. "I can't leave until my girls are at peace."

I wind my fingers through her hair to calm her. "We're good, Mother. I promise."

"Arizona?"

No matter how much I have tried to prepare myself, I still can't accept the inevitable. I don't want to let my mother go, but I've done as my father taught me, and I've made a plan. When I tell her so, she summons a bright smile, the biggest one I've seen this week.

"Your father's daughter." She brushes her hand across my brow and holds my cheek in her palm, then looks at me with eyes that seem at once misty and clear, weak yet fully and completely here with me now.

I lie next to her, sharing the pillow, stroking her hair as she did mine when I was young, wishing more than anything that time would give us more than it takes.

"The Jansana offer was a good one." I provide all the details she's after. "But with the bonus I got from completing the campaign in time for Prague, I'll be able to retire early. Leave the advertising world behind for good."

"Proud." Her voice is weak, almost a whisper. "You'll move home? Grow flowers?"

"I've given it a lot of thought, actually. Talked to my friends in Arizona. Think we've got it all worked out."

She moans a bit, a long, slow roll of pain, and I help her adjust again, wishing I could stem her suffering. I try to give her another pill, a glass of water, but she's unable to swallow, coughing until she pushes both away.

"Tell me more," she says, once resettled.

"Well, Marian will use my home in Sedona to open that spiritual center I told you about. I may go teach a few yoga workshops for her throughout the year, but the property will be hers to use as she sees fit. She'll keep the Seniors at Sunrise class and create an entire catalog of services. We'll operate it as a nonprofit, write the house off as an expense."

Mother smiles. "Think of the good she'll be doing."

"I hope so," I admit, grateful Marian came into my life.

"And Brynn?"

"Brynn, well, she's finally ready to settle down now that she's landed the job with Jansana. And that dentist she's been seeing? They're engaged."

Mother's eyes suggest she's smiling even though her lips barely move.

"He's just getting his practice off the ground, so they'll be renting my Phoenix house with plans to buy."

"So you'll stay?" She lifts her voice, hopeful.

"I'll stay, yes. I'm ready." I can't hide my grin, and Mother responds in kind. "Fisher and Finn closed on their farm, all thanks to Chief. Turns out he nudged the attorneys to finally do the right thing. Even put in a word with the loan officer and agreed to fund any excess they couldn't cover."

Mother nods knowingly.

"Fisher plans to move into the guesthouse. Gave his mom the big house. Said he couldn't stand to see her in that little apartment anymore."

"Your father would be so happy."

"He would, wouldn't he?"

She nods. "What about *this* farm?" Her words are strained, so I do most of the talking.

"We've already drawn up the plans. Fisher will help manage the irrigation. I think it can work."

"Flowers?" Despite her weakness, she's alight with curiosity, making me wish I had done this years ago with her at the helm. So many regrets.

"Yes. Flowers." This elicits an even brighter smile. "I plan to expand your greenhouse. Add some hoop houses too. Cycle through a big crop of sunflowers, with smaller plots of zinnia, mums, and lilies for a start. I'll also have dahlias, hydrangeas, and cosmos, a few hardy plants like that. I'll add more once I learn the market, but I've got a business plan in place, with goals already set for one-year, five-year, and ten-year profits."

"You were born for this, Lovey."

"I don't know, Mother. But it's the first time in my life I feel like I'm on the right track."

She kisses my hand, says she loves me, doesn't let go.

"The florists are already interested, and I hope to sell direct to consumers through the farmer's market, maybe even online. We'll probably offer some pick-your-own options and host events, bring in school groups and the like. Plus yoga retreats, of course, maybe some herbal classes, art workshops, etiquette teas. A little bit of everything really, just to keep the income flowing in."

"I'll be with you, Lovey. Every step. Never doubt it." Her lip quivers. I can't bear this. In recent weeks her hair has become thin and brittle, her nails yellow and cracked. With little strength to leave the bed and very limited caloric intake, her muscles have all but disappeared, and her eyes say in every way possible she is tired. "You'll need help."

I rub my fingers against hers. "Bitsy's going to partner with me. She needs something to focus on moving forward, you know?"

Mother nods, tears welling.

"And get this . . . We're hiring Trip and Mary Evelyn."

Her brows lift slightly. She's pleased.

"I think they'll be happy to drop a few of those structured activities."

"Good. That's good."

"I'll handle the flowers. Bitsy will help me with events. Figure we can host weddings and private parties out here, farm-to-table kind of stuff. In time, I hope to use Fisher's produce, partner together for the long run."

She smiles, nods again. It takes all her strength, but she's offering approval. Her blessing.

"I owe it all to you, Mother. I found that notebook. The one from when I was little."

"Your flower farm book?"

"Yep. It was in my desk drawer."

She smiles again, and I suspect she left it there for me to stumble across, knowing it would help me find my way. With tattered pages, it still holds the hand-printed cover: *My Flower Farm Book.* Doodles fill nearly every space, with drawings of daisies and roses, violets and tulips.

"You were right," I tell her. "I knew the answers from the start. Just lost sight of them for a while."

"Some of us take the long way around."

I rub my forehead. "All that time I could have been here, with you and Chief."

"And Fisher?"

"And Fisher." I sigh.

"Not the way the story goes." She exhales hard and takes her time to say all she wants to say, breaking sentences into short, clipped phrases. "Forty years in the desert. Or a few days. In the belly of the whale. We all get lost, Lovey."

I trace veins across her wrists, a map of blue-green tunnels as if entire worlds exist within her. Who is this woman who guided my soul into this world, who cared for me and nurtured me and loved me through it all? I want to examine every piece of her journey, learn all I can from the one who gave me life.

"You're finding your way. Back to your true self. That sweet, brave, beautiful little girl. She's a soul worth fighting for. Never forget that."

It's taken me all these years to return to Oxford, but now here I am, sharing a pillow with my mother, watching the leaves fall from the trees outside her bedroom window. The air is quiet, and the house smells of homemade cider. Dolly P. is at Mother's feet, and Manning rests on the floor beside the bed. Chief has gone ahead to hold the door, and Mother is traveling back to him. We all seem to be finding our way home.

When Bitsy and the kids arrive, I grant them privacy and take a walk with Manning. Another Faulkner phrase comes to mind as I climb the hill: "It would be nice if you could just ravel out into time."

We're nearly to the memory garden when my phone rings. It's been years since I've seen this number on my screen, and it's the last thing I expect today, but there it is: Meghan, Reed's wife.

She greets me kindly. I exhale. "I'm relieved to hear from you, Meghan. Reed seemed so angry that day you called."

"Police came," she admits. "Someone reported a disturbance."

I don't tell her I'm the one who called the cops. Nor that I flew to her home, spying from a distance just to make sure she was alive and well. It was a jolt the first time I saw her. I'm not sure what I had expected when the private detective gave me an address. Perhaps a part of me pictured her as some crazy, bitter woman whose cold heart had turned her husband to another bed. What I found instead was a selfless mother, shuttling her children to school with home-packed lunches and freshly washed clothes.

Surely she was falling to pieces from her husband's choices, and yet, somehow, she was finding the strength to hug her children, to check their backpacks and tie their shoes and send them out into this dangerous world with all the hope she could pour into their fragile little souls. She had chosen love, and in that choosing, love survived. It was there, passing through her wounded heart straight into her children. I watched her that day in awe, feeling so much admiration and respect for this woman I had never known. But I don't say any of this now.

"You won't believe it," she continues. "He convinced the cops I was the one having an affair. That he'd lost his temper because he caught me with another man. And they bought that!"

"Did you show them the texts? Tell them the truth?" I sit on the wall, lean against the stones.

"Honestly, no. I guess you can't understand until you've lived it. If you'd called it abuse at the time, I would have thought you were crazy."

I think of Bitsy. Of Meghan. Of me. Three women who did nothing but dare to love the wrong man. I've learned enough now to understand how someone can lose perspective. Before you know it, you're living in a jar, forgetting there's a whole big world on the other side of the glass, relying on a few pierced holes in the lid to keep you breathing. Sometimes it takes an outside force to shake you free. "Did you file charges?"

"Oh no. I never would have shamed him like that. My focus was on protecting him, all while he was out to destroy me. I just couldn't see it. But it's like people always say. You put a frog in a pot of water, and she has no idea she's being boiled."

Hearing this, I realize Fisher and Finn weren't the only ones to survive a fire. We've all been caught by the flames at some point in our lives. Some of us aren't able to escape, and for those who do, scars remain. Some visible. Others hidden deep inside. Either way, we are changed.

"Meghan, I'm so sorry."

"It's okay. I'm not angry. Not anymore. In fact, I called to thank you. I know that's the last thing you'd expect."

I get up from the wall and walk the steps around the labyrinth. Think of all the hurt we've survived.

"Thing is, I tried to convince myself that Reed was just going through a midlife crisis or whatever you want to call it. I hoped we could work through it. But the more I discovered, the less I could deny the truth."

I want to say yes, I learned a lot too. About Reed. About myself.

"Honestly, Eva, I've come to understand . . . you're as much a victim as I am. We both loved a man who never existed."

I look to Mary, her arms outstretched, and I think of Chief, Fisher, and Finn. The love they offer.

Reed is nothing like these men. Never was. Instead, he is a master of disguise. A man so broken, his form shifts completely based on the angle of the light that meets him. He's like the cleome that bloom here in Mother's garden, changing from dark pink at night to pale come morning, then to white again before the bloom falls. Or the heirloom petunias. Or the Confederate rose. Never know what we might find when we visit them. Fickle flowers, they behave as if they've forgotten who they really are, always hiding, fooling us by showing only what they want us to see.

I now understand there have always been men like Reed in the world. A Judas. A wounded soul who causes tremendous harm for his own gain. My mind shifts to Mary Evelyn and Trip. *How can I shield them from the danger?*

When a rabbit hops out to explore the memory garden, I'm drawn back to Meghan. "Are your kids okay?"

"They're still caught in the spin. Reed knows there's no better way to destroy me than to hurt my children. But now we know, don't we, Eva? Now we know what people are capable of."

My hand moves to my heart. The idea of Whitman doing such a thing to Trip and Mary Evelyn . . . It's too much. "He has to stop this."

"I don't think that'll ever happen. He feeds on power, takes pleasure from pushing other people down. But I'm moving in the right direction now. The kids and I have come back to California, near my sister. In time, we'll be okay. All that matters now is that we're finally free."

I sit in Mother's memory garden for a long time after Meghan ends the call. Around me, rabbits, birds, and squirrels carry on their normal activities, searching for food, cleaning their nests, preparing for the change of seasons. I used to think the garden of Eden story was all about Eve breaking the rules and eating the forbidden fruit. Church lessons taught us that her selfishness and deception resulted in great suffering for every generation to follow.

That's the guilt we have been taught to carry as women. The serpent tricks us, and it's all our fault. Others are harmed by our naive choice, and it's all our fault. Our children stray from the right path, and it's all our fault.

Truth is, the dangers were here from the start. But so was the beauty.

Now I realize the story is not about punishing all of humankind for Eve's mistake. It's about relationship. It's about gratitude and honesty and choosing the right person to be by your side in life. It's about trust and partnership and loyalty. It's about love.

Now, as the garden comes to life around me, I no longer think of serpents and betrayals and lies and shame. Instead, I see what God sees. I see that it is good. All of it. Good.

THIRTY-FOUR

May 2017

In Mother's prayer garden I walk the labyrinth, slowly moving around the spiral of stones. I inhale and exhale my way through steady steps, grounding my thoughts in the hilly red soils of Mississippi the same way I did on the desert sands of Sedona a year ago, when I circled the medicine wheel with Marian as my guide. Today, I walk alone, focusing on one stone at a time, round and round until I reach the center of the spiral. There, I lift my eyes to the sky, finding focus on the resurrection ferns that grow lush and green from the oak limbs above me.

One such group of ferns grows from a different white oak down by the house. It's the one that held our tire swing as children. Mother would push us, pointing to the rope that was looped and double knotted from a branch where the ferns grew green.

"You see that fern?" Mother would ask. *"It's magic."*

Bitsy and I would cling to the rope, her legs balanced on top of the tire, mine threaded through the opening as Mother pushed us, her floral skirt flapping in the wind.

"Doesn't need any soil, for one thing. Grows right there on the branch without any dirt at all. Survives against all odds."

Mother would go on to tell us the fern could lose up to 95 percent of its water, wither and curl into dry, brown twists, and still come back to life when the rains finally returned. Nothing could stop it from doing what it was born to do.

I sit at the foot of Mary, centered within a spiral of stones and blooms. I fiddle with my silver charm as I focus on the ferns. *Your time is now.* That's what Mother and Chief wanted me to know so long ago. I thought that to mean I should rush out and claim the world as my own. Dive headfirst into the deep end of life and not let anything stop me. And maybe that was what I needed to do. But when Reed shattered my world, everything turned upside down. By the time I escaped, I no longer recognized myself on account of all the scars. I had become nearly dead inside, as Mother would say.

Mary watches over me now, reminding me it's never too late for a person to rise again. I lie back against the ground where autumn's leaves crinkle crisp beneath me. Manning nuzzles my side, and I close my eyes, resting in the warmth of the sun. When Marian told me we limit things by giving them a name, I didn't fully understand. But now I get it. I've been called so many horrible things in my life: Liar. Cheater. Unwanted. Unloved. The list goes on, and most of those have been hurled from the lips of my own sister, a person who was supposed to be on my side in life.

But what I've forgotten is that I've been called other names too: Loyal. Generous. Honest. Compassionate. This list also goes on. In the end it's like Marian says. I am everything it means to be fully human, alive, and moving through this world in the best way I can at any given moment in time. That is enough. I am enough. And nothing anyone says can change that.

With my eyes closed, my breath echoes within me and I am met again by the ancestral woman from Sedona, the one who came to me in a vision back on the noonday mesa. With each step closer, she becomes more defined in my mind, and just like the first time, I feel as if I know her, as if I have always known her. And she knows me.

Her name no longer matters. Whether she is Kachina Woman, Hera, Kuan Yin, or Mary, she is here, timeless and omnipotent, representing all things feminine and calming, wise and eternal. And she is searching for me. Just as she did before, she walks with arms outstretched. As she spins slowly, white feathers spiral out around her, drifting down, clipping the wind. And as she spins, she is surrounded by a radiant glow of light, her raven hair falling long against her back. Very clearly, I hear her words:

Strong. I am strong.

And then she is no longer a wise, mysterious ancestor. She is me. She is me.

I open my eyes, and I rise. Below me, dying leaves are working their way back to the soil, surrendering to the ruin to make way for new life. As the sun washes over me, warm light flows through, heating my cheeks, my lips, my neck. I begin to spin, slowly, the same way the woman in my vision has done. Mary watches over me and Manning barks as I turn 'round and 'round, right here where flowers bloom among the stones.

I soak in the light, and I absorb my mother's love, Mary's love, ancestral love, all the love that has come before and will continue to come. It is flowing through me now. Here. In my mother's garden.

The one my father and Fisher and Finn built together with their kind and generous hands. Hands that are both strong and gentle, loving and scarred.

If only I could have realized the truth years ago. But now I know. And now I see. Love is what strengthens and remains of me.

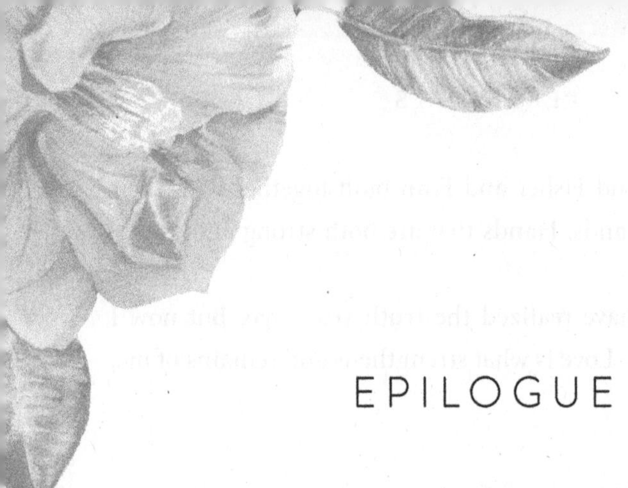

EPILOGUE

"Do not let kindness and truth leave you."

—Proverbs 3:3

Summer 2017
Oxford, Mississippi

Fisher meets me at the gate with a kiss, pulling my hand to his as Manning barks his own affections. It has been more than a year since he helped my parents book an online flight to bring me back to Oxford. In that time I've scattered the ashes of both Chief and Mother. I've helped my sister file for divorce and sell the home of her dreams. I've helped Fisher and Finn move their mom back to their family farmhouse. I've bonded with Manning and Dolly P. as if they were always my own, and I've removed the mementos from my childhood bedroom, passing the space to Mary Evelyn who, along with Trip and Bitsy, seems happy to make this farm her home now. Somehow we've all come full circle, entering another loop around the wheel.

I've stayed here in Oxford as the seasons have changed, watching summer turn to autumn turn to winter turn to spring. And in the coming cycle, I will be here once more. Season after season, year after year, as crocuses make way for summer honeysuckle, as sun-loving lantana ease out for the quieter mums, as pansies blanket the wintry town and as spring beauties burst forth again behind the snow. I'll still be here with Fisher by my side. Because this spring the stars aligned, as Marian promised they would. I picked a mid-March spray of spirea, made myself a bridal bouquet, and gave my whole heart to the man whose heart was given whole to me.

Today, as we walk through our first young yield of blooms, hand in hand, husband and wife, I'm reminded of all the F-words in my life. Fisher, Finn, Farm, Friends, Faith. Even Finances and Future don't draw Fear now. I've chosen Fact over Fiction, and I've Fertilized the Fallow Fields—Flower Fields, that is.

In the barn I feed a feisty tomcat I've named Phoenix. And what I've learned is that Bitsy was never a Feral, Ferocious predator. She was simply Fragile. Now, after a long life of imprisonment and insecurities, she is finally finding her way into the Free. As she softens, I have learned to Forgive and to move Forward and to Focus on the good again. Together, we are putting Love First. Healthy, balanced, safe, and secure love.

In the field Chief's and Mother's ashes have settled into the ground, and today, the wildflower patch is home not only to black-eyed Susan but to her one true love, Sweet William, a beautiful reminder that my parents are still with us. And always will be.

High on the ridge overlooking both of our family farms, Fisher and I are building a home. From the front porch we can see his crops, my flowers, the memory garden, and the perennial blooms. If we're lucky, we'll spend the rest of our lives watching the sunset from our front porch swing, counting fireflies and stealing kisses as the clock slays time. And when life cycles round again, we'll be right here, walking hand in hand as the fields sing out with color, reminding us that now is the time to choose love. That is the truth.

AUTHOR NOTE

Dear Reader,

Thank you for taking time to enter Lovey's world. I hope you've enjoyed the adventure.

One of my favorite parts of writing a novel is conducting research. I love to learn, and this story has taught me a lot. Of course, I have relied on many experts to help me with specific details. Please know, any mistakes you find are mine and should not reflect poorly on the professionals who advised me.

Those of you familiar with Oxford, Mississippi, may wonder why I referred to two special locations as Bailey's Woods and St. Peter's Cemetery. While locals frequently refer to these locations in this way, scholars argue the accurate names are Bailey Woods and St. Peter Cemetery. This discrepancy fuels many a debate, resulting in signs and brochures printed both ways. As a nod to Faulkner, I opted to go with the most common pronunciation, capturing the way people talk instead of what may be officially accurate.

Another detail is in regard to the clock tower. Oxford does have a beautiful clock tower and it is, in fact, centered in our town square. However, because it is frequently in disrepair, it does not always chime. For the sake of the story, I made the clock chime.

That, my friends, is the magic of fiction! For the record, I think Faulkner would find great pleasure in the fact that the town's clock has stopped, allowing time to finally "come to life."

Readers familiar with New Albany may remember the literary garden was in disarray during the time frame of this novel. In fact, the museum was under construction, and as the beautiful new expansion was being built, the garden suffered a bit. However, the Garden Club has done a wonderful job restoring the flower beds, and they are once again ready for visitors. As with Oxford's clock tower, I played with reality to make my fictional version of New Albany suit my needs. I appreciate your understanding.

I encourage you to visit the communities mentioned in this tale and to read the works of Mississippi authors, both past and present. I also hope you'll plant a flower garden and that it will offer you a place of comfort as well as an opportunity to keep your own family stories alive.

Here's to the garden. Here's to finding the good.

ACKNOWLEDGMENTS

Many wise experts, nature lovers, and friends helped me conduct research for this story. I thank each of you for your incredible kindness, support, and generosity.

Special thanks to Angie Barmer, who got the story brewing; Jill Smith, director and curator of the Union County Heritage Museum; Sherra Owen, chairman of the Faulkner Garden Project, along with all members of the New Albany Garden Club and caretakers of the William Faulkner Literary Garden; Jay Watson, Howry Professor of Faulkner Studies at the University of Mississippi; William Griffith, curator of Rowan Oak; and Ed Croom, ethnobotanist and photographer, whose book *The Land of Rowan Oak* proved to be a stellar resource.

Tremendous thanks also to Mitch Robinson, conservation education manager of Strawberry Plains Audubon Center, along with Kristin Lamberson, interpretive garden specialist; Bob Brzuszek, extension professor, along with Sadik C. Artunç, FASLA, professor and head of the Department of Landscape Architecture, Mississippi State University; Daniel J. Doyle, executive director of the Mississippi Sustainable Agriculture Network; Benjamin Koltai of Mississippi Ecological Design; Will and Amanda Reed of Native Son Farm; Katie Naron of Oxford Floral; Jane Perini and Wib Middleton, caretakers of the Amitabha Peace Park; Bob and Sam Fox, owl specialists with Wild at Heart; Becky Nichols, entomologist for Great Smoky Mountains National Park; and Kenneth "Tuk" Jacobson, raptor management coordinator for Arizona Game and Fish Department.

My heartfelt gratitude goes out to Bridget Edwards, director of the Eudora Welty House, along with Lee Anne Bryan, Bernie Lieb, and Molly Knight. Thanks for preserving such a beautiful space and for sharing Welty's works with the world.

Tons of thanks also to Sarah Colombo, head of Adult Services and main branch manager with Livingston Parish Library; Laura Beth Walker, branch manager of the Lafayette County and Oxford Public Library, along with Corey Vinson, reference librarian, and Dorothy "Dotsy" Fitts, who gave us all our start. Also thanks to Kim Austin, David Carter, Lisa Carwyle, Shannon Curtis, Regina Daniels, Carol Dorsey, Nicole Green, Richard Mabry, Gail Magee, Jordyn Redwood, Felder Rushing, Katie Schroder, Kelly Simmons, Marin Thomas, Claire von Dedenroth, Todd Winant, The Hike House, and countless friends who answered questions about flowers, wildlife, cancer, advertising, event planning, literature, Mississippi, and Arizona. For answers, I thank you. For friendship, I thank you even more.

This story was shaped and polished thanks to my savvy critique partners: Christa Allan, Rob Bradford, Cindy Perkins, Larry Wells, Kathleen Wickham, and Lisa Wingate, as well as my talented editors Amanda Bostic, Mary Ann Bowen, and Julee Schwarzburg. I simply cannot write a book without you.

Stories don't become books on their own. BIG thanks to

the entire HarperCollins/Thomas Nelson team: Daisy Hutton, Amanda Bostic, Paul Fisher, Allison Carter, Kristen Golden, Meghan O'Brien, Becky Monds, Karli Jackson, Jodi Hughes, Kim Carlton, Kayleigh Hines, Mitch Davis, and the proofreaders. Thanks also to Kristen Ingebretson and Mary Hooper for the beautiful cover design, and to my agent, Greg Johnson, with WordServe Literary.

I could not have made it to the finish line without the generous support of Carmen and Michael Thompson of Rivendell Writers' Colony and John Dreyfus of St. Columba Memphis who gave me quiet sanctuary. Thank you for the tremendous support you offer writers and for all you do to make this world a better place. You are saints, all of you.

Also thanks to Kathy Murphy and the Pulpwood Queens; Wanda Jewell of the Southern Independent Booksellers Alliance; as well as Amanda Borden and Carrie Steinmehl of the Hoover Public Library. You fierce literary leaders have kept my fire burning.

While much of the writing process is a solitary endeavor, publishing is a team sport. I am eternally grateful for the booksellers, book clubs, libraries, schools, churches, women's groups, and readers of all stripes who dare to enter these stories. Thank you all.

I'm especially grateful for the gifted women writers who have welcomed me into the fabulous Tall Poppy tribe, as well as my Writers Summit gals (Carla, Christa, Jenny, Judy, and Lisa), who hold me accountable each day and offer salve to my soul. Also thanks to the Southern Belle View girls (Amy, Denise, Eva Marie, Jolina, Joneal, Kellie, Lisa, Nicole, Shellie) who have wrapped their hearts around me from the start.

Last of all, many thanks to the people of Oxford, who have

given me such a beautiful and welcoming place to call home. And to Rob, with all my heart, thank you. And most importantly, thanks to my two children, Emily and Adam, who make every step of life's journey worthwhile.

DISCUSSION QUESTIONS

1. We start the book with Lovey, Bitsy, Fisher, and Finn catching fireflies during their Mississippi childhood. The scene depicts an innocent, happy group of friends, a safe and loyal family home, and a strong connection to the landscape that has formed them all. Yet when newcomer Blaire Dayton arrives in her fancy dress, Bitsy crumbles. Why do you think Bitsy was affected so significantly by Blaire's critical comment? Why did Lovey present an entirely different reaction? How have you reacted to criticism in your life?
2. Throughout the book we witness sibling rivalry between Lovey and Bitsy, some of it particularly cruel. Do you believe Bitsy loves her sister? Why does she treat Lovey with such contempt? How healthy are your sibling relationships? What steps can you take to improve them?
3. The book explores family relationships, including that of Chief and Mother, a happily married couple celebrating fifty years of matrimony. Do you know any couples who have achieved such a harmonious partnership in real life? What do Lovey and Bitsy learn about love and marriage from their parents? What mistakes do they make in trying to replicate

that ideal family model? In the end Mother explains what Chief really meant by his mantra "Family First." What does Family First mean to you? What do you want your children and grandchildren to know of love?

4. What meaning do you take from the story of Judas? Have you ever been betrayed? If so, have you forgiven the person who hurt you? Have you ever betrayed anyone? If so, have you forgiven yourself and/or asked for forgiveness?
5. Lovey's favorite *Wizard of Oz* character was Glinda, the Witch of the South. She was described as being "kind to everyone . . . a beautiful woman, who knows how to keep young in spite of the many years she has lived." How does each woman in *Perennials* try to stay young? What does it mean to be young of heart?
6. Chief and Laurel gave the girls a wonderful, supportive family, but they weren't always able to give the girls the emotional support they needed. How can we offer healthy emotional support to the people in our lives? Why is such support so important? What characters offer this to one another in the book?
7. Fireflies play an important part in Lovey's life. She realizes that even when the lid is removed, the fireflies don't always leave the jar. How does this apply to Lovey's life? In nature, fireflies light in order to find their mates. Sometimes a firefly shines her light only to discover that no light is signaled in return. How does this relate to Lovey's attempt to offer love to people who aren't always able to give or receive love in return? Discuss other lessons nature teaches us.
8. Lovey discusses F-words throughout this story. In the end she names her barn cat Phoenix, a play on the F-word theme.

In literature the phoenix must burn to emerge from the fire. Who has emerged from the fire in this novel? How have you survived your own "fires" in life?

9. When The Dragon is defeated, Brynn acknowledges that she never could have survived the "fight" without Lovey on her side. Lovey doesn't begin to heal until Chief finally says he believes her and believes in her. How important is it to have one "constant" person in our lives to help us remember our own truth? What does the story of David and Goliath teach us about fighting such monsters even when we have to face them on our own?
10. The book presents many symbols. In the prayer garden, new growth surrounds the hardened stones of the labyrinth. The memory garden includes a four-tiered wall of stone. Lovey visits statues of the White Tara and Mary. She wears a timepiece charm. The medicine wheel incorporates the cross and the circle. The Reed Incident takes place in the Tortolita Mountains, which is Spanish for novice or beginner. Lovey works for a firm named Apogee. And, of course, flowers play a predominant role, including the resurrection fern, the cleome, and the scentless rose. What do each of these symbols represent?
11. Despite the reconciliation between the two sisters by book's end, Bitsy has yet to confess to starting the fire, nor has she apologized for many of the destructive choices she has made to harm Lovey. Mother tells Lovey that we don't always get the apology we need. How does Lovey learn to forgive Bitsy in spite of this? Do you believe Bitsy has changed? Will she continue to hurt Lovey? How do you think Lovey might respond differently now that she has learned to reclaim her

own truth? How does this relate to the advice Eudora Welty supposedly offered Lovey from the sketched portrait ("Liars only have as much power as you give them. Claim your own truth.")?

12. Adam and Eve's story begins in the garden of Eden. Lovey remembers that God called it "good." What does Lovey come to learn about "the garden" by the end of the book, and how does this relate to her life as a whole?
13. Mother tells the girls they have been giving too much of themselves to the wrong people, the wrong goals. Have you ever been spread too thin, trying to nourish too many things in your life's garden? Would you benefit from a little weeding in your own life? How does Lovey learn to make wise choices, understanding when to say no and when to say yes? What do Lovey and Bitsy learn from the "hardening" season?
14. In the end, Lovey learns from each of the people and experiences in her life. What have you learned from reading this novel? How might your life change as a result?

ACTIVITY SPARKS

- What is your favorite scene in *Perennials*? Why? What is your least favorite? Rewrite that scene to create the outcome you desire.
- Create a "Fifty Things I Love About You" list for someone special in your life. Now write one about yourself. Which of the two was a greater challenge?
- Consider building your own memory, prayer, or literary garden. What flowers, quotes, or stories would you include?
- At one point Lovey considers the timeline of her life. Make a timeline of your life. What key moments have you included? Notice the high points and the low points. Do you notice "seasons" in your own life: growth, bloom, loss, ruin, rebirth?

"Feathers—no matter what size or shape or color—are all the same, if you think about them. They're soft. Delicate. But the secret thing about feathers is . . . they are very strong."

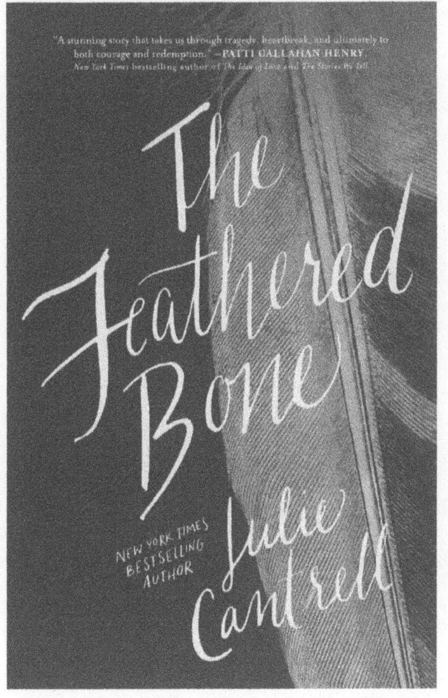

"*The Feathered Bone* is a rare find, a beautifully written page-turner that left me stunned and breathless."

—CASSANDRA KING, bestselling author of *The Sunday Wife*

THOMAS NELSON

Since 1798

AVAILABLE IN PRINT, E-BOOK, AND AUDIO!

9780718037642-A

ABOUT THE AUTHOR

Author photo by Andew McNeece

Julie Cantrell is the *New York Times* and *USA Today* bestselling author of *Into the Free*, the 2013 Christy Award–winning Book of the Year and recipient of the Mississippi Library Association's Fiction Award. Cantrell has served as editor-in-chief of the *Southern Literary Review* and is a recipient of the Mississippi Arts Commission Literary Fellowship. Her second novel, *When Mountains Move*, won the 2014 Carol Award for Historical Fiction and, like her debut, was selected for several Top Reads lists. Her third novel, *The Feathered Bone*, was named a Best Read by *Library Journal* and is currently a finalist for multiple literary awards, including the Southern Book Prize.

Visit Julie online: JulieCantrell.com
Facebook: Julie Cantrell Author
Twitter: @JulieCantrell
Pinterest: Julie Cantrell
Instagram: JulieCantrell

www.ingramcontent.com/pod-product-compliance
Ingram Content Group UK Ltd.
Pitfield, Milton Keynes, MK11 3LW, UK
UKHW020223190625
459827UK00006BA/790

9 780718 037642